WITH
THE VICTORS

WITH
THE VICTORS

●●

BY MAX GALLO
TRANSLATED FROM THE FRENCH
BY NANCY AMPHOUX

Doubleday & Company, Inc., Garden City, New York

1974

NOTE: Real and imaginary persons mingle in the book; the former belong to history, in other words to everyone; the latter to imagination. I have taken liberties with them all, seeking only, as Aragon wrote, to allow "the novel's falsehood to show truth in all its nakedness."

The Author

WITH THE VICTORS was published in France by Éditions Robert Laffont. *Le Cortège des Vainqueurs* © Éditions Robert Laffont, 1972.

Library of Congress Cataloging in Publication Data

Gallo, Max, 1932–
    With the victors.

    Translation of Le cortège des vainqueurs.
    I. Title.
PZ4.G168Wi   [PQ2667.A419]   843'.9'14
ISBN 0-385-05471-8
Library of Congress Catalog Card Number 73-10536

CONTENTS

"Great God! Why am I me?"

—Stendhal, *The Red and the Black*

"A life is built upon a series of decisive acts which are often throws of the dice, in which there is always an element of chance."

—Roger Vailland, *Diary*

PART ONE

G·I·U·L·I·A

1

Giulia's hair was soaked; she undid it in the shed while I shivered, my jacket weighted down with the cold rain that had been drowning Magliano and Venice for days, swelling the woods, rotting the apples. The meadows were turning into marshes, water was breaking through walls, paths, and roads. Giulia's fear, the shake of her head to turn me away, made me let go of her hair that I held tightly between my hands, her hair that hung in long, straight locks.

"If my father finds us he'll kill us, you first," she said.

In the distance, behind the poplars on the Venice road, the trucks on their way to the front sent up sprays of muddy water and we could hear their wailing motors and the noise of their tires churning on the pitted road.

Giulia, pouting, biting into an apple or an ear of fresh corn, pushing me away but leaving her hand on my chest.

"He made me swear, you know, swear never to see you again. He wants to kill you. 'I'll be back with the gun, I'll kill that cocky little brat, it's as good as shooting Austrians. He'll never marry you, he's got the land, we have nothing': that's what he said, and then he made me swear."

"Did you swear?"

"I swore."

Giulia, that was the autumn of '17, the end of October, maybe November already. Cannon fire came every day and every night with the rain, rolling in from the east. They said the Austrians had broken through the front; the stream of convoys along the road never stopped.

"Do you think they'll get this far?"

The women were afraid, Giulia laughed at them; but the

Austrians, the Germans, the *tedeschi*, they were the old occupier, the former master, still remembered by the old folk.

"Did you swear?"

"Yes, but I crossed my fingers."

She moved closer, we forgot the cold, and lay down on the
layer of straw covering the earth.

"Marco, mind the apples, Marco."

Hours went by, the rain drummed on the plank roof of the
shed, fog came with the night; we could feel it rising because
the silence spread with it, leaving only the deep rumble of the
cannon to the east.

"Giulia, what if I swore to marry you later, when I'm twenty-
one?"

"You'd cross your fingers."

"Hold my hands."

"In four years you'll have forgotten me."

"I swear anyway."

She put her hand over my mouth, she stifled me with an
apple that smelled of damp and earth.

"Don't swear, Marco, it brings bad luck. Let fate take care
of things, I trust it."

We met every day despite the weather, our watchful mothers,
the war, the cold. I lived for that moment, for her wet hand
against my mouth, her low voice, her refusals, her reticence;
one look, the lightest pressure of her fingers, and I moved away,
stopped what I was doing, breathed more heavily while she
laughed. But one day my mother's voice came, sharp and raw,
distorted by the wind, "Marco! Marco!"

The voice climbed as though it had to rise forever, then broke
off, began again, "Marco! Marco!"

A voice of mourning, anguish, terror. Giulia, next to me, began to tremble. And still the cannon, like something beating
in the sky.

"My father," I said.

"Marco, Marco!"

My mother was wailing in the rain. We began to run, Giulia by my side; I fell down, my whole body was covered with sticky mud.

"Marco, Marco!" repeated Giulia like an echo.

I saw my mother coming down the middle of the path, bareheaded, her fists clenched, her arms gripped to her chest, a black shawl over her shoulders. In front of the entrance to the farm an officer, leaning against a car, the flap of his cape thrown over one shoulder, smoking, unmoving, as though the rain weren't there at all. He watched me come, I stopped running and held my mother close to me, I felt her fists, I began to shiver from her shivering.

"I am Captain Ferri; are you Marco Naldi?"

It was the autumn of '17, the Austrians were advancing on Venice, their shells were falling on routed regiments and the men were pounded into the mud that mixed with their blood.

"Your father is in a hospital in Venice. You will come with me. Your mother is to stay here. Get a coat."

I ran through the house.

In the big room mother had slumped over our long black table where father used to write, working out his accounts, how much was owing to the farmers. They would wait silently outside the door with their straw hats in their hands, Nitti—Giulia's father—was always last to come in and every time I heard father snap at him, "Nitti the proud, Nitti the red, he comes for his share all the same."

"Why, sure, Mr. Naldi," Nitti would answer, "my share, my little share."

Then father would strike the table. "You old mule-head," he would say.

"Are you ready?"

Captain Ferri had come indoors. Mother cried out and ran to me.

"Take his coat too, his coat."

The captain gestured in annoyance, what's the point, waste of time, then shrugged.

"I'll wait for you in the car."

We started, driving down into the rain and fog and night; water came in through the sides, covering our knees and lashing our faces. We overtook convoys moving forward between the shuddering walls of gray water, we met fugitives, refugees, old people draped in black, weaponless bareheaded soldiers, we overtook a bony horse with no saddle and two men clinging to it, one hanging to the back of his sleeping mate. It was the autumn of '17, defeat, the débâcle. Captain Ferri said nothing, I watched the retreating troops, the population like a muddy flooding river. Just before we reached the Mestre road some *carabinieri*, their two-cornered hats glistening in the rain, barred the way. They were aiming their guns at some men lying in puddles on the ground. The officers were shouting orders and in the yellow lantern light I saw them shaking the soldiers and dragging them into the fields behind the trees. There were shots. We went on. On the road, soldiers with their hands tied behind their backs were walking between mounted guards. I began to shiver, hugging my father's coat, imagining him as one of those men who were hobbling like animals.

"How old are you?"

Ferri's first words to me. Now we were alone on the road. He stopped, lit a cigarette, I caught a glimpse of his sleepless feverish eyes. He held out a cigarette to me.

"You smoke, I hope?"

I saw the furrows on his forehead in the matchflame, his short mustache, the stubble covering his chin; I tried to remember my father's face and found nothing: erased, washed out of my memory.

"How old are you?"

"Seventeen."

"Say, 'Seventeen, Captain.'"

We set off again, Ferri talked. The front was broached, the flanks were collapsing.

"The bastards ran like rabbits, they've been turned soft with words, ideas, they crumbled like stale cake. But we'll take them in hand. Too much freedom is what's wrong with this country. They've ruined it. A country of old women."

I listened, seeing Giulia, hugging the coat; I was with mother and father in our apartment on the Grand Canal. Father was talking about the news, the stock exchange. He sat me on his knees and made me repeat numbers and English or French words after him. In the summer we would go to Magliano, his parents' farm, and then we went to live there permanently. I used to follow him along the bare paths between marshes and rice fields, putting my feet in the prints made by his blond leather boots, and sitting with him in the blind at dawn when the wild geese would rise with a flurry of wingbeats into the holes in the fog. We would go back to the house, Nitti raised his hat, father stopped and showed him what he'd shot and I would watch our farmer's face, the folds narrowing his eyes, the beard already gray, covering the furrows of his cheeks. I was afraid of Nitti. Beneath his look, gestures, I sensed another world, deep as a well. Leaning against a wall watching us, Giulia, dark-haired with sparkling eyes and an apple or an ear of corn in her hand.

The car lurched, Ferri braked savagely. We were at the entrance to the Ponte Sulle Laguna, barricaded from side to side by rolls of barbed wire guarded by helmeted soldiers and carabinieri. An officer, his leather throat strap cutting into his skin, stepped forward to look at our papers.

"Sorry, Captain; deserters. We'd never find them once they got inside Venice."

He raised his lantern to look at me.

"Who's this?"

"His father is dying; my comrade, Major Naldi."

One man more or less in the great massacre, in Europe plowed up with mass graveyards, what difference did it make? But it was my father and the words broke me in half. I was swinging on the trapeze that hung from the tree and then I fell, fell forever, fell on my back, my head hit the ground and the black veil covered my eyes, my lungs were squeezed in an implacable vise, I screamed without a sound and woke up in the arms of my father who was running for the village doctor. The vise wouldn't loosen, the one man less in the great massacre was my father, the world had exploded like a flock of wild geese in the white smoke of a gunshot.

"Buck up, Naldi?"

Ferri took me by the shoulder. I was hugging my father's coat. We had stopped at the far end of the Ponte Sulla Laguna. Soldiers were loading the wounded onto a motor launch by lantern light. Vans stood in rows by the quays, filled with men leaning against one another, covered in black bandages, splattered with mud and blood. It was still raining, the cannon thundered steadily in the east.

"Rotten town, rotten weather," Ferri cursed.

He hurried me along, we went down dark canals and sticky streets across a dripping Venice leaking from every seam, wounded, pus-infested Venice. We reached the hospital, I recognized the quay, the Fondamenta Nuove where I often used to play with my father running behind me.

"Come on."

Ferri went in. A warm odor of blood, yellow lights like dirty, oily water. The hospital, stretchers, the wounded, voices crying out, on our farm at Magliano it was in an almost dark room that Nitti killed a pig once a year while an iron cauldron filled with thick liquid boiled over the fire, it was the same smell, the smell of slaughter I shall never forget, that had been drifting over Europe for three years and would stifle the whole century, asphyxiating all men, I was going to meet it everywhere, in Ethiopia and Berlin and frozen Russia. The smell that rose from the Venice hospital wards, the smell of my father dead, would never leave me again. I followed Ferri. We were crossing wards, I was running away from the screaming, but it was my own voice. The captain stopped a doctor.

"Major, what's Major Naldi's condition?"

An evasive gesture.

"Brought in yesterday," Ferri went on, "you told me he could live a day or two, I promised to bring his son."

The doctor looked at me. I saw the deaths of hundreds of men in his eyes, my presence was like an insult; then the expression faded.

"Naldi, Major, you remember," Ferri urged.

Then lowered his voice.

"A shell, both legs, an arm, a miracle he got this far alive, you said."

It was morning when we used to go out along the dirt paths among the marshes and rice fields. I would put my feet where he did, following his blond leather boots, he leaped from one path to another and I saw his legs rise, when he held out his arms I flew over the obstacle with one bound.

"Both legs and an arm," Captain Ferri repeated.

"Naldi, yesterday, yes, of course. Died an hour or two ago."

The major turned to me.

"It's better, you know," he said.

Somebody screamed in a ward. A nurse ran between us, her hands over her eyes, running away. I wanted to cling to her, bury myself in the straw in the shed, bury myself in the sand.

"You heard? It's better."

Ferri took my arm.

"You want to see him?"

I hugged the coat. I was holding the material to my mouth, breathing the smell of the wool. It was years before, all three of us had gone into a shop near the Piazza San Marco, me between my mother and father.

"You should have an English coat," my mother told him. "Something elegant."

Father nodded. He towered over the salesmen, he was huge. In one movement he picked me up by my armpits and swung me onto the counter among the samples.

"You're taller than I am," he told me, "look at yourself in the mirror."

I saw the man, so strong and tall, my father, and then my mother so frail at his side and me taller than her too, her hair pulled back, her long eyes. Everybody laughed. It was years before.

I began to cry, saying over and over, "Poor Mama, poor Mama."

Now she was waiting for me at Magliano, death had hit her and she had clung to me, had slumped over the long black table and held out my father's coat, the one she had chosen.

"All right," Captain Ferri said. "Let's go."

In the vaulted cellars of the hospital the dead were separated from the living by a dirty curtain. They were lying stretched out inside gray sacks, many blood-stained. I read the cardboard labels: Muratore, Grassi, Galeotti, Ottavi, Molinella, Oberti, Naldi. Naldi, Naldi, Naldi. They were my father killed a hundred times.

Ferri stopped by the short shape and uncovered the face. But it wasn't his face, lost to me forever, it was a piece of stone with a sickly vegetation growing on the cheeks. Years ago I had rubbed against his prickly beard, I learned what my skin was by feeling his, in the burn that stung my forehead and chin.

Nothing was left of all that except a vise that was strangling me, a stone consumed by black moss, the rotting body. I learned that death leaves nothing behind.

"So that's it," said Ferri.

I was still holding the coat. I walked beside the captain, we went past beds, between the dead, the screams.

"If you want war, Naldi, you have to know how to look at death."

That wasn't death, it was a hole in me, an empty coat, wanting to vomit, to sleep, it was a stupor, my father, gray stone in a gray sack; it wasn't death, it was a life in which everything was blurred, like when your eyes are full of sand.

"You'll sleep here, I'll give you a car, a soldier to take you back tomorrow. But first you're going to eat and drink something."

I ate and drank. The Palazzo Dandolo was filled with officers, with soldiers in white jackets running from table to table among voices shouting orders; a woman went past laughing, with her hands over her eyes, bumping into us as we came in. She was laughing loudly as though something was hurting her. The tablecloth was red with wine.

I drank, it was autumn, the season of the new wine, my father held out his glass, ringed with pink foam, then I put my head on my mother's knees. I heard father talking, I heard Captain Ferri talking.

"Don't forget Russia," he was saying. "There was already one uprising in June. The gangrene must not spread all over the country. If we have to thin out a few regiments, we'll thin them out, cut out the dead wood; if someone has to command a firing squad, well, I'm ready, every day if I have to."

Late that night, Ferri shook me.

"Naldi, I'm leaving you with Carlo, my orderly. Here's your safe-conduct for tomorrow. If you want to fight someday, come see me. Good-bye, boy."

I followed Carlo down deserted corridors cluttered with crates; he made me a bed in a drawing room. I heard the waves slapping the quays, the light hiss of rain mingling with the howl of the wind.

"A dirty year, sir," Carlo said. "They'll remember '17. A dirty year."

In that dirty year, '17, while the war was rotting, the rats, in those muddy trenches where the living were being buried, the rats were feeding on dead men and on the eve of lost battles and futile assaults the rats were full. From the Baltic to

Flanders, from the Piave to Champagne they were running in millions over the cadavers, and on that November night as I lay in the drawing room of the Palazzo Dandolo on the Grand Canal in Venice, I dreamed of them. They swarmed up my legs and arms, tore off my limbs, and to get away from them I huddled inside my dead father's coat and breathed in the smell of the wool until I choked in my misery. I bit the cloth to keep my teeth from chattering, to keep from drowning in my sobs. It was cold and damp in the Palazzo Dandolo, the wood creaked, noises came crawling toward me. Somewhere a woman laughed nervously, and I was afraid of the rats as though I had been a wounded soldier, abandoned and bleeding in the trench. Then, in a room nearby, a low, monotonous voice began humming a peasant's lament that seemed to come from across the fields on a foggy morning at Magliano, when my father would shake me by the shoulder and wake me up to go hunting with him.

"Here, drink this."

Carlo was there with a jug of scalding coffee in his hand.

"You need it, I heard you crying out all night long."

He was bustling about, already folding up the blankets.

"Don't worry about it, it's always like that the first time you see dead bodies. You get used to it."

I tried to drink, I was still choking, I wanted to vomit.

"The same with everything, you get used to it, even war. Haven't seen my wife since May 1915, sir, two and a half years."

He had a heavy peasant's head, reddish skin, thick lips, and short arms. He heaved a sigh. Noisy.

"You get used to it all right, but what a lousy war."

We started soon after, crossing the carabinieri's barricades and going against the current of columns of soldiers and refugees fleeing the front. We met trucks loaded with casualties and carts filled with old people pale in the rain.

"Lousy war, damn them all," muttered Carlo.

I asked him to stop near the shed because I wanted to be

alone when I got to the farmhouse, to walk, to compose a brave face for my mother.

"Good luck, sir," said Carlo. "Lousy weather."

He left in a hurry, the car digging into the ruts and yellow mud spurting out of the road. I was alone. Silence and rain on the planks of the shed roof, soon mother weeping against me and the dark room. I could see her half-lying on the table saying "Aldo, Aldo" over and over in a flat voice, my father's name, the first man in my universe, my strength, my protection. The war destroyed him; I had to convince myself, to face the emptiness, the fields and house and deserted beach and the death that left me on the edge of a chasm with my back to a whole wall of my life that had just collapsed, a chasm and in front of me many days, and roads to travel that would never let me escape from the overwhelming emptiness, my father dead. I pushed open the shed door to gain time before going back to the house and mother, and in the gray light I saw them squatting against the wall, Nitti—Giulia's father—and another soldier, their coats covered with mud, their high collars turned up over unshaven cheeks and their eyes glittering with fear or anger; then I saw the bayonet, the long slender blade in Nitti's fist. Nobody spoke for a few seconds, stunned, observing one another while my eyes grew used to the darkness and saw the haversacks and helmets on the ground.

"Shut the door," Nitti said.

I obeyed, leaning against it with father's coat in front of me.

"The boss's son," Nitti told his mate. "The boss isn't here."

"Father died yesterday."

I showed them the coat like a shield, an excuse. Nitti lowered the bayonet and walked up.

"If this goes on any longer we'll all die and I don't want to. So we've cleared out. Mr. Naldi, he wanted his war, if you die for what you want, after all . . ."

He was coming close to me, I recognized the tight mouth I had always seen wearing the beginning of an ironic, almost scornful smile. "Yes, Mr. Naldi," he used to say, "my share, my little share," and father would place the coins on the black table, our farmer's share.

"I've had enough of being made a fool of, you understand, kid, getting myself killed for the gentlemen, enough of it. It's not my war, Mr. Naldi."

I hugged the coat.

"Leave him alone, Nitti, leave him, let's get the hell out."

The other soldier came up and spoke quietly.

"If we hang around here they'll get us."

I saw the carabinieri's faces on the Venice road, I heard Ferri's voice: "They ran like rabbits, they crumbled like stale cake," he said, and we had overtaken the soldiers with their hands tied walking between the mounted guards.

"We've got the carabinieri on our tails," Nitti said. "You hear me, Naldi, if they get us it's twelve bullets in our hide then and there."

He waved his bayonet.

"But I'll get one or two of them first."

"Let's get the hell out," the other man repeated.

"Naldi."

Nitti was looking at me, standing close to me, thin and bony, wrinkles all over his skin, his face inches from mine.

"Naldi, not a word, not a word to Giulia, not a word to her mother or yours, not one word you hear? If the carabinieri come you've seen nothing, understand, kid? Don't forget it, I'll come for you in hell if you talk."

I threw myself at him, the coat first, fists clenched.

"Cowards, cowards, you let the others be killed, rotten, rotten peasants, cowards, I'll denounce you."

He flung me back against the door.

"Let's get the hell out, Nitti, out of here," his mate said.

Nitti hurled the door open, pushing me out into the muddy road.

"Get out before I kill you."

Father's coat was covered with mud. I picked it up and hugged it and ran across the courtyard to the farm. Mother was standing at the door all in black with a black veil over her head, she held out her arms and we cried there in the doorway in the beating rain. Then the carabinieri came, four men on horseback with their guns slung butt upwards across their backs and long sabers hanging at their sides. We were still in the doorway. One stood in his stirrups and hailed us. They were looking for some deserters who had been seen going across the fields, two or three soldiers, Giulia and her mother had come out.

"Where's your husband?" the carabinieri asked.

"At the front for two years now, you think it's fair, not one furlough."

Giulia's mother waved her hands as she spoke.

"You haven't seen him since?"

"How could I have seen him, they took him away from me."

The carabinieri turned back to us.

"And you, madam?"

I stepped forward.

"She is my mother, I am the son of Major Naldi, who died yesterday, I am his son and I am going to enlist this week. I have seen no one, there's nobody here, no deserter."

"Excuse us, madam."

The man saluted, gave a signal, and all four went away again, passing close to the shed, crossing the bridge, heading toward the poplars and the Venice road.

Later, indoors, I sat across from mother at the end of the long table, in father's place. She talked and cried and called me Aldo, then Marco, and Aldo again.

"Enlist," she said, "you want to die too, to kill me, Marco." She was shaking with sobs, hiding her face in her black veil.

"Mama, I have to, I have to."

I didn't know what else to say because that is what I felt, the need to take my place, and father's place and Nitti's because I hadn't turned him in: there were empty places in the front line and I was responsible for them. "It's not my war," Nitti said, "he wanted his war," he said, about my father. So it was my war, for I was not on Nitti's side or Carlo's side, I sat next to Captain Ferri and we went through the barricades of carabinieri against which columns of disarmed soldiers broke and scattered. At that same table, there, I had heard my grandfather, authoritarian, sitting erect in the same armchair, his gray hair short and bushy, reading the *Memorial of Saint Helena* in a deep voice. "Napoleon," he said, "is the greatest Italian of all, our first liberator." The farmers came in, there was old Nitti, Giulia's grandfather, with his hat in his hand, but my grandfather didn't stop reading, he went on, and I ached for the old peasant standing there, his bent back hurt me. Grandfather erect in his frock coat seemed not to see old Nitti, but I couldn't listen any longer, I was ashamed. Once I tried to stop grandfather by standing up and pushing my chair over to old Nitti. Grandfather put down the book.

"You sit back down," he said.

Then he went on reading. He led me to his room, mine now.

"Marco, you're big enough now, you have to understand, you belong to a different race from the peasants. Don't ever weaken in front of them, or they'll eat you up. Never forget that, the land belongs to you." ———

I thought of all that while I looked at my mother, I saw Nitti's bayonet, the dead men in the hospital cellar in Venice, "lousy war" Carlo kept saying. Since it was our war, my father's, Captain Ferri's, I had to fight it. Then we could look the Nittis and Carlos in the face, and all the men my people had dragged into the trenches. The land was not all I was inheriting: the war, too, the blood-gorged time.

There was a knock at the door, Giulia came in with a big coat over her shoulders.

"May I, Mrs. Naldi?"

"Giulia, Giulia, he wants to enlist, he wants to go away!"

I didn't look at Giulia but I said, "Maybe tomorrow, before the end of the week anyway."

A sob came from my mother and the door slammed. Giulia was gone. I was only seventeen, she was hardly fifteen. We had inherited a sad autumn.

Two days later I left, harnessing our last horse to the trap myself, the one the government hadn't requisitioned. The women were standing around, mother crying, Mrs. Nitti holding the lantern and mumbling.

"They'll take them all away from us, all."

Giulia was quiet, leaning against the stable door, and I avoided her staring eyes. The horse was nervous and fidgeting, I was clumsy, I couldn't manage to fasten the last girth.

"Leave it alone," Giulia said in a commanding tone.

She pushed me away, stroked the horse's neck and soothed it by whispering a few words into its ear, harnessing it easily, her movements precise.

"I'm going now, Mother."

Mother stopped crying and hugged me, stroking my hair.

"Come back, come back," she said.

Dawn came with neither rain nor fog, suddenly it was winter. Giulia climbed up first and took the reins, she would bring the trap back to Magliano. Her mother gave her advice but she didn't listen, she uttered one short sharp word and the horse jerked the trap into motion. Mother walked a few steps behind us.

"Marco, Marco!"

Mrs. Nitti cried out:

"Look out! Be careful!"

Giulia flapped the reins, the horse broke into a trot. We passed close to the shed and then the poplars, the trap jolting in the ruts. I tried to move closer to Giulia but she pushed me away with her elbow.

"Let me drive him," she said.

A lurch threw me against her and she let me stay. I put my

arm around her shoulder and we went down the Venice road like that, not moving or speaking, she calling out now and then to the horse, who slowed to a walk behind a column of refugees or trotted ahead to overtake the truckloads of wounded. When we came to the barricade across the Ponte Sulla Laguna, Giulia jumped down with me. Civilian vehicles could not go any farther. The soldiers, their long rifles at their shoulders, whistled ironically and exchanged gleeful comments about Giulia.

"Come on, miss, come with us, leave him, leave the horse and the man too."

The officer was beating his hands together in front of the hut.

"You want to freeze me to death?" he shouted.

A cold wind blew across the lagoon.

"Go on," said Giulia, "you know I'll wait for you and if you want to—"

"I swore," I said.

"You always cross your fingers."

She kissed me in a hail of soldiers' catcalls and I crossed the bridge over the lagoon.

2

Venice, the winter of '17, I was learning how to kill, waving a sword.

"Kill! Kill!" shouted Captain Ferri.

I sliced open the dummy and sand poured out like blood. We started for the lagoon in the black dawn, our boots drumming on the pavement, we sang; in front, his long cape flapping in the wind, marched Captain Ferri. We threw ourselves into the waves, crawled through the gray sand, held ourselves like knife blades to keep from shivering.

"Boys!" Ferri said as he moved along the ranks, "I mean to make warriors out of you, you hear me, warriors such as the earth has never known since Caesar's centurions."

We flourished our swords, repeated the battle cry of the volunteers: "A noï!" We were the Arditi, the bold, the commandos, destined for death and glory and in the evenings our bodies burned with fatigue. Giulia and my mother wrote, their letters were opened before I got them and Giulia's sentences blacked out by the censor. I wrote a few words back before sleep overcame me and it was morning again, the shrill whistle, the races across the dunes, Ferri's voice reading the King's Appeal.

"Any act of cowardice is treason, any quarreling is treason, any dissent is treason. That is what our king says. Be loyal."

We raised our swords and swore.

We often met units coming from the front; the muddy men hardly looked at us, a few spat without raising their heads in our direction, we went on faster. One evening, near the hospital, I had to run through the narrow alleys to get away from some soldiers who were chasing me without a word. I knew what it meant, some of the enlisted men had already been beaten up two or three times. Within the war another war was being

waged, against us, the men who were going to become officers.
Ferri had warned us. He came into the room and sat on one of
the beds.

"Boys, don't mix with the regulars. You are different. You
will be the heart of the army."

He took me aside, led me down corridors with his hand on
my shoulder.

"So, Naldi, you're made of good stuff, you're losing your fat,
in a few months you'll be up to scratch."

Soldiers saluted, we came to Ferri's office. A black flag bearing a skull was nailed to the wall.

"Sit down, Marco."

He smoked slowly, his legs crossed, his thin body stretched
out in a chair.

"How's the morale in the unit?"

He asked me questions about various men, kept coming back
to Alatri, a silent Roman who scorned enthusiasm and who
would sometimes mutter, when Ferri was lecturing with his
lawyer's stance and rhetoric, "He thinks he's still in the court-
room, what a whore, Ferri!"

"Alatri is gangrene," Ferri told me, "and I don't want any
gangrene here."

In the evenings Alatri would read, not far from me. All around
him the men were shouting, some singing, others mulling wine,
Alatri was an island of silence. My bed was next to his and I
knew he didn't miss a thing, his ironic glance moved from one
to another before returning to his book. On Christmas Eve,
when we put on our black uniforms and capes for the first time,
he lay on his bed, his hands flat on the blankets, a book propped
in front of him. I kicked him.

"What the hell are you doing there?"

"I was reading."

Ferri had given us three days' furlough, I thought of my
mother amazed and weeping, Giulia, whom I would wrap up
in my cape and we'd roll together on the apples in the shed.

"You staying here?"

"I'm staying here."

Somebody was shouting my name in the corridor, Captain Ferri wanted to see me. I ran to his office and saluted.

"Drop it, Marco, you're on furlough."

Ferri turned me around in front of him.

"I don't want any soldiers in rags. You look well in uniform, Naldi. I want men women like to look at. Going to Magliano? Your mother?"

He held out a cigarette.

"I remember our first meeting, Marco, a filthy day. Tell me, that little peasant girl I saw at Magliano, you do fuck her at least?"

He hadn't raised his voice, he tossed off the words like a sword slash. I didn't say anything.

"I see; be ready in an hour. You're coming with me. You can spend the last day at Magliano."

I clicked my heels and saluted. Ferri caught my sleeve.

"Naldi, I want men at the front, you understand, men. And in one week we'll be at the front. Be ready in an hour."

Men were running down the corridors shouting my name, Naldi, Naldi, capes were flying, they were pushing and shoving. There was nobody left in the room except Alatri, immobile, questioning me with a look.

"Ferri's taking me with him."

Alatri whistled.

"You'll discover the brothels of Bologna. A Jesuit warrior is our Captain Ferri, he leads you by the hand from the cradle to the grave."

I shouted.

"Shut up! What the hell are you doing here anyway, Mr. Alatri, you pest, you bloody censor, what are you doing here?"

I leaped at him, knocking his book over, grabbed him by the shoulders and dragged him out of his blankets. He wrenched away, trembling with anger, and turned on me.

"So you've been humiliated by that slut of a Ferri and you want to take it out on your mates, do you? Watch out, Naldi."

Alatri had grabbed his sword.

"I know how to use one too."

"But what the hell are you doing here?"

I kept repeating the same sentence, the same question, to this new Alatri, tense and violent, whose brutal energy had taken me by surprise and disarmed me. He held his sword against me and I remembered Nitti in the shed, his bayonet in his fist.

"What the hell am I doing? Why, I'm going to kill you, Naldi, since they're making us into killers and Ferri is a killer and my father is a killer."

He was speaking softly, pushing me back toward the door.

"You know General Alatri? Most heroic general in all the army. Attack, attack, those are his orders, get it, Naldi?"

I was against the door. Alatri abruptly dropped his arm.

"Such a shame, old man, such a shame," he said. He tossed me my cape.

"Now don't forget to come when you get on top of her, Naldi, that's an order!" he shouted as I went out.

I ran down the hall because I didn't want to hear him any more, and crashed into Carlo, who was looking for me.

"The captain is waiting for you at Maghera."

Carlo winked.

"You won't be bored with him, I know him. Ah, he's no ordinary man!"

Carlo never stopped talking all the way to Maghera, laughing noiselessly, showing his black teeth.

"The colonel was asleep," he told me, "and the captain came in through the window and—bang!—into bed with the colonel's wife while the old guy was snoring away beside him!"

We made our way along the canals. The water was greenish, the boat pitched, the tide was going out, showing the cracked, gnawed bases of the buildings, I wanted to vomit.

"He'll take you to the Aquila Nera, there's girls there but only for officers. Us? Pfft! Nothing doing, and I haven't seen my wife since May 1915, May 1915, takes some getting used to, I can tell you."

At Maghera, Ferri was already in the car. He ordered Carlo into the back seat with a jerk of his head, I sat next to the captain and we left for Bologna under a limpid wind-swept sky. Convoys were moving northward, and now and then we were stopped for a road check. At Santa Maddalena, on the near side of the Po bridge, we had to wait over an hour. Carabinieri were searching the trucks carrying the wounded. I saw some men in red bandages put on one side of the road, with an armed guard by them.

"The bastards have wounded themselves on purpose," Ferri said. "The guts of convent girls."

Now we were driving through the night, the road and the poplars hardly visible in our bluish headlights. Ferri had begun to soliloquize.

"We've become a nation of women, Naldi, our mothers stifle us, don't let yourself be caught, my boy, they squeeze you between their breasts and you die smiling like an angel. You've got to lie down on top of a woman, pin down her arms and dig in your spurs. You'll see, they jump for joy, they love it."

I could imagine Carlo's smile, my throat was in knots, I wanted to say something but what, Giulia's eyes, my arm on her shoulder in the trap taking me to Venice, her last words on the Ponte Sulla Laguna.

"You'll learn all that, my boy, in less time than it takes to tell you, because you're made of the right stuff, I don't make mistakes about men. Do I, Carlo?"

The orderly gave an obedient grunt of assent and Ferri continued.

"Ah, Marco! What splendid animals women are, you won't be able to do without them afterwards."

He began to sing, a happy, strong voice.

"Captain," Carlo murmured, "what a voice you've got!"

Ferri roared and began again. At last we reached the forts defending Bologna and the last road check. In front of us lay the town's winding streets, we drove along the arcades of a black, deserted Bologna. A few silhouettes of mounted carabinieri stood out in the squares, barely moving shadows among the statuary.

"I'm home, Naldi, you feel it, the air's different, you won't forget Bologna the superb, I promise you, my boy."

He speeded up, the noise of the motor followed us, swelling, down the long narrow streets. Then we stopped in front of a tall building, over whose door I made out a black eagle with spread wings and an inscription, Aquila Nera. Ferri gave Carlo some brief instructions, which I didn't hear, I was listening to Alatri's voice shouting, "Don't forget to come, Naldi, that's an order!" and remembering the fear that glued me to the sand when we were crawling under the barbed wire and Ferri opened up real machine-gun fire over our heads. Then I had wanted to dig into the sand, prayed for it to swallow me, and that night in Bologna I felt the same fear.

"Naldi, this is no time for sleeping."

Ferri shook me, I jumped out of the car. The captain thumped on the door with a metal knocker that rang flat and dead against the wood. Some words were exchanged, then he pushed me in front of him into the pink, warm light of the entrance where a woman in black stood smiling.

"Captain," she said shaking her head, "Captain Ferri, at this time of night . . ."

"It's wartime, Signora Maria, wartime . . ."

He kissed her on both cheeks and she laughed, her mouth open, a laugh in her throat that was soft as a dove's coo. She took his arm.

"You never change, Mr. Lawyer."

"I want you to look after this little soldier, he's new, new, you understand, don't spoil him."

Ferri gave me a thump.

"Uphold the honor of the Arditi, Naldi."

They both laughed.

"I've got just the thing but I was saving her for you, Captain."

Signora Maria turned to me. "If the captain . . ."

"Let him have her, let him have her first," Ferri said, "I'm going to drink."

He rolled off his cape with a swirl, tossing it on the floor, running up the stairs and disappearing into the shadows, up there where women's laughter began to rise.

"This way."

Maria took my hand and spoke softly:

"You're so young to be in the war. Enlisted?"

I still couldn't speak, I felt her soft skin against my hand, it seemed as though I was going into a long corridor and at the end there would be the priest my mother was leading me to, in front of whom I had knelt for the first time. "Marco," she said, "you have to tell everything, otherwise you sin." She had left me and I had waited there on my knees, my hands on the soft red velvet, listening to the priest's murmur, and I told him that some schoolmates had tried to get me to go with them into the cellars where a woman from the working-class district of Venice came and took off her clothes if they paid her. But I hadn't gone. "Well done," said the priest's voice, "well done, my boy." He absolved me and I had pulled aside the heavy curtain of the confessional.

Maria pulled aside a hanging behind which was a door. She opened it, a gas lamp lit up a bed covered in white lace, a Virgin and Child, shades of blue in a gilded oval frame, above the tall headboard of the bed.

"This is my own room, for you, for Captain Ferri, he's a friend and I'd do anything for him. Before the war I always used to go to hear him in court, what a voice, he ought to have been in the opera but he was too intelligent, too educated."

She fussed about, carefully folding the white lace and I stood watching her, sweating under my heavy cape. Signora Maria smiled and shook her head.

"Relax, now, I'll send her in right away, here."

She took a bottle of liqueur and two glasses out of the bedside table.

"Drink, like before you go into battle."

She went out, quietly closing the door, and I remember grabbing the bottle and pouring a long gulp straight down my throat, a sweet, strong smell of fruit. I sat down and listened to horses trotting over the paving stones, carabinieri no doubt, and laughter, and one high voice singing and some quickly stifled applause. Suddenly I was cold and wanted to be sick again, then the door opened and the girl gave me a cheerful smile. Her blond hair fell over her breasts and she was wrapped in a long, light gown.

"So I am to teach you everything? Such a pretty little soldier."

She came toward me shaking her head, holding out her hands to my neck, unfastening the chain of my cape.

"You're mad, you must be dying of heat, look, look, I've nothing on. . . ."

She lifted her gown to show her white flesh, her buttocks, she came nearer again and then, suddenly serious, took my hands and placed them on her breasts.

"Here, soldier, feel how I'm alive."

I remember that sentence and the life vibrating under my palms, I remember the alcohol taking the place of my blood, the burning along my arms and in my skull, how she pushed me onto the bed and I can see her breasts over my face in the yellow light of the gas lamp. We slept, then we fought and she uttered little cries in the silence.

"But you're an old soldier," she said.

I was being born, from then on I knew what the world was because I knew a woman's body and through it discovered my own; the heaviness in the hollow of my back that was pleasure coming again, rising from the deepest part inside me, and she brought it leaping out again, I laughed and clung to her, I was a happy animal, I wanted to shout, wave my fists, shake my head. Like coming out of the water in summer when the storm smashed over the lagoon and father and I threw ourselves against the waves and came up in the foam, he with his round head in his white cap, I with hair in my eyes, dazzled by sun and the joy of being with him.

In the morning she woke me.

"You're going to have to go," she said.

I stretched my arms and legs, my body felt as though it covered the whole earth.

"Who are you, I don't even know?" I asked.

She was standing putting up her hair in a bun, I saw the reddish hair in her armpits and could remember the strong scent that came from under her arms, in the soft folds of skin.

"You didn't need to know my name to do what you did, eh?"

"My name is Marco, Marco Naldi."

"So?"

She leaned against the bedpost, thoughtful. "Do you suppose I'm going to remember you?"

"I'll remember you."

She went back to doing up her hair, humming, suddenly quiet.

"All the better, soldier, all the better, that'll mean you're still alive. Go on, get dressed and scat."

I put on my uniform, it seemed heavy, stifling, scratchy. She came to the entrance with me; the house was dark and silent. When she opened the door, cold clear daylight crept in.

"Good-bye, soldier," she said.

I tried to take her hand and said, "But I don't even know, I'd like to thank you."

Her face went suddenly harsh, there were wrinkles in her cheeks, I saw her old and ugly.

"And maybe pray for me too?"

Then she was sweet and beautiful again, running her fingers over my face.

"Come on, run away now, little boy, I'm sleepy, you've killed me, soldier."

Firmly, she pushed me out. A cyclist nearly knocked me down and then swore at me, I walked away wanting to laugh and cry both at once, like that time when I was a little child and fell down in the gravel of the courtyard of the farm at Magliano, and father called out to me, "Marco, come on, on your feet, you haven't hurt yourself, up you get, Marco," and I stood up and ran to him and burst out laughing, and sometimes if mother was there tears came instead. That morning in 1917, I walked through the streets of Bologna with hesitation in my heart; I bought some fried bread from a street vendor, warming my hands over his coals.

"Cold, eh, soldier?"

He winked at me, pointing to the end of the street where the Aquila Nera was.

"Better there than in the trenches."

My body chose to laugh, the bread was crisp and fiery, I was hungry. He made an obscene gesture.

"Those nights of battle give you an appetite, don't they, soldier?"

I laughed with him, bought another piece of his bread; the keen air was food too. I paid and left to conquer Bologna, the squares set like the squares on a chessboard, the towers, ice-imprisoned fountains, and to drink sickening sweet coffee in low-ceilinged smoky cafés. It was as though Bologna was the first city I had ever seen, and these hurrying women clutching their shawls with both hands were the first women of my adulthood. I roamed for hours, measuring the length and breadth of this new world, then went back to the Aquila Nera, where I was to meet Carlo. He was there, leaning against the car, stamping the paving stones and grumbling:

"Captain Ferri said I was to take you home and then to Ven-

ice, he'll manage by himself, he's spending Christmas here, nice
and warm, with a girl on each side of the bed and him in the
middle."

I jumped into the car.

"Let's go, Carlo."

We started, overtaking convoys; soldiers in the trucks hailed
the peasant women who were riding their bicycles across the
fields.

"How come it's always the same ones, eh?" Carlo asked. "I
haven't laid a finger on my wife since May 1915 and I send her
all the money I get, precious little of it; so a whore costs too
much for the likes of us. Captain Ferri's different, sure, a big
guy, I'm not comparing him with us soldiers, but, I mean,
we've got the same as him, we're all men and get the itch as
bad as anybody else."

I listened to Carlo and little by little my joy wore away;
maybe, too, it was because I began to recognize the roads and
rivers after the Po and the Adige, chapels on a hilltop on the
horizon above the fields, alternating with vines as tall as trees
and long rows of mulberry trees between poplars, and because
at the end of the road were mother and Giulia, women of a
former life who had been altered for me, perhaps, by one night.
We went past the shed, Carlo was talking:

"You remember the first time I brought you back, what lousy
weather it was with all those poor sods on the road, ah! Italy
wasn't much to look at then."

"Come with me."

The courtyard was empty, a few hens outside Nitti's house.
I tried to imagine Giulia crossing the courtyard but all I could
see were the breasts of the girl in Bologna, and her buttocks, all
I knew of Giulia was a face, hair, the warmth of a body against
mine, her shape sensed for one instant and then snatched away,
a cool cheek, a look that offered a whole life; and it was all nothing to me any more, scarcely an image. I pushed open the door

of our house; what kind of look did that girl at the Aquila Nera have, I couldn't remember, was there even a look?

"Marco! Marco!"

All three of them were there, sitting at the long black table, mother in mourning just getting up, Giulia frail in a woolen dress with braids over her ears, Mrs. Nitti crossing herself, mother already upon me and calling me by my name and father's, enfolding me in her arms and her suffering, in the emptiness I had tried to escape.

"I don't know what I'm saying, you look so much like him in that cape, it's him."

She wept and Mrs. Nitti came up. Giulia hadn't moved but her eyes were laughing, quick, alert. We sat down with the women around us, Giulia brushed against me as she passed, her silence speaking to me, running to fetch eggs. I talked, Carlo ate, I was coming from the world of men and I was one, I told them about the barracks, about Alatri and Captain Ferri and morning drill along the sea front.

"When do you have to leave?"

Those were Giulia's first words, a silence fell, I was afraid; if I were alone with her what would I say, to hide nothing and yet tell nothing.

"In a little while, don't we, Carlo?"

He looked at Giulia and then shook his head like a peasant who knows when the weather's going to change from signs other people don't see, the edges of leaves curling, the way a dog sniffs the earth.

"In a little while," he said, "can't help it, can we?"

Mother began to cry again, Mrs. Nitti cursed the war. Giulia stood up and took down my cape, held it out to me.

"Come on," she said, "we'll go for a walk."

Night was falling, the poplars in the distance were almost invisible.

"I didn't want to talk in there," she said. Our arms touched, our hands brushed each other; the solitary barking of a dog in the muted countryside. Cold, silence, our footsteps.

"They cry and cry, that's all they do." Giulia kicked at the dry winter ground.

"Are you going to the front?"

She was just asking a question, stubborn and precise as she had always been, proud like Nitti. I raised one side of my cape to cover her shoulders.

"I'm not cold," she said.

I could feel her shivering.

"We haven't heard anything more of father. The carabinieri came several times, they don't know."

I might have said something but the door of the house opened, Mrs. Nitti was calling us. Giulia put her arms around my neck, her body had never been so close to mine.

"Marco, the war is going to end one day?"

Her face, her look, were held out to me. That night I didn't seem to have the right to kiss her, and we went slowly back indoors.

Later, on the banks of the Piave, that river of mud, pebbles and blood where the Austrian offensive was stopped; later, when I was standing sentry behind the parapet, I sometimes heard a dog barking on the other bank and I thought of Giulia while machine-gun fire broke out somewhere, bullets ricocheting off the pebbles and thudding into our sandbags, and a few men emerged from their holes; and Alatri, a heavy woolen scarf wrapped around the lower half of his face.

"What do they want?" he asked.

The whisperings must have run the whole length of the trenches, then the night swallowed up the noise again and I dreamed of the Aquila Nera, Giulia, her look, that walk, the last we had together. She wrote regularly, about what was happening on the farm, one word would show me the corner of a field, a tree we used to chase each other around, before, in a country of memories; she talked about my mother, the cold. "Soon," she would put at the end of her letters, and sometimes added, "I'm waiting for you." One morning the Austrian artillery went for us; we burrowed into the ground, were flung up with every explosion as though the earth were an injured man somebody was finishing off. The bombardment ceased abruptly early in the afternoon; a few men stood up, Ferri gave orders. Bent double, leaping over scattered sandbags, a soldier came running with a packet of letters and tossed it at us. There was a vibration in the air, we threw ourselves down, covering our heads with our hands, hugging the earth, and one last shell burst, cleaving the space overhead. When I looked around, a long time later, the post orderly was lying near the packet of mail, his face halved as though by a meathook and his uniform covered with blackish pulp. Alatri dug his nails into my hand.

"Look, Naldi, look, another hero."

"Bury him," Ferri shouted. "You've seen dead men before. Alatri, get him out of there and distribute the mail."

There was only one letter for me, from mother, telling about the influenza epidemic, it was spreading into every chest, she was afraid, for me, for herself. "Giulia's been evacuated to the hospital," she wrote at the bottom of one page. Days passed, the front was busy, attacks, patrols; card games under a blanket, Arditi quarreling among themselves. Ferri shouting. When we were relieved we sang on the big canvas-covered trucks going down to Treviso; Alatri read a book. I tried to get him to come with me to the Stella d'Oro, where a few women had set up in business, we drank, I learned that life existed again, holding a warm body against mine.

"But what if you die tomorrow, you idiot?" I shouted at Alatri.

He smiled.

"So you want me to act like an animal because I might die?"

Days. No letter came from Giulia; I asked mother, she didn't answer. I played cards, went on patrols. One evening while we

were waiting to slip out, our faces blackened with soot, somebody handed me a letter, I didn't recognize the writing. It was
Giulia telling about her illness, the hospital ward. Everything
is fine, she said, the war is surely coming to an end. The lines
were barred with a purple stamp that said in big capital letters
DECEASED THE and the date was written in by hand.

"Let's go, boys."

We had to bring back prisoners, find out what they were
planning on the other side. Following Ferri, we slipped through
our barbed wire, wormed down the pebbles, slowly sank into
the water. I thought I heard a dog barking again in the distance,
back at Magliano. Giulia had raised her face, was looking at me.
The Piave was icy, Alatri was crawling in front of me. Before
we even reached the other bank they were sending up flares
that sifted slowly down like calm, certain death. I became a tree
trunk in the water. Bullets began to ricochet, boring into the
air and water. Ferri had moved back; we'd been seen, no
point in going on. Between two flares we leaped, in the pocket
of darkness that was our hope. A machine gun, Alatri on his
knees. Idiot, idiot, I screamed inside. I lay beside him; he was
moaning quietly, I put my hand over his mouth to silence him.
Then dragged him, yard by yard, toward our barbed wire, hands
reached out, I pushed him over and fell into Ferri's arms, who
held me to him.

"Good, Naldi," he said, "good. Drink, boy."

The bottle was icy but the liquid burned like at the Aquila
Nera, some strong-scented fruit liqueur. I would have nothing
more to hide from Giulia and I would never know what woman
she was. The next day I wrote to Mrs. Nitti, then I went to see
Alatri at the first-aid post. He would make it.

"It's over for you."

I shook his hand, made jokes.

"Your father will be proud, you're going to get a pretty medal."

"If you can, don't forget my books," he kept saying.

The first-aid post smelled of death and the filth of pain. I left, that evening Ferri and I went down to Treviso. The captain sang on the road, then broke off.

"We're going to win, the front's collapsing up there."

"All those dead men."

The soldier with the cleft face, the smell of the Venice hospital, the gray sacks of bodies, father's shorter than the rest, and Giulia unfulfilled, hardly a memory.

"All those dead men, Captain."

He began to sing again.

"Naldi," he said, "we're alive; and you'd better learn, boy, that you make history and empires with blood."

That was his lawyer's voice, the voice that made Alatri fume. We stopped in front of the Stella d'Oro. He pushed me toward the door.

"Later, Captain, I'd rather go for a walk first."

"Too bad for you, then, I'll take the blonde."

I sat down next to Carlo, who was drowsing.

"Are you sick?"

I held out a cigarette and we smoked a long time without speaking.

"You remember that girl, at home, at Magliano?"

He nodded and I knew he had already understood.

"Pass me another cigarette," he said.

Then, after a pause:

"You get used to anything, but what a lousy war!"

I didn't get used to Giulia's death and the country hadn't gotten used to war. On November 4, when the bugles sounded the cease-fire in the fog that was sliding like gray water over the Piave, their voices struggling to break the silence, and we heard them answering from camp to camp and no explosion shattered the soft morning peace, at first not one of us moved. Then a human voice shouted words that were not fear or death, one voice then a hail of voices, I jumped onto the parapet with the rest, threw my helmet in the air, shouted, and all along the front those who had survived were screaming with joy. You don't get used to massacre.

"Calm down, boys, it's only the armistice," said Ferri.

We carried him on our shoulders and he laughed, too, making us sing patriotic songs and our battle cry, "A *noï! A noï!*" and we chanted it with the fury of survivors. The next day I went down to the first-aid post, Alatri was sitting on the edge of a bed with a wide white bandage across his chest, struggling to talk to other injured men who listened with their eyes half shut and their big red peasants' hands on the blankets. Alatri hardly looked at me, I sat down near him.

"Now you've got to get back the land," he was saying, "they owe it to you, you've given your life, your blood, it's yours, you've got to take it."

He coughed, dropping his head, leaning on me with one hand.

"And you think they'll let us?"

A soldier stood up, balancing on one foot, and hopped back to his bed, clumsy with his crutch; he called out:

"They're keeping my leg and my gun and you want me to take the land with my crutch? They'll have my other leg and then spit on me!"

He spat fiercely, threw his crutch to the floor, carefully arranged himself on his bed.

"You talk like a lawyer, you know how to read; come out to the fields and you'll see," he went on.

The others turned away and Alatri looked at me coldly.

"The armistice," I said, laughing.

"And that's all you want? Bravo, Captain Ferri, bravo, you know how to handle a jackass!"

He started coughing again and in the whole ward I couldn't hear anything except that cough that shook his entire body, forcing him to hold his chest with both hands to keep it from being torn apart with every heave. Alatri closed his eyes, the nurse wiped his brow.

"You, clear out of here or I'll have the major throw you out."

I took Alatri's hand, leaning over him. "If you don't have anywhere to go afterward, come to Magliano, there's a house and land."

"You're just a landowner. . . ."

He smiled, shaking his head to show he'd heard and he might come. We had never talked about his family but I had seen him tearing up letters that came with the seal of General Alatri's headquarters. "I refuse to be the son of a butcher," he told Ferri one day when the captain asked, on his father's behalf, why he never wrote. "If General Alatri orders me to write, Captain, that's different, I'm a soldier, I'll obey."

"That's enough, you're sick in the head," Ferri had said, and Alatri got no more letters.

When I came out of the post I promised myself I would write to him, and try to tell him that now that victory was at hand we could all build another country together, a more just one, it was the duty of all of us who had been chosen, generation after generation, by events, by destiny, by God perhaps, to own and to know. We held the land, true, and before giving it up we had to make sure the others wouldn't ruin it.

I remembered a short summer night, luminous as an endless dawn, the air laden with the smell of wheat; one hardly slept at all, and in the evenings I walked under the poplars with Giulia. The war had already begun on the Marne, but we were still at peace. Suddenly I heard shouting, the air grew hot, horses were neighing and pawing the stable floor. I ran to the window; in the middle of the field our combine, the only one in the district and my father's pride, was burning, and the standing wheat around it was catching and sending up tall flames. Father and Nitti and I came running but water was a long way away and in the morning, haggard and black with soot, we looked at the scorched earth, the carbonized stalks and the black, twisted carcass of the machine.

"They're brutes," said father. "Destroying, smashing, pillaging, they go crazy if they aren't kept down."

The fire had been set: in a corner of the field and over near the combine we found holes that had been dug for petroleum and paper.

"They're afraid for their jobs," Nitti had said, looking at the ground. "If there are machines, what are they going to do, eh?"

Father turned on Nitti, grabbed his shirt and shook him. "You're on their side, you bastard, and what about me, who's going to pay me for the wheat and the combine, you think the insurance company will?"

He shook him. Nitti stared back, his jaw tight, and said nothing.

"Oh, what's the use of telling you? You're just like them, you're longing to do it, dying to, you're still barbarians!"

He turned around to me.

"Look, Marco, see the kind of work they do, destruction, they've got to be kept down."

I wanted to explain that to Alatri, to tell him how grandfather had struggled for years, during the hard times when Canadian wheat began coming to Europe, to keep the land, our land. "You can't understand," he used to tell me, his forearms leaning on our long black table, "it was in January of '87, I was alone here, a cold spell . . . and I didn't have a cent, nothing left, nothing, all around they were waiting and watching, sell off a piece, sell, there'll be enough left for your son. I didn't give in, we gritted our teeth. I was the whole squadron, just me, like the imperial guard at Waterloo." Grandfather laughed. "I defended the land of the Naldis, one tiny piece of Italy."

Alatri had to understand this land, our fields, held by main force, for which father had died and I had fought.

"Defend the land, Marco," grandfather used to tell me, "it belongs to the Naldis, believe me, we are the ones who made it."

He showed me the trees he had planted, the canals he had dug. I often used to stop and look at the peasant women, the hired hands bent over the rice, their faces completely hidden under wide straw hats.

"Come on," he'd say. "We worked harder than they, for centuries. It's their turn. If they want land let them take it somewhere else. All we have to do is colonize Africa. It wouldn't be the first time."

He was excited by the fighting in Tripolitania, read the papers and dispatches aloud.

"And the socialists don't like it; there'll be work out there and land for everybody. But they don't understand anything, the illiterate brutes!"

Now that we were victorious we would wrench off a piece of that Africa and our peasants could go there to become Naldis, with their own land. I wanted to convince Alatri, to write him; but then we went to Milan to find the city gone mad, the streets around the Duomo filled with a screaming, dancing throng. Women leaped onto our trucks, we sang, the drivers kept time with their horns, we went into the cafés and stormed the bars, swirling our capes, carrying off women. I kidnapped a little nurse from a *farandole*, two blows with the heel of my hand on the wrists of the people on either side, and I held her close to me, forcing her into the truck; she laughed anxiously, her hair in my neck, her face tight against my chest, abandoned.

"Drinks, drinks for the Arditi," cried Ferri.

The bar owners grumbled and scowled, but there were so many of us, we stampeded their customers, one of us climbed onto a table. "*Viva l'Italia!*" he shouted and we howled our fury at being alive and young, our joy at having women in our arms. Under the Gallerie Vittorio Emanuele, where we were marching arm in arm, twenty abreast, singing and sweeping the people and goods along with us, intoxicated by liquor and the light of the glittering glass corridor after the fog that was beginning to come down over the city, we saw a column marching toward us behind flag bearers, civilians and soldiers together. They were shouting, "Hurrah for the Arditi!"

We screamed with joy; a small, gesticulating man climbed on a platform and began to speak:

"We are fellow soldiers," he said in a harsh, cutting voice, "you are the conquerors, you have made the victory with grenades and sabers, long live the Arditi, long live great Italy. Never forget our victory, our dead."

The two processions mingled together and we set off again; I clutched the nurse to me, I knew she would not escape.

"You're hurting me," she kept saying.

"It's love, signorina."

She laughed and relaxed her arm and the body she had been trying to free. Captain Ferri was near me. "Did you hear that journalist?" he asked. "There's a real Italian."

He saw the nurse with me and winked. "Overnight furlough, Naldi."

I left the procession a little later, making my way into the empty narrow streets behind La Scala; alone with me, the nurse stopped laughing.

"I have to go home," she kept saying, pulling at the arm I was holding.

"But I'm going home with you; you're not going to leave a soldier alone on such a cold night."

I had been drinking all day, and then, all the women I'd had before had given themselves for money. She was my first conquest.

"I can't, I live at the hospital."

She refused again and again, I held her arm more tightly, brushed against her breasts, felt her body yielding, so that words didn't matter any longer.

"You'll have to be quiet, there's the head nurse, it's against the rules."

I promised. We went along dimly lighted corridors, wards with bluish lamps scarcely aglow, I followed her among the beds, recognizing that smell of wounds and death. At the end of one ward was her little room, white, with a washbasin and an iron bedstead. She stopped in the doorway.

"I've got to leave you here, there are the patients, I'm on duty."

I pulled her into the room, stopped her from crying out, locked the door, shoving her down, repeating, "But what did you think, what did you imagine?"

I searched for the warm skin under the wool and silk, I tore at her, she was moaning, fighting but only with words.

"You mustn't, I don't know you."

Did I know her, does shrapnel know the flesh it pierces, the heads it cuts in two, did death know Giulia? I took her and then I went, leaving her on the bed, running through the wards, finally finding the street, a café full of soldiers where I stayed until dawn drinking little glasses of fruit-flavored spirits and dozing off now and then. Huge words across the front pages, "VICTORY," a photo of the crowd in the Piazza del Duomo; the accounts said that the editor of the *Popolo d'Italia*, Benito Mussolini, had addressed the populace on several occasions.

I wandered the streets a few hours longer but the city was wearing its gray face again, only the newspapers showed any excitement and in these streets where everybody seemed to know where he was going I felt lost and useless, encumbered by my cape, my black uniform, the sword hanging from my belt. Outside the barracks the men were already boarding the trucks, but they weren't singing any more—like me, suddenly awake in an indifferent atmosphere. Then the army took over: we were the undisciplined, the pirates, the enlisted; they had put up with our pranks, called them acts of heroism in staff press communiqués, but now came the day of the regiments. We had left our quarters in the villages behind the lines, the open-doored houses where we had sung and drunk, Ferri sitting with us to play cards. Now a mounted colonel was reviewing us.

"You have been warriors," he said, half-standing in his stirrups, "now you are going to become soldiers."

We began a slow march southward across the muddy plains in the driving winter rain; the infantry watched us go by with sneers on their faces, making obscene gestures.

"One-two, one-two Arditi," they shouted.

Captain Ferri marched alone in front without so much as turning his head, and in the evening we couldn't get a word out of him. He commanded with gestures, stepped aside for the colonel who joined us at the halt, a dilapidated barracks where we half froze to death. By mid-December we had reached Bologna and camped in one of the outlying forts, an ancient stone prison undermined by damp.

Only one year since the Aquila Nera; the icy water of the Piave had run all through that year and the girl Ferri had bought me in the bed with the white lace bedspread was a long way away, carried off in the current of the war; one year, I had learned about women and the death that is dealt and the death that strikes, and Giulia lost too.

Captain Ferri came into the barracks with the seeping walls where we were trying to warm ourselves. He sat at the table between the beds, playing with his sword.

"Boys, I'm leaving you," he said abruptly. "I am going to say good-bye to you. You fought well. For Italy we'll fight again if we must. Boys!"

He stood, extended his sword with upraised arm. "*A noï!*"

We gave our battle cry and he went out, I walked alongside him.

"Captain, why?"

"Naldi, you can't mix gold and lead."

We crossed the rain-swept courtyard.

"We're a nuisance to them, all these music-hall soldiers, careermen, midgets. They've always been beaten, for centuries. They're scared."

Carlo was waiting for Ferri under the high postern of the fort.

"Get your discharge, Marco. Go home and keep yourself in

shape. The time will come, and then we'll have them crawling to us. See you soon, Marco. Take my advice."

He embraced me, Carlo loaded his bags into a car.

"I'm moving into the Aquila Nera; more comfortable than here, you know?"

He winked.

"Come see us one of these days."

We loafed around the courtyard, went to roll calls, drilled for fancy officers who seemed never to have heard the sound of a bullet ricocheting off the pebbles. A few days before Christmas the colonel called us together. It was snowing. He stood under a postern and we got the snow in our faces. He announced that volunteers under twenty years of age could be discharged before the end of the year. There were enthusiastic shouts and we broke ranks despite the lieutenant's orders. I looked at the colonel: a thin little man, smiling sarcastically. The next day I left the fort, in uniform but free. I tried to hitch a ride to Bologna from farmers going to town in their carts loaded with milk churns. They didn't even answer, whipped up their horses; and I went on on foot, slogging through the snow banked up at the roadside. I wanted to go back to the Aquila Nera, I was hoping to see that nice girl again, and Signora Maria's bedroom, and I was curious to find out how Ferri lived in his rather special hotel. But just as I reached the Strada di Circonvallazione I saw the procession: it was coming out between the high walls of the gasworks, the black cylinders covered by a deep layer of snow, coming toward me crowned with red flags, preceded by running urchins, by young people walking backward as though they couldn't stop looking at it; it seemed to move forward in jerks, I could see women, soldiers arm-in-arm, and I heard shouting.

"*Avanti, popolo,* forward, people, long live the Soviets, long live the Revolution!"

It filled the road. A song rose.

La bandiera rossa la trionfera,
La bandiera rossa la trionfera,
E viva il socialismo e la libertà.

The gasworks employees cheered, standing on the walls and waving red flags too. There wasn't time to run away, the youngsters were already upon me, soldiers were breaking out of the procession. People began pushing me.

"So you're happy now, you've had your war, your victory, you're proud to be a hero!"

"He's got medals. . . ."

Somebody was pulling at my cape.

"Where did you earn those, in the 'back-line brothels'?"

One soldier, an old man who looked like Nitti, spat in my face.

"It's because of the little gentlemen like you that we got ourselves slaughtered."

I was backed against a wall with faces, hands, insults all around. A man came up, he looked like a shopkeeper, wearing a broad-brimmed hat and a wide red scarf.

"Comrades, comrades," he shouted, "leave him alone; not people, no: attack the ideas, not the men, leave him alone, the guilty ones are in Rome, he's only a victim too; fight ideas, not men."

"It was men who died out there," the soldier cried.

But he turned away and the rest followed him, running to catch up with the procession, which was moving away, followed by workers on bikes. I was left alone with the man who had rescued me. Then I saw his round face, schoolteacher's spectacles, gray beard on his cheeks and chin.

"Don't hang around Bologna today," he said. "There've been too many killed in this war, too much injustice the last three years, so your uniform, you know, you have to understand them. We didn't start the violence."

I mopped my face and straightened my uniform.

"You think I did?"

He raised his arms:

"We're all caught by history, it sweeps us all along if we don't choose our camp. Excuse me."

He raised his hat to salute and hurried away, a heavy, clumsy figure, stopping suddenly and calling back, "If you have any trouble say you're a friend of Calvini, the Socialist representative."*

He shambled off.

I didn't feel like going to the Aquila Nera any more, maybe it was fear, fatigue maybe, or frustration at not being able to tell those maddened men spitting in my face that I had seen my mutilated father stuffed into a gray canvas bag, had crossed the Piave at night with a knife between my teeth and my body covered in black soot, with instructions to cut the sentries' throats on the other side before an attack, that the blood of the first dead man in my arms made me vomit and that I was going back home now to my land and had the right to look any man on earth in the face. I had, we, the Naldis, had earned the right.

The railway station was occupied by carabinieri; the railwaymen stood in a threatening knot at the end of the platform. An officer looked at my papers.

"Discharged? You're in a hurry."

"I've just been spat on, Lieutenant, and had my decorations torn off."

"I know, they're a bit excited today, it'll pass."

"What if it doesn't?"

"You're a civilian now anyway, all you have to do is change your clothes, none of this concerns you any more."

That evening I was in Venice, there were girls selling themselves in front of the hotels. I took one into a shabby room where the paper was peeling off the walls. She started to undress.

"Don't . . ."

---

* Translator's note: "representative" here refers to elected members of the national parliament.

I held out my pack of cigarettes.

"I'll pay you anyway."

Then she lay down and began to talk and that was what I needed, an anonymous voice uttering words that were not full of resentment, that had no importance.

"You look gentle," she said, "you're nice."

I fell asleep and when morning came I saw her rolled up in my cape, still sleeping. Later, I got a lift in a truck going up toward Magliano.

Nothing had changed at home, every object was in its place. Only father and Giulia were missing. It was winter, rain, snow, wind, the season matched my mood, I walked, the days were gray, I set out early with father's gun and dog, the dog bounding in ecstatic circles and running wildly down the paths and snow-thickened hedges, then looking back perplexed and brushing against my boots, for I never fired a shot. Sometimes I didn't come home until after dark, and the exhausted dog collapsed in front of the fire, mother talked, Mrs. Nitti sniffled, shaking her head.

"We've got to hire somebody," mother kept saying, "it's for you to decide, or else let's sell here and live in Venice, you can go back to your studies, father took care of everything, there's money, shares, some gold, and then the land."

Months of sleep and silence. I hardly read a paper, avoided the neighbors. Mother nagged at me with questions and advice.

"We can't wait, the work has to be started, we can't just leave the fields empty."

She wept, called on God, the calamity of father's death; she started on me before breakfast. To get away I went out earlier, came back later. One evening, it was already springtime, the dog suddenly set off at a run toward a man who was coming from the house, he must have been looking out for me. The dog barked and jumped up at the man's face in a frenzy. I almost began to run too, to cry "Father, Father," for an instant of joy.

The man came toward me, behind the wriggling dog. I recognized Nitti's slow steps, short arms. We stood facing each other in the middle of the path, silent and unmoving.

"You and me, we're still alive," he said after a long pause.

"What do you want?"

"My job back. There's been an amnesty."

The dog lay down between us and his tail thumped against my boots.

"And if I refuse?"

"You're not to refuse."

"Why?"

"Because it's my right, Mr. Naldi. You know everything has changed in the last four years, a lot has happened."

I couldn't see his face but I remembered his look, his sarcastic smile when father used to give him his share at the long black table. I cocked the gun and placed the barrel against his chest.

"And what if I decided it was my right to kill you, Nitti, just like that, because you're a deserter and this land is mine?"

He slowly pushed the barrel away.

"Come now, Mr. Naldi, now, now, I don't think they've made a murderer out of you."

I didn't resist the pressure of his arm but I kept the gun ready.

"Don't you think there've been enough people killed?" he asked.

I put the rifle back on my shoulder with the same sense of embarrassment I used to feel when old Nitti stood waiting with his straw hat in his hand while grandfather read from the *Memorial of Saint Helena*.

"Tomorrow you'll tell me what you've decided," Nitti added as he turned.

The dog frolicked behind him.

The next day I left for Bologna without seeing him, but I told my mother:

"Now you've got Nitti, he'll take care of everything."

Where was there to go, except the Aquila Nera? Signora Maria remembered me perfectly.

"The lawyer was always talking about you, and then how could one forget you anyway?"

She minced and laughed. "I gave you my bed, you could almost say you were baptized in my bedroom."

But Ferri had gone to Milan.

"He's going into politics, writing in the papers. Here, the Reds tried to kill him."

She lowered her voice.

"Bologna is in their hands, but Mr. Ferri has sworn to get rid of them all, then we can breathe again, the idea of striking a man like him, a lawyer, and them only peasants and factory workers, they can't even read."

She gave me the address of the *Popolo d'Italia*, where Ferri could be found, and I hung around Bologna for a few weeks. I had money, the days were long and the nights short, I changed hotels and women, bought newspapers, installed myself in hotel lounges, drank a little. In the *Popolo* Ferri wrote, "Yes, we are fascists because we are loyal to our dead, because the fascist is the fighter of yesterday who wants his comrades' sacrifice not to have been in vain, who wants respect for Italy, work for everyone, and no hero, no uniformed officer ever to be insulted or struck again—as happened only yesterday in Genoa. Gentlemen socialists, gentlemen defeatists, you who did not fight the war, our memory is long and we will settle our account with you one day soon."

I learned that the Arditi were joining the combat units formed by Mussolini; in the pages of the socialist newspaper *Avanti* I discovered a whole world of conflict, insult, confrontation, and passion; I became worried, uncertain, I thought of Nitti and Alatri, and Captain Ferri, I imagined father alive, taking sides in these quarrels. Then I went out and buried myself in the country. I had bought a motorcar from a wealthy livestock dealer I met at the Aquila Nera, and set out along the empty white roads, feeding myself on wind and independence. It was as though I were still on furlough, a long empty period after the strain of the war and before other battles I would have to choose for myself: a job, because father's money would run out, a wife maybe. I stopped and lay in the grass by the roadside, looking at the clouds and trying to see nothing but sky, to forget the earth. Then I went back to Bologna, overtaking groups of peasants on their way home from work; some saluted, many insulted me, and sometimes threw stones and shouted, "*Viva la rivoluzione*, death to the rich!"

Often, in the heavy heat of the evenings of the new summer I would walk through the Piazza Vittorio Emanuele before knocking at the door of the Aquila Nera, where Signora Maria now welcomed me with respect. I mingled with the groups gathering under the arcades, there was talk of peasants brandishing red flags, occupying the land; of strikes in La Spezia and Turin. In the center of one attentive group I found Calvini, foretelling the revolution, punctuating his sentences with upraised fist:

"When schoolteachers are marching in Milan in rows of fifteen abreast, fifteen abreast you hear, and the priests are on strike and the peasants are organizing, what does it mean, it means socialism . . ."

"And the end of Italy."

I had made my way to the middle of the group and faced Calvini; immediately there was muttering, whistles.

"Let him speak," Calvini said.

"Provocation," someone called out.

"And who is going to run the country then, who, your striking workers, your stone-throwing peasants, you know them?"

"The people, mister."

"Go out to the country and look at them, they know how to set fire to a combine, and then what?"

We were under the arcade and daylight had faded.

"He's a fascist, got to be, a fascist."

People started shoving and pushing.

"Leave him alone, leave him alone," Calvini shouted.

"They burned the *Avanti* in Milan, they killed people."

My legs were being kicked, then there were shrill whistles and people running down the arcades, the carabinieri around me, a courteous sergeant checking my identification.

"Go home, sir, would you like someone to escort you?"

I went alone. Always two camps in life, like on the Piave, two sides, if you went forward by daylight the other side opened fire, no mercy, either the knife sinks home with one stroke or the sentry calls out and kills you. The law nobody chooses, your country, the side you inherit, Austrian on one side, Italian on the other, beaten on one side, victorious on the other, peasant on one side, landowner on the other. The law, the war.

I drank a lot that night at the Aquila Nera, I said my farewells, sang, the girls hovered around, laughing, Signora Maria whispered in my ear.

I woke in the morning in her bedroom and above my head saw the Virgin and Child in the oval frame. Signora Maria came in, opened the shutters, the sun burned my eyes.

"You're not much fun when you're drunk, you cried all night long."

She went out and returned with some coffee, sat down on the bed.

"Listen, Mr. Naldi, who is this Giulia who made you so unhappy? You were sobbing, truly, you were calling her."

Signora Maria shook her head:

"I've seen all sorts, I know men; you're a sentimental type, you'll never be like Captain Ferri, never, you're trying but you can't do it, nature's against it, he's tough and you're all tender inside, drink some coffee, you need it."

I hardly listened, I was reliving the nightmare, Giulia on the other side of the Piave, we had to cut her throat because that was the law, that was war.

I left Bologna that afternoon for Milan. It was a stormy day, dust whirled in cyclones on the roadway, peasants were driving the animals in from the fields with long sticks and the grass was flattened by the wind. I knew the brutal squalls of the Po Valley, the sky goes dark in seconds and rain and hail lay waste to the crops. I decided to stop at Reggio. The long Via Emilia was deserted, I found a hotel, the Albergo della Posta, on a square near the church. Almost the moment I parked the car, the storm broke and a cold wind drove the rain down the street. I ran for the arcade, a car turned into the square sending up a spray of water; its passengers rushed for cover too. We entered the hotel together; there were two young men in black shirts and a woman wearing a cape, which she removed with one flourish as she came through the door.

"The prince," she asked, "where is the prince?" She had a strong French accent.

"Ah, I was worrying about you."

I turned. An elegant old man came in behind me, he smiled, wiping his face.

"What a storm, a genuine tornado," he said. "Elsa, you're not cold?"

"Excuse me, you are traveling by car aren't you? Have you come from Bologna? Or Parma?"

She was speaking to me, her accent made me smile, she sounded as though she was trying to exaggerate it; or maybe it was the way she was looking at me that made me smile.

"We've lost a truck with several of our people," she went on, "we don't know whether they have gone ahead or haven't reached Reggio yet because of the storm."

I had met no one and seen nothing. The prince stepped forward. We introduced ourselves.

"May I invite you to join us until this tornado is over?"

The waiters hurried forward, lighting lamps, but it was as gloomy as ever. The two young men in black shirts never took their eyes off Elsa. They resembled each other, both thin with narrow mustaches, the same nervousness of look and gesture, the same way of picking up a glass, ordering another drink. The prince talked about his wars, this vulgar age, the peasants who think they own everything.

"The Russian example, extremely pernicious because the press, our little masters, make such a mountain of it, my wife who is French will tell you that if we are not careful we'll have another 1789 before long. But *they* are here, and they are tough."

He waved at the young men.

"Prince Missini is, too, I can assure you," one of them said. "And here's something to persuade even the hardest head."

With a smile he showed the handle of a dagger pushed down inside his boot. I recognized that smile and dagger, I had met them on the Piave. Among us there had been some who liked to kill.

"Were you in the war?"

Elsa Missini was sitting next to me, I watched her long fingers playing with her glass, I could see the extremely white skin of her wrists and hands.

"I beg your pardon."

I couldn't answer him for a moment, she had sent my thoughts spinning, the insistence of her look, the freedom of her movements, that way of crossing her legs, smoking, throwing back her head and showing her throat.

"You are a dreamer, sir."

"Marco Naldi," I said, "second lieutenant in the Arditi. I was in the war, yes, like everybody else."

"Arditi? Then you must be a fascist?"

I shook my head, neither yes nor no, my doubt.

"Not yet, then," she said, smiling. "You don't like to commit yourself?"

She took little sips of her drink, her eyes on my face.

"I am a friend of Captain Ferri, I was under his orders."

The prince gave an exclamation, Ferri had just been through

his province, he was helping the landowners to form combat units, the *squadre*, to fight the peasants.

"We must break their backs," said the prince, "you understand, destroy the carriers of the germs, then the rest will keep quiet."

"Were you on the Piave?"

Elsa Missini questioned me in a low voice, creating a complicity between us underneath the surface of the conversation.

"My brother was a French military adviser on your front," she went on.

I had not known Major Pierre de Beuil.

"Ferri is remarkable," the prince continued; "an organizer, a leader, and he has *virtù*. You've been to a good school, sir. You will always be welcome, we need young men for our squadre, especially here in a Socialist stronghold, they are putting up quite a fight."

There was a racket at the entrance, loud voices; a dozen men carrying cudgels, wet black shirts clinging to their skins, burst into the room. Elsa Missini leaned toward me and whispered, "The truck I was speaking of a moment ago, there they are. What part of the country are you from?"

The prince and the two young men had gotten up, we were alone.

"Venice."

"The most beautiful city in Italy."

Then quickly, emphasizing her words with a frown.

"Come see us in Rome, we are there most of the year, we only live here in the summer, my husband is fond of his estate but the city is the only thing that exists for me, you know." She said, even more softly than before, "I was born in Paris."

The prince was coming back, Elsa turned away. "Gentlemen, here is a second lieutenant in the Arditi, a friend of Captain Ferri."

They gave the battle cry we had so often shouted in the war, "A *noï!*" and I took it up with them. We drank. The storm had interrupted their expedition in the Parma region, they were laughing at the terror of a peasant woman: they had forced her to drink two liters of castor oil, tied her skirt down around her calves, and made her dance in the middle of their group until the laxative took effect.

"But then this damned rain came, the show was just beginning," said the loudest member of the group.

His cudgel was attached to his wrist by a leather bracelet and he twirled it continuously, stopping only to drink.

"Who was it?"

He looked at me and shrugged:

"Some peasant woman, the wife or daughter of a leader of the union or co-operative, I don't remember. A Red, for sure."

Giulia, if she hadn't been dead.

"We're going now, Mr. Naldi. You were dreaming again."

Elsa Missini had put her hand on my shoulder, the lightest touch, a warmth spread through me.

"Come see us."

She was putting on her cape.

"Or who knows, we will meet again, everything is possible, isn't it?"

I went outside with her, after the others. The motors were idling, their headlights shining on the wet paving stones and probing under the arches where silhouettes passed swiftly; the truck moved off first with a great grinding of gears, the singing *squadristi* hanging to the rails and waving black flags. The car drew alongside us.

"An age of violence," Elsa Missini said.

"Elsa, we'll lose them again."

Prince Missini, who sat in the back with one of the young men, had opened the door but Elsa went on as though she had not heard.

"You're a strange people," she was saying, "we cut off our king's head but when all is said and done, we are the moderates. We don't have your passion."

She sat next to the driver, holding out her long white hand. "But then, I too have lost my moderation since I've been living here. Come to us, Mr. Naldi, I'm counting on you."

She pressed my fingers, soft and imperious. In the hotel, customers I had either not noticed before or who had preferred to keep out of sight were observing me coldly, talking too loudly. I left, driving through a landscape that rustled in the moist cool of the night. Faces jumbled together in my mind, the unknown peasant woman they had compelled to dance, the young killer with the dagger, Elsa Missini, a woman unlike any I had met, neither submissive nor mercenary, she seemed to scorn both tears and complaints, to have chosen her life. "There are the masters and there are the others," my grandfather used to say, "and you don't become a master overnight." Elsa Missini had been born among masters.

I reached Milan at dawn, overtaking clusters of workers riding their bicycles through gray suburbs, head down like those others back in the rice fields whose faces were also bent to the earth. Life had not chosen them to reign, they were on one side, Elsa Missini on the other. Was I responsible for the choice, the allocation of fate that made some men conquerors and others the conquered? On the Via Paolo di Canobbio I found the offices of the *Popolo d'Italia*. Men in black shirts were sleeping on chairs, there were weapons lying about on tables among newspapers. A black flag with a skull on it hung on the wall. I was searched and given permission to wait for Ferri.

"You know, we have to be careful," explained one fascist with a revolver stuck in his belt. "Sit over there."

I looked through back numbers of the *Popolo*, then there was a burst of loud voices in the staircase and some fascists came in, Mussolini in their midst, talking, shaking his fists. I saw his heavy head, square and bald, his black suit and off-white collar. Ferri came in soon afterward, gave me a hug.

"Marco, at last . . ."

He introduced me to various people.

"There's as much action ahead as back there on the Piave, and we need boys who know how to fight."

He had put on a little weight but seemed to have more energy than ever when he laughed, his close-set white teeth sharp against the black of his beard. From the back of the office, behind a guarded door, angry voices could be heard. Ferri winked.

"He makes a lot of noise, but he knows what he's talking about. I want you to meet him."

When Mussolini came out, Ferri pushed me forward.

"Here is the son of a hero who died for the fatherland, an Ardito, Second Lieutenant Naldi."

Mussolini stared at me, took me by the shoulders, laid one hand on my neck, his eyes unmoving.

"Fine, fine, it's what has to be done for Italy, for your father."

Then he took Ferri into his office and I heard his clipped, sharp voice hammering out sentences, detaching every word:

"It's no longer a government, Ferri, it's some kind of foetus, half democratic, half legislative, and I want you to be there for the abortion."

They laughed and joked.

"Leave the squadre to the others and go to Rome," Mussolini went on. "You're a lawyer, Ferri, you'll know how to talk to them."

I stood aside and stopped listening, I was dreaming of Giulia, a smell of apples and death, of father, of the peasant woman dancing with her mouth full of castor oil; I was waiting for Ferri and for months I had been waiting, waiting for the fatal bullet, the fateful woman, waiting to finish spending my inheritance. Ferri called me into the office. Mussolini was sitting, elbows on the table and head between his hands, watching me come in.

"What are you doing now?" he asked.

I was going from woman to woman, from day to day, I was

fleeing Magliano, Nitti, Giulia, father, despair, and my mother's arms.

"Nothing?"

Mussolini stood up; he was quicksilver, his expression changing continually, his hands moving.

"Captain Ferri has told me about you. You'll go to Rome with him. Fight well, as you did on the Piave."

"Come see us in Rome," Elsa Missini had said. I had no choice to make, Rome was coming to me. Had I ever made a choice? I had inherited the land and the war and the money that brought such a honeyed smile to Signora Maria's lips and made the Aquila Nera girls so tender, I was born on that side of the barrier and Giulia was on the other shore, in a country where people stoop over rice fields.

That evening, Ferri took me into the busy streets in the center of Milan. He squeezed my arm.

"You'd have rotted away at Magliano, Naldi, widows always rot their sons."

We crossed the Piazza del Duomo; Ferri showed me the Corso, where the fascists had fought the socialists one April evening.

"They were scampering like rabbits, they can talk but they can't fight, they haven't got the determination, Naldi, they're afraid to be hit. And politics is determination above all, and then hitting and getting hit. You remember Alatri?"

Ferri had seen him among the socialist demonstrators.

"He was running like the rest. He's founded some little communist group, and it was you who brought him back through the lines!"

I remembered: the first-aid post, Alatri's cough, the listening soldiers.

"Alatri, a real gangrene."

We had been going to meet again, I was going to write, to explain; now he'd crossed the barrier, he was on the other side and I was with Ferri, who was talking:

"It's an iron century, Naldi, there is no middle way, it's either them or us, that's the way it is."

We left for Rome the next day.

At first, Rome was the searing sirocco, empty streets, a long, long twilight, yellow and purple streaks, and then it was the stench of garbage piled outside doors and in the gutters, spreading over the pavement of the Campo dei Fiori, dogs scavenging in the rubbish and cats watching them from a distance. Rome like a red ripe fruit, half-splitting, open streets with striking garbagemen and cab drivers; fights broke out sometimes, figures collided and other figures parted them, shouting, muttering, and the carabinieri in pairs, erect and unseeing beneath the arches. Ferri squeezed my shoulder and laughed nervously.

"The government's letting it rot," he said, "it's their strategy, but they've got some crazy idea that the war never happened. They've forgotten about us. Naldi, we're going to hold their heads down in the shit until they cry for help."

We moved into a big apartment on the Piazza Barberini and from our windows we could see Montecitorio, where the parliament sat. Ferri paced through the rooms with folded arms.

"They won't stay in power long, believe me, Marco."

Then I began to learn what a city was, a country, power. I escorted cautious politicians into Ferri's office and he ushered them out again, smiling.

"My dear friend, really, whom do you take us for," he would say. "Legality is sacred to us, the interests of Italy come before all else. Think it over, do you honestly believe the situation which the president of the council is tolerating can endure? Come, now!"

"He's a fox, he's maneuvering," they answered.

With modest conviction Ferri repeated, "Think it over, think it over, look at the spectacle in the streets."

They would leave and Ferri would curse.

"Scum."

He pulled me over to the balcony. We drank and looked at the city.

"They're scared, Naldi. They're hesitating. They're all coming to see us."

Ferri consulted his diary.

"They've all come," he said, "all of them. They're shitting in their pants."

He gave me a thump on the back and we went out. Cafés on the Corso, the Via Veneto, Piazza Colonna.

"We'll fuck them, Marco," Ferri said when we got back. "We'll fuck this city, believe me."

I was growing up fast, discovering the spider web that covers a city, a country, and Ferri fascinated me here even more than he had in Venice or on the Piave. Out there I'd seen him hurl grenades, unfurling his arm at the end of his taut body. Here, just as precise and violent, he spied, intrigued, paid.

It was my job to listen to the debates in parliament, to read the papers. A representative would get up and address the house, swearing unconditional loyalty to the government. I knew the other side of his words, I'd seen the man shaking Ferri's hand. In a notebook, a sum of money facing a name. The price of a vote. I was acquiring a taste for the shadows, I liked to slip through the streets among the crowd when the fascists were parading, bareheaded and hairy in tight-fitting black or sometimes blue shirts and wide belts over their riding breeches; their furious songs, their death's-head flags, their cudgels and riding crops. I was anonymous. Violence in their eyes, fear on the spectators' faces. I knew the underside of things, I knew that in order to assemble those fifteen thousand men in Rome every one of them had to be paid three hundred lire; four and a half million, they cost.

"Harder work than clearing a trench, Marco," said Ferri.

A sympathetic industrialist came in. Ferri received him deferentially, then, once the door was closed behind him, bawled, "He coughed up!"

Now fifteen thousand fascists were parading through the streets; their clubs threatened spectators who didn't take off their hats when the black flag went by. They glowered, shouted, "*Abbasso il cappello!* Hats off!"

I remove mine, too, who knows me? I'm just a young man, too tall, too thin, I don't wear the fashionable short beard, I'm smooth-shaven, almost fair, and sometimes the children who beg in the streets speak to me in English. I pass by, I remove my hat, but I know. I sat in Mussolini's office in Milan, listening to Ferri.

"They're shitting in their pants," he said again. "We're the only ones they trust."

Mussolini, nervous, rubbing his hands, pacing in circles around Ferri.

"We must maneuver, wait a little longer, play a close game, frighten and reassure," he said.

Later, Ferri in the train, pensive, smoking a cigar.

"It's coming, Naldi, it's ripening."

I was learning about reality. The truth about words, their weakness and their strength.

When I saw Prince Missini come into the apartment on the Piazza Barberini I knew the words I was about to say would commit me; I had the choice, I could say nothing, but once I had identified myself my life would take a new turn. I hesitated, I wasn't used to making decisions. The prince didn't recognize me, we were waiting for Ferri, who was late.

"I know the king," said the prince, "he won't dare proclaim a state of siege against us if we make a move."

He was looking out the window, slowly pacing around the drawing room.

"Mussolini must be convinced of that; the army, you know, will never open fire on the fascists without an order from the king, and the king will not give that order. So we've won. Besides, between us and the revolution how could he hesitate?"

He sat. I was beginning to be familiar with that indolent way

of moving, that relaxed self-possession of men who are at home
inside their skins. The prince leaned his head against his left
hand and smoked with a half smile and I thought of Nitti's pon-
derous walk, of Carlo, of all those men of the country and those
who labored, dragged down by weariness, I saw Giulia again,
not yet bogged down in the mire but she would have been, in-
evitably. Whereas Elsa Missini had this same way of moving,
carrying her head and throat, her long white hands.

"Revolution," the prince was continuing, "or the specter of
it, but the king and the Italians don't need to know that, do
they?"

"In other words," I said, "it never would have been 1789 here;
but didn't Princess Missini believe it might, at one time?"

"Do you know her?"

One sentence; I had taken the turn. I recalled the stop at the
Albergo della Posta, summer, the storm, Reggio nell'Emilia.

"Good Lord, I remember perfectly, we were coming back
from a little expedition to Parma, quite dreadful weather, night
in broad daylight, yes, of course, you were a friend of Captain
Ferri, how could I have . . ."

Ferri came in, apologized, his voice was loud and excited.

"Prince, I had no idea; you know the decision has been taken,
I've just seen General de Bono . . ."

"The end of the month?"

The prince remained utterly calm.

"After the Naples Congress, which is set for October the
twenty-fourth," Ferri went on. "At last, Prince, at last!"

Ferri had tossed his briefcase on the desk and was pacing,
talking quickly, his face flushed.

"Everything depends on the king and the army; the socialists, the communists are wiped out, the church . . ."

"My dear captain, come now, I was just explaining to your
friend Naldi that the king is ours, of course the legal conven-
tions must be respected."

"We'll respect anything you like, what do we care."

Ferri had let himself go a little too far, but the prince seemed not to have heard.

"Mr. Naldi," he said turning to me, "we are at home on Tuesdays after six, will you do the princess and myself the honor of coming this Tuesday?"

I bowed and withdrew, leaving them to discuss the details of the March on Rome, which we had been planning for weeks. And now it was finally about to begin, it would give us the power, "All the power, Marco, imagine!" said Ferri. In those days I had no political imagination. I was learning to know men, dreaming about women, hearing Elsa Missini's voice under the rain-washed sky, "Come to us in Rome."

"We always meet in a storm, is it a sign?" said Elsa Missini.

I was in the Palazzo Missini at the end of the Via Giulia; I had meant to walk there in order to calm my nerves but the storm broke and I took a cab that went down the Via Giulia in a raging downpour, the driver cursing the sky, his words mingling with the splatter of the rain. October 1922 in Rome was a month of thunderstorms and wind. I kissed Elsa's long white hand and walked on with her beneath crystal chandeliers. There were a hundred people there, some in evening dress, others in suits, many in uniform, black shirts and women's bare shoulders. Servants moved about, there was a knot of people in front of the long white buffet, and drawing rooms opening off the sides of the great hall with the pink marble floor.

"I knew we would meet again, everything is possible, isn't it?" murmured Elsa. "I have great faith in chance."

She smiled at the others, looked at me and did not smile; I was intimidated, dazzled, could hardly find my words.

"You're with Captain Ferri here, what great work he has done, I think we're nearing the goal."

She frowned to emphasize certain phrases, extending her hand right and left.

"I'd like you to come back, but not on a Tuesday, so we can

talk quietly; this evening—perhaps it's the storm—I find this crowd oppressive."

She hurried over to a French officer, very tall, a thin black mustache cutting across a rectilinear face.

"My brother, Major Pierre de Beuil, military attaché at the embassy, we've become neighbors, the Palazzo Farnese is just around the corner."

She left us; my French was clumsy but Major de Beuil took such a passionate interest in fascism that he understood every intimation and was soon telling me how badly France needed a movement like ours.

"When Mussolini writes that the nineteenth was the century of revolution and the twentieth will be that of restoration, dear sir, he is in the mainstream, the tradition of Joseph de Maistre and Maurras."

I was not paying attention, I was following Elsa's shoulders; I recognized politicians and businessmen I had ushered into Captain Ferri's office on the Piazza Barberini; they nodded to me. Now I was learning that Rome is a village, and power is a few men connected together. Toward the end of the evening Elsa came back to me and drew me into a room dimly lit by candles. We sat facing each other in two huge armchairs.

"Are you going to the Naples Congress?"

I was staying in Rome to replace Ferri, keep an eye on the press and government circles.

"The prince will be there," she told me as she rose. "Come to me, we can have dinner here on the twenty-fourth."

That was the opening day of the Congress. I left with Pierre de Beuil, we walked up the Via Giulia in semidarkness.

"You're going to win," Beuil said, "and Italy needs you, and you'll set us an example. There has always been an exchange between France and Italy; you brought the Renaissance, we gave you Napoleon. Today it's your move."

He stopped in the middle of the Via Giulia, lightning was flashing in the distance.

"It will be contagious, Mr. Naldi, and this contagion is the only way to stop the Bolshevik contagion, the only way."

This passion for power and politics, Beuil, Alatri, Ferri, Mussolini, I couldn't understand it. I was involved in the movement, of course, and felt I was going to become more and more deeply involved, it would become my occupation; but what would be my passion? I wanted to keep my place, no more. Maybe I was not ambitious enough, and maybe I felt that if father and Giulia had lived I would have stayed at Magliano and my life would have gone another way.

"You have a great future, Mr. Naldi, you're young and you're at the heart of things, where the decisions are made," said Major de Bcuil as he turned to enter the Palazzo Farnese.

What was the future? I carried that question inside me all through the end of that October 1922. Our apartment on the Piazza Barberini had become a headquarters; delegations from right-wing and moderate parliamentary groups were coming in a steady stream, last-minute allies came running with some new tidbit of information, Ferri couldn't handle them all so I saw the unpaid informers who drew me aside in a corner of the room to relate some confidential remark made by General Badoglio, one of the leaders of the army.

"I assure you," one representative repeated with alarm in his voice, "the general said and I'm quoting word for word, 'Five minutes under fire and fascism will collapse.'"

They watched my reactions as though I were some source of truth, they questioned me anxiously, wanting to make sure they had bet on the right horse. I said nothing, letting their anxiety mount, then I would get up without a word, usher them out, take their arms:

"We know all that, my dear sir, and much more, have no fear, we're ready."

I discovered the power of words, played with it, sometimes gave out Ferri's remarks, criticizing some politician or other, as though they were my own:

"The most that old crook can hope for from fascism is the firing squad."

They listened to me; and these men laden with honors showed their fear. Had they never faced anything? Had the men who sent us out to the Piave never seen a head explode in the black dirt of the trenches? I exaggerated our strength, our violence, out of sheer pleasure, I liked to see them quaking at the tips of my words.

On October 23, Mussolini stopped off at Ferri's for a few hours on his way to Naples: he was already the power in the state. I saw yesterday's presidents of the council coming to pay court, and paying court to me because I held a fragment of that power. In the main drawing room Mussolini spoke to a few of his journalist friends. He was playing with a long-stemmed rose, inhaling it affectedly, walking back and forth in the room.

"We have no intention of coming into power by the back door," he said. "Either they give us the government or we take it, it's a simple problem."

It became even simpler once we knew the army would not interfere. After the departure on the following day, October 24, Rome was quiet; the fascists were gathering in Naples and I walked through the empty, village-like streets to the echo of horses' hoofs. The footman at the Palazzo Missini guided me through a labyrinth of inner courtyards, limping as he walked. He was wearing decorations, talked about the war, the Carso plateau swept by snow and machine-gun fire. He took me to a little hallway lined with gilded mirrors where pink cherubs chased one another across the ceiling. Elsa Missini came in almost at once, her hair loose on her neck, a white blouse hugging her waist and black trousers making her figure appear more slender.

"Venetian mirrors," she said, taking my hand. "You're not too busy with your politics?"

She was talking quickly, leading me into a drawing room hung with blue.

"Tell me; for me politics is a drug, you must know everything."

I talked, she laughed, we drank, I knew a few secrets, I watched her breasts under the white silk, if I was there it was because she wanted me to be, but I'd have to take the plunge like at night on the Piave; when we went over the top there had always been one moment of doubt, fear falling upon me, a painful question—why jump?—a longing to lie down on the ground, cling to the earth, refuse to follow Ferri, and then the captain would give the signal and we would move out silently one behind the other, crawling toward the river.

Elsa Missini stood up.

"Here we are talking," she said, "and I've forgotten all about our supper."

I stood too; she was tall, maybe the tallest woman I had known until then, she passed me on the way to the door, I reached for her arm, waist, shoulders, she was only a woman, pulling her close, finding her mouth that did not pull away, the lift of her breasts, sliding my hand under the white silk, finding the cool skin of her back and her scented neck. I squeezed as though I wanted to break her, she was my first woman, I knew that through her I had just entered a new world, a phase had ended. She pushed me away, I reached for her again, she gave me her mouth again and then pushed me away once more.

"Come," she said in French, "we'll eat afterward, all right?"

I put my hands on her hips. She was Princess Elsa Missini but she was a woman like the nurse I had thrown down on her brass bed in the Milan hospital the night of the victory. The only light in the bedroom came from a candelabrum with three tall red tapers, her bedroom was a forest of hangings, rugs, cushions, and she said in French:

"You're being brutal, wait. . . ."

But she was laughing, letting me undress her, she was white, full, silky, she had the boldness and freedom of the girls of the Aquila Nera and the nervous, impatient eagerness of women who give themselves for pleasure. Now it was her turn to squeeze me hard.

"You're young," she said.

Then came a laugh from her throat, and she added in French, "But skillful."

We ate and drank in her room. She had put on a lace peignoir and I remembered the girl in Signora Maria's room: "Look, soldier," she had said. I was naked, I drank.

"You're shameless," murmured Elsa Missini, "I thought you were shy, you're an old veteran, a true fascist."

We came together again, she let herself go entirely, I rediscovered her body, playing with her. We slept, a little.

"We'll have to arrange something, the prince is coming back from Naples."

She was smoking while I dressed.

"But don't worry, we have our rules."

"Is this a habit?"

She laughed.

"Have you ever looked at the prince, and have you looked at me? He knows how to behave and so do I. We loathe scandal. It doesn't add anything, does it, Marco?"

The Palazzo Missini had many doors, one whole wing overlooked the Lungo Tevere, Elsa led me there. There was an apartment with walls of dark carved wood.

"This is my kingdom, here I have extraterritorial rights. You can wait for me here."

Life was simple. I took a long way home, following the river to the Isola Tiberina; a bitter wind was blowing down from the Apennines and the sky was pale blue. Then I turned into the narrow alleys of the poor people's Rome where tradesmen were opening their dark shops, I walked down the middle of the streets. I had seen through the façade: I knew that everything was a stage setting—power, the respectability of women, I knew there were two worlds, one laid on top of the other. I was initiated, thank you Captain Ferri, thank you Princess Elsa Missini, there would be no scandal, I would not be late for my rendez-vous in the palace apartment overlooking the Lungo Tevere.

At home a stack of messages had piled up in a few hours, Ferri was issuing instructions. I ran to see our informers; they were quaking. The king, it appeared, had declared a state of siege after all; Facta, the president of the council, an absurd little man, was posturing on the platform, appealing to the nation: "In the face of an attempted uprising," he wrote, "it is the duty of the government to maintain order by any means and at any cost."

Soldiers were already piling sandbags outside government buildings and setting up barricades across the bridges. In the evening, Elsa Missini was laughing in my arms.

"The king is just putting on his little show, the prince saw him today, he's going to give in as usual."

I made love to her violently; perhaps I wanted Elsa, someone, something to resist, wanted one statement to be true; but when I left in the middle of the night in the rain, the soldiers had already disappeared and I crossed the bridges over the Tiber without seeing a single sentry. Ferri was back from Naples, jubilant.

"Marco, this is the last act, they're going to call him, you'll see, they're falling apart."

On the twenty-ninth the headline of the *Popolo* read "Fascism Wants Power, It Will Get It" and the next day the press published the king's confidential telegram to Mussolini: "His Majesty the King, wishing to confer with you, requests you to come to Rome. Yours. General Cittadini."

Preparations had to be made for Mussolini's arrival, conferences with the military authorities, I followed Ferri, took notes, was unable to get to Elsa until late that night. She was waiting for me, asleep, lying among her cushions in the soft light of the red candles. I sat down facing her, without waking her. What would Giulia have become over the years, what was hiding behind father's reassurances, what face, what passions, were there no alternatives but nonexistence or duplicity?

"Marco."

Elsa awoke, voluptuous, holding out her arms, truthful in her calculated abandon.

"I've got to leave again, Mussolini is coming tomorrow, there are still things to be done."

She pulled me to her.

"You're a good fascist," she said, nibbling at my ear.

She had taken to speaking to me in French and I liked it that she kept that less public part of herself for me.

"A good lover."

I was late, I found a cab in the Piazza Farnese, it was still raining; I heard shouting in the streets around the Campo dei Fiori, shots were fired at long intervals. I questioned the driver. He shrugged, answered in Roman dialect.

"Some of them are playing heroes as if there was anything they could do about it. The fools'll only get themselves shot; as if you didn't die soon enough anyway."

Groups of Black Shirts were crossing the Piazza Venezia, singing and waving clubs and black banners. At home I assembled the news. There had been fighting in the poor parts of town all night, the offices of antifascist newspapers had been raided. A representative of the liberal faction came to Ferri to protest. He was grave, moderate, respectable, with his heavy ivory-headed cane.

"Public opinion," he was saying as we were getting ready to leave for the station to meet Mussolini, "will be shocked."

"Perhaps you'd rather we let the *Avanti* pull a strike on us," shouted Ferri on his way down the stairs.

"But we are not socialists, my dear Ferri, and you know it, we support the movement for renovation."

He was trying to keep up but we walked too fast.

"Loose threads, there are always a few loose threads," Ferri snapped.

We jumped into a taxi. At 10:42 on October 30, 1922, Mussolini got off the train from Milan. The troops saluted him.

Fascists were shouting with outstretched arms. He and Ferri got into the first car, I was in the third.

That evening, while the center of town was overrun by squadristi celebrating their victory, arrogant, threatening people in the streets, I took a cab to Elsa's.

The rain that had flailed at the city most of the day had stopped. I got out at the end of the Via Giulia and walked down the long straight street. This was another world, silence, paving stones with moss creeping between them, the austere façades of palazzi and, at the very end, the river, the Roman hills half-seen through the mist. I walked slowly. During the day I had learned that Calvini, the socialist representative from Bologna, had been manhandled outside Montecitorio. Young fascists had made him drink castor oil and cut off his beard. I could still hear him near the Bologna gasworks shouting, trying to protect me, "Comrades, attack ideas, not men!" Other fascists had painted the face of a young communist journalist, son of a noted general, in the colors of the national flag, green-white-red. The papers didn't give his name.

Elsa was in her room, naked on the bed among the cushions.

"You don't look very cheerful for a day of victory," she said when she saw me come in.

3

I left Elsa Missini, as usual, at dawn. Without opening her eyes she murmured a few words, the same every morning. Rome was silent, only the cry of a cab driver along the Tiber and my footsteps on the paving stones of the Via Giulia. Habit. Nevertheless, there had been a change. From that day forward I belonged on the side of the conquerors, I marched in the procession of power, I was one of those who are deferred to and feared. The very first day Major Pierre de Beuil came to the Piazza Barberini. I supposed he wanted to see Ferri and began making the captain's apologies.

"An audience at the Quirinale with the king and Mussolini."

Beuil, in civilian dress, smiling, had laid his gloves on the arm of a chair.

"But it's you, my dear Naldi, I wanted to congratulate, you personally, I know all you have done in these past weeks for the victory of fascism and I was anxious to tell you so."

I listened, what had I done? Nothing but use words, meet a few people who were said to be important, play on their fear, transmit information to Captain Ferri. Beuil was talking about my future again.

"My dear fellow, you are the new generation, you are the power, not today perhaps but tomorrow. Would you please give my respects to Ferri?"

I accompanied him to the door.

"In my own name and also on behalf of all fighting Frenchmen."

Pierre de Beuil took my arm in the doorway, and leaning toward me he said, in a low voice, "Give my respects to my sister as well, I think you see more of her than I do."

He had the same trick of frowning as Elsa.

"Be careful of Pierre," Elsa told me that evening, "he wants to be the French Mussolini, he has the pride of the Beuils, he believes . . ."

She interrupted herself. "Why not, after all, he'll shower you with favors, he thinks you're important."

She looked at herself in the mirrors, arched her back, puffed out her breasts, walked over to me naked, rubbing herself along my arm:

"But you are important, you're going to be very important, aren't you?"

They saw me as grasping a piece of the scepter: I was Ferri's private secretary, Ferri was a secretary of state and an adviser and confidant of Mussolini in the Consultà, seat of the ministry of foreign affairs. From his windows he could see the obelisk of Dogali, the roofs of Rome, their baroque alignment. I came into his office; Ferri seemed to be dreaming, sitting erect in his tall armchair facing a huge portrait of Cavour. I waited, laid a file on the desk. At last he saw me.

"Naldi, my dear Marco."

Ferri. Power changes men; only a few days had passed, and he was swathed in layers of ceremony.

"Ah, Naldi," Ferri went on, "government, first and foremost, is foreign policy. That is what draws the portrait of a country; never forget it."

He was addressing an invisible audience; Alatri's words came back to me, when he sat grumbling on the edge of the lagoon in Venice: "Lawtalker!" But I was catching the disease, too. In the drawing room of the Hotel Savoia I too was making speeches to journalists, collecting my share of the friendly regards, conniving smiles, mute signals. They all wanted to see Mussolini, the Duce.

"Gentlemen, Minister Ferri is with him at this moment."

I was the substitute for the Duce, for Minister Ferri, I smiled, eluded, invented. I held them in my hand. I took one over to the Duce. Mussolini raised his head after a long pause, stared at us with his unmoving eyes, then began to talk, his whole face contorted to shape the sentences he was uttering too loudly, as though to a crowd.

"The Italians have never obeyed," he said, "that is what we lack, obedience, order."

He struck his chest.

"But I am here, fascism is here, I swear that from now on things are going to be different."

I was different. Mother wrote regularly, telling me about the land, the Nittis. Farm prices were falling, machinery had to be bought, fortunately Mussolini had stopped all plans for land reform. "At last we can forget that worry, but we are short of cash, the lawyer . . ." I sent back a few lines, I didn't need anything from home now, power was money too, and the apartment on the Piazza Barberini, which Ferri had left to me, where Elsa sometimes came in the afternoons. I would find her dozing in one of the armchairs near the balcony, I looked out to the piazza, the Via del Tritone, the crossing cars and horse-drawn cabs, my official car on its way back to the Consultà, the langorous woman awakening. I was indeed on the side of the conquerors, I remembered that first evening when Ferri and I had left the Quirinale after the fascist parade outside the royal palace and the straining crowd was still held in check by carabinieri and Black Shirts, I saw the faces and outstretched arms again, the hands waving little flags, I heard the voices shouting "Mussolini, Mussolini, Mussolini," and other voices between the hooting horns and bugle blasts chanting "Viva il fascismo, viva il fascismo." I was sitting beside Ferri, who was smoking, his head thrown back against the seat while the driver tried to force a way through.

"Listen to them, Naldi," he said, "listen to them bleating: sheep! If we had lost they would hang us with exactly the same enthusiasm."

Then he sat up and put his arm around my shoulders.

"They have no idea, Marco, they think they're going to assim-

ilate us, they're all hoping, the king, the politicians, the damned
fools don't even know what they want, but we're going to dig
in and hang on with tooth and nail, and we won't let go, and
we'll stick in their throats like chicken bones."

That was at the very beginning, when the truth was still naked,
Ferri still resembled the captain I had met for the first time
outside our house at Magliano with his cape thrown over his
shoulder, seeming not to notice the rain; he was still the man
who had pushed me through the door of the Aquila Nera, Signora Maria's friend, the lawyer who had such a lovely voice.
Then came power, a few short days, the cheering squadristi
bawling in the gardens of the Villa Borghese, surrounding us,
"Mussolini, Mussolini, Mussolini," their black banners lowered
as we passed, their salute with outstretched arm, and Mussolini
solemn a few yards in front. A few short days, the time of the
ceremonies, we were kneeling in puddles of water in the Piazza
Venezia in front of the Altar of the Fatherland, I looked at those
men in evening dress, their top hats in their hands, ministers,
austere generals, their eyes fixed on Mussolini's stocky figure,
bending down with him, rising at his signal, I listened to the
swelling waves of applause rolling down from the Corso. We
were the official train of power, we moved down the roadway,
arms reached out to us, we were becoming symbols, mirages.
Ferri wasn't Captain Ferri any more, he was His Excellency
Secretary of State Ferri. And I was his secretary, the young lover
of Princess Elsa Missini.

"I must run," she said, "you're coming tonight."

She was wearing a tremendously wide-brimmed hat, a fur
collar hid her chin, all I could see were her lips coming toward
me. She pushed me away.

"Marco, I haven't time, the chauffeur is waiting."

I accompanied her to the car and wandered through the
streets, down the Via del Tritone to Montecitorio. The House
was in session, I strolled along the corridors, the representatives
of the government majority saluted me, mostly diffident, the

socialists ignored me. I caught sight of Calvini in his eternal red scarf, and of Matteotti, thin, hollow-cheeked, with sunken eyes. When Mussolini had grasped the edge of the rostrum in both hands and challenged "I could have turned this roomful of deaf men into a camp of maniples" and the fascists had stood and cheered for minutes on end, Calvini and Matteotti, both on their feet, had shouted, "*Eviva il parlamento!* Long live the parliament!"

Ferri, in the galleries of Montecitorio after the sitting, joked: "Oh, a fine gesture, they think they'll get us out with words, with their vaudeville heroics!"

He pointed to the armed fascist militia patrolling outside parliament.

"But the show is over, Mr. Public Menace, take care, take care, machine guns speak louder than words."

He was standing in the center of a group of self-satisfied representatives and squadristi, and he still had his voice from the days when we were recapturing outposts on the Piave. One soldier had hung on alone, senselessly and hopelessly defending a few square yards of gray earth. We found his body, I had to pry apart the fingers clamped around his gun. "A fine, futile gesture," Alatri grumbled as he came back into the shelter.

It was there at Montecitorio, in the dim gallery where Ferri had been orating, that I saw Alatri a few days later. He was coming toward me in the din of an interval in the sitting. Thinner, wearing a light gray suit even though it was winter, and coughing, walking with a stoop, turning the pages of a newspaper. I stood in front of him. He wore glasses now. He bumped into me, raised his head, showed no surprise, as though we had parted the day before.

"Well, well, Naldi."

My hand reached out to take his arm, his hand, his shoulder. He forestalled me, disengaging himself. The tone of the meeting was already set.

"You made it, that's good," I said.

"You saved me once, now I'm waiting for your friends to kill me. They'd like to take back what you lent me. Fascist justice, isn't that so, Marco?"

He was nervous, stinging, a few steely, precise words, whether they were fair or unfair I didn't know but they hit me and I couldn't tell him anything; I should have written those letters before the victory, should have told him; but what was the use, he'd already chosen. So I talked about his injury, the front, Magliano, he was taking his glasses off and putting them on again, hardly listening. I kept talking, beginning to feel more and more ill at ease, I wanted to shake him, we could take a walk outside, sit down in a café, was I trying to kill him? I was ready to protect him, hadn't I dragged him yard by yard out of the Piave? I kept talking, useless words, the only ones possible. Suddenly he interrupted me, tapping my shoulder with his newspaper.

"My dear Naldi, you're a curious fellow, I've never figured out whether you are naïve or an imbecile or a cynic, probably a little of all three. But what does it matter, eh?"

He smiled for the first time, already moving away.

"Excuse me, but I don't suppose you people will let us hang around parliament much longer so I don't want to waste my time, and you're only a walk-on."

The bell to resume the sitting had already rung and the ushers were calling the spectators back to their seats. Alatri turned around. "Regards to Ferri."

I stayed in the public gallery listening to Mussolini's voice punctuated by applause. I was standing near one of the entrances observing the representatives' tiers, Calvini making wild gestures of protest, Matteotti rising to his feet now and then, and the Duce cutting off his partisans with his hand.

"We are being slandered, they are adding up, counting the so-called victims of fascism," he was saying. "Gentlemen, you forget one very simple thing: the fascist revolution is entitled to defend itself, and it will defend itself."

The representatives rose, I saw Ferri cheering on the ministers' bench, hands over his head; when the uproar died down Mussolini began to read out the orders of the day:

"This House, confident in the destiny of the fatherland, approves the declaration . . ."

His voice was again drowned in applause. There would be a division, a vote, I left, why bother to wait? The scales had tipped weeks before, who could conceive of an opposing vote? The naïve, Alatri perhaps, with his mouth full of sarcasm and his head full of illusions. Under the arches of the Piazza Colonna, Black Shirts were marching arm in arm, chanting "Mussolini, Mussolini, Mussolini!" Passersby saluted, arms outstretched. "Calvini and Matteotti to Russia, Calvini and Matteotti to Russia!" some young people were shouting in the street. At the corner, Manacorda, a young diplomat from the Consultà, joined me.

"A historic sitting," he said, "we have just witnessed a turning-point in history. For Italy, for the world."

He was speaking loudly, his features serious, eager to please, inviting me to the Café Doria with him.

"A meeting with a friend, a woman, mad about fascism, perhaps you might . . ." he said in a lower voice.

I refused, leaving him uncertain, wondering whether he had made a mistake with this Marco Naldi, secretary to Secretary of State Ferri. But I only wanted to be alone, far from the historic, from these words they were all squeezing to death, Manacorda, Alatri, Ferri, words dripping blood; I wanted quiet for a moment, an end to words, shouting, grand gestures, one moment. I went down the Via del Corso, squadristi everywhere, filling the alleys, bellowing "Mussolini, *viva il fascismo*, Mussolini, Mussolini!" The man who would remain only a name for them, they saw him at a distance, a moving figure whose intentions they would never know, but they would acclaim him with the blind faith of the believer. They were the real walk-ons Alatri was talking about. I knew that behind the word "Musso-

lini" was a man who, while the journalists were waiting for a
political statement in the drawing rooms of the Hotel Savoia,
had shut himself into a room with a red-haired Englishwoman,
the heavy-fleshed, worthy spouse of an embassy councillor, and
that he had laid her on the rug. I knew. Outside the Hotel
Savoia the squadristi were shouting "Mussolini, Mussolini, Mussolini!" I had ushered out the Englishwoman, wrapped in her
coat, holding her hat in her hand, her face lowered, red. Mussolini was back at his desk:

"What a pig!" he said.

A reporter came in.

"Mr. President," he began.

I did not shout "Mussolini, Mussolini," I did my job like a
Magliano peasant.

I walked to the Coliseum, it was cold but at last I was out
of the crowd, the ruins of the Forum like a plowed field, and
the lines of columns, the marble standing in rows like trees
snapped off in a hurricane. I wanted to see the poplars at Magliano again, to hide in the fog, to forget for a while. But trucks
filled with Black Shirts were going by. "Eia, Eia Alala" they
sang; the result of the vote must have been announced, they
were celebrating. Alatri, furious, was contemplating his defeat.
It was history, the furrow being plowed. Why change its course?
I hadn't converted anyone, I hadn't caused the war or fascism,
I had come to life with a few acres of land around me, father
showing me how far our fields extended, to the hummocks
hiding the horizon above the rice fields, all I'd done was take
my place, and it happened to be in the field of the conquerors. I
was there. What was there to do about it? Neither joy nor resentment. A life to follow like a furrow in a field, in the land of
the Naldis at Magliano. For what, for whom should I give it
up? For others who weren't as good as us? Naïve, cynic, imbecile, Alatri said. Let him.

I had gone along the Tiber and was now across from the dark

mass of the Castel Sant'Angelo. I retraced my steps as far as the Via Giulia, and went into the Palazzo Missini.

There was a reception that evening: glitter, reflections of the high crystal chandeliers, on a platform violinists in powdered wigs trying to make themselves heard over the racket. I saw Elsa in a long black gown, back and shoulders bare, she saw me too and came over, distributing smiles, a few sentences here and there, not looking at me but offering herself already and my whole body filled with a physical joy, delight ran down my muscles, my skin knew her, Elsa, my first woman, the one I had not left after a single brief embrace, the one I hadn't paid, my first woman-habit, with whom I was learning that time is part of pleasure, that a body begins over again every night, all the more secret for being already known. She came toward me, holding out both hands, taking me aside into another room.

"Marco, I must know the truth. Has Ferri really mentioned the prince for one of the big embassies, for Paris, they say?"

I knew nothing of Ferri's intentions.

"But you must know, Marco, you must act, you must talk to Ferri, why doesn't he ever come, make him come with you, you're the only person he listens to."

I watched her, what did I know about her? We met in her room on the Lungo Tevere, sometimes in the Piazza Barberini apartment. We were the happy, fulfilled encounter of two bodies, but beyond that? We seldom talked, our mouths refused words, mingling in silence, afterward a few names, gossip, a few sidelights of Rome, she dropped off to sleep, I left, we had never opened our memories to each other, we remained mirages too. That evening I was discovering her, listening for the first time to an angry, insistent, passionate voice, seeing her face without that half-smile, the little frown that hid the years and the heaviness of her features. Her words came out in a rough, swift, new French.

"You don't understand, Marco, but I hate Rome, it's so

provincial. In Paris, thanks to the Beuils, the prince could have some influence."

"This palazzo," I said pointing to the hall, "these receptions, your life here . . ."

She came closer, with a smile.

"You'll come to Paris," she said, "if the prince is ambassador, a word will be enough."

Then the harsh expression again:

"Marco, I want that embassy, I want to see Ferri, to talk to him about the prince."

"Such passion, such ambition, you're burning!"

She squeezed my hands as though to force a promise out of me.

"Speak to Ferri."

"I thought you . . ."

Fiercely, she cut me off.

"What do you know about me, do you know that I am going to be thirty-five years old, Marco, and the prince is twice that? You only take, you're just passing by."

"Elsa . . ."

"Before you another Marco, after you another Marco, and then another one. Receptions, chatter, Parma in the summer. Peasants. In Paris I would have a real role to play, a real role."

"I'll speak to Ferri, you'll see."

She stroked my cheek with her fingertips, smiling again.

"Come tonight, Marco, come."

She went back to her guests, I saw her smiling, merging into groups, holding out her long white hand, sometimes throwing me a secret glance, playing her part, keeping the place that was no longer enough for her. Perhaps a day would come when I, too, would have to change scenes, to choose. I had already left Magliano.

"Why, Naldi, you're hiding."

Pierre de Beuil entered the room in full-dress uniform, with Prince Missini.

"Do sit down, Prince," he said.

The prince appeared tired and Beuil fluttered over him, helping him undo his vest and talking to me at the same time, his head toward me.

"What a triumph in the House, they positively lay down and wagged their tails in front of him. Those bastards start to quake every time they see someone with balls."

The prince tried to smile, cheeks very scarlet, forehead very pale.

"He may not be Napoleon," he breathed, "and he isn't Cavour, but he's a leader."

Beuil straightened.

"Naldi, I hear the prince is being spoken of for the embassy in Paris?"

I had learned how to listen, to imply with a look that I knew and approved.

"Elsa must have told you, it would be very important for relations between our countries and also, I assure you, for the future of fascism. Naldi, you're on intimate terms with Minister Ferri?"

Beuil drew me into the great hall.

"I should so much like to meet the Duce, I don't mention it in front of the prince, he talks too much, in Paris Elsa would be the real ambassador, you know what that can mean for you? In your position?"

"I've promised to speak to Ferri."

"Bravo, bravo!"

Elsa passed near us and came to my rescue, taking my arm:

"Pierre, please, leave Marco to our guests."

I moved from group to group, people detained me, I leaned toward them, listened to their secrets; abruptly facing me was a very dark young woman with short hair curling over her forehead and a face full of laughter.

"Merry Groves of the New York *Times*, please, they tell me

you know everything, you're a hero, tell me about your life, it must be fascinating, we're so ignorant in America."

We went out and walked up and down the inner courtyard, hearing the distant hum of conversation and violins. She did all the talking, I had only a few words to say, she expanded them into long paragraphs.

"In other words it was out of loyalty to your father, patriotism, to uphold your idea of society and history that you became a fascist, is that it?"

How to answer? I would have needed to see inside myself, calmly untangle my destiny, and I was hardly twenty-three years old, how can anyone have a past at that age?

"And the violence, do you accept the brutality, people were killed in Turin. It's your personal feeling I need to know."

She had a little black notebook in which she scribbled jerkily from time to time.

"Were you ever at the front, Miss Grove? Shells land, shells are fired, you are no artilleryman, you don't give the order to fire, you don't select the victims, and then they fall on this side and on the other, it isn't very nice to look at when one of your comrades has his face cut in half by shrapnel. But it's war."

"So you do accept, you say that violence is unavoidable, like evil in humanity and in history?"

"Miss Groves, I don't understand a word you're saying, I left school at seventeen, after that the war came and we had other things to do."

We went back inside, she was tiny, trotting along, a steady stream of words.

"How do you see the future of Italy and fascism?"

I burst out laughing; who did she think I was?

"You know, Miss Groves, my name is not Mussolini, it's Marco Naldi, just Naldi."

I left her with more words on her lips and went back to the Piazza Barberini. Ferri had sent a message: "Urgent, come to the Consultà." He was fond of these impromptu summonses, the silence of the ministry at night, the echo of his own voice, the atmosphere of secrecy. Rome was deserted, Elsa must already be growing impatient but she would soon fall asleep and it was one of my greatest pleasures to surprise her then, abandoned. At the Consultà I found Carlo outside Ferri's office. A short while before, Ferri had dug him out of his regiment where they were putting off his discharge, trying to ship him to Albania or Greece, and now Carlo had traded his uniform for a black shirt.

"The captain is waiting for you, Mr. Naldi."

Ferri was smoking, his face in darkness, a green-shaded lamp lighting the desk surface.

"How are things with you, Marco?"

The tone was confidential rather than official.

"You saw that sitting in the House, incredible, they'll let go of the lot, they always do. Where were you now?"

"Prince Missini's."

"Ah!"

He rose and walked to the window.

"An odd couple, that Frenchwoman and her old man."

"She wants to see you, she insisted, pleaded."

"Me?"

"You're powerful."

"Tell her to ring the ministry, I'll see her. I met her in Parma, I was in a hurry, on my way through, you know her well, I hear?"

I said nothing.

"You must never say anything about women, you respect what is sacred. Perfect. Come here, Marco."

He had opened a file on his desk, letters, telegrams, a passport.

"Starting tomorrow your name is Parri, you're going to Geneva, it's all in here."

There was a fat envelope containing a reservation at the Hôtel du Lac, the name of a Mr. Karl Maestricht, whom I was to meet. He would make the contact.

"You'll wait for him, listen to him, and tell me what it's about," Ferri said. "He says he represents a German fascist party. They want funds, weapons. And then you'll bring him to me, maybe, quietly. This is a reconnaissance, Marco, you're used to them. Not a word, of course."

As I was leaving, he called me back.

"Not even to a woman."

Carlo was nodding in the entrance, half-lying on the sofa, but he felt like talking and came with me as far as my car.

"Do you know what, she didn't wait for me? Imagine, since May 1915, she went to America, she had relatives over there, I felt like a widower all of a sudden so I stayed in the army, I took it for three years and after that I'd had enough, luckily the captain was there, he didn't forget me, do you think it's right for her to go like that?"

He closed the car door and leaned over.

"I can't get married again and yet I'm like a widower."

"*Addio*, Carlo."

In those days the nights were like days to me, I was never tired. I found Elsa, loved her, afterward she lay close to me, a supple, relaxed body.

"You'll see Ferri," I told her.

She hugged me, my head against her breast, between her arms.

The wind was blowing down Lake Geneva from the north, icy, raising choppy waves and beating at the lakefront. I waited for Karl Maestricht, walking beside the lake where clusters of black swans let themselves drift as the wind pushed them; I visited the old town, sat in the Cintra, drank, picked up lethargic women, awoke in unfamiliar beds, placed bank notes on a table, moved on to a different bar. One evening I went to a meeting of the Swiss Socialist party: "Solidarity with Italy" said the poster. In a badly heated hall a few souls sat listening to speakers telling about the crimes of fascism, the workers in

Turin who had been beaten to death and dragged through the streets behind cars. I left before the end, it was just words to me. I was bored. I asked Ferri what to do, he told me to go on waiting. I waited. One day when I came in from a walk a fat young man rose to meet me. He wore round, gold-rimmed glasses.

"You are Mr. Parri, from Rome, aren't you? Karl Maestricht. I think I am very late."

His Italian was slow but very fluent.

"Shall we go outside?"

We walked.

"The German police, you understand, I had to make a detour. You're taking me to Rome, aren't you?"

"There's plenty of time."

I was supposed to make him talk and pass on information to Ferri, who would decide.

"You want to know first, before you make any commitments?"

"Does that surprise you?"

We sat down in the back room of the Cintra. His hands were stubby and manicured, nails cut short, pink-skinned.

"We are still only a small party," he said, "but we've adopted your fascism as our model. We shall take Munich and from there we'll march on Berlin. You marched and took Rome, didn't you?"

Was it all so simple, then? I remembered the interviews, back-room negotiations, the squadre scouring the countryside, the processions. Karl Maestricht was telling me. They needed money, first of all.

"When you can't persuade people, you have to buy them. And then there's propaganda, arms—"

I interrupted him.

"Were you in the war, Mr. Maestricht?"

He had fought in France, then with the commandos on the shore of the Baltic.

"Never against you," he said, laughing, "never against the Italians."

He was on the other side, an ally of those who were firing as we crawled along the Piave. Now we drank together, we were going to give them arms. Everything was shifting, moving. I wrote a long report for Ferri, summarizing what Karl Maestricht had told me about the National Socialist party, the officer they had chosen to lead it, a trench fighter, Adolf Hitler, who requested, for himself personally, a signed photograph of Mussolini. They coded my message in the consulate and the next day I received orders to escort "our cousin" to Rome. The trip seemed endless. Karl Maestricht chain-smoked and read German magazines full of pornographic cartoons and photos. He laughed to himself, held out the magazine, translated the captions. Carlo was waiting for us in Rome.

"The captain wants to see you immediately."

Ferri was wearing his command-performance expression. Sitting erect at his desk, chin raised, adopting the postures of the Duce.

"Your Excellency, here is Karl Maestricht."

I stepped aside, Maestricht stood at attention.

"So," Ferri began wryly, "you want to copy us, it seems, and make your March on Rome. You've even unearthed some German or Austrian duce?"

Maestricht coughed. "Without your help, Your Excellency, without the example of fascism and the Duce's advice, nothing will be possible in Germany. Adolf Hitler is convinced of that. Otherwise, why would I have come?"

I went out. Maestricht had found the right tone to take with Secretary of State Ferri. He would get his funds and his arms. History would follow its furrow. At the Piazza Barberini a pile of correspondence was waiting for me. I turned over the letters without interest, looked at the apartment without pleasure and at Rome, in its winter gray, without joy. There were letters from Elsa, from mother, which I didn't want to open. I telephoned Elsa, her voice was sharp. "Marco, where on earth have you been, you just disappear . . ."

"Have you seen Ferri, he could have told you."

She began to laugh too loudly.

"He's discreet, you know him, I'll tell you about it."

"What about the prince?"

"I think you'll be coming to Paris, Marco."

I said nothing; it had probably been a mistake, in Geneva, to have found other bodies, known other women.

"Marco? Did you hear, Ferri has promised me, for the prince."

"Are you seeing him again?"

"Jealous," she said, laughing.

So she had slept with him or was planning to. I had done as much to her, after all, and she had made me no promises. Why then this taste of dirt in my mouth, like the nausea that used to come over me when I lay on the ground and the explosions of shells landing nearby forced my mouth open in spite of myself, filling it with mud.

"You're coming tonight, aren't you?"

"Tonight, of course."

Mother's letters lay in front of me, I knew the sloping round hand, the yellow envelopes from father's desk, bottom right-hand drawer. There were treasures in there, sheets of white paper, pencils, envelopes, erasers. Sometimes I had dared to open it and make off with my booty.

I tore open an envelope: "Magliano." The word at the top of a page brought the fog, the poplars, Giulia. How would our lives have been spent if we had ever brought our bodies together one night, many nights? The question was still in my heart. "Dear Marco," mother wrote, "the house is so empty, so dead. Mrs. Nitti spends the evenings with me. Your friends came to question Nitti several times. Last week they took him out on the Venice road and made him walk home again in the rain. Can't you do something? Nitti has his ideas, but he's honest and loyal.

And what would become of me if they left? Father would not have permitted him to be molested."

Always the same tone, dreary, drowning me. There had to be an answer, I'd have to go through Ferri to make sure Nitti was left alone. Didn't the Venetian fascists have anything better to do?

But day-to-day events caught me up, the unexpected that was forever occurring, and I forgot Nitti and Magliano. I accompanied the Italian delegation to London and met Merry Groves again in the lounges at Claridge's, where Mussolini and Ferri were staying. She was full of sprightly good cheer, she took me to pubs, I read the stories she wrote on her knees: "An energetic profile, virile features, a glittering, determined expression; to English eyes, that is the Duce," she began. I laughed.

"You like that, don't you? That's how I see the Duce, as a Renaissance condottiere. And besides, the readers have to have images, they love heroes."

Why contradict her? We drank sirupy brown beer and went home early in the morning, as the first editions of the papers were coming out. I was laughing to myself as I pushed her up the main staircase of the hotel in front of me.

"Tell me, Merry, how can your readers still believe what they read? Are they blind, or just sheep?"

Merry protested. "We tell the truth," she said seriously.

I followed her into her room, we found ourselves together in the dark, and she who always seemed so gay, with the smile that wrinkled up her whole face, was sobbing raggedly.

"I'm so lonely, I'm sick to death of this traveling circus act, sick, sick, sick."

She was a little drunk, dropping her mask. When I bumped into her late the next morning she threatened me with her notebook:

"Marco Naldi, you're not to get me drunk any more, I wonder what I said last night, it's my job to make you talk, not the other way around."

I reassured her, drew her into a corner of the hall and "leaked" a little secret to her, Their Majesties' decision to visit Rome the following spring.

"I don't know anything, of course, I've told you nothing."

She laughed and ran to the telephone, drawn like me into the whirlpool of events, faces, mirages. From time to time, during a trip, the pace slowed and I could try to understand them, Ferri or Manacorda, Mussolini himself. Sitting in a train next to Ferri, the Duce would soliloquize to the members of our delegation, looking at each of us in turn, leaving long pauses between his sentences for our laughter and murmurs of approval.

"These English are the Chinese of the West," he would say, "or maybe Germans who have traveled."

Manacorda asked permission to take notes. "For history, Duce."

"Outside history, man is nothing, gentlemen."

Enthusiastic groups awaited us in Rome, chanting the same eternal slogans, waving Italian flags and the black flags of the squadre. Mussolini leaned over the Pullman door to salute the crowd and then turned back to us.

"Myself, Italy, fascism, we're all one to history."

I could never manage to talk or ask questions, I just paid attention. In the station we were caught up by the eddying crowd. At my side Manacorda kept saying, "What enthusiasm, the Duce is right, Italy and fascism are no longer separable."

Ferri was going to the Consultà with the Duce, I was alone in the ministry car. Carlo, wearing a fascist militia uniform, drove.

"Italy's still the most beautiful country, isn't that true, Mr. Naldi? I've never done any traveling, but I never get tired of Italy. It's home, you're always glad to get back to it."

Via del Corso, Via del Tritone, Piazza Barberini, Carlo was talking. I looked at Rome, the posters on the walls, Mussolini's face again, the writing: "Anyone who harms the fascist militia will be shot. Mussolini." I was not glad to get back to Rome, Italy, my mother's letters certainly waiting for me, the offices of the Consultà or the Palazzo Chighi—the new headquarters of the ministry—the galleries at Montecitorio where an electoral reform was being debated. I already knew the words they would volley back and forth and the outcome of the fight and the contented smiles, Ferri, who would summon me in the middle of the night. Elsa Missini herself, who might be being unfaithful to me? Was that why I felt no joy at coming back to Rome? The night of my return from London, and all the other nights of the long winter of 1923, I kept asking myself questions. Elsa was radiant.

"It will be in thc spring of '24," she said. "Ferri has promised. Thc Duce is to see the prince. You'll be our secrctary at the embassy, very private secretary. Just for me, we'll move around, Paris is not a city, Marco, when you go into a different part of town you go into a different world."

Sometimes I tried to imagine my life there with them. The prince, Elsa. Then there would be other countries, it would be a way of escaping Rome and the tedium that was beginning to infect me. I lay beside Elsa, she stroked my chest, scratched my skin.

"I find you rathcr cool, Mr. Naldi," she said. "Have you changed? Are you playing around behind my back?"

"Are you still seeing Minister Ferri?"

She put her lips to my chest. "Idiot, idiot . . ."

I relaxed, she swept me away into a pleasure that was sharp, clean and painful as a bite. Only a few months had passed but I no longer loved her in the same way, maybe it was the passing of time, or my imagination that wandered when we made love, but I couldn't drive out the images of my other women, or of her other lovers. She forced me to a climax and we fell back heavily, not turning to each other with the old tenderness.

So I took every opportunity to get out of Rome. Ferri was representing Italy at the League of Nations in Geneva, and I

went with him. Our fleet had bombarded Corfu, Ferri was denouncing the assassination that had provoked our military inter-
vention.

"This murder of defenseless Italian officers," he stormed from
the platform, "whose faces had been hammered with rifle butts,
gentlemen, is an unprecedented political crime in the contem-
porary history of civilized Europe."

Even the grandiloquence of the speeches no longer amazed
me; I watched the delegates whom we would be meeting a few
minutes later in the bar, calm and amiable gentlemen who carried on like prosecuting attorneys when they mounted the
rostrum. I was listening to Ferri while we prepared our briefs in
his hotel bedroom:

"Now I entertain them, Naldi, but if we were strong enough,
and one day we will be strong enough, then, like with the gentlemen at Montecitorio, the show's over, curtain!"

I went back to Rome ahead of him, with a report to be
handed to the Duce in person. I waited a long time in the
Palazzo Tittoni, Via Rasella. There were plants along the marble staircase, a red rug leading to the Duce's office. One of the
militia opened the door. Mussolini was sprawling across his
desk, a newspaper open in front of him. I stood. He was scoring
heavy blue marks across the columns, suddenly he straightened,
his face red:

"You think we're going to put up with that much longer!"
he shouted.

Pushed the paper away.

"Treating us like that, listen: 'The Italians show proof of
great naïveté in their negotiations.' You've just come from
Geneva, you tell me what that ass Ferri is up to there, that pretentious little lawyer, what the hell is he playing at, all he does
is talk, he's got to flatten them. He's not on the stage!"

I held out the report. Mussolini dismissed me with a jerk of
his head. The guard saluted. Outside in the Via Rasella, a
group of loiterers was waiting for the Duce to come out, ogling

the red sports car in which he sometimes went roaring through Rome.

"Did you see him?" Carlo asked me as he drove me home. "Did he talk to you?"

We went along the Piazza Venezia. The long fascist streamers were waving over the palazzo and portraits of Mussolini adorned the façades of the buildings on the Via del Corso. It required an effort to remember that this same huge face rippling in the wind I had just seen snarling in anger or grimacing with stomach cramp: only a man, true, but with a split personality. One, they whispered in the ministries, toppled women onto the rugs, the other accepted the homage of the masses.

"Ferri talks to you, why shouldn't the Duce talk to me?" I said.

"If you look at it that way . . ." said Carlo after a pause.

That evening was the first big fascist rally on the piazza. Barricades were erected, the militia lined up in rows. There would be rhythmic chanting, imprecations, an announcement about the new electoral law that parliament had accepted, giving the fascists an absolute majority, there would be the whole superproduction and the voice of the Duce, the voice of power, deciding lives and decreeing laws.

"Only thing, Mr. Naldi," Carlo resumed, "there's nobody above him. He's the last one, at the top. And since God doesn't talk very often, he can do whatever he wants; but the captain, even the captain . . ."

What was the use, it was human history, Caesar, Napoleon, all of them, and now the Duce. That was all you needed to know in order to keep out of the trap where Carlo was and the actors in Merry Groves' articles.

"Aren't I right, eh, Mr. Naldi?"

I was tempted to explain, I liked Carlo, his good faith, he was woven into some of my memories, the Palazzo Dandolo, the front, Giulia's death, Bologna; but I didn't. He was in his place, he needed to believe. Old Nitti had to stand there while grandfather read the *Memorial*. Afterward, in some other unforesee-able history, things might be different. It wasn't for me to alter the present. It existed. I existed with it, molded myself to fit it. I resumed my Roman habits, the Consultà, Montecitorio, the Palazzo Missini, ceremonies and demonstrations. Ferri, back from Geneva, was worried about his ministry. I discovered an-other aspect of his personality, there had been changes in him since he had grasped a wisp of power.

"But did you tell him," he insisted, "that it's the diplomats, that bunch of impotents, who paralyzed me. They hate us."

I tried to make him understand that the Duce had given me little time to talk.

"The article irritated him," I said again.

"What bastard showed it to him? Naldi, Naldi, I don't trust anybody. They want my head."

News of the nazi failure in Munich was another blow.

"I told that stupid fool Maestricht that you can't take over a government with some unknown agitator for a leader. The Ger-mans will always be barbarians."

A group of nazis had come to Venice. Maestricht was asking for money, and for an interview between Mussolini and Cap-tain Hermann Goering, their leader, a war hero who had just been wounded at Munich.

"Go see what they want, Naldi. We can't make a single false move, the Duce would never forgive it."

I was glad to go to Venice. I meant to stop off at Magliano, return to the world of my memories, see my mother again, face the unbearable past I couldn't seem to get rid of, it kept coming back whatever I did, like some ache I could hold at bay only by cramming my life with activities, alcohol, new scenery, women's bodies.

Spring had taken over the country, I was alone in the com-partment. After the Apennines—the countless tunnels, villages clinging to bare brown heights still showing occasional patches of snow—we entered the Po Valley and made a long stop at Bologna. I stepped out onto the platform, hesitating to go on into town, I was in no hurry, I could have taken another train, visited the Aquila Nera again, the hotels I had haunted during those weeks between lives, idle weeks, laboriously emerging from my war and my adolescence. The train backed and lurched, every time they announced it would depart in another half hour. Platform vendors uttered their piercing cries, like whistles: "*Cestini, cestini!*, box lunches, box lunches!"

The air was cooler and sharper than in Rome. A crowd had gathered at the far end of the platform and I strolled over to it, carabinieri standing in two lines between a shed and a carriage at the rear of the train. The crowd drifted away and I was left with a group of loudly joking fascist militia. Some prisoners came out of the shed. A dozen, in single file, linked together by a long chain binding their wrists. Most were awkwardly grasping large bundles knotted at the top, like the ones peasants carry. The militia began spitting at them. Some of the prisoners ducked their heads, others looked defiant. The indifferent carabinieri pushed them toward the carriage.

I looked back and saw Alatri, separated from the rest of the prisoners, emerge from the shed after them between two carabinieri, he was wearing the same gray suit but his glasses were gone and his head shaven. He was looking straight ahead, walking like a free man alone. He didn't see me. We left soon afterward. The plains were waterlogged, reflecting the sky. Sometimes we slowed at a level crossing or going through a station, I heard the voice of a peasant woman lying on a heap of sacks on top of a cart, hailing us with a cheery wave of her hand. At Rovigo night was falling, and fog, pierced by the shrill whistle of steam, was gradually overtaking the railway. What was one supposed to do? Alatri had chosen, he stood up on top of the parapet, he was in the other camp: all's fair in war. But what was one supposed to do? I tried to convince myself, word by word, that that was the law, and he knew it, if Alatri were the conqueror he would play the same rules. I felt like shouting, as I had done back on the Piave, "Idiot, what if you die tomorrow!" The train moved on, the windows steamed over. I began to cough and heard Alatri's cough in the first-aid post and the dim corridors of Montecitorio. At Padua I ran the length of the train that was slowly maneuvering in the station. Carabinieri and fascist militia were pacing the platform in pairs. At the rear of the train an inspector and a linesman were watching the signals, scarcely visible in the fog.

"Where's the carriage with the carabinieri?"

The inspector looked at me cautiously, the linesman raised his lantern to show my face.

"What carriage?"

"You took on some prisoners at Bologna, you know what I mean. Tell me the number of the carriage."

"That carriage was detached at Rovigo, sir."

"Rovigo?"

"That's all I know, sir, let us get on with our work, go back to your seat, the train's about to leave."

I stayed with them. I felt the chill in my shoulders.

"The train for Milan goes through Rovigo," said the linesman without looking at me.

He moved off, rhythmically tapping the wheels. The inspector shook me.

"The train's moving, sir, hurry."

I climbed into the first carriage, the train was already gathering speed. My seat was at the other end, I walked down the aisle. Peasants, soldiers, crying children, an odor of sweat, a gray light in the damp, workers asleep on their feet, their foreheads against the windows, people sitting on piled-up suitcases. It felt like war and it was only a few carriages in a train on a peacetime night, but in the past few years I had been living at a distance from other people and I remember that walk through the over-crowded train as a discovery of something new. I finally found my seat, the compartment, a high-ranking officer had moved in and saluted me. I had nothing to say or do except sleep until we reached Venice, while Alatri was on his way to Milan.

At Venice, Valsecchini, the Fascio delegate, a spare young man in a tight-fitting black militia uniform, was waiting for me with a motor launch. He was full of respect and consideration, talking about Minister Ferri and the Duce, with whom I had the privilege to associate.

"In Rome they are not sufficiently aware of our difficulties here," he added, "there is still opposition, and we can't relax for a minute or everything will go, the elections were a real struggle . . ."

He leaned contentedly against the back of the seat.

". . . which we won."

"Using what means?"

"Fascist means, Mr. Naldi."

And he laughed, telling me the story of the socialist candidate they had thrown in the Grand Canal on the evening of his campaign rally.

"A cold shower, that's not too serious."

We were slowly making our way down the Grand Canal. I recognized the broken reflections on the black water, the echo of the motor as we went under the Rialto bridge, the breeze laden with sea smells, growing stronger after the last loop when the Grand Canal widens out and the dome of Santa Maria della Salute comes into view, and the dock lights far away on the San Marco Canal. The Germans were staying at the Palazzo Zucchelli, across from Santa Maria. In the lobby, rising as soon as he caught sight of me, I recognized Karl Maestricht. He came forward holding out his pink hand, even plumper than in Geneva.

"My dear Mr. Parri . . ."

"Naldi here, Naldi."

Valsecchini stood to one side, disappointed at being left out of our secrets, stiff, hands behind his back. I liked making him wait, dryly asking him to make a car available to me the next

day so I could go to Magliano. I was using him as Mussolini could use me, and I felt him bending, he was a malleable,
servile piece of clay. And so was I. I suddenly saw myself in his
face—different, but like me in his silence, perhaps in his revolt,
I could interpret them as respect and fear. I was the Duce, he
was me. So that was all I was, a mirage to be summoned and
dismissed.

"Naturally, Mr. Naldi, your car, with a chauffeur, of course."

"Of course."

"Please give my respects to Minister Ferri."

He clicked his heels, saluted, I was already turning away. In
his room at the Hotel Savoia and his office in the Palazzo
Tittoni, Mussolini never looked up until several minutes had
gone by. Ferri at the Consultà adopted the same attitude. They
reduced me to the level of existence of an object, and I reduced
Valsecchini.

"I must tell you," said Maestricht.

He took my arm, we went outside to the quay.

"An ambush, treason. We passed the first barricade thanks
to General Ludendorff. That was a great moment, he went up
to the officer commanding the troops on the Ludwigbrücke,
magnificent, Ludendorff, with his Order of Merit on his chest,
the officer let us through. I thought we had won."

Maestricht was a short man, holding my arm tightly, looking
up at me, his quick eyes seeking out mine.

"Were you there?"

"Of course. We wanted to get to the ministry, where Roehm
had barricaded himself in. But the army opened fire near the
Marienplatz. The Reichswehr, Mr. Naldi, and Ludendorff was
with us, Hitler called out to them to surrender, they fired. Men
of the Reichswehr. My own comrades, Mr. Naldi."

We had gone some distance, the water was lapping the quays,
he stopped talking. Men aiming at one another everywhere, plotting their revenges, preparing to cut more throats.

"You will meet Captain Goering, he is very weak. He was seriously injured. Minister Ferri must be convinced, by you, Mr. Naldi, by you."

He turned to face me, his forefinger pointing at my chest.

"A meeting between Goering and the Duce is vital to the future. We need fascism, Mr. Naldi, we need you."

I spent the entire night at my bedroom window, watching for dawn, the fog lifting, the first noises on the canal. Cold and weariness numbed me but I didn't want to fall asleep, I was trying to fit the pictures together: Alatri with his shaven head and bound hands, the long, crowded train, and me in this mirror, this other, my brother, Valsecchini who obeyed me. Slowly the sun turned the fog to pearl and the breeze lifted it in slices; the main cupola of Santa Maria della Salute appeared all at once, rending the veil, powerful as a jutting cliff. It was day, and I was a chaotic jumble of memories and unfinished ideas. Suddenly the sun broke through. I pulled the curtains, hid my face under the pillow and went to sleep.

I was to meet Maestricht and Captain Goering at lunchtime. I was late, joined them on the enclosed terrace where I saw Goering first, enveloped in a long camel's hair coat, white face, legs stretched in front of him and an expression of strain chiseling his features. Maestricht spoke in a low voice.

"His injury, he's still in terrible pain."

Next to Goering was a woman who hardly looked at me, lowering her head by way of greeting, with huge eyes and tense features, a frightened expression. Maestricht drew me aside.

"Mrs. Goering is ill too. She can't bear to see him suffer. He had a dreadful night, she called me, morphine is the only thing that calms him at all. Two months ago his leg was still full of pus."

We sat with our backs to the sun, waiting for Goering to wake.

"He was saved by a miracle, a bullet in the groin wasn't properly taken care of. But, Mr. Naldi, we won't forget, we shall find von Kahr again. To keep his position in the ministry, he

put down a national revolution. The national revolution will
put him down, Mr. Naldi."

Goering stretched, summoned us with a smile. His skin
seemed bloated, his eyes glittering, feverish. He had taken his
wife's hand and gripped it in his fingers. I saw two large rings,
one above the other, digging into the flesh between the joints.
Maestricht translated, Goering spoke persuasively, of the Italian sun and the museums they were beginning to visit.

"What a treasure, Venice, the Grand Canal is like a necklace."

Maestricht, admiring, translated with nods of approval. At
last, Goering began talking about the Duce, his stay in Italy,
his friend Prince Phillip of Hesse, who was on the best of terms
with Princess Mafalda, the king's daughter. I must tell Minister
Ferri all that, I must stress the confidence of the Nazi party.

"Adolf Hitler is imprisoned at Landsberg, I am in Italy, but
you may be sure, and tell Minister Ferri this as well, Germany
will follow us as we followed you."

Maestricht came into the hall with me.

"When we are in power, Mr. Naldi, you must come to Berlin, we will decorate you."

"You'll be a minister, Mr. Maestricht."

"Why not?"

He didn't laugh. Nobody jests with power, ambition. Was
that my real weakness, uncertainty about what I wanted, I had
no longings to become a minister or ambassador. I had neither
Elsa Missini's passion for the roles she wanted to play nor
Ferri's appetite for honors nor Alatri's convictions nor Maestricht's aspirations nor those of Major Pierre de Beuil. I drove
to Magliano, maybe I was a country man who liked to walk alone
along the side of a field, to look and know when the weather
was going to change, detect the signs. But war had uprooted
me, war had laid waste my country. What could I do at
Magliano with those voices echoing around me, the past still
living in my mother? "Widows rot their sons," Ferri had said.

I knew the past would rot me. I was condemned to walk among other men, but alone as at the side of a field.

I told the black-shirted driver to wait for me on the road beyond the poplars, and I walked to Magliano, past the shed. Mrs. Nitti was in the courtyard and came rushing over, wringing my hands, hugging me.

"Mr. Marco, Mr. Marco, you've got to do something to help us, they're going to kill him, they came again yesterday. They hit him, you'll see. After Giulia, now they want to kill him."

She kissed my hands.

"Maddelena!"

Nitti's voice was harsh, imperative.

"Maddelena, stop that foolishness!"

Nitti came out of the granary with a fork in his hand, and as he drew nearer in the sunlight I saw his blackened face, the eyelids swollen so that his eyes were almost shut fast. Mrs. Nitti went away in tears and Nitti and I stood looking at each other, just as we had done that other time when I saw him on the path after the war. Then he turned away and crossed the courtyard. I followed and caught up with him.

"Nitti, come on, tell me."

"Tell you what?"

I pointed to the face, the torn lips, the black skin.

"We lost, they're making us pay for it," he said. "Only, we won't always lose, Mr. Naldi."

Goering and Maestricht were certain of their revenge, too.

"But there must be a reason, Nitti."

"There are always reasons, Mr. Naldi. You know, they know me, I bother them, I'm alive and I get in their way. As long as I'm alive, Mr. Naldi, they'll be afraid."

"They can't kill you, Nitti."

"Are you sure?"

All day long, while mother was unreeling her sentences, tears, laments, memories, I was unable to forget Nitti's question. What could I be sure of? Men were killed in Turin and dragged through the streets, the ones the speaker in Geneva had talked about in the chilly hall. Words for me, then. Now there was Nitti's face, and Alatri's.

"You're not listening any more," murmured mother. "I can feel it, your mind is on other things. Talk to me, Marco, what is wrong, aren't you happy?"

She hounded me with questions, intuitively, and her eyes went even further into me than her words.

"These politics," she said, "all this violence, you weren't made for it, Marco, neither was your father. He loved peace and quiet and order. He would have wanted you to take over here after him, at Magliano, and then there was the war."

She began to cry again.

For me, I could feel it, Magliano was a swamp, and the water in the rice fields was limpid from afar but fetid and treacherous when you went in it up to your knees and your legs became heavy, black, stinking.

"You're going?"

"Sell Magliano, Mother, sell. Move to Venice and live with your brother, sell."

"Why are you shouting? I'll never sell, Marco, never."

Suddenly she was very calm, speaking in measured, decided tones.

"I shall never leave Magliano, not even for you."

She came into the courtyard with me, wrapping a black shawl around her head and shoulders, her hand on my arm.

"Marco, don't become like the rest. Stay, you're better than the others, I know it."

She had begun to weep again, softly, without sobbing, tears she wiped away with little dabs of her handkerchief, they kept coming back again. We walked down to the road. Night was falling.

"For Nitti," she said, "don't forget."

I had myself taken to the Fascio headquarters in Venice. Valsecchini had a huge office overlooking the Piazza San Marco.

He showed me portraits of the Duce, a photograph on the wall across from his desk, of Mussolini in a black shirt at the Naples Congress, just before the March on Rome. I felt ill-tempered and aggressive.

"You were in the Arditi, weren't you?" I asked.

Valsecchini apologized, he had served in the infantry, on the Carso. I asked other questions, insidious and cunning. It was easy to manipulate a man, drive him to ridicule, compel him to humiliate himself. All you needed was power. When I had Valsecchini where I wanted him, I spoke about Nitti.

"If any Venetian fascist touches that peasant, I'll touch *him*. And he'll remember it for the rest of his days. Take note of that, Valsecchini, I don't care how you manage it. Leave Nitti alone."

He floundered through explanations, the electoral campaign had been arduous, new recruits were not sufficiently supervised, sometimes members of the opposition went to extremes simply in order to discredit fascism.

"Who could know, Mr. Naldi, that you were the owner of Magliano, of Nitti."

"You have to know, Valsecchini, always."

I took a train back to Rome that evening. The lights filed past in the water of the lagoon, oblique, I was leaving, I was running away. Sometimes at the front we would abandon the injured in the night on the banks of the river, they were dying but they reached out to us and we left their hands empty, muttering to ourselves, "Don't worry about it, we'll come back, don't worry, mate, it'll be all right." We didn't come back. That evening I was abandoning Magliano, mother, Nitti.

In the days that followed I ran from one reception and meeting to another. Elsa, whom I glimpsed in Ferri's waiting room at the ministry, rose and came over to me, indifferent to all the watching eyes. Still lovely, lovelier than ever perhaps, with a new hunger on her thinner, taut face.

"You're avoiding me, aren't you?" she said.

"I've been traveling, Venice, Palermo yesterday for the Duce's speech. Your embassy?"

"After the opening of the parliamentary session, Ferri swears it's certain. We have to wait."

She frowned, smiling, but her lips stayed clamped together. "We're leaving for Paris in September. Will you come?"

I made a movement of uncertainty.

"You see, you are avoiding me."

We met again one evening at a reception Minister Ferri was giving in the huge tapestry-hung rooms of the Palazzo Chighi in honor of Payern, the new Belgian ambassador. Elsa tried to join me but I kept moving from group to group, bowing, picking up snatches of sentences, all centered on the Duce, who was to come at some point in the evening. "He must guard against attempts on his life, these reforms will be held against him, this is a country of vendettas," one rasping old senator was saying. Then the Duce arrived, occupied one of the rooms, arms crossed, unmoving, eyes and features rigid. Ferri presented the most important guests, the Duce gave a slight nod. "He has a profound understanding of the psychology of the Italian nation," a French diplomat murmured near me. Prince Missini and Elsa came forward in due course; I thought the prince looked much older, his cheeks hollow and his nose pinched, a skull almost, but he was still erect and smiling. Elsa like a fruit at his side and I wanted her. I joined her as she was leaving the palazzo behind the prince, who was leaning on the arm of Pierre de Beuil.

"Already?" I said. "Going so soon?"

"I tried to find you, the prince is tired, come tonight."

I kissed her hand. Ferri kept me a long time, he had spoken to the Duce about Captain Goering.

"The Duce has agreed to see him, he was very pleased with your report."

We were sitting in a room off to one side. The last guests

were departing, Ferri, his legs stretched out and spread apart, was smoking.

"If the prince gets that embassy," he said after a pause, "will you ask to go to Paris? I know you're very attached to him."

He was scrutinizing me through half-shut eyes, smoothing the short beard that lengthened his round face.

"I don't think so."

"Well, well . . . you know the prince is counting on it."

"Things change, Your Excellency."

He yawned, pressing his face between his hands.

"What a life, Naldi, what an effort, to imprint the seal of fascism on our foreign policy."

"Apropos, Your Excellency, might I hope for a post abroad one day, in the service of your ministry?"

He burst out laughing.

"Silly Marco, in Paris of course. Why couldn't you just say so?"

"No, Your Excellency, somewhere else, Africa, why not?"

The words were out, I hadn't even thought them, now they were between us, little bricks that could dam up my destiny. Ferri stood up and took my shoulder.

"Marco, Marco, what is this mad idea?"

We walked slowly out of the room.

"Here you are at the center of government, where we are making policy with the Duce and you want to go bury yourself thousands of miles away, a little intelligence work, some propaganda, do you know what you're saying?"

Carlo in the militia black dress uniform was waiting for Ferri in the middle of the empty great hall.

"Carlo, here's our Naldi with sentimental problems again."

He turned and gave me a thump on the back.

"Naldi, women are all whores. All of them. Don't make a fuss about it. Please. Isn't that right, Carlo?"

It hadn't only to do with women, it had to do with whether I should go on living as I was, between my desire for Elsa and

my contempt for her, my pleasure at being on the side of the
conquerors and my disgust with Valsecchini and the rest of the
flunkeys; it had to do with whether I could go on wavering between my muffled remorse, the faces of Nitti and Alatri, and
my belief that history would have its way in spite of me and
them; it had to do with my belief that people were on different
sides and my longing to escape the law of their warfare. My duty
was to carry on here, feeling that I belonged to one side, had
inherited it, had to accept it. My duty, which I did not want to
perform.

Rome, that May night, its ochre stones, old people sitting
on straw chairs outside their doors, the thousand noises, Rome
was quivering, intent. I crossed the Piazza Navona where the
cabs were loitering and finally reached the Palazzo Missini without being aware of it, because for months my nightly wanderings had taken me to that apartment on the Lungo Tevere and
because I wanted Elsa's body. She was waiting for me. She
wanted me too. Months of mingling, months of learning the
labyrinthine paths of pleasure, learning to guess, to sense, weeks
of discovering the acidity of a more bitter kind of love, you
didn't forget all that in a few days. And each of us, part of us,
the part of habit, was reaching for the other.

She was almost naked, I sought her skin, her smell, I rolled
on top of her without stopping to take my clothes off.

"You're here at last," she said almost furiously, "you're here."

I took off my jacket without letting go of her body. I bit her
neck, her chest, her ripe breasts, I found her silky skin, we made
love with the violence of discovery and the accuracy of habit.
Then, exhausted, we fell back side by side as though the force
driving us toward each other had finally worn itself out in that
headlong plunge. I had nothing to say to her. She said nothing.
It might have been one of those anonymous rooms you enter
for an hour or a night to satisfy a need. Then get up. A woman
is there whom you no longer see. And go away. And forget. Elsa
was asleep. I couldn't make up my mind to leave. Someone

knocked at the door. A servant was calling Elsa. I woke her, we dressed hurriedly.

"Signora, Signora!"

The panic-stricken voice kept repeating the word. Elsa yelled at her.

"What is it, come in, you idiot!"

A small dark-haired woman came in, head down, not looking at us:

"The prince, Signora, the prince is very ill. . . ."

Elsa pushed her aside, screaming in French:

"No, he can't do that, not now!"

There was a growing clamor inside the palazzo, I followed Elsa down the corridor leading to the main wing on the Via Giulia side. Behind her, I entered the prince's rooms, small dark chambers decorated like candy boxes. At last the bedroom, a high canopied bed and in one corner a girl hardly fifteen years old, black hair hanging loose, sobbing, biting her fingers and trembling. At first I didn't see the prince, only the half-dressed girl with a flowered shirt hanging out of her skirt. Then I saw him, sitting naked, a servant had put a white towel over his thighs. The thin, bony head lying on the hollow white chest, a stream of saliva running from his mouth.

"A doctor," Elsa cried.

Then she saw the girl and flew at her:

"Whore, whore, you'll pay for this, I'll have you arrested, whore!"

She was screaming half in French half in Italian, twice she slapped the girl. I grabbed her arm, she struggled.

"Let go of me, let go!"

I held her by the waist and pushed her down on the bed.

"Clear out, quick, out of here!"

The girl left. Her sandals forgotten in the middle of the floor. Now Elsa was shaking with spasms.

"The swine," she kept saying, "the swine. He's had everything, me nothing, and now."

She clutched me.

"The embassy, Marco, the embassy."

A doctor came. He had the prince laid out, examined him superficially, raised his eyelids.

"My condolences, madam. He had better be dressed."

He sat on the edge of the bed filling out the death certificate and a prescription he held out to me.

"For the lady's nerves, she needs to be looked after."

Elsa was prostrated, bent double, crying soundlessly. Was this the same body I had held against mine hardly an hour before, greedy and full of strength? She stood up. The doctor had gone. The servants were watching her.

"Pietro, summon the prince's secretary, he must take care of everything. I will see no one until the funeral."

She straightened, biting her lips, her jaw advancing determinedly. I recognized her.

"Do you think the Duce will come?" she asked.

"Ferri will, certainly."

We went back to her room on the Lungo Tevere. The red candles were burning out. She sat down, her arms hanging limp and her eyes closed, talking to herself, surprisingly calm.

"He always deceived me," she said. "About himself, about his fortune, his position, his influence, he lied. A powdered nonentity riddled with vices. A coward. He hardly dared to be a fascist. Lip service, because I was pushing him to commit himself. That embassy, he didn't want it, I forced him, I did all the work, me alone. All of it. Without him. And the pig, with those girls, little sluts, impotent, Marco, that's what he was."

We faced each other, I mute, she telling her life in bits and pieces, pell-mell, frustrations and hatreds. Angle by angle, the sun flooded the room.

"I have to go," I said.

"Go. We said everything there was to say last night, I think."

Almost touching me, circles around her eyes, no smile, no little frown. Someone else.

"You won't come any more, Marco."

"Why?"

"I know, I knew before he . . ."

I interrupted her, I didn't want to hear her say the word death.

"Will you stay on in Rome?"

"I'll have to think everything over, work it all out again," she said.

She came with me along the main corridor. I could go through the palazzo now.

"Do you want me to tell Ferri?"

She hesitated, stared at me unblinking.

"I'll do it," she said.

The prince was given a state funeral. A senior official carried his decorations on a red cushion, all the ambassadors and ministers were there. The Duce had signed the guest book at the Palazzo Missini. In the first row of seats in the church of Saint-Louis-des-Français: Princess Elsa Missini, on the arm of Major Pierre de Beuil. I sat next to Manacorda behind the dignitaries, in Ferri's shadow.

"The fight over the embassy has already started," murmured Manacorda.

When I came up to Elsa Missini she smiled at me under her black veils.

Ferri and I stood waiting for the cars outside the church, he turned to me, crossed his arms, serious, trying, with jutting jaw, to assume a Mussolinian air.

"She must get out of Rome, Naldi, for a few weeks, she needs to forget."

I didn't go to the cemetery. At Montecitorio the new parliament's debates were stormy, I was Ferri's eyes and ears. From the opening sitting he had been worried, there was talk of a cabinet reshuffle.

"Something's in the air," he kept saying. "I get in the diplomats' way, I prevent them from fawning and scraping."

He had been pacing back and forth in his office, Carlo near the door, I in a chair. His loyal spectators.

"Those fancy gentlemen turn up their noses at us, Naldi, we smell of gunpowder, the Duce is not an aristocrat, ah, the king, His Majesty the King, that's what gives them a thrill. But we've cleared a path before, haven't we Naldi?"

Then his anxiety returned.

"They're more dangerous than those high-minded socialist asses, and the communists; for them . . ."

He raised his arms as if taking aim.

". . . bang, bang! But these monarchist lords . . ."

On one of the benches at the parliament debates at Monte-citorio I saw Calvini, thinner and more stooped. Despite the stifling heat in the house he always wore his red scarf, sometimes mopped his brow with it. He had tried to intervene in a storm of jeers, the fascists shaking their fists, Mussolini smiling on the front bench, Ferri yawning, leafing through a newspaper. Cal-vini's voice was too high.

"We were assassinated!" he cried.

A roll of laughter. "But you're still there, alas!"

Calvini wiped his forehead. "My comrade Piccini shot down at Reggio Emilia with three bullets in the back."

"Like a traitor," bawled an anonymous voice.

Applause swept through the fascist benches. Reggio Emilia, the hotel on the square, the arches and the fierce rain driving sideways in the wind, Elsa turning to me, the prince and his fascists laughing, "She danced with her mouth full of castor oil, a peasant . . ." Who could have been Giulia.

"Enough, enough, enough!" Calvini let the wave pass.

"The opposition journalists arrested, Alatri of the *Unità* beaten and sentenced without cause."

I went into the gallery, walked, I wanted to go away, see different people, a different geography. Snatches of the speeches drifted out through the open doors, I recognized the calm, grave voice of the socialist Matteotti.

"Nobody was free in these elections," he said. "There is an armed militia."

"Go to Russia!" one voice answered.

Away, to find some calm place and silence, a village; not to be at the heart of things any more but on the edge, a walk-on, to stroll along the side of a field.

"I can supply details and facts," Matteotti went on, "to prove these crimes."

"You insult Italy and the king."

Get out of this country, these quarrels, go toward the horizon and lose myself there, find a new land, plow a new furrow, leave the rice fields, Magliano, the addled mud.

"We are defending the free sovereignty of the people, we demand the nullification of the improperly elected fascist representatives."

I went back into the hall. Calvini was embracing Matteotti amid shouts and threats. Then Matteotti walked past, an ironic smile beneath his sad eyes.

"A bullet in the back!" One fascist representative was shouting, standing on his bench and waving his fist. Matteotti did not turn back, Calvini took his arm.

"They'll have to be shut up," Ferri told me in the car. "The Duce can't stand them any more. They're like mosquitoes. They don't realize that we can . . ."

A slap of his hand.

"They're insane, insane!"

Once again, the game was over before it began. The fascist government obtained a large majority. One morning in the ministry, Ferri held out a newspaper.

"They're being stubborn," he said.

Matteotti had announced his intention of challenging the government on the subject of fascist financial abuses. In the cypresses outside Rome—the city's cupolas shone far off in the sun, the city glittered under a bright haze—Ferri had just bought one of those summer residences with marble columns and water flowing cool in pink basins. Carlo had driven me out there one day with a report to hand in, and I thought I recognized, walking head down in one of the paths with an armful of flowers, the small dark woman who had come that night into the apartment on the Lungo Tevere to tell Elsa Missini that the prince was dying. Ferri was not formal at all, was almost too friendly.

"I had you brought here," he said, "I wanted you to see it, you can spend the summer months here if you like, plenty of rooms."

He guided me to the door, paternal, arm around my shoulders.

"Watch the debates this evening, telephone me if anything comes up, I'll be in Rome tomorrow, Carlo will bring me down."

Carlo held open the car door. In the red twilight the cypresses stood out against the crests of the hills, black shapes twisting toward the sky.

"Carlo, take good care of Naldi, he's almost my son."

Now, in his office, Ferri was annoyed by my silence.

"Did you hear that, financial abuses, tell me, Naldi, what do they imagine, the prigs? That we're living on onions and salt? We risked our lives, why?"

He tore the paper out of my hands.

"They'd better not go too far."

That July was too hot. Rome seemed to be exploding, cracking open under the sun, the darkest streets like gaping wounds in the heat, the white summer glare. Slowly, cooler air irrigated the city at night, street by street, with difficulty reaching the higher floors. I came home late, left the windows open, stayed out on the balcony, sometimes with a woman I had picked up in a bar or on a street corner. Then I would send her away and listen to the fading noises. One night the telephone awoke me, the ring seemed to be coming from the street.

"You recognize my voice? I have to see you, right away."

I tried to place a face, a name.

"Merry Groves, don't you remember?"

What time was it, three in the morning?

"Please, I have to come."

She waited, the silence heavy with anxiety and expectation. In London she had told me, "I'm sick of it, sick, I'm so alone . . ." A little voice.

"But of course, come."

"Wait for me downstairs on the pavement, please, I've got a white convertible, I'll be there in ten minutes. If you don't see me, please, telephone the embassy. Tomorrow."

She hung up. I dressed quickly, not thinking, almost as soon as I got outside I saw her car coming up the Via del Tritone, turning around the fountain and parking. She leaped out and pushed me into the doorway.

"There they are," she said, "I knew it."

A car was creeping along, I made out a man leaning forward peering out, then the car accelerated. In the elevator Merry grew calmer, I looked at her, the little black curls on her forehead, her short pleated skirt scarcely covering her knees. I had always wanted to know her better, a few nights half-drunk in London, here, sometimes Piazza Barberini when we left a reception together. I took her by the waist.

"You've awakened me in the middle of the night."

She twisted away, I felt her hip under my hand.

"Please, Marco Naldi, not now."

We sat down facing each other near the balcony, leaving the apartment in darkness, the night was so light.

"They've been following me since this afternoon," she explained. "At first I couldn't figure out why. Then I saw them. They're killers, I know it."

She was talking rapidly, chain-smoking.

"When I tried to telephone the embassy there was no one there but some idiot caretaker."

I gave her a drink, stroked her hair, half-wanting her to stop talking because it was a hot night and I wanted her, half-wanting to listen and understand.

"But why," I said, "you're American, an accredited journalist."

"Naldi, nobody else knows yet but me."

She began to tell me. That morning she had decided to go to Ostia. She was driving along the Tiber and suddenly, on the bridge, a car that had been parked along the sidewalk pulled out in front of her, a Lancia. She had had to swerve to miss it, had overtaken it, and inside she had seen:

"A man struggling, Naldi," she said, "he even kicked through one of the rear windows just as I was passing. And I saw the driver's head, I won't forget it. This afternoon I saw him again with the others, the ones who were following me. They must have investigated. I'm a witness, Naldi."

She remembered the first two numbers of the license plate of the Lancia, 55.

"Afterward I couldn't, if I hadn't swerved . . ."

She had seen only the arms and legs of the man struggling inside the car.

"In other words, you don't know anything."

She went on talking, guessing. We were leaning on the balcony, silence and the immobility of dawn enveloping the town, the roofs turning gray. It was cool. The telephone rang, an angry jangle.

"It's them," Merry said.

I recognized Ferri's voice. Hard, his commanding voice.

"Naldi, are you with the New York *Times* reporter? Good. That's one thing, anyway. Don't let her go out or make any calls. I'm cutting your line. Lock her in and come to the ministry."

I said nothing.

"I give you my word she won't be hurt," Ferri went on. "Lock her in. Fuck her to keep her quiet if you like. I'm waiting."

Merry came over. I hung up.

"It's about me, isn't it?"

I had to lie, find out first, protect her too, and I knew she would be safe in my place. Ferri would keep his word.

"Here they can't do anything," I said. "Wait until I come back. Sleep. I'll go find out."

She wanted to telephone her newspaper, the embassy. I managed to convince her it would be better to wait, to make sure. She might be deported, make a false step. I would find out, I promised to let her know.

"Merry, you trust me?"

I was playing my part and it worked. She trusted me and she was wrong.

In Ferri's office General de Bono, the chief of police, was sitting on a corner of the desk. A small man, bald with a short white beard, he had helped to organize the March on Rome. He turned his quick eyes on me.

"Naldi, Naldi."

Ferri had stood up and was coming toward me.

"You've got a load on your hands now, you've walked into a hornet's nest."

I didn't understand, didn't know anything.

"Tell us what the girl told you."

De Bono cut me off:

"He'd better know what's happened, Ferri."

"The cunts," Ferri began, "the cunts!"

A few of them had got together, a Polish killer, Thierschwald, some squadristi, Dumini, Volpi, had lain in wait for Matteotti and overpowered him on the Arnoldo da Brescia embankment.

"The cunts wanted to teach him a lesson but the great fool tried to fight."

"Is he dead?"

Matteotti had walked past me, the weary smile, the sad eyes, the disdain.

Ferri burst out:

"Maybe you think they offered him a box of chocolates and de Bono and I are here because we're worried about his liver! Of course he's dead, the ass!"

Ferri had been alerted at dawn. The killers had been frightened, they had seen Merry Groves' car, confessed. Another witness, a janitor, had already given the police the car number: 55-12169. Merry had been right.

"The Duce's right," Ferri was shouting, "all the fools had to do was piss on the number plate!"

"They don't know what they're doing," murmured de Bono. "They've turned that scum into a hero."

Both of them were silent. The telephone rang. The police had found the car, cushions covered with blood, its owner, Filippelli, a personal friend of Mussolini, was being questioned. He had just given Dumini's name.

"They're not wasting time," de Bono said. "You'll see the rats start to leave the ship if they think we're going down. It's beginning."

Ferri was sprawled across the desk, his eyes staring, breathing noisily. He looked from one to the other of us. Suddenly he struck the desk with his fist.

"And that's all you can think of to say, I thought you were chief of police and you're going to let them get away with it? You've lost your mind, de Bono, your mind!"

"You should have kept a closer eye on your killers, my friend," de Bono retorted.

I was in a corner, listening, watching. As though he were standing in front of me I saw Nitti's face, the broken skin and half-shut eyes. "You can't be killed," I had told him. "Are you sure?" Nitti had asked. He could be killed.

"My killers!" Ferri roared; "you might as well say the Duce's, because Filippelli is no friend of mine, he's the Duce's friend. The Duce, you hear, de Bono?"

The telephone rang again.

"A fine start," Ferri said when he hung up. "We've got the family, the socialists, the liberals on our backs already."

He went to the window, pulled back the curtains. Rome, dead for Matteotti, whose body Dumini and Volpi had shoveled into the earth behind the hills. When Ferri turned back, his expression had altered. He was stroking his beard.

"De Bono, why are we arguing? You want to stay chief of police, I want to go on being minister and the Duce wants to be Duce. So there are no traitors among us, right? For them, we're all in it together."

He sat down at his desk.

"Let's just accept it, accept it. All we have to do is stick together, not give way. Not an inch, you hear, de Bono. Let them come out of their holes, we just sit here and put them to sleep. They'll waste all their ammunition, they'll stick their heads out too far, and bang! Point-blank. Put them to sleep. Not one word, de Bono. Shut up your police. Let them investigate, but quietly. We gain time, they'll grow impatient, we'll tell them a few soft words and when we're ready . . ."

He rubbed his hands, leaning against the back of his armchair again.

"The king won't dump us, de Bono. If we're killers, what's he? The king who chose killers to run his country."

If they were killers, what was I? The man who had chosen to serve them.

"Anyway, do you lose control of a government because one representative disappears? Who would ever stay in power on this earth at that price, who?"

I stood, mute and motionless.

"Ah, Naldi! You too have got a part in this play. You take the American and you go for a trip. Don't let go of her. In a week, maybe sooner, everyone will know about it, you can drop her. Whatever she says won't matter any more. Until then, silence."

Know, and everything is different. I drove slowly toward the Piazza Barberini. You think you're outside other people's games. Walk-on, Alatri had said. Then you're splashed with blood, your hands are tied, you're chained to Dumini, Ferri, de Bono, the Duce, one of the line, like those prisoners coming out of the shed in the Bologna station and walking across the platform in single file. To know means to be unable not to know. I was angry with Merry Groves for coming to me and talking. I ought to have put her down under me and screwed her into silence. I was already at the Piazza Barberini, turned around the fountain, drove toward the Tiber, crossed the bridge after the embankment where the Lancia had pulled out in front of Merry with Matteotti fighting inside it, kicking out the glass, and the dagger Dumini or Volpi stuck into him, or maybe it was Thierschwald, or all three of them, blood spurting. "Kill, kill!" Ferri had shouted while I stuck my dagger into the sandbag. The war had taught us to kill, I had killed. One man more or less? Why so much noise inside me? Often, after a bombardment, when we found our trenches exploded, we would see the tangled corpses under the earth, hands, a helmet, the end of a gun hardly visible. And when we were digging out new trenches our shovels would gouge into mixtures of cloth and flesh that used to be called men, remnants of another bombardment. Millions of men. Today, Matteotti. I went back to the apartment with nothing decided. I opened the door. Merry was standing there.

"The telephone's been cut," she said. "Did you know?"

I slowly pushed her back in. Her hands were fists, she was brandishing them in my face.

"Naldi, I am American, you hear me, a citizen of the United States, a democracy, a great country, Mr. Naldi. I am going to make a scandal, you hear me?"

I pushed her away, what had she come here for, why hadn't she run to one of her admirable colleagues who kept saying how we had found our way back at last to the tradition of Roman civilization after a century of decadence. Merry cried:

"Mr. Naldi, you're going to let me out!"

I took her by the wrists and began to shake her, I was shouting too:

"Miss Groves, you're going to shut your mouth, there is no such thing as a scandal in the country of the condottiere of the Renaissance, you understand, just shut up!"

Then I pushed her onto the bed and locked the bedroom door. Sun, noise, car horns, the unbearable growl of the city in the heat. Behind the door Merry Groves was calling:

"Marco, explain, have you gone crazy Marco, what's wrong?"
I paced.

"I swear I won't make a scandal, but explain."

I took bottles, everything I had, fruit liqueurs from Magliano,
wine, an armload. "You've got a load on your hands," Ferri
said, a load of shit, problems, blood. I kicked open the door.
Merry shrank back. She stared at me with huge eyes.

"Marco, please explain."

She was talking gently, calmly. I closed the door, put the bottles on the floor by the bed.

"Merry, listen to me carefully. You telephoned me, right? I
didn't come looking for you?"

"Of course, Marco, I told you so."

I filled a glass with sparkling wine, a plains wine, slightly sour,
pink like the wine father used to give me.

"All right; we're going to drink. I'll tell you later."

"I don't understand anything," she said, "anything. You've
gone mad, Marco."

But she drank and drank again because it was hot and the
wine was good and I was there threatening, joking, drinking too,
and there was a shared past between us and because drinking
makes you thirsty.

"I don't understand anything," she kept saying.

But she was hot. She drank.

"Marco, you're crazy, crazy. Marco, tell me. I can write the
best story of my career, Marco, you've been so nice to me, lots
of times."

She sniffled and clung to me, we rolled together on the bed
in an aura of wine and sweat, the damp heat of ending days.
Then she was just a disjointed form, one of those dead soldiers
it was so hard to pull out of the mud, her face swung from side
to side, she vomited in a hiccough. Then she began to snore,
her mouth open, and I tried not to pass out with her. I chewed
handfuls of coffee beans, took a cold shower, was sick too. Then
I went out. The evening papers talked about Matteotti's disappearance. In the "anxious" House of Representatives, as he

put it, Mussolini had demanded to know "the fate of Representative Matteotti, unexpectedly vanished." I drank a coffee on the Piazza Colonna, trying to fight off the nausea that was overwhelming me. Manacorda came in with a woman, he ignored me. I walked over to him. He had already removed his fascist buttonhole insignia. A rat.

"Well, Manacorda, how's the political climate?"

He smiled, embarrassed.

"Nasty business," he said, turning to his companion. "The Duce obviously is not implicated. But his entourage, you know, has not always been irreproachable."

He had raised his voice.

"Naldi, I think we must look to the king. He is the conscience of the country."

The nausea. Sometimes I liked the killers better than these gray jackals padding in their wake, sniffing the remains, scattering at the first sign of danger. I went home. Little groups were arguing under the arcades on the Piazza Colonna. Not one fascist to be seen, not one cry, no gang filling the roadway shouting "Mussolini, Mussolini, Mussolini!" in the people's faces. Was it possible that one dead man could have so much importance, that this cadaver could unseat fascism, the mirages could vanish with Matteotti? I approached one group. Beating the ground with his walking stick an old man in an alpaca suit was hammering out his sentences:

"The king, that is our recourse. If Matteotti has been assassinated the king will unmask the killers, but we mustn't play into their hands by creating disorder."

Two carabinieri, their long gleaming sabers slapping their thighs, calmly dispersed the loiterers without a word, moving slowly forward. Nausea. "The king won't dump us," Ferri had said. Ferri was right. They would all wake up one morning in single file with a chain between their legs and they would never understand anything. Why should I complain, since they were already beaten, self-blinded?

Merry Groves was asleep. I had played my part in the play.

The next day I took her to Ostia. We ran down a deserted beach.

"You still haven't told me," she said. "I haven't even been able to read the papers."

I drew her under water, she was spluttering and laughing. Then we lost ourselves in the Roman hills. We slept at an inn far to the south, near Frosinone. I was still playing my part. Finally, we went back to Rome.

"You're very quiet all of a sudden, Marco."

In the Piazza Colonna, outside Montecitorio, people were shouting, "Light and justice, light and justice." I bought an armful of papers and we went up to my apartment, Merry dunning me with questions. I saw the headlines, the story was spread all over the *Corriere della Sera* and the *Stampa*. Merry howled.

"Bastard, bastard!"

She leaped at me:

"You knew, didn't you?"

I shrugged.

"I'm going to write it all, sequestered, you sequestered me!"

"Come on, Merry, you're not going to write anything."

Standing on tiptoe, she slapped me.

"Bastard!"

"You're not going to write anything, Merry. And listen, I'll tell you, here's a very good story."

"Bastard," she repeated, but she couldn't make up her mind to go.

"You'll write that despite all appearances and shouting in the streets, fascism is going to triumph. You hear, Merry. Because it is in power. There. That's all. Power is something you keep. And there is the king, the army, the militia. You understand, Merry, power."

She slammed the door. I knew she wouldn't say anything. She was tied, like me, she would play her part. For me, though, that was the last part. I would play somewhere else. Far away. Far from Rome, Ferri, Magliano.

The game went as Ferri had predicted. Heroic words uttered by the opposition, the king mute, the Duce strengthened by his silence. And on January 3, 1925, when I was in Ferri's office at the Palazzo Chighi, the Duce came in. He had grown balder, which made his head seem even heavier. Ferri hurried forward, raising his arm:

"Duce, Duce."

"How do you work here, like fascists?"

"Like fascists, Duce."

He was preparing his speech for that afternoon at Monte-citorio. The opposition was already broken. He stayed only a moment.

"Ferri, I'm going to talk to them with my balls on the table," he called out as he left.

Ferri came back rubbing his hands.

"The buggers are going to wake up now, believe me," said Ferri. "The age of the little Italian with a thousand opinions and not one real one is over, Naldi, dead and gone."

My role in Rome was finished. I couldn't do any more. Each day smothered me. I drank. I changed women every night. The city seemed shriveled to me, shrunken, I kept stumbling into the same scenes, the same men, the same women. I knew the swamp, I was bogged down in it. Ferri was laughing. I took advantage of his good humor.

"Your Excellency . . ."

He seemed to notice me all of a sudden, he was talking to himself, my name uttered at the ends of his sentences was just one word among the rest, a refrain. I explained. I needed space, Africa. Now that the crisis was over, I was leaving.

"It's true, you didn't try to get out when the ship was in the storm, it's true. But what do you want? Africa? Why not?"

I was surprised, he seemed delighted by my request. Perhaps he, too, had had enough of my face and eyes following him since those nights in 1917, since the Aquila Nera.

"You could go to Tripolitania, Somalia, press service, prop-aganda, a little intelligence work for us."

He took my shoulder.

"Naldi, Naldi, I think you've got the right idea."

So he wanted me to go.

"But don't be in too much of a hurry. I won't forget you. Too many things between us, Naldi."

It was only a phrase, not even a reference to our past. Gradually I understood, as I watched his painstaking preparations for my departure for Somalia, that he wanted to cut loose, quickly. The Duce didn't give his ministers much time, though. He was speaking from the balcony of the Palazzo Chighi to a big banner-waving assembly of *squadre*, and he said, "Black Shirts of this city, there is fine weather ahead for me and for you, there is going to be a complete renewal of the whole fascist movement, at all times and places against any opponent, do you want it?" The crowd roared approval. Ferri and the other ministers saluted, loyal to the Duce. But Ferri turned to me:

"I haven't forgotten you, Naldi."

He relieved me of my duties and appointed Manacorda, fascist insignia in buttonhole, to replace me.

"You're right, Naldi," he said, "if only I could too."

A jackal. I sat in my apartment on the Piazza Barberini and waited. I followed the fascification of my country. Calvini and other representatives had fled to France. Mother was worried again. Nitti, summoned to Venice, had been interrogated at length, ordered to present himself at the *questura* every week. Valsecchini must have heard that I had dropped out of the procession of power. Nitti was paying. At last, one morning, Carlo himself brought my orders.

"There must be land out there," he said. "Let me know, Mr. Naldi. Who knows, maybe me too, one day, if I can find a woman, a real one."

I wanted to see Magliano one last time, I didn't intend to come back for years.

"Of course," said Ferri. "Go on up there. What is a day or two?"

So he didn't want me to hang around. I quickly packed two cases. It must have been in 1915: mother had laid them open on our long black table, she was folding clothes with slow gestures. Father was fussing around her. "I won't need all that," he said, "honestly." She said nothing, went on folding. Then the cases came back. There they were in front of me, half-empty. I had nothing to take. The telephone rang. I knew the voice.

"I know you're leaving," Elsa said. "Let's meet in Venice, at the Palazzo Dandolo, all right, tomorrow. I'll wait for you."

She had already hung up.

I was seeing my city once again, pale sky playing with the water in the canals. Here, at the Palazzo Dandolo, I had listened to Ferri at a long table, seen the tablecloth stained with red. The war. Carlo shaking my shoulder in the morning after the nightmare rats had gnawed through my sleep. And the sounds of rain and water. At the desk Elsa Missini had left orders for me to be shown directly to her room. I knocked. Her joyful voice. She was in white, bare-armed, bare-throated, and her hair piled high. I knew I would not leave that room without making love to her, and she knew and wanted it.

"Marco, you don't think I would have left you just like that, after that night . . ."

"You disappeared."

She put her hand on my mouth.

"I knew what you were doing."

We tumbled together onto the huge bed and lived, slept, loved to the boatsmen's cries, the hailing gondoliers. I forgot mother. My boat was leaving from Naples, no time to go to Magliano.

"After all these years the least I could do was give you a farewell party. Are you sorry?" said Elsa.

She was returning to Rome by car. She came to the station with me. We went up the Grand Canal, I was happy, life was a circle about to close, I was leaving Venice again.

"My town," I said, "the palazzi, dirty water, marble and the sewer."

"Do you know," said Elsa, "I'm marrying Ferri next month?"

PART TWO

M·A·U·D

4

Later, months or maybe years later, I've lost track of those confused days, the heat like a veil blurring time, erasing milestones,
those days at the end of the trails with Marghella, the years,
Eritrea, Somalia, when the nomads surrounded the post, a dom-
ineering *ascaro* translated our speeches, money was handed to
the chiefs and a girl with naked breasts and copper rings around
her ankles was thrust toward us, Marghella starting to laugh
while I ran my hand over the deep arch of her back, the girl's
vague eyes. Later, was it at the embassy at Addis Ababa in the
garden under the eucalyptus, Provi, my friend then, explaining
that we had begun our long march toward war.

"The Duce wants to conquer Ethiopia," he said, "and the
King Tafari will go down, emperor or not."

Or perhaps it was at Massaua, even later, looking at the steam-
ing sea, hardly grayer than the desert it continued. At Massaua,
or at Assab, or perhaps beyond the Strait of Bab el Mandeb
already, Obbia or Mogadishu or in Djibouti, in the marble building, the monument to pride that the government had erected
and forgotten among the dusty streets: headquarters of the
Italian delegation. Where, when, I can't remember and who
cares, but later, in an illustrated French magazine, I saw a photo
of Ferri and Elsa. They were arriving at one of His Majesty's
receptions in Rome, she was wearing a long gown with a train
that I imagined white and he was in uniform, a dress sword at
his belt. It must have been years later because both of them
had changed, she was heavier, a woman slowly used up by the
years, Ferri angular, concerned only to make an appearance,
pausing and posing for the photographer, Elsa still moving, her
head half-turned toward him in irritation or scorn, perhaps.
Years later, or was it just distance and unexpectedness, reveal-

ing them to me all of a sudden as though I was seeing them for
the first time, because of my departure and time passing, the
pit, between them and me.

Also, the cliffs with their blurred outlines, swathed in a searing haze, the basalt tables cut by gravel-sided faults from which
the heat rose up. Sometimes a trace of water meandering, a
few tufts and the assembled nomads sitting silently on white
stones. Marghella took topographical readings, imagined roads
to climb the mountains, to slither through the faults and crawl
toward Addis Ababa, the sources of the Blue Nile, Lake Tana;
I talked to the nomads, gathered information, paid, recruited.
I listened to their long monologues, lost my bearings in the gesticulations of their hands and the interpreter's translations,
the war I was preparing on the Duce's behalf and on Ferri's,
spreading my snarcs around the realm of King Tafari, Emperor
Haile Selassie, King of Kings.

I moved from a post circled by shattered stones to the sandy
streets of Massaua, Assab or Mogadishu. I found old friends,
Provi, who was preparing to leave for Addis Ababa. We played
poker under a noisy fan. Provi had left Rome after me, had been
seen by Ferri and the Duce, been given final instructions. I had
been there for months but a few days here were enough to abolish distinctions, Rome withdrew behind a horizon from which
an occasional ripple came, bringing letters, a few newspapers and
the telegraphic messages they uncoded for me in a dark room
smelling of wood and moldy paper.

For months I was numb, surrounding myself with silence, setting out for the base of the cliffs to meet the nomad tribes who
shifted from side to side of what was called the frontier but was
really only a line on a map. I followed them, learned to recognize their expressions, tents, sometimes a girl would lie down
next to me, shifting to her back a necklace of big white balls.
One after the other I bribed irresolute tribes away from the
Ethiopian influence, Marghella noted waterholes, trail intersec-
tions and peaks that would enable troops to orient themselves

in an armed combat once they crossed the unreal line dividing the chaotic desert.

I was acting in the superb illusion that I was free because there was no known face to send back a reflection of my actions, neither Nitti's nor Alatri's, and along those trails I did not meet the silhouette of father or of Giulia. I roamed, at peace and uprooted, far from my rice fields and tall vines, my fertile, curried, plowed land, I was without soul in ephemeral towns born yesterday that made me forget my timeless city, motionless in the moving waters of its canals. I had wanted this break, this impression of being nowhere, this absence of mirrors and points of reference. I spent months, years of peace in a land without echoes. I drifted under the sumptuous eucalyptus of Addis Ababa, days linked themselves together without the anguished interruption of questions. I owed nothing to this setting, it had given me nothing. Maybe because the war had thrown me too early among men, I needed this scorching sanctuary that was, for me, a return to a late, postponed adolescence. An age of irresponsibility regained.

I spent almost a year at Djibouti: an incandescent plate; then Provi, the embassy councillor, joined me and we left for Addis Ababa. The King of Kings had just visited Italy. In Rome the Duce himself had welcomed him and shown him every courtesy.

"Ferri," Provi told me, "has been instructed to get Ethiopia into the League of Nations, while we prepare it for invasion by our troops. Fascist diplomacy, Naldi."

Along the streets of Addis Ababa we both dreamed of a great colony populated by our landless peasants who would cut roads and sow wheat. Haile Selassie received us in the semi-darkness of his palace, a tame lion lying on red rugs, the imperial guard barefoot, wearing leggings wrapped around their calves and tight dress uniforms, holding curved blades over our heads. Then we went outside and the endless sky enveloped us. How could anyone sleep during the throbbing nights of the high plateaus? We smoked, side by side, talking quietly. Provi went to Rome regularly and brought back echoes of the struggles between Ferri and Manacorda and their rivals in the corridors of the Palazzo Chighi. It was like watching a play. Month by month I watched the rise of the fat young man named Ciano, son of a government dignitary.

"Ferri managed to ship him off to China as consul in Shanghai, but the fellow has long teeth and Ferri's right to fear him."

Then came the announcement of the marriage between Ciano and the Duce's daughter Edda, a nervous, dry, precise young woman.

"Now Ciano is really a threat," said Provi. "Poor Ferri, he's losing weight, the princess keeps pushing him. Odd couple."

I was far away, learning to fly a plane. I flew over the plateaus, dove down to the shores of Lake Tana, flushed thousands of birds. Marghella already imagined our troops at the lake, holding the sources of the Blue Nile, controlling the supply of water to the Nile. We landed in a cloud of yellow dust, he pounded me on the back.

"You're making out fine, Naldi, perfect. Understand," he added, spreading out his maps, "we'll have England by the throat."

It was like a long vacation in which the consequences of my acts were lost in some indefinite future. Sometimes I would get bad news from Magliano, but it came so long after the event that I was hardly concerned. I could do nothing any more: Nitti had been arrested, accused of antifascist propaganda, deported to a work camp on one of the southern islands. Mother regularly sent packages to him, Mrs. Nitti was still living at Magliano, where there was a new farmer, mother liked Nitti better, of course, but was getting used to this new one. She had even stopped complaining about my absence, accepted my silence, my refusal to go back to Italy although I was entitled to a long holiday every year. But I wanted to discover the diversity of the world. I had faith in new scenes, I drifted through the streets of Cairo and the hotel bars; I had faith in new faces, I loved

easy women who offered themselves between two whiskies and
made love under lukewarm showers. I went to Beirut and Jerusalem. One spring I boarded the *Colonel-Ferré* at Djibouti. A
southwest wind swooped into the Red Sea, churning up angry
waves; the tug rammed the steamer's side. Then the sirens'
scream, the open sea, a fresh departure. I intended to disembark
in Bombay and come back after a month. Maybe, as Provi said,
it would have been better for my career if I had gone back to
Rome to see Ferri or Manacorda. Request an interview with the
Duce. But what was a career? I let other people decide for me.
I saw Bombay, the English streets and alley wounds of wretch-
edness and death. I took another French ship back. In the
lounges where fans futilely kneaded damp air I kept looking for
women who were alone. I had to kill time, the days of the trip,
imprisonment on a boat. At the corner of a deck one morning
the past suddenly burst into life: Pierre de Beuil stood in front
of me, in civilian clothes, a white suit, broad-brimmed hat, walking stick. Overflowing with friendship.

"I can't believe my eyes, did you get on at Bombay? I should
have seen you."

Poured out his life, a sudden transfer to Indochina, a command in Tonkin.

"After a post in Rome, can you imagine, Naldi? You, of
course, your disappearance was something else again, I know,
I understand. There are wonderful things about Elsa but she
has great shortcomings too. You were right to go. But me,
Naldi . . ."

According to him, he had been the victim of a radical plot.
"You know the procedure, I was promoted, made a colonel
and moved to Indochina where I wouldn't be in anyone's way,
but now I have applied for early retirement, Mr. Naldi, and I
swear you'll be hearing about me."

Farewell to the women, farewell to watching the sea, the
sharks' fins slipping along in the wake of the ship. Beuil stuck
to me all the way to Djibouti. He disembarked with me. Mar-

ghella was waiting; he was now our military attaché in Addis Ababa.

"Gentlemen, believe me," said Beuil, "you are fortunate, your country is well defended. What is there left for me? France is rotting from the top down, like a dead fish."

Luckily the ship stopped only a few hours in Djibouti, but meeting Beuil had spoiled my peace. I had reached the end of it anyway, no doubt; when a phase comes to a close some event occurs, a sign, an almost imperceptible coincidence yet everything follows from it. Marghella told me an official delegation was coming to Addis Ababa, led by His Highness the Duke of the Abruzzi and his retinue, journalists, the colonial minister, and Manacorda, now director general in the ministry of foreign affairs.

"They want to put King to sleep," Provi said, "they take him for a savage, a little flattery, a sugar lump and the savage sits up and begs with both paws in the air, and drops his bone."

They landed one morning in the dust, a few weeks later. The imperial guard turned out for them, the emperor hieratic in a black cape, Manacorda servile, the Duke of the Abruzzi distant and bored. They were there and Merry Groves with them, Manacorda protective, spreading his arms.

"Naldi, Naldi, how wonderful, why don't you ever come to Rome? We'd like to give you a post big enough for you, but you've exiled yourself, you just travel about, India, Jerusalem. Ah, Naldi, what wisdom!"

There was the past, in the eyes and voice of Merry Groves.

"Years, Naldi," she said, "it's been years since your ghastly performance."

She put her arm through mine.

"Tell me, how do you live here? You're preparing an invasion, aren't you, everyone in Rome says so, the Duce wants his empire."

There was no out-of-the-way place, no escape, death maybe.

I had thought I was taking a vacation and I had gone on following the furrow of history in spite of myself.

"And you?"

"Still Rome," Merry said, "the Ferris' receptions, an extraordinary pair, two birds of prey."

The shadow of Galeazzo Ciano looming, backed by the Duce.

"They're trembling for their lives, Elsa and Ferri, the Duce's sick of them, they're the biggest gossip item in Rome. But they're hanging on, both of them."

We were separated by Manacorda, who was positively oozing, he took me into the ambassador's office.

"Marghella tells me your reports on the military situation in Egypt and the Black Sea are models of exactitude."

He took off his jacket.

"How have you managed to stay out here so long, almost five years?"

We went outdoors, the air was heavy with the sweetish scent of eucalyptus.

"You know there are going to be big changes at the palazzo? Ciano has been talking to me about you."

Pause. A glance to see how much I already knew.

"He regards you as one of Ferri's victims," he went on. "There was that marriage with Elsa Missini. It didn't do him any good in the eyes of the Duce. She's French, after all. You know her brother. He claims to be a fascist, of course, but he's an officer. Who can tell . . ."

Manacorda never spoke unless he was sure, and he only ran up his sails once he knew which way the wind was blowing. Those few words were Ferri's funeral oration, and Manacorda had already changed camp.

After the receptions came the parade. Thousands of barefoot warriors in white shammas, obsolete guns raised, sabers waved, dust floating above the long column. The Duke of the Abruzzi presenting the emperor with a tank, a present from His Majesty and the Duce to the King of Kings.

"Good thing they only gave him one," Provi murmured.

In the evening I met Merry, we sat apart from the others while the embassy gardens slowly emptied.

"How can you live here?" she asked again. "This silence."

"I wanted a calm place."

She shook her head.

"You weren't made for calm. People who want peace and quiet find it anywhere. You threw yourself into it, here, violently. . . . You are an extremist, Marco Naldi. An extremist without a passion. You haven't found and maybe never will find your passion, so you're an extremist about peace and quiet. I watched you in Rome, during the Matteotti affair. You frightened me."

She had turned toward me as she spoke, her hands around her knees.

"But I forgave you," she went on. "I'm still fond of you. You gave me a few good tips."

We let the silence grow between us, the breeze in the high branches. One gesture from me would have been enough, for her to be as before in London or at the Piazza Barberini. But I had no desire for her, I felt like talking, wanted her to listen to me talking about myself.

"Are you going to stay in Rome?" I asked.

"Maybe Berlin this year. Rome has become an iceberg, there's nothing more to see or write there. One word and you're thrown out. In Berlin everything is on the move, fascism is going to win there."

Maestricht, Captain Goering, Venice. You think you're doing nothing, being a cog in a machine. Then the machine starts to turn.

"You've changed, Marco Naldi, you're serious, quiet."

"I've grown old, Merry."

"Brrr, Africa is no good for you. You're morbid. Don't ever talk to me about growing old."

"You're just a girl, Merry, a young girl."

I took her to her room in a long tree-framed building the emperor had turned over to the journalists. On the terraced plateaus the warriors could be seen lying wrapped in their shammas, white spots on the gray earth, as though mown down by machine guns. And we had plenty of them.

"Stay," Merry said, "stay."

I lay down beside her and she went to sleep almost at once, curling up, fists closed, her head against my arm. Afraid, she was afraid; needed to touch a body, only touch it, to believe in the apparent fraternity of a skin, an arm. Who would she have picked up if I hadn't been there, already familiar? Provi, Manacorda, one of the reporters with whom she'd been laughing on the airstrip before she saw me. Anyone, a body, someone else. I kept quiet in order not to wake her, listened to the night and the rustling of insects and the far-off cry of an ambushed bird dying in one crunch of a pair of jaws, all woven together into the breeze. Night, the age-old terror. I was like Merry, the memories, at night, with the implacable sharpness of detail, an exploded face, hospital corridors, an outstretched hand, Giulia crying for help and only her mute mouth, desperately open, and the gray sacks, father's shorter than the rest. Night, the false come true, the half-formed questions, visions of today endlessly prolonged, why take a step tomorrow, and tomorrow again, and in what direction? I was like Merry. A foreign body, a woman, it had weight, you took hold of it with both hands, felt the nape of the neck under your fingers, buttocks and breasts under the palm, crushed, arms enfolding life arching up. Then sleep came. Then morning, acts, gestures, words, the machine, oblivion, peace.

Sometimes when I knew I wouldn't find a woman I walked toward the bush, after the last shanties, the last stockades, where the bush begins and shadow suddenly covers the trail. Walking, an act, a slowly mounting fatigue. I came back exhausted, dogs barked as I passed, some animal crossed my path belly to the ground and I lay down on my bed on the edge of sleep, still hesitating. I dredged up prayers, the ones mother used to say at Magliano when she leaned over me, her lips hardly moving, and I recited them with her, then she was leaning over me again but it was morning. The night was gone. I went over the words of the past, back to a time without memories, my lips were mother's and my voice hers, I felt her warm breath on my face and plunged down into the murmur.

Childhood, women's bodies, I used them in the months following Merry Groves' departure, for peace had left me. Too many signs, words, Manacorda giving me a wink as he boarded the throbbing twin-engine plane that stirred up clouds of yellow dust.

"See you soon, Naldi, we haven't forgotten you."

Since then a mounting impatience. If the time for change had come, let it come quickly. Provi was summoned to Rome, Marghella went off into the highlands with two guides for a season of shooting that was really a mission to see that maps were filled in, tribes located, liaisons set up. I stayed alone with my waiting. The weather turned sultry. To the south, beyond the volcanic bars standing like purple shards, rose the black protuberances of the rainy season. Gradually they drew nearer, let them drown this town in which I no longer had anyone to talk to. They came, the inverted image of the basalt plateaus, I waited for the crack that would open the sky. I waited for Provi, Marghella, the weary smile of the wife of a German embassy councillor I'd had my eye on since I had been alone, but she shied away, her function in life was to provoke desire and then refuse. At last one night earth and sky met, the water erupted in a roar of white lightning, trees bent double, trails transformed into torrents, the rain front filling the entire horizon in the morning.

Provi returned from Rome on the train up from Djibouti

that came slowly in the rainy season. He talked and talked, about Rome, the big trial of the anarchists who had tried to assassinate the Duce, the prisoners deported to the southern islands who had been pardoned for the tenth anniversary of the fascist victory. Nitti must be back at Magliano. Perhaps Alatri had been freed too. And Ferri about to topple, Provi said.

"Ciano is boss now," he added. "Insanely vain, juggling with the succession."

He had caught a glimpse of Mussolini in the gardens of the Villa Torlonia, the Duce's residence, where Ciano had seen him.

"Caesar," Provi said, "a fat Caesar but a Caesar. Head shaved, hardly speaks. He told me that Bulgarian yoghurt is an excellent remedy for tropical diseases and promotes longevity."

Provi laughed. Marghella had joined us.

"You poor bourgeois," he said, "corrupt bourgeois; he's got that and that." Showing his fist and his prick.

"What else does a leader need?"

"An idea or two, sometimes," said Provi. "Although the game he's playing here is not crazy. Pluck Ethiopia slowly like an artichoke, then swallow the heart in one gulp."

War soon. We watched the soldiers of the imperial guard march past on their way back from the palace of the King of Kings. Their bare heels slapped the mud.

"Musical comedy," Provi said.

War. Its net was spreading and I was one of the threads. Sometimes I'd have liked it to break out, like a storm. Everywhere. So everyone could know that all there was to do was fight on one's own side. Then die. Provi was unconsciously stirring up my impatience.

"Ferri goes down, you go up, Naldi. Ciano spoke to me about you, the unfortunate victim of Ferri's jealousy, the fascist hero driven out. And then, you're hot stuff, our first contact with the Germans."

Maestricht, Captain Goering, Venice. Everything in a life adds up, the total is drawn in an instant.

"Ciano wants to play you off against Ferri," Provi went on. "He imagines you're nursing a deep hatred. Don't undeceive him. This is your chance, take it, Naldi."

My chance or Ciano's. I was always caught in the web, one of the threads, a cog. Pawn in a game.

"It's your chance, take it," Provi repeated.

He knew me well, too many days and nights spent side by side drinking and talking about women.

"Don't forget," he went on. "If it isn't you it'll be somebody else. There's always somebody, believe me, Naldi. You're naïve, you don't know enough historical background. All the dice are loaded. So play with loaded dice. Take your chance."

I took it. A physical impulse more than a reasoned decision, maybe. Because I already knew the color of the sky once the clouds would disappear toward Eritrea in the north. Because Rome had become foreign to me after all these years and I now had too many roots in the Ethiopian soil. And had made the rounds of all the women and all the trails. And then, I was being called. A cable came from Ciano, Provi came running to me with it.

"He's minister, and you're his first act. Good sign, Naldi."

A few days, farewell drinking bouts, solemn or raucous, black female figures with pointed breasts coming up to us, Marghella sprawling on the ground and Provi dignified, elegant and drunk. Then Djibouti, the sea, Naples. Rome as though I had never left it. The "Imperial Ways" that had been opened up near the Forum, the Duce's portrait everywhere, proclamations about the tenth anniversary. Militia parading across the Piazza Venezia. Ciano at the Palazzo Chighi. Manacorda ushering me in. Ciano like Ferri's rejuvenated double.

"So you are Marco Naldi," he said.

Hair brushed back, a chubby child's face, flabby features that an expression was struggling to harden. Haughtily polite.

Pages of a file he leafed through, a gesture to tell Manacorda to withdraw, and the rapid step, scarcely audible padding, of Manacorda receding.

"Naldi, why nearly six years in the desert? Oh, I know, it's the fascist front, the battle will take place there. But why?"

A mild, soft voice, veiled eyes, hands enveloping words. Galeazzo Ciano is observing me.

"You could have aspired to an important position, you had performed difficult missions, Karl Maestricht, Goering. You know Goering? What do you think of him, let's see, it was in Venice wasn't it? Tell me about it, Naldi."

To size me up, that's what he wants. Or make me feel he wants to size me up, establish a dependent or insecure relationship between us. I talk. I remember the terrace in the sun, Maestricht, Goering's wife.

"I have your report here," Ciano interrupts. "You're repeating it word for word."

Disappointed, pleased? Let nothing be seen, that's his strategy. He stands, shoulders thrown back, uniform too tight, crosses his arms. Like Ferri—like the Duce. All of them copying the original.

"Now, Naldi, are you aware of the situation in Germany?"

The voice swells, he walks slowly, chin raised, keeping his arms folded.

"Things are deteriorating rapidly there, Naldi, they're back to 1921. Nobody believes in the republic any more. Hindenburg is going to pass the deal. The Reichswehr will obey. There will be a Nazi government before the end of the year. Then the Europe of Versailles, Naldi, will be dead. Really dead. The Duce can play his fascist card. They'll all be hanging on our apron strings."

Silence. The parquet creaks.

"I want somebody there. Someone reliable. With good connections. Not a diplomat, not a journalist, not a spy, Naldi, someone respectable. A representative of the ministry of press and propaganda who will keep me informed directly."

Me, naturally. I had been Ferri's eyes at Montecitorio. I will be Ciano's eyes now.

"Without going through channels. Directly. Berlin to Rome. Sealed letter, diplomatic bag. You talk freely, about everything and everybody. Everybody, I repeat, Naldi."

Ciano goes back to his desk and sits. Closes my file.

"You should be there in a month, at the beginning of November."

Gets up. Hand on my shoulder. The same gestures as Ferri, as the Duce maybe.

"I'd like you to meet the Duce before you go. We'll arrange that. And then, rest. You're from Venice, I believe?"

A few sentences about eternal Venice. I am caught. Have been chosen, pushed out on the slope again, and it makes me angry, afraid, and glad.

"See you soon, Naldi."

The steps move away. Footmen hurry in. Manacorda already at my side.

"Well?"

"Berlin."

Handshake.

"Bravo, Naldi, bravo. Right now it's the key post. Everything is being decided there. Everything. You know who is ambassador there? Ferri, of course. He couldn't be given less, a former minister."

Manacorda leans toward me.

"But not for long, perhaps. One mistake, and the count . . ."

Outside, Rome, which I had hardly seen yet, Rome in the autumn vagueness; uniformed schoolchildren singing their way down the Via del Corso. I had sworn to fall in love with the twilit stones again, to forget the solar white of Ethiopia and the empty austerity of the plateaus. Had wanted it. What was left for me to do? I went upstairs to the apartment on the

Piazza Barberini. Their moves were so clear, so simple, Ciano was sending me there as pawn, dynamite, spy. Sending hatred to its foe, he thought. My chance. I had only to play the game, say what I was expected to say. Provoke, invent. Here in Rome, Ciano would accumulate files. And if Ferri became threatening one day, then, in the Sala del Mappamondo of the Palazzo Venezia, the evidence would be laid out on the Duce's desk.

I'd been back only a few days and was already disgusted. Wanting to leave again. Not even to wait for November but to plunge far from Rome into this frenzied Berlin the newspapers were talking about. To see. And then, I knew what they were up to.

Outside, Rome. I loafed. Via Giulia, the Palazzo Missini looked abandoned. An enormous inscription across the road: FEDE, faith. In front of the palazzo on Piazza Venezia, fascist militia stood guard, frozen in their black uniforms. I crossed the empty piazza slowly, heading for the café Faraglia. Suddenly there were three of them hemming me in, in civilian clothes, one pushing and the other two already pinning down my arms. I shouted. A blow on the back.

"No noise, your papers."

Hands wrenching my passport away. Rudeness, then the craven humility of flunkeys. The oldest, a massive fellow with a round face under a hat with a turned-up rim, kept saying, "Sir, excuse us, the Duce is in the palazzo, we have orders. The attempts, you know . . ."

I took their names, to make them worry for a few days perhaps. Then went back home. Staying on the balcony, trying to telephone Merry Groves, other women I had known before. No answer. Rome had become my new desert. I couldn't stay in that silent apartment. Going out again. Aggressive, restless, hanging around the streets. At last, two women, one tall, all in black, with a curving supple body, the other heavy, a stifled laugh. They stopped when they saw me in the empty street, walking toward them. Then when they understood, the smaller one shook her head. The other one looked at me. A Roman type.

"Don't go," said the first.

The woman shrugged.

"Leave me alone," she said.

Took my arm, decisively.

"Take me with you, if you want."

At last an arm, a body, at last a voice that was not play-acting. At last. She came upstairs with me. I looked her over: a Roman nose, high cheekbones, lips too thick. Ugly but full of life. She had taken off her shoes.

"My feet hurt."

She rubbed one foot against the other, slowly, immodest, her legs spread apart, her skirt above her knees.

"What do you do?" I asked.

"I'm a widow," she said.

Then laughed: "Not an occupation, being a widow; I'm an unemployed widow. You see, that's why I'm in black."

I sat down across from her. Made her drink, like Merry Groves, long ago.

"And you?"

She drank in little sips and grimaces. She wasn't used to alcohol.

"I travel."

"You're a reporter?"

I said yes, it was simpler.

"What paper?"

"Italian, American."

A fairy tale for camouflage, so that I could see her more clearly, since she couldn't see me.

"Could you get me to America?"

"Depends."

I tried to approach her. That's what she was there for, she knew it.

"Are you in such a hurry? Can't you talk a little? Only fuck? What do you write in your paper?"

"That everything is going just fine."

I gave her another drink, then began to undress her. She let me for a while, then suddenly resisted.

"You said yes," I said.

"I still do. But I'd rather do that myself."

And she continued to undress, without a glance. I went out on the balcony. Empty streets, empty sky, silence. Sometimes at night, a few weeks before father died, I would sneak out. Giulia was waiting for me. We hardly touched each other, sitting side by side in the stable in a cone of shadow, the moon lighting up the countryside with a blue glow. Giulia would talk, sometimes reaching for the tips of my fingers, what did she say? Miracles, how mad it was to meet there. For hours. Her murmur. Then my lips on her temple and we parted. Time had had its way with me. There I was, holding out bank notes.

"All right," said the girl tonelessly.

I went back inside. She was lying under the sheets. Modest.

"Well?"

I had sat down. In the end it was enough for her to be there, to have come. Thanks to her my thoughts had swerved away.

"You can go. Here."

I put down the money.

"As you please."

I went back onto the balcony. Was that the law, day after day, a blow to knock you down to size, some part of you chipped or worn away, day after day. The girl came out to stand by me, leaning on the balcony too. It seemed as though one could hear the water in the fountain on the Piazza del Tritone. Then the roofs, interlocked surfaces on which reflections passed briefly.

"Pretty, Rome," she said.

Silence, perhaps the sound of water. She stayed there, her eyes unfocused like mine, staring at the geometry of roofs, terraces and tiles dominated by the hills.

"It's pretty at night. Too much dirt in the daytime," she went on. "You shouldn't look at things in broad daylight. You know what they say in Rome: how lucky to be blind, then all women are beautiful. You're not Roman?"

"From Venice."

Silence. Two carabinieri going down the Piazza Barberini.

"My husband was from Turin."

"Have you been a widow a long time?"

A laugh.

"You know, I got married young. He died in '22."

1922. I was waking up on the Via Giulia, Elsa was murmuring a few words. I was learning about power. Ten years.

"Don't you want to know how it happened?"

In 1922, in the streets of Turin and the courtyards of farms and outside factory gates and in Genoa and on the paths along the rice fields men had fallen, maybe hers.

"1922, in Turin and other places," I began, "it was easy to die if you weren't lucky."

"Lucky? What he wasn't was smart enough to keep his mouth shut, he talked too much, you know?"

She turned away.

"Since then I'm a widow. Unemployed. So, you see, when some jerk like you comes along and doesn't look too much like a cop . . ."

I said nothing. She was speaking loudly, from the other end of the apartment, running water.

"Because *he* isn't too keen on people doing that in Rome."

She said it again, aggressively, to make sure I understood it was the Duce she meant:

"*He* doesn't like it because he's afraid he'll run out of women one day. One every afternoon, you know, they say, a different one, proper women."

"You talk too much too."

A few words made the silence again. I turned around. She was picking up her bag, head down.

"You made me drink," she said, "you made me talk."

"Don't forget your money."

She hesitated, slipped it into her bag. I saw her running down the Via del Tritone. Perhaps it was that night that I lost the habit of whores, the first unfamiliar body I saw became incapable of pacifying me, I could no longer find sleep by holding a head in my fingers or feeling a breast under the palm of my hand. I had wanted to begin again with this woman, I had done it so many times, from the Aquila Nera to Geneva, Rome to Cairo, so many bodies, the gleaming Somalian girls with their heavy necklaces, women in bars and on ships, wives driven toward me by boredom, who talked of London, Paris, or Berlin, the posts they coveted for their husbands. Then the lassitude with Merry Groves and this woman, the gestures to make, to impose. My rejection. Perhaps it was the age of maturity that had come.

"He's really a man now," said mother.

I had left Rome for Magliano the next day and was in the ground-floor room of our house, mother holding my arm, hugging me, standing back to see me better.

"Marco, what a man you've grown into, look, Maddelena!"

Mrs. Nitti wept, smiling. She stood near the door, a handkerchief to her mouth, in black like mother, then burst into sobs and I went over to her, took hold of her shoulders.

"Aren't you glad to see me, Mrs. Nitti?"

She nodded yes.

"Excuse me," she said, "excuse me, Mr. Marco, but I can't help it."

I was the years Giulia would not know. I had left them both with their few words to share, both of them driftwood in the stream that carried them, both now smaller, shorter, gradually burying themselves in black cloths, shawls. I saw my room, then the fields, paths, poplars, the shed, another dog that didn't know me; Matteroni, the new farmer, was lifting huge forkfuls of manure in front of the barn.

"And Nitti?"

Mother shrugged.

"He's wilder than ever. He goes off in the morning, no one

ever sees him. He comes back at night. Maddelena doesn't know what to say to him. He won't talk at all."

Sitting at the side of the road beyond the poplars one morning I found him, watched him coming forward, head down, a spade on his shoulder. I stood up and went to meet him. A glance, a movement of the hand toward his hat, measured tread. I walked alongside him.

"What are you going to do this morning?"

"I'm digging out the canals, sir, we agreed, Matteroni and I."

Nitti was thinner, stooped, breathing noisily. We went along among the rice fields, a thin layer of ragged gray mist was clinging to them.

"When did they let you out? Was it hard?"

He raised his head, looked me in the eyes, a snort.

"Canals, you know, they've got to be kept up, sir, otherwise the earth goes hard, like cement."

Another look, my urge to shout that he had to talk to me, I had spent those years a long way from Italy, I couldn't have done anything, after all he had made a choice, then I stopped, why go on? He hardly turned his head, touched his hand to his hat, walking on to the end of our fields.

I went back to Rome a few days later, Mrs. Nitti and mother coming as far as the road with me.

"You must forgive my husband," she murmured, "he doesn't realize what you and Mrs. Naldi have done for him."

She had her handkerchief in her hand.

"We did nothing," I said roughly.

Rome, Manacorda after Nitti, Manacorda congratulating me in his office in the Palazzo Chighi.

"The Duce will see you on the twenty-eighth, the date of the tenth anniversary, Palazzo Venezia, here are the instructions. Vital for you, Naldi, Ciano will be there."

There I was, in a black uniform, bronzed skin, hair short at the temples, pronounced jaw, the same chin as father I had, and the swollen vein on the side of the neck like his that I used to trace with my finger when I was hanging to his shoulders.

There I was, at eight o'clock in the Duce's waiting room, with others from different parts of Italy, others like me, as unsure maybe, as ready as Manacorda was in June 1924 after Matteotti's assassination to remove the party insignia from his lapel. But today like me, there in the waiting room, leaping to our feet at the footman's call under the suspicious eye of the Duce's *moschettieri*, sword in belt, immobile, arms folded, eyes following as we rose and walked toward the tall doors of the Sala del Mappamondo. Behind which the Duce, the summit of our pyramid of hesitations, scruples, remorses, refusals, the Duce like the King of Kings in his palace at Addis Ababa. Myself, others, myself an other since I was caught up in the compact agglomeration called fascism, government, power, and since in the end what importance did they have, the words that welled up for me alone, screaming in my head, on my lips becoming a resigned smile.

I followed the footman into the vast room where, at the far end, was a table in a corner by a window. Ciano standing beside it and the Duce watching me come, Ciano halting me at a respectful distance.

"Duce, this is Captain Naldi, whom you met before in the heroic days, second lieutenant on the Piave, enlisted at seventeen after Caporetto, an official in my ministry. He is just back from Ethiopia, en route for Berlin."

There I was, in the sentence Ciano had just pronounced, and the annihilation of my life, the forest of images, trenches, Giulia and the stopping train and Alatri walking between two carabinieri and Nitti's silence. And the gray sack, the shortest one where father lay. My forest pruned in those few words.

The Duce rises. Goes to the window. Folds his arms. The same fixed stare, face a little heavier and paler than when I saw him last on my return from Geneva. Ciano smiles.

"He had a little unpleasantness, of a personal nature, Duce, with Ferri," he says.

The Duce frowns, his footsteps ring out.

"Naldi, I remember you," the Duce begins, "Naldi, personal

matters must always come second to the state. The state, the great word of our age. Nothing exists outside the state. That is fascism."

He leans both hands on the desk, his face still raised to me.

"In Berlin, Naldi, as on the Piave, your duty, your sole duty, is to serve the state."

Each word detached from the rest, the expression suited to the word and freezing between each word. Words for history. I seem to recognize them, my whole childhood was framed by them. Old Nitti, his bent back, standing, and grandfather reading the *Memorial*. Napoleon was only that too, a few grandiloquent words at the summit of a pyramid of men like me.

"What does the King of Kings say?"

The Duce does not wait for an answer, bursts out laughing, Ciano laughs too.

"He's grumbling, isn't he, the wrinkled old monkey? Give me two years, two years. And we'll have an empire."

He sits heavily, a motion of the head, Ciano signs that the interview is over. About-face, sound of my footsteps, the Duce's voice stopping me.

"You're not married, are you? I don't want any more single men. We need children. Hurry up."

I wait in another room. All around me, these images I could no longer bear to look at: men in uniform, their chests striped with decorations. Outside the windows I see the crowd massed on the Piazza Venezia. Soldiers, children, thousands of upturned faces. In a group of journalists near the entrance to the hall Merry Groves, a wave, she comes over.

"Marco, Manacorda told me you were going to Berlin. Maybe we'll see each other there."

A wink, a smile.

"You're going to think I'm following you."

She goes on talking but I've stopped listening: the fanfares, bugles, rhythmic drum rolls, chanting, and the upraised faces, a stir among the uniforms, Merry Groves pulls my sleeve, I salute, the others salute, the Duce walks between us to the balcony, turns to an officer, shouts:

"Tell those stupid fools to stop playing."

Merry and the other journalists cluster around, he straightens, points to the crowd:

"What about the war, Duce?" one reporter calls out.

"The war?"

"Ethiopia, there have been troop movements."

The reporter has a strong English accent. The Duce shrugs:

"The war? I would not presume to describe war to conquerors, to warriors like the English, would I?"

A glance at us, at the place where the fanfares gradually die off.

"But I have said it before, war is to man what maternity is to women, am I wrong?"

A silence on the square, as before a gathering wave. The Duce is on the balcony, I see all those upturned faces, round white pebbles shaken by a cry. The Duce leans both gloved hands on the balcony. He is on tiptoe, turns right and left, the cry mounts, silence.

"*Popolo*, people of Rome and Italy!" he says.

The loudspeakers brassily send back the first words to fill the piazza, the room where we stand; then a pause, a single loud voice shouting up from the piazza:

"Duce, give us a smile!"

Mussolini raises his arm, the crowd shouts, then once more: "*Popolo*, people of Rome and Italy!"

That evening the town was illuminated, processions paraded through it singing. I was to meet Merry Groves at the Excelsior, Via Veneto. Other faces, shouting voices, a woman I thought I recognized on the arm of an officer, perhaps someone I'd met at one of Elsa Missini's receptions. Merry came in with an American, thin, an extremely long face, who smiled.

"Norman Strang from the embassy, he's going to Berlin too," said Merry, "all Rome is going to Berlin."

"It's because things are happening there," said Strang, "so they're sending the best, the good newshounds. Do you like to shoot, Mr. Naldi?"

He talked about the Catskill Mountains, forests, lakes.

"Merry tells me you know Ferri well, your new ambassador?"

His anecdotes splintered into pointed questions, then his smile became a grimace, wrinkles freezing in the corners of his eyes. He seemed old. Merry interrupted him:

"Norman, I don't want this evening to turn into a working conference, you promised."

He apologized:

"You know how it is, don't you, Mr. Naldi, the machine keeps turning, hard to stop it. You must have hunted in Ethiopia, big game surely."

His archaic tactics amused me. I ordered another round of drinks.

"Listen, Strang, tell me frankly what you want to know and I'll send you a report tomorrow, drafted under my supervision, to the embassy, that'll be simpler."

We laughed, Merry shook her head, repeating, "You've disappointed me, Strang."

I ended the night alone.

They were my last days in Rome. I tried to retrieve my schoolboy German, read the *Berliner Tageblatt* and the *Frankfürter Allgemeine*. They were awaiting the elections of November 6. Berlin was paralyzed by a strike. Hitler was touring the country predicting a Nazi victory but I sensed uncertainty in his speeches. Little by little I became interested. It looked as if I would be reliving the days of the March on Rome but this time as a member of the audience in a theater that was no concern of mine. And then Italy, including the women at the Excelsior, the Manacordas, Piazza Venezia, Ciano, the moschettieri, their ambitions and uniforms, had all become foreign to me. I needed exile.

I left Rome early in November. It was to be a long voyage.

5

A few steps in the train station, the Bahnhof Friedrichstrasse, and Berlin has caught me, only a few steps along the emptying platforms, in an icy mist under steel and concrete vaulting where the echo of a distorted voice resounds, repeating that this is Berlin, that the journey ends here, a few steps, my first steps, and Berlin is clutching me, pressing down on me as on the Piave when a mud shelter collapsed on top of me and the fear that I would never get out alive, the pain that scars through my chest like shrapnel.

Bahnhof Friedrichstrasse, perhaps it was just the unsettling effect and fatigue of a long journey: at first I thought the square in front of the station was empty, but it was only drenched in moisture, lit by the intermittent flashes of a red and green sign. Suddenly, silhouettes emerging from streets, men in helmets with raised fists, jackets too short and collars turned up because the cold was sharp, and police whistling shrilly and running, their long black bayonets covered by the folds of their gray capes. Exile in a hard, cold land: Berlin as I felt it after my first few steps in the Bahnhof Friedrichstrasse. Apprehension, too, at having to meet Ferri and Elsa again, their indifference or their hatred, I didn't know which I feared most. Then those processions the first evening, dark compact masses that invaded the bridge over the Spree near the station, outstretched arms wearing the red band with the black design. More police, *Schupos* in round caps, throat straps cutting their cheeks, others in civilian clothes, wrapped in long cloaks, coming up to me in the lobby of the Central Hotel as I went in.

"You're the French journalist Laborderie, no?"

I had hardly begun to speak before they tried to drag me away, saying:

"Police, police, you are not allowed to remain in Berlin."

I finally managed to show them my papers, their apology was curt. In the hotel lobby, men, a few women, faces tense, listening to a speech punctuated by high-pitched roars, being transmitted by radio from some distant meeting. I recognized the words "soul," "destiny of the German fatherland"; I recognized the upturned faces, like those looking up at the Duce on Piazza Venezia, some tide seemed to have washed them all this way. A young bellhop in blue livery with gold epaulets and blond hair took my suitcases with a swift, energetic motion; a girl's face, the only thing masculine about it was the short hair. He turned to me in the corridor where carpets muffled our footsteps.

"You heard the radio," he said, "that was Hitler. This evening he's speaking in Hamburg. Before the elections I heard him in the Sports-Palast."

He set down my cases in the doorway, didn't even wait for a tip.

"Excuse me, I want to hear the end."

He ran back down the corridor.

Here as in Rome, the power would be taken: in Hitler's harsh voice I had recognized the Duce's determination, I was discovering the faces that were going to be piled one on top of the other, consenting, hesitant, fearful, blind, living stones of the pyramid of power. Karl Maestricht and Captain Goering, now reaching the end of the road that began back in Geneva, Munich, and Venice in the days when I had known them. The squares of Berlin were already full of shouting, like the Piazza Venezia, I could already sense the mutter of intrigue that precedes the fall of a government. They had all come to the Piazza Barberini, generals, moderate politicians, monarchists, and I had only to look at the papers to see that the tin soldiers —von Papen, the old aristocrat of the club of the lords; General von Schleicher; Field Marshal Hindenburg—had already been swept away. Once again the game was over before it began.

"All the dice are loaded," Provi had said in the embassy gardens at Addis Ababa. So why not let go, history was going to abandon itself to the same men here too, and I was with them, risking nothing because they couldn't hear the murmur inside me, my questions. But the questions, the anguish when I had seen those brown men emerging from the mist and marching rhythmically forward over the Spree, how could they threaten me, Marco Naldi, fascist civil servant? What rebelled in me, making me shiver with joy when I heard, in the lobby of the Central Hotel, that the Nazi party had just lost over two million votes in the elections, and maybe . . . Yet I had to convince myself, turn to my memories, that those two million votes would change nothing. A few determined men were all that was needed, a few threads woven in the shadows, a fine dignified stage prop like His Majesty the King of Italy or Field Marshal Hindenburg, and the doors would open as they opened in Rome. In those days I would wait at the foot of the stairs in the Quirinale for Mussolini to walk out of the royal palace with Ferri.

"His Excellency Ambassador Ferri has instructed me to take you up at once," said the embassy footman as he stood up.

I had crossed the Tiergarten in its russet and black autumn hues, a Berlin of straight-backed horsemen cantering down barren paths heaped with dead leaves. It was morning, a gray sun, and my brisk walk had made me forget I was about to meet Ferri in the embassy on the Matthäistrasse, a street of middle-class town houses hidden behind gardens. My name, a footman hurrying up the marble staircase ahead of me. Another footman in black shirt, sitting under a portrait of the Duce. My name again, a click of heels, and the door opening.

Ferri was leaning on his desk, slightly stooped, older, his forehead higher, wrinkles around his mouth, an expression of resolution, sarcasm, bitterness. Not one word. I stopped facing him.

"Your Excellency," I began.

A violent gesture, the features exploding:

"Naldi, if you try to provoke me, if you have come for that purpose, then listen, it will be war."

I waited. Ferri sat heavily, pushing back the armchair whose feet scraped on the parquet.

"You've become a spy for Ciano, that intriguer who turned the Duce's head, that conceited fool, you've come to spy on me, Ferri."

He struck himself on the chest, stood again, came over to me:

"I'm going to talk to you like a soldier, a fascist soldier, an officer."

Now he stops, paces around his office. Through the windows I see trees in the garden. Before, it was the roofs of Rome, outside the windows of the Consultà.

"Naldi, it was a mistake to accept Ciano's proposal. He'll go too . . ."

He brushes Ciano away with a breath.

"You know me, Naldi, we were on the Piave together, can you forget that? We risked our lives together, you and me both, in the same mud."

Silence.

"Because I don't forget anything, Naldi, nothing, I know you're a fighter, I'll remember it but Ciano, Ciano . . ."

He takes me by the shoulders, forces me to walk with him.

"You weren't born yesterday, Naldi, why has he dragged you out of the depths of Africa: because he thinks we'll tear each other apart. Well, Naldi, let's join forces, you and me, the old guard, the first fascists, you understand?"

His eyes question me, his arm, I know the passion for power that is crippling him.

"Your Excellency, the Duce, who was good enough to see me before I left, made it very plain that I was in the service of the state alone."

He moves away, takes a few steps, sits, points to a chair facing his desk. He watches me.

"So the Duce saw you?"

Power: words, mirages. From top to bottom of the pyramid a chain of words, subterranean linkings, chains of fear and obedience. Subjections, from top to bottom.

"And, Naldi, come now, what specific instructions? I am ambassador here, I must know."

"The press to watch, direct relations with Rome."

His fist thumped the desk.

"You have direct relations with Rome, and what about me? Where does the hierarchy come in? What am I for?"

Power: a series of links joining each to the next, if one breaks the whole chain goes. I was a missing link, escaping Ferri's control. Therefore I was a threat to him. He spoke, switching from rage to menace, seduction to indifference. Then suddenly, after another pause, he made up his mind, resuming the tone of jovial friendship, paternal:

"Marco, do your job, you've proven yourself, haven't you?"

He laughed.

"The days of the Aquila Nera are a long way away, finished and done with, now you fly alone."

So far the name of Elsa had not been mentioned.

"I trust you. See Antonetti, the first councillor, he knows Berlin society, all of it, Naldi, the Fräuleins, the embassy misses, and the journalists, of course."

We were at the door. He was holding my elbow as he had so often done, wasn't he going to say anything? Would he dare? He paused.

"Marco, of course . . ."

A moment of silence.

"Elsa will be happy to see you, the past is over and done with, isn't it?"

The black-shirted footman stuck out an arm. He resembled those in the Palazzo Chighi or the Palazzo Venezia, Berlin in the grip of the nazis was an overenlarged reflection of Rome, a hard, systematized outgrowth of the 1920s. My years. The past, exile, does such a thing exist? Rome in Berlin. Ferri marked, embittered, but similar. "The past is over and done with," he said. Easy, too easy to dispose of things that way, set up a frontier, I too had believed in clean breaks, had needed them, had gone off to the chaotic desert, gone to Berlin, had wanted —still wanted—to put my past, my country, my thoughts, in exile. How long can an exile endure?

Antonetti, Count Antonetti, was a diplomat—a real one, he intimated. Ferri and I were mere parvenus who had entered the career by accident, clumsy buccaneers, vulgar and ignorant. He was a head taller, hardly dropping his eyes to me, forcing me to raise mine to look at his heavy face, broad jaw, and the scornful pout it displayed permanently.

"My dear friend," said Antonetti, "His Excellency was quite right to send you to me, but what can I do? Berlin society doesn't let itself be invaded overnight, you need roots. Do you know Auwi?"

Antonetti was playing with a long letter opener, he had sat down, for him I was old Nitti, cap in hand.

"Auwi, Prince August Wilhelm, one of the kaiser's sons, is a turntable, through him we can gain access to Hitler, Hindenburg, General von Wirth. And then there's Putzi, Phillip, he will make your work easier. . . ."

Putzi Hanfstaengl, Prince Phillip of Hesse, Auwi: Antonetti's world, that of Prince Missini or Elsa de Beuil. Not Ferri's world, nor the Duce's, nor mine. Ferri had squeezed his way in, the Duce was at the top of the pile and for a time princes served him. But what was I? I belonged and wanted to belong only to myself, my land at Magliano. I had probably been wrong to think I had a camp, that there were camps, sides. My camp was myself. Pride, madness, naïveté.

"My dear count, I'll go straight to Goering, I knew him in 1924. Very well."

I left Antonetti gaping. In the embassy courtyard I recognized Carlo washing Ferri's car. Past, present, exile? Carlo, in Ferri's shadow forever. He had hardly changed at all, glad to see me, the same quiet smile. The same questions.

"I was going to get married, in Rome, then the captain came here and I didn't want to go through that again, I didn't know if I could bring her with me and now—pfft!—vanished. . . . I can drive you, I'm going to pick up Madame."

We left, driving along the canals.

"She likes to go for walks by herself in the morning, I pick her up at the end of Unter den Linden."

I didn't ask any questions, didn't want to know, not yet.

"I can tell you," murmured Carlo as I got out, "you didn't miss anything. Have no regrets."

The phrase took root in me during the weeks I spent discovering Berlin, following day by day the asphyxiation of the government, the ballet of the tin soldiers, Papen-Schleicher, their moves toward Hitler. It was as though I was reliving that Roman October, I could feel the government cracking on all sides beneath the unseamed façade of legality. Then some Matteotti affair would occur and Hitler, like Mussolini, would talk with his "balls on the table." The furrow of history. Straight. The rest, writhing like drowning men, gradually being covered over by a layer of black fuel oil, trying to signal for help. And speaking out would get one nowhere, except down in the mire with them.

Weeks. I moved into a sculptor's studio on the Dorotheenstrasse. Behind the glass wall a corner of the Tiergarten was visible. Von Baulig, a Wilhelmstrasse official, rented it to me around mid-December. He was showing me around it.

"My former tenant preferred to move to London."

We were looking at the trees.

"He was very fond of Berlin, this is a wonderful place to work in. Only, his name was Karl Meyerson. Such a nuisance . . ."

We talked later, in his library on the floor above. He spoke of Venice, its attraction for the German spirit.

"Venice is a mad whim that worked, and we love madness, it fascinates us, we're too rational to be able to resist insanity, if you see what I mean."

He walked me to the door.

"I hope I shall not have to leave Berlin and go to London," he was saying. "Anyway, I should prefer Venice or Rome, but just now . . ."

"Your name isn't Meyerson?"

"It's so easy to become a Jew today, perhaps I already am one without knowing it, and you too."

He opened the door. In front of us an officer with a broken nose, hardly any lips at all, sunken eyes, indeterminate age, too thin for the years to have left any imprint on his skin. At his side, hatless, blond hair cut very short and a lively expression, what seemed to me to be the first woman I had seen in Berlin. General von Wirth and Frau Ingrid von Wirth. Introductions, a few words, Ingrid's laugh that stayed in my memory and came back when I saw her again a few days later at the embassy New Year reception.

Throughout those weeks I had avoided the Matthäistrasse, Ferri, the memory of Elsa. I invented excuses, I had to learn about Berlin, von Baulig was taking me on a tour of the best society, I was following up the threads, from conversation to confession, that wove the web of power in which a bare hundred names crossed and recrossed, always the same: von Papen, General Schleicher, Field Marshal Hindenburg, Goering, Maestricht, von Wirth, Goebbels, and also Kurt von Schroeder, the Cologne banker who was said to be acting as go-between for Hitler and von Papen, Voegler, Thyssen, Schacht. The power, the future in their hands, and the others? The groups colliding on the Berlin squares in the fog, assembling in front of the Kaiserhof, filling the Wilhelmplatz and Ziettenplatz and overflowing onto the Wilhelmstrasse, brown shirts, arms raised, members of the Storm Troopers hoping to catch a glimpse of Adolf Hitler coming out of the Kaiserhof. The others: whom those few names, silhouettes in a drawing room, had succeeded in capturing and transforming into a compact, black, brown, noisy, determined, obedient mob, shouting a name in the Berlin fog: "Hitler, Hitler, Hitler!" and the other name on the Piazza Venezia, "Duce, Duce, Duce!"

I couldn't avoid Elsa. She stood at the entrance to one of the drawing rooms, hidden by Ferri, and I was following the receiving line of guests through the hum of conversation and the poignant purr of a cello, suddenly alone, cutting through the sugary violins and I remembered the musicians of the Palazzo Missini. There she was in front of me, pallid, face bloated and skin too white, chalky, and her cheeks that seemed to fall into her neck, her lips too red like a bloodstain. I kissed her hand, idiotically afraid she might clutch my head to her chest, to the voile dress, hold me to her amid a roar of laughter. An irrational panic that made me straighten quickly.

"We must see each other," was all she said.

She still had the same frown, but now her face seemed like a mask, a cracking glaze. The word "past" must have some meaning for her. Unless she had always been like this, walking out of that photo I had happened upon in some forgotten post or office in East Africa when I seemed to see her for the first time.

Later in the evening she came up to me, tense and smiling, taking my hand, and against my palm was this icy moving object, her hand.

"Marco, you've matured, Africa, talk to me."

I wanted to get away, withdraw my hand, my presence.

"You find me changed, don't you?"

I followed her along corridors where groups of guests parted and bowed to us.

"I can't bear Berlin any longer, an odious city, I am French, you understand, they are so vulgar here."

We were in the shadows of some office.

"Marco, I hate him, you hear me, I hate him, he's a peasant. He's so narrow."

I couldn't see her face but I could guess the look on it, that hungry expression she had worn when she was urging me to speak to Ferri. "I want that embassy," she had said.

"You've got your embassy."

"A slap in the face, we were insulted, Ciano made a fool of him, and me too, and you've come to spy on us, Marco, isn't that so, you're jealous?"

She moved closer, holding my hands.

"You're jealous."

Low voice, that wants to speak and give a whole body, hands opening the better to take you with, and in me uneasiness and revulsion; between us something like a thick pane of glass that kept me from hearing and touching her: the past.

"I must see you again," she said, understanding at last.

I returned to the drawing rooms and to Ferri, caught his eyes on Elsa, an instant of interrogation between them, of collusion perhaps, get me involved again and disarm me, their fear of losing this embassy too, this crumb of power, these chandeliers and smiling faces moving past, Phillip of Hesse, von Baulig.

"Ah, Naldi," he said, "you must come with me to the von Wirths', we're celebrating the New Year there, you'll see Potsdam."

In one corner a laugh that vibrates in my mind, Ingrid von Wirth tossing her head.

Faces, Strang introducing me to a French reporter: "Laborderie, I'll tell you, Naldi, because you're a friend, Laborderie is a confirmed antifascist but he drinks the embassy champagne."

Jerky gestures, nervous tics:

"My job, my good Strang," said Laborderie, "I have to be at home everywhere."

Further on, Ferri observing me and talking to François-

Poncet, the French ambassador, then Karl Maestricht hailing me, shaking my hand.

"Mr. Naldi, I heard you were in Berlin, we've come a long way, haven't we, since Geneva?"

"You promised me a decoration, and I predicted a ministry for you."

It had been in Venice, Captain Goering had been half asleep. Karl Maestricht squeezed my arm and raised his goblet.

"Promise kept, prediction come true, who knows? The press gives us the victory, you know?"

The present. January 30, again January 31, I saw them, Karl Maestricht's comrades, coming from Charlottenburg, seeming to pour out of the forests of which the Tiergarten was a dark outpost, I saw them from my Dorotheenstrasse studio, heard the deep rumble of drums and the dry hammer of boots, I went down and mingled with the crowd, carried along in the current. I saw the brown front lines of the procession pass under the Brandenburger Tor, thousands of torches weaving down the Wilhelmstrasse, pause for a moment under the windows of Hindenburg's residence, whose façade seemed to ignite in the yellow reflections, then voices, shouts, chants, the black glittering stream trickling on, invading the city. Adolf Hitler was chancellor, Goering minister, Karl Maestricht *Obergruppenfuehrer* SA responsible for keeping order in Berlin. Almost a minister. The tin soldiers, von Papen, Field Marshal Hindenburg, were still standing, set up in the middle of the field, still useful props in a stage setting. Only General Schleicher had been removed, he was traveling, a holiday, and his deputy General von Wirth had been given a mission to Japan.

"They didn't even give him time to say good-bye," said von Baulig.

He often invited me up to his library.

"Japan," he went on, "suddenly seems to have acquired a considerable importance. The truth is that they're afraid of the Reichswehr, or the part of the Reichswehr that might stir up the main army. You know, Blomberg and Reichenau are not typical of the *Offizierkorps*."

The main thing for me that day was not in the Reichswehr. It was Ingrid von Wirth. I had seen her again at the end of December, at that New Year's party von Baulig had mentioned, in their huge chalet above the Griebnitzsee at Neue Babelsberg, one of Potsdam's fingers reaching out to the forest. Snow and fog, water and the nearby forest all together. Von Wirth silent and austere, stiff as a scaffolding; Ingrid near us, sitting on the floor on the bearskin that had a history, she told us, her father had brought it back from a shooting trip in the north of Sweden.

"For I am not German, Mr. Naldi, I am Scandinavian."

Nothing between us, just two or three sentences, looks, each keeping his eyes open, unblinking, a turn of the head interrupted by our eyes fastening to each other's face, then conversation resumed, the turn of the head completed, each seeming to forget the other and plunge into a lively dialogue with someone else, then the look again. I saw her two or three times in January at von Baulig's, the Prince of Hesse's, at Goering's too, he was still president of the Reichstag and entertaining the cream of Berlin society and, fists on hips and body shaken by a resounding laugh, he called me to witness.

"Frau Wirth, you know that General von Wirth and the Reichswehr were not so gentle with us once, ask Mr. Naldi, I was not in such good condition in Venice. Ah, sometimes the Reichswehr aims at the wrong target, but at least it never misses."

General von Wirth made no reply.

"But that's all in the past, isn't it, General?"

Goering remained urbane.

"United for Germany, you and us."

General von Wirth left for Japan, and that February evening I was driving toward Neue Babelsberg, the chalet on the Kaiserstrasse. A decision taken after that sentence of von Baulig's.

Desire for a woman, after weeks. Memories mingling with desire, the dream of a body, the joyful, exalted certainty that the woman was going to accept, the looks were a subterranean dialogue and we were already moving forward side by side. The telephone, a few words, a hesitation, more words.

"Why not?" she finally said.

Road, sleet, trucks, the Berlin Opera, to which I did not want to take her, had she really believed we would leave the chalet? Haste in me, not love, but haste to bend her body, see her eyes close, the certainty that after these slow, almost imperceptible gropings our bodies would catch fire, as they say, with one glance; the certainty broken for a moment by a memory of Elsa's body, my desire for it, the peace it had given me and the ashes left today. Then take without thinking, let go, enjoy, let yourself slide, be pushed, follow the procession, grab the women, stay on the side where they are beautiful, bejeweled, easy, where they lie down on furs and smell good. Content yourself with bodies, mirages, take.

"I'm not ready," Ingrid called from her room. "You've taken me by surprise."

As life did me.

I went up the stairs quietly, toward her voice. Her door was ajar and she was speaking loudly so I could hear from below, what was she saying, how she loved Italian opera, maybe, or Stockholm, how she missed it, her husband had been military attaché there and she had been seduced, Germany, the Reichswehr, fame. I went in. She was sitting in front of a dressing table, her bare arms raised. I put my hands under her arms, in the moist secret warmth. She cried out and I knelt behind her, kissing her throat, the back of her neck, while she let herself sink backward and gave me her mouth, which I kissed on the side. Then we went up to the attic.

"The maid is coming back," she said. There were big thick eiderdowns on the wooden floor and we buried ourselves in them.

I drove to Neue Babelsberg many times. I would stop at a distance from the chalet, at the end of the Kaiserstrasse, and walk the rest of the way, stumbling in the snow massed at the side of the road, then push open the door Ingrid left unlocked for me and go up to the attic. The rooms I walked through were silent. In the pantry, Ingrid talking to the maid, and in the attic at last the eiderdowns, which I piled in one corner where the beams met the floor, waiting. Ingrid. Our language was our movements, immediate, no exploration, movements that I recall as curves, spirals, endless whorls, circles. Sometimes in the middle of the night we would go into the forest of Babelsberg, toward the height from which one could see the shining spots of the Havel waters and the lights of Potsdam. I drove slowly back at dawn, trying to reconstruct the hours that had just gone by, to re-create my other nights in the apartment on the Lungo Tevere with Elsa, to understand, to measure the distance. Then too there had been joy in my muscles, and the Via Giulia was as fine as the paths of Babelsberg. So was Ingrid another Elsa? Another happy habit, then erosion, curves becoming angles, the loyal body an enemy to be vanquished, Ingrid today, Elsa tomorrow? But today joy, the car window down, icy air stinging my face, wasn't that enough?

One February morning, because Ingrid was sleeping at my side, her warm naked body stirred by her slow breathing, because I had been watching her a long time, not wanting to wake her, wondering whether one day I would make up my mind to stay with one woman, not just at night, whether I would manage —I had done it with Giulia in a period already farther away than a dream—to talk to her about myself, to tell her my memories, whether I would ever find the one woman who would be the last for me, my wife, as mother was for father at Magliano; one February morning, because I was so comfortable in the warmth of the eiderdown, because it was cold outside, I stayed later than usual at Neue Babelsberg.

When I reached Berlin the fog was thinning over the Spree.

First, in the Dorotheenstrasse, I saw the crowd: workers in caps pushing their bikes by the handlebars, office workers with their leather briefcases, then groups of Storm Troopers. They were occupying the roadway: shoulder straps and belts pulling in their new uniforms, some assembled in squadrons, chanting angrily:

"Punishment, punishment, out with the Reds, out with the Reds!"

I slowed, then at the corner of the Wilhelmstrasse a barrier of Schupos forced me to stop. A policeman checked my papers.

"You'd better walk home, sir, you won't go any farther here, the Reichstag burned last night."

I saw the big building at the corner of the Tiergarten surrounded by a cordon of Schupos and SA: the tower had blown up, iron ribs rose skyward amid columns of smoke and flame climbing as though from an open crater. Traces of fire on the façade; patches of plaster or cement had cracked and fallen off, forming a heap of rubble that police were poring through. An occasional shatter as panes of glass broke or exploded spontaneously in the heat where the fire was still burning. SAs were going through the crowd; one, near me, hailed a group. A violent voice, gloved, clutching hands.

"We've got to get rid of them," he said, "they destroyed the Reichstag."

A whistle blew and the SA stopped talking. At the corner of the Dorotheenstrasse someone, bareheaded, was struggling with the SAs who were dragging him away.

Soon Matteotti. The same scenario over again. Inexorable.

I went up to von Baulig's apartment. He was drinking his morning tea in his library, windows open, we could see the crowd milling in the Tiergarten.

"My dear Naldi, you missed the show."

He was pale, still in his dressing gown, his voice weary.

"The symbol of the German parliamentary system consigned to the flames."

"Arson?"

"Beyond doubt. You heard the SAs, come over here."

We walked to the window, Schupos and SAs were linking hands to keep back the spectators. At a distance, apart from the tower, the Reichstag did not seem seriously damaged.

"We called it the *Schwatzbude*, the chatterbox; still a fine figure of a building, isn't it?"

SAs were grouped at the entrance to the Wilhelmstrasse, joking and slapping each other on the back to keep warm. At a signal they began to shout, marching rapidly toward the chancellery.

"Communist crime," they were shouting, "communist crime!"

"You see," von Baulig said to me, "it's all perfectly clear."

He closed the window, poured out tea for me.

"Devilish cold in spite of this fire, it's true that a tall stone building like that doesn't burn very well."

Then we drank in silence. The servant brought the papers. Black headlines on the front page: "Communists and Socialists Set Fire to Reichstag" and below, Hitler's first orders: "Boycott the Jews, Defenders of the Arsonists."

"All so simple, isn't it?"

Now von Baulig was smoking, letting his head sink back against the edge of the armchair.

"I shouldn't like to shock you, Naldi, but I do believe we will be better at fascism than you, we're more methodical."

I stood up to go.

"Or less civilized," he said at the door.

He took my arm.

"I hope you are not unaware of the fact that the residence of Goering, president of the Reichstag, is linked to the Reichstag by an underground passage?"

A question, an item of information. Von Baulig repeated, holding me back with his hand:

"An underground passage, dear Mr. Naldi."

Goering responsible? Why not? I knew too much about mirages to be taken in by the slogans of the *Sturmabteilungen.*
"Red crime," they bawled.

At the corner of the Matthäistrasse and the Tiergarten they had gathered outside their headquarters; other SAs were waiting in the Matthäistrasse, leaning on the wrought-iron fence of the garden of their leader Captain Roehm's house. I saw him come out, red face, a purplish scar across nose and cheeks. Maestricht in his uniform of Obergruppenfuehrer stood next to him. He stopped in front of me.

"We're almost neighbors, Mr. Naldi," he said happily. "Today we begin our clean-up."

The SAs were chanting Roehm's name.

"Follow our example, Mr. Naldi, as we followed yours."

Maestricht set off at a run. Uniform, boots, armband: Maestricht was no longer the dim figure I had first seen in the lobby of the Hôtel du Lac in Geneva, an isolated individual looking for help. He was wearing the insignia of violence, violence was his commander and he its servant. In his office at the embassy Ferri was jubilant. He pulled back the curtains, showing me the SAs forming up into ranks.

"'There, Naldi, there are true fascists. And they're going to go all the way. We squadristi let ourselves be pushed aside, we ought to have . . .'"

Every minute of his life was undermined by remorse and regret; he tried to encircle me with consideration, allusions. He was afraid of the reports I was sending directly to Ciano, in which I never spoke of him or Elsa; but the sealed envelopes I regularly placed in the diplomatic bag haunted him. I was Ciano's spy, with orders to shoot him down. Then he would try seduction, pushing Elsa at me.

She came a few weeks later, unannounced, to the Dorotheenstrasse.

"Carlo's waiting for me," she said, frowning.

She came in, went through the rooms and over to the glass wall.

"Marco, what a wonderful place. You know, Ferri doesn't know I'm here. He's afraid of you."

She sat, I remained standing in front of her.

"Aren't you going to offer me a drink? I'm very thirsty, thirstier and thirstier."

Her laugh was too loud, the motions of her head too abrupt.

"How do you like Berlin, the women here, tell me, Marco, this is a love nest."

She drank, her lipstick marking the glass, greedily.

"This city's turned me into an alcoholic," she said suddenly. "I need some kind of passion. What is there here? So I drink."

She didn't seem to want to leave, she posed and postured. Available, a red and white made-up face, a body I found too heavy, and sometimes her eyes glazed with a feigned tenderness or regret, for there was nothing between us any more except her vain, obstinate attempt, like an insect against a window pane.

"I'm boring you," she said.

Then her expression hardened, her teeth clenched, and she dropped back again:

"Marco, you're so indifferent!"

I pushed her away, a sigh.

"I must go, Carlo's waiting."

She had masked her defeat, come back, pushed by Ferri no doubt, allied with him to compromise me. I watched her going along the pavement, weaving a little, mildly drunk, Carlo held the door, she let herself fall, I could imagine it, and the car drove off. The game of Elsa, Ferri, my games in the evening when I left for Neue Babelsberg and Ingrid threw an eiderdown over my head, laughing, and then dropped down on top of me. Back in the morning, the streets of Berlin, a report to draft, Ferri to see, who started off again: "Ciano—you know, Naldi, in my view he isn't a true fascist." Our lives continuing while history rotted around us, sometimes I wanted to throw them off with

one toss of a shoulder. Commit myself with my body, my whole
body, open it up to blows and kicks, stop administering my
days and joys, stop enjoying, dive in headfirst and let death
come if it liked. But doing what? Strang took me to the Taverne
one evening, an Italian restaurant run by an authoritarian German, where the American journalists used to gather. In one
corner of the room they had their *Stammtisch*, their regular
drinking table. Smoke, smells, voices.

"I've got a surprise for you," Strang said, "a nice one, I hope."

Merry Groves was sitting laughing with Shirer of the *Herald
Tribune*. She kissed me.

"I left the New York *Times* in order to come to Berlin, are
you glad, Marco?"

She talked nonstop. Shirer, mute, chewed at his pipe. I didn't
stay long but Strang wouldn't let go, came home with me, we
walked along the Spree. People were loitering by the banks.

"More and more arrests," Strang began, "they've set up a
political police force."

What did he expect? That the opposition would be allowed
to remain free? Hadn't he learned yet that the law was to slay
your adversary?

"Listen, Naldi," he said abruptly. "I've had a piece of confidential information. You see a lot of Ingrid von Wirth? In
Berlin, they know about it."

"Who is they?"

"The Gestapo, the secret police, Heydrich, Himmler. I
wouldn't like you to fall into their clutches."

"So I can fall into yours? Thanks, Strang. Good night."

History surrounds me. A swamp. I don't have to make a move,
it comes to me and buries me. I can see the threads twisting
together. What should I do? One time I hurled my life into the
heart of the game, on the Piave. Duty, heroes, fatherland, my
father to avenge, Ferri haranguing us. The gun they gave us:
I seized it with both hands. Two camps, black, white, the Piave
between us. The enthusiasm of beginnings, my joy, sometimes,

when we leaped back into the trenches alive, still alive. Victory.
The chant "A *noï! A noï!*" Then nothing, ever again, a tangle
of intrigue. Loaded dice. Negotiations. Why stick your neck
out? You have to let yourself float in the changing times, the
lengthening days, the coming spring, snatch a woman's body,
her look. Then it's not very much, this rotting history and the
processions beating time to the seasons. "*Sieg Heil, Heil* Hitler!"
The voices burst forth, Labor Day, day of heroes. Fanfares, black
uniforms, fair-haired children stretching out their hands. "*Heil*
Hitler, Fuehrer, Fuehrer, *Sieg Heil!*" Banners across the fronts
of buildings and the sign in its white circle bordered by red,
on the walls, on arms, faces, in eyes, the black sign of a grim
time coming, I feel it coming.

"Do you have a moment?" von Baulig asks.

We go up to his apartment; I recognize Laborderie standing
by the bookcase, leafing through a book.

"You must have met M. Laborderie of *L'Époque.*"

"The police thought I was M. Laborderie, coming out of the
Bahnhof Friedrichstrasse, when I first arrived in Berlin."

"I am not popular here," says Laborderie.

He sits, cracking the joints of his fingers, crossing and uncross-
ing his legs.

"Fortunately, François-Poncet intervened. I have the personal
authorization of Hitler, an extremely understanding, fine chap,
the Fuehrer."

Von Baulig serves us a liqueur. It's already the end of the
Berlin summer, the trees in the Tiergarten shudder in the breeze
chasing down the Spree in the late afternoon. Red sky.

"You are an antifascist journalist, I am told."

"Strang exaggerates. I'm not enough of one."

"Antifascist, antifascist, words," says von Baulig.

He has lighted a cigar.

"I owe you a few explanations, Mr. Naldi. I need a neutral
witness, it may be useful one day. M. Laborderie is French,

isn't he? You are Italian, almost an ally, but if you'd rather back out?"

Why back out. If that's the furrow of my life. Make no moves, but don't take back your bets, your life, if it's in the game. Otherwise, what's left: cowardice, a body that is nothing but a mirage any more, an empty shell.

"Thank you, Mr. Naldi," von Baulig goes on. "You see, I am in possession of information and I should like it to be known in Paris and perhaps in Rome. I have just come from Sonnenburg, 120 kilometers from Berlin, a friend in the ministry of information took me there. It is a camp for improvement by work, a model camp."

Laborderie has stopped fidgeting, he listens, chin on hands, leaning forward. Von Baulig stops only to draw on his cigar. A calm voice to talk of Sonnenburg, bodies struck down by blows, faces beaten, Jews on all fours in the mud.

"It is the SA who are doing this work."

Obergruppenfuehrer Karl Maestricht, met in the Matthäistrasse, had been coming out alongside Captain Roehm. My friend Maestricht had said, "We're beginning the clean-up."

"I think the method is going to spread," von Baulig continues. "But that is not the most important thing. The most important thing is a settling of accounts that is being planned, the clans are going to kill each other off, and Germany may be plunged into bloodshed and the mire."

Laborderie asks questions; there are Goering, Himmler, and Heydrich on one side, against Roehm and Maestricht. Hitler is hesitating, playing off one group against the other.

"Naturally," said von Baulig looking at me, "if one group liquidates the other, the nuisances in the middle will be done away with as well. Schleicher, von Wirth. You know, Naldi, that General von Wirth is coming back from Japan?"

So Ingrid and I had changed our routine. Now she came to the Dorotheenstrasse, I pulled the tall blue curtains and we forgot the day for a few hours. Afterward, we lay side by side, then I watched her moving around the room, dressing, her flawless figure.

"I wonder if they've been waiting?" she said.

She was sure she was being followed. A car that hadn't even tried to pass unnoticed was parked at the corner of the Kaiserstrasse in Neue Babelsberg, and followed fifty yards behind her on the Berlin road, never dropping back. I urged her to be careful, for herself. What was I risking? She shrugged.

"Werner couldn't care less what I do. He doesn't mind. I'm sure it isn't him. It's the others, the Gestapo. It's Werner they're after. I warned him but he already knew. He's waiting for the field marshal to give the signal, then the Reichswehr will liquidate Hitler, Roehm, all those pimps. Werner says they have to wait."

I was still lying on the bed. She came over:

"Day after tomorrow, Marco. At teatime."

She laughed at her joke. Werner von Wirth wanted to wait. He still had confidence in the tin soldiers, Hindenburg, von Papen. How could he be so blind? I went to open the curtains, sat facing the trees in the Tiergarten. Von Baulig himself had the courage to leak secrets, but didn't go far enough, I thought.

I was coming back from Nuremberg, from the party congress. Goebbels had seen me before I went, in his big office in the Wilhelmplatz. Gaunt face, mobile hands playing with a bronze swastika, penciling nervously on a blank sheet of paper, crumpling it, taking another sheet, his eyes going from me to the score of telephones ranged on a little table.

"You will study our organization, Mr. Naldi. I believe Mr. Ciano could profit by it. Propaganda is essential, Mr. Naldi, you will judge for yourself. Wasn't it your Duce who said the people are like a woman you have to seduce? Well, we're trying."

Nuremberg red and black. A fine rain, projectors catching faces in their shafts of light, women screaming, "We want our Fuehrer, we want our Fuehrer!" The white beam seems to be pushing them, lifting them toward the balcony of the Deutscher

Hof, where Hitler steps out for a moment, saluting, and the crowd hurls me forward shouting and laughing, "Fuehrer, Fuehrer!" More projectors like columns aimed at the sky in the big stadium where thousands of muscles contract, shining, swollen, brandishing steel shovels, pounding the shuddering earth: "We want a Fuehrer, Fuehrer, we want a Fuehrer!" The tiers explode, arms rise like weapons about to fall and in the Luitpold Hall military marches and the high-pitched voice of Putzi Hanfstaengl shouting, "History alone, in a thousand years, can judge the events taking place now under the government of the Fuehrer." In the lobby of the Deutscher Hof I met Karl Maestricht.

"You have come to the source, Mr. Naldi, remember, I told you we had begun the clean-up. . . ."

Goering, Goebbels, and Streicher, shaven head and riding crop in hand, and the faces of the crowd being held back by the SA and pushed into the square again. The mob saluting the conquerors, the masters—those men I first saw in Venice or Geneva, transfigured by power.

I return to Berlin. General Werner von Wirth is waiting, von Baulig gives more information. A thin barrage of words swept away by the flood now beginning to rise. Laborderie wrote an article for *L'Époque,* I sent a report to Ciano, Merry Groves cabled the Chicago *Tribune.* Words among more words, the bottom of a page, a few sheets in a file. Nothing. There would need to be another mob, a madness to stand up against the other madness. Those men on the boulevards of Bologna who had shoved me up against a wall and begun to hit me until Calvini stopped them. Violence against violence? Perhaps it really was better to take back one's bet, save one's little joys. Ingrid's body. And then, all mobs seemed to go the same way. In Paris there was shooting on the place de la Concorde, groups trying to invade the Chambre des Députés and throw the representatives into the Seine. In a corridor of the embassy I met Elsa, sway-

ing a little, her eyes too big, struggling to control the tongue
that sometimes refused to obey, stammering.

"In Paris, Pierre has come into action. Did you see, Marco;
Pierre de Beuil, Duce of the French? That would be funny.
We'd go live there. I'd advise him."

Ferri opened his door, waving the footmen away and inviting
us into his office.

"Elsa, please, do not come to the embassy when we're working, please."

She dropped into a chair, her head drooping on her chest, a
half-smile, hands open.

"You bore me, Ferri, you bore me, this city bores me, if Pierre
succeeds . . ."

Suddenly Ferri shouted:

"Be quiet, be bored, go wherever you please!"

"You're a failure, Ferri, a little provincial lawyer, you'll lose
your post here too."

Elsa went out, stiffly. One must never be a witness, witnesses
are hated. Ferri sat at his desk.

"Make your report to Ciano, make it," he began. "Say we're
tearing each other to pieces here, it's the scandal of the diplomatic corps. Shall I dictate it to you?"

I was just back from Nuremberg. Von Baulig, in his library,
talked about the new camps, men standing in the snow, cap in
hand, for hours, blows, preparations for war. But Ferri, and
Elsa, and Ciano and I as well, all of us glued fast in our daily
lives. Unbearable images. What else to do? The ambitions,
fears, glories, sordid struggles between them, between ourselves,
and under the balconies faces shouting "Duce, Duce, Duce,
Fuehrer, Fuehrer!" Unbearable to know, to go backstage and
then return to a crowd on a square applauding its masters and
kneeling.

Elsa came in again:

"You humiliated me," she said, "in front of Marco Naldi.

You humiliated me, Ferri, and I will not allow myself to be humiliated by a peasant."

She walked toward Ferri with her hands closed into fists. He had shrunk down behind the desk, his head between his shoulders, as though he didn't want to hear.

"You're not going to make me pay for your failures, Ferri. To Ciano you're nothing any more, nothing."

He leaped at her and grabbed her wrists, shook her, stopping her from crying out.

"Shut up, shut up," he said, between his teeth.

She wrenched away, slapped him savagely. I moved between them, Ferri shoved me aside.

"Go away, Naldi."

"Marco, he's crazy," Elsa was screaming, "don't leave me."

"The slut's been drinking," Ferri said. "Bitch and whore."

Lines in his face, fury and hatred. He took hold of Elsa again, throwing her into a chair.

"If you move, if you speak, I'll kill you. I'll kill you."

A murmured roar:

"I'll kill you."

I left. Their mud on me. I was with them. I was them too. I had followed Ferri, loved Elsa. They, my world. I walked along the paths of the Tiergarten to the Reichstag still guarded by Schupos. At home a note from Laborderie asking me to meet him at the Taverne. He was alone at the Stammtisch, the Americans' table reserved for Merry Groves, Strang, Shirer.

"This Colonel de Beuil, do you know him?" he asked me. "What kind of man is he?"

What kind was I? Was Ferri? The man who cried, "Kill, kill!" in the Venetia dunes, the man who embraced Signora Maria, the secretary of state with his top hat in his hand, welcoming the ambassador of France, and this reviled man returning to the language of war and the brothel. What was Colonel de Beuil? What were we? At what moment was the truth of a man laid bare?

"He believes in himself," I said.

"I fear," Laborderie went on, "I fear that his stay in Rome and his contacts with fascist circles have made him lose his sense of French reality. We have a taste, a habit of democracy and freedom. Those are our roots."

Can a taste and a habit stand up to the projectiles fired from guns?

"Frankly, Mr. Naldi, I want to tell you, I've been watching you, listening to you."

Laborderie moved closer, his head toward me:

"I think that like me, you see the danger, you've fought in the war, you know what it is and . . ."

What trap was he setting for me? Slowly, I drank the brown Berlin beer.

"I'm sure you are not a man of violence. Do you know Alatri?"

Alatri on the station platform in Bologna between two carabinieri, his head shaven.

"Alatri?"

"He escaped from Lipari, he's in Paris now. It was he who mentioned you to me."

Laborderie looked at me over the tops of his glasses, his eyes insistent.

"He told me you weren't exactly a fascist. A patriot, yes."

Silence is a weapon, let Laborderie show himself.

"Alatri and the antifascists, they are patriots too," he went on. "Between you and them there is common ground, especially as . . ."

He waves at the room. Members of the SA sit at tables, others stand in the entrance asking customers to show their papers.

"One day France and Italy will have to join forces against Germany. The threat is here."

"What do you want?"

"Nothing, my dear Naldi, nothing, except to know whether Alatri can get in touch with you."

He leans back, spreads his hands:

"This is something between Italians, I'm only in it to . . ."
I stand up.

"You're wasting your time, Laborderie, Alatri too. You see, history will decide. I try not to lean on it very heavily. I don't count for much and I try not to count. What do you see coming after fascism? For me, the time has not yet come to look for other solutions."

Laborderie gets up too.

"In other words, you refuse."

"Call it that. I abstain. I let myself float where the current takes me. In the name of what, of whom, do you want me to intervene?"

We show our papers to the SA by the door. They stare at Laborderie, hand around his passport, keep us waiting, take down his name. At last, the street.

"But Naldi, these brutes, you heard von Baulig, there are principles, rights one can't permit to be violated."

"Have you been to Bombay?"

Laborderie shrugged.

"You see people dead in the streets, kids sleeping in garbage, so what are you waiting for to protest? But you'd have to change everything, everything, you understand, and I see no solidarity anywhere. In Bombay they die. In Berlin they kill. They kill in Moscow. They kill in Paris. They kill in Rome. They're going to kill in Ethiopia. I killed at the front."

"You're hiding behind these noble arguments, my dear Naldi. In reality, and it's your right, you are simply on the right side, the winning side, and you want to stay there. That's what it is."

"If you like. I didn't choose. Inheritance. Why should I squander it when I know it won't do any good?"

"Naldi, you're an egotist, a cynic."

"Sorry I can't be any better. Believe me, I wish I could try."

Strang, Laborderie, Alatri, Ferri, they were all men of certainties. I had none any more. Only refusals. A refusal to believe, to accept symbols. I was trying to move forward without bumping into other lives, and to defend my own.

Spring came. The lakes around Berlin: Ingrid von Wirth and I went sailing in the afternoon, white pebble clouds floating overhead, I trailed my arm in water that was still ice-cold.

"They've stopped following me," Ingrid said. "Werner's worried. He'd rather they kept it up."

She came close, we held the rudder together, the boat heeling in the breeze, then I went back to the car with her. We lingered.

"Werner thinks they've decided on some policy for us. Otherwise they'd still be following me. Since they've stopped and haven't changed their minds, they must have decided. They're going to arrest us, Marco, kill us maybe."

"They don't kill generals of the Reichswehr."

I pronounced the words and saw Nitti, I heard von Baulig talking about the underground passage from Goering's residence to the Reichstag. Then there had been Matteotti, Merry Groves had been followed too. Every time, history deposited me on the fringe of the event. Von Baulig, when I asked him, thought the time for swordplay was coming.

"I have an informer in the Gestapo. Heydrich and Himmler are drawing up lists. Who?"

Von Baulig was speaking from his balcony. A June sky over the Tiergarten, cantering riders bending under the branches.

"Me, of course."

I shook my head without conviction.

"And also of course, I'll fight back. Von Papen and Hindenburg are preparing a counterattack. We could win, take them by surprise."

Von Baulig explained; the setting sun was in my eyes, all I could see was his outline, his delicate hands occasionally emphasizing a word. Dead, von Baulig. Already dead to me. Conquered.

"Go abroad," I said suddenly, cutting into his words. "I can help you. An Italian passport. You'll get through easily. Austria, Denmark, Italy. Go, they're stronger and you know it. Don't be deceived, you know them."

I had stood up and was walking around the library, the words came.

"Your hands are empty, you talk, you talk, they'll shoot and your great figures, Hindenburg, von Papen, will collaborate to save their skins and stay in power. Choose, von Baulig, either get out or be an accomplice, but don't let words go to your head. Or else shoot first, first, you hear. Don't hope for anything."

At first he didn't answer. Noise of cars on the Dorotheen-strasse. I sat down again. Von Baulig held out a cigar, slowly lighting his.

"And what if, sometimes, losing, dying was the only answer, the only possible victory?" he said. "What if it was too late now?"

"I'll have a passport for you tomorrow morning."

"Who's talking about me? Do I count, dear Naldi? Is it possible to be concerned about oneself at this time, wouldn't that be truly pitiful?"

I stubbed out the cigar.

"Von Baulig, I am concerned about myself and myself alone."

"You've just offered to get me a passport."

"A mistake, since you've refused it."

"The kind of mistake that makes a friendship, Naldi."

"Maybe this isn't the time for friendship."

I walked across the room slowly.

"Are you really a fascist?"

"I don't want to be taken in, or be a victim either. Good night, von Baulig."

"May I add that if an accident did happen to me it would not be suicide?"

I was in the doorway, von Baulig leaning against the bookcase and I saw him already a standing target.

"If you don't go tomorrow, von Baulig, you'll have chosen

deliberately, suicide. And nothing is more stupid than that."

"Matter of opinion, my friend."

He was accepting, he was one of those who decide to be conquered, to pay for defeat with their lives, that soldier clutching his gun on the Piave, Alatri, Calvini, and Matteotti uttering words at Montecitorio after telling Calvini himself they were his death warrant. They knew, and yet chose to be in the losing camp. Or did they still hope to win, in the depths of their hearts? Victims of their illusions or of their loyalty? These questions, old now, the true questions of my life: I carried them around inside me again all through the Berlin June, fragile and porcelain blue, days it seemed that one cry could shatter and bring back the fog and cold northeast winds, taut, shrill days suspended between two seasons, to be melted and liquefied by heat or hardened into winter again. Slow, light days. Ingrid and I went out on the Griebnitzsee, naked at the bottom of the boat, drifting almost motionless in the breeze. Werner von Wirth was directing Reichswehr maneuvers on the Baltic coast. He wouldn't be back until the end of the month. Days of anguish, because the season was short and the telephone ringing at Ingrid's.

"Another warning," she said. "An officer in the ministry. Refuses to give his name. Just a few words, always the same. I know the voice. Leave, he says, leave. I'm beginning to be afraid, Marco. Werner laughs at me. He says the Reichswehr is behind Hindenburg and the officers. He's not afraid of anything. What do you think, Marco?"

Signs on all sides, creakings, cracks in the façade. I met Karl Maestricht in the SA headquarters on the corner of the Matthäistrasse, he broke the news.

"My dear Naldi, don't leave town in August. We're going to finish off the clean-up."

He was the boss in this office. Young men came in, clicked their heels, voices, arms stretched out, brown, black and red, and the smell of leather, sweat, gun oil.

"We are the strength, do you see, Naldi? Without us Hitler can do nothing. We are loyal but we'll fight for our rights. Against the Reichswehr and those puppet officers who lost the war, against the traitors."

I knew the language, the language of men in power when they come together to fight, and power lies between them like a bone they scrap over.

"But we're in no hurry, Mr. Naldi. We have the strength. August. Stay in Berlin in August."

Maestricht ushered me out, arms were raised as he passed.

"I'm leaving for my honeymoon in the Canaries at the end of June. Madeira. You see, Obergruppenfuehrer Maestricht has no worries. But in August . . ."

A machine gun stood in firing position in the courtyard.

"If you have any influence over General von Wirth, my good Naldi, do urge him to retire."

A laugh, a friendly squeeze of the hand.

"Of course, it might be delicate for you. But tell him anyway."

Signs. Laborderie had been deported. The Ministry of War, on the Bendlerstrasse, was under heavy guard. Von Baulig was urging von Papen to take action.

"They're quarreling among themselves, Goering against Maestricht and Roehm, Hitler still hasn't made up his mind, we could win, Naldi," he said. "Restore a civilized order."

Perhaps I was wrong, perhaps he would win? I wasn't sure any more. I hardly listened to Ingrid, who had come to see me at home and was trying to distract me from my questions.

"Let's just live, Marco. You aren't in any danger, I trust Werner."

She gave herself, spontaneously, to joy, a healthy, serene body, like an opened flower.

"Have you ever wondered why I am unfaithful to Werner?"

Those were her questions, running in and out of mine.

"I love him, you know. He has integrity. An officer."

"And he doesn't mind that . . ."

"He's not very clear why he married me. At heart, he's a bachelor. A friend. He doesn't like to make love. It bores him."

Ingrid moved on top of me.

"All he cares about is politics, and the army. And he doesn't need much. You understand, you're different."

I kissed her whole body. She laughed.

"You know how to take your time. It takes time to make love. Werner doesn't know how, he refuses. You know, you want."

Or was it that I had nothing else to fill my mind with? My time was available, to offer to my body and Ingrid's.

I left her for a few days. Hitler was meeting Mussolini in Venice and I was part of the retinue. Ferri had summoned me, anxious, thinner, nibbling at his lips, clenching his hands.

"Naldi, you'll look after Elsa. She has to be with me in Venice, but you've seen her, she can't control herself any more. I ask it of you, Naldi, I won't forget."

We landed at San Niccolo outside Venice the day before the Fuehrer's arrival. The city in front of my eyes again, pearling in the sun, our motor launch passing the island of San Giorgio Maggiore. Manacorda falling all over himself with courtesy.

"Ciano is very, very pleased with your reports. Much better than Ferri's," he said, "you've succeeded in getting into Berlin society. Ciano appreciates it, believe me. Tell me about this woman Ingrid."

He moved aside laughing, winked at me. We turn into the Grand Canal, gray-green water reflecting my memories, my nostalgia for a secret life at Magliano with Giulia by my side, a life like a series of intimate seasons, preserved.

"Marco, you remember, what a coincidence, a sign."

Elsa was leaning on the rail near me.

"Here we are in Venice again. You remember, I'm sure."

She challenged my look.

"It was our farewell. But a man and a woman who have loved never say farewell."

A low, whispering voice like a prompter in a theater, the play of over-made-up eyes, a look that no longer deceives, withered by time. She takes my hand.

"I'm going to leave Ferri. I won't go back to Germany with him, you hear Marco? I'll speak to Ciano, to the Duce if necessary."

I push her away.

"I need you," she says.

The hall of the palazzo, my footsteps in the huge room, down the corridors. I can't stay alone in this room. My memories come over me like rats, the nightmare rats. Hours to strangle. So then girls, a bar, clink of glasses. Strang, Merry Groves, Laborderie.

"You see, Naldi," Laborderie says with a laugh, "I need Hitler, he chases me out the door and I come back through the window."

We drink. Strang takes me outside, where the cool air and sea breeze sober me a little.

"Naldi, I've got my information from a good source. Directly from the Gestapo. Trust me. They're going to act at the end of this month. Against the SA and all other opposition. Von Wirth is on the list. Trust me. Don't hang around Berlin. Posthumous diplomatic immunity isn't much use to you. And if you care about Ingrid . . ."

I don't care about anybody. Reflections in the water, palazzo façades bending and wriggling, I want to throw up, I don't care about anybody. I make the clean break, the war makes it for me, breaks legs and arms, two legs, two arms.

"Let them slit each other's throats, let them kill each other."

"You're drunk, Naldi, drunk as a pig."

I drink glass after glass of water, throw up. Merry Groves wipes my mouth.

"That's ugly," she says, laughing. "Very ugly, Marco, I've never seen you like this."

I left them, refused their help.

"You'll fall in and drown yourself," said Laborderie.

"Leave me the hell alone."

I knew Venice, wandered through the narrow streets behind the Piazza San Marco, an unknown girl takes my arm.

"You want," she says, "you want, you're English?"

I say yes. English, Turkish, not of this country, Venice and Magliano.

"Have you got money?"

She murmurs thick, fat words in my ear. We climb a staircase; a room with an enormous bed. She murmurs some more. Another girl comes, they laugh together. Fall over, let my eyes turn white, no more pupil, let me lose eyes and memory. I left later. Weary. Slept until morning.

Hitler arrived at nine. An unglamorous figure in the doorframe of the plane at San Niccolo. Hat in hand, hair flying in the wind, a wrinkled gray gabardine. "*Sieg Heil, Sieg Heil!* We want our Fuehrer," screamed the crowd outside the Deutscher Hof in Nuremberg. Here, facing our group of diplomats and journalists, Hitler is nothing, without those faces screaming obedience; here he is clumsy, climbing down the metal ladder, smiling timidly at Ferri, crosses the field, head down, the hat going from one hand to the other. Manacorda in his black uniform guides him to the landing. In front of the gangway Hitler struts, still smiling. Merry Groves pulls my coat sleeve.

"A German salesman," she says. "Where did you spend the night?"

"Looking for you, like every night."

She laughs. Hitler salutes awkwardly before disappearing into the motor launch. The fate of men, of all those swelling bare chests brandishing shovels on the Nuremberg stadium field. Insanity of history. Merry still laughing at my side.

"You can't have looked very hard, Marco, because I'll tell you a secret, I was waiting for you in the hotel lobby."

Handshakes, trivial words, other words deciding life and death. At the Villa Royale, Mussolini and Ciano welcome the Fuehrer. The Duce, his broad gestures, in uniform, booted, wearing a black fez; Ciano haughty and servile and Hitler between them, hat in hand, his dark suit too big for him. The Duce stops in front of the Tiepolo frescoes, speaks German, the Fuehrer listens, hands folded, a grave, timid nod of agreement. I remember Nuremberg, the projectors aimed at the sky and the Fuehrer nervous, mounting the platform. Here he plays the modest pupil. Ferri comes over to me, draws me aside. He rubs his gloved hands together.

"Naldi, Marco, I don't see Elsa, she's got to be at the luncheon. Go, I'm counting on you."

He pushes me:

"Go on . . ."

Around the Villa Royale young men in black shirts chanting "Duce, Duce, Duce!" Then the tranquil canals and façades. The past making a mockery of their chants, yet they can destroy it all. Lives, Venice, Ingrid, von Baulig. At the Palazzo Dandolo, Madame Elsa Ferri has not been seen. She doesn't answer the call from the desk. I go up, second floor, her door, and the key on the outside. An intuition. A cleaning woman goes by.

"Come with me."

I open. Bed hardly rumpled, a dent in the pillow. Nobody. Water running in the bathroom.

"Knock."

The cleaning woman, with her white band in her hair, hesitates. I shove her aside and push the door ajar. Water running in the handbasin. The light on. On the tile floor, Elsa in her peignoir against the side of the bathtub, her face blue. In his armchair, Prince Missini one night. I grab the cleaning woman's arm.

"Don't move from here."

I telephone. Doctor, hotel manager, police, Ambassador Ferri at the Villa Royale. I talk, the porter repeats my instructions. But the words are only the surface, I try to find Ferri's eyes sending me here. A trap or pure chance? I hear Elsa in the motor launch: "I'll talk to Ciano, to the Duce if necessary." "Kill, kill!" Ferri shouted in the dunes of Venetia.

I wait. I look at Elsa. All one side of her face, from temple to chin, is bruised as though she had struck the floor or the bathtub, or been hit. Her face is still made up, but her mascara has run into black wrinkles. The room fills. Diffident policemen.

"Certainly a heart attack."

A fat man in a uniform:

"We've met before," he said, "then I was head of the Venice Fascio. Valsecchini, secretary of the Fascist Federation of Venetia, general of the militia."

He shakes his head.

"An attack," he goes on, "and then the shock, hitting the floor. What a misfortune for His Excellency the ambassador."

Elsa is laid out on the bed. Years ago in the Palazzo Missini they had laid out the prince on his bed, Elsa was sitting. I sat. I was watching her death with no emotion. Dead to me for so long, Elsa was, dead to my flesh, still alive when I saw her in Berlin but so different.

"An attack wasn't it, Doctor?" Valsecchini repeated.

The hotel doctor looked at the manager, glanced at me, nodded. He had pushed his glasses up on his forehead.

"Obviously," he began.

Ferri came in, stopped by the bed and clutched the posts with both hands, his face contorted. Minutes passed. Then he turned to us:

"The Duce and the Fuehrer are waiting for me. Do the best you can. I insist upon absolute discretion. Absolute. My name belongs to fascist Italy."

Valsecchini saluted.

"His Excellency can . . ."

"I'm counting on you."

The doctor put his glasses back on, then slowly packed away his stethoscope.

"Obviously," he said, "she is dead."

Ferri had already gone. Valsecchini was telephoning. I looked at the body. Trying to remember. She had been my first real woman. Had it been so many years ago, to make me this indifferent to her death? There was a dull weariness, though, a sense of being weighted down, an accepted despair. Perhaps from learning that I felt nothing, that she was any anonymous woman, or from realizing that the inquiry into this death was closed. No one would ever try to find out whether an underground passage existed, like the one in Berlin from Goering's residence to the burning Reichstag. "Red crime," the SAs shouted in the streets. "Heart attack," Valsecchini repeated. No one would ever know, about Elsa. Accidental death, the medical report would conclude.

I returned to the crowd, Merry Groves, Laborderie, Ferri, Strang; we visited the Biennale, following the Fuehrer and the Duce. I lunched at an official table at the Alberoni golf club.

"What do you know, Marco? They say Elsa committed suicide."

Merry Groves and I were walking along the canals.

"She wasn't the kind of woman to commit suicide," Merry went on. "Too eager for pleasure, fame, come now, Marco, you know that better than anyone else."

"There are lots of ways of committing suicide. Who knows? Living can be a kind of suicide too."

"You're becoming paradoxical."

She came to my room with me. We helped each other to sleep. Ciano summoned me on the last day of the Fuehrer's visit. He was staying in one of the suites of the Villa Royale. In the late morning the gardens were full of sun, the gravel of the paths crunched underfoot, in the distance the cupolas, marble, and sky like a faintly tinted watercolor sketch. Ciano was sitting in the sun, eating his breakfast.

"Some tea, Naldi? What a supernatural splendor, Venice, don't you find? There are no words for it!"

He drank carefully, appreciatively, holding his cup in both hands.

"Your reports are excellent, I value your sources."

A smile, he sets down the cup, rises, takes a few steps.

"I hear you are on the best of terms with the Reichswehr."

His hand on my shoulder:

"Your private affairs are no concern of mine, but Ferri's here, when they turn into front-page stories during this conference . . ."

Ciano smooths his hair, raising his face to the sun, eyes half-closed, lower lip pouting.

"What do you think about this death, Naldi, you were the one who found the body?"

"The inquest concluded that death was accidental."

He watches me, eyes still half-closed. The bottom half of his face is heavy.

"Do you really believe there could be any other conclusion?"

Ciano, Ferri: I had seen them flanking the Duce on the balcony of the Palace of the Doges, leaning toward each other, looking like allies, the crowd on the Piazza San Marco could hardly make out their faces. It saw a group of uniforms, it saw power, and it shouted, gullible. At the end of the Duce's speech young fascists had stormed the doors chanting "Duce, Duce, Duce!" The police barricades gave way, the doors were broken open, the carabinieri and the Duce's moschettieri fought them step by step on the staircase: "Duce, Duce, Duce!" One group managed to break into the room where we were standing and suddenly, seeing us, seeing the livid Duce, they stopped: "Duce, Duce!" a few of them went on shouting but they let themselves be driven back unresisting. They had seen that power was only a bunch of men, the Duce was nothing but a muscular fifty-year-old exhausted by a speech. I listened to Ciano.

"Don't misunderstand me, I have no criticism to make of Ferri, but at my level I must know, the Duce must know."

Power was decomposing in front of my eyes: men who hated

each other were trying to murder each other. Ciano was playing me off against Ferri, Maestricht in Berlin was allying himself with Roehm against Goering, von Baulig against Hitler. A rivalry the mob would never discover. For the mob, power was a group of black uniforms on a balcony. I didn't answer Ciano. Manacorda was coming. Ciano relaxed, stretching.

"It's so mild here, the air of Venice is like silk."

He took my arm and accompanied me back to the entrance to the garden.

"I need your opinion, Naldi, never hesitate to get in touch with me directly. You can count on my support. Do you know Ferri asked me to recall you to Rome? The Gestapo was concerned about your relationship with . . . what's her name? But I opposed them, general's wife or not, she's a woman . . ."

Traps, allusions, I was not surprised. Ever since the war I had known that other people broke into one's life like burglars. It was the rule. The time of diffidence was over, of secrets shared with Giulia and the world that seemed to end at the end of our fields, behind the poplars.

"Those are my sources of information, Your Excellency," I said.

"Bravo, Naldi! If you could put me directly in touch with this source . . ."

He laughed, including Manacorda in his joke, wished me a good trip back. I went away slowly. It was my last day in Venice, I was returning to Berlin without even stopping at Magliano.

In Berlin they were still waiting. I was walking with von Baulig to his office on the Wilhelmstrasse, he pointed to the Reichswehr soldiers guarding the ministries.

"It'll be soon," he said.

The battle between the clans, the SA against the army; Goering, Himmler, Heydrich against Roehm and Maestricht; Hitler trying to strengthen his personal position; Hindenburg, von Papen hesitant.

"I don't give them a moment's peace," said von Baulig, "they'll act. Von Wirth is with us."

He grew excited:

"This is the historic moment, we'll take advantage of the nazis' internal rivalries to play our own card."

"Do you have arms?"

"They'll all kill each other off and then we'll pounce. And there's the army, Schleicher, von Wirth."

Too simple.

"You're a pessimist," he went on. "All you need is to want badly enough."

"What do you want?"

He looked at me in astonishment, then laughed:

"You're an odd fellow, Naldi, for weeks I've been explaining that our aim is the restoration of liberal principles and you . . ."

He shook his head.

"You're teasing me, Naldi."

"Von Baulig, you've got to want power, for yourself, power."

He shrugged.

"Power, a word, my dear fellow."

A passion. Von Baulig didn't have it. For him power was only a way of governing, not a way of possessing, of being. But that passion was consuming his adversaries. They held power in their hands and wouldn't let go of it until they were dead. And were ready to kill to keep it. Only other men with the same passion could do battle with them.

"Do you think people fight for liberal principles?"

"You are a fascist after all, Naldi, I do fear it. I've already told you so."

Fascism showed me men naked, it had been my lesson in reality. I left von Baulig outside the Ministry of Foreign Affairs and went on to the embassy. On the Leipzigerplatz, Goering's residence was guarded by SS, those soldiers in black uniforms one was beginning to see in increasing numbers. What could von

Baulig do against them? Or von Wirth, who respected the rules?

"The army serves the state," Ingrid told me. "Werner doesn't believe it will intervene. If Hindenburg ordered it to, Werner . . ."

She stopped.

"Why talk about all that? Werner has thought of everything. Hindenburg will make a speech and Schleicher will be chancellor again. Werner doesn't want anything himself. He's not interested in politics. But stop asking me questions, pay some attention to me. I'm here."

Summer had struck Berlin. In the evening, the red sun beat into my studio. Ingrid lay motionless on the floor, arms flung wide and legs apart, naked, giving herself to the sun.

"This is life," she said.

She had to dress and leave. She sighed.

"I was born for the sun, I'd like to live in the south, far away in a land of deaf mutes. Sun and silence. You talk too much, Marco. Always your questions. You must just let things come."

The last evening of June I drove her to Neue Babelsberg and left her on the road on the shore of the Griebnitzsee. She wanted to get out before the last bend in the road and walk the rest of the way in order to arrive home alone. Shadows were already covering the lake but Babelsberg hill was ablaze in the sun. I drove along toward the Havelsee, watching Ingrid in the rearview mirror, walking slowly, swinging her bag. Outside the von Wirths' chalet I saw two cars parked, the doors of the house open, men in long gray gabardines going in and out. I speeded up, made a U-turn after the crossing, passed in front of the chalet and braked when I drew level with Ingrid.

"Get in," I shouted, opening the door.

Startled, she hesitated. I grabbed her arm and pulled her into the car. I drove to Berlin.

"Not safe to stay. We'll telephone."

She was angry. Nobody had the right to enter the home of General von Wirth, I had too much imagination, like all Italians. We telephoned from the Tiergarten station. Someone took the receiver off the hook but didn't answer my questions. Ingrid, at my side, had begun to perspire, big drops were running down her forehead.

"But Werner's there," she said. "He is there. He was supposed to be writing a report on the maneuvers."

On the landing of the Dorotheenstrasse apartment von Baulig's servant was talking to mine, waving his arms, running to meet me. We followed him: everything in von Baulig's apartment had been searched. Open books littered the library rug, drawers had been thrown out upside down. The servant kept saying dully, "I don't understand, he should be here, I had gone out. I don't understand."

We went through the apartment. Disorder, files strewn about the floor, clothes thrown on the beds. On a wall of the bathroom I saw a hastily scribbled word: "Gestapo."

"Notify the police," I said. "But try to reach von Papen first."

I took Ingrid away. Now she was quiet, wiping her forehead with the back of her hand. They had begun, they would have no mercy.

"I must see Werner."

I didn't even bother to answer, shoved her down the stairs. They knew Ingrid was seeing me, they might come and my diplomatic status would be no obstacle to the men in gray gabardine I had seen on the Neue Babelsberg road. We left on foot, mingling with the crowd of sightseers who were pouring into the Tiergarten paths.

"You'll wait at the embassy until we know."

"Nothing can happen," Ingrid murmured.

Trees, the crowd, the warm summer night, children running from tree to tree, women with bare arms, what could happen? Nevertheless, Matthäistrasse was barred by a cordon of troops, SS were guarding the Storm Troopers' headquarters, they had set up a machine gun in firing position outside the door and were waiting, arms crossed, black gloves, leaning against the front of the building in which I used to meet Karl Maestricht. He wouldn't be having his honeymoon in Madeira. The settling of accounts had begun and he was not on the winning side. I took Ingrid's arm.

"Don't say a word."

An officer saluted coldly: face cut in two by his helmet, an anonymous expression. I spoke Italian, showed my passport, pointed to the embassy flag, which was visible from where we stood. Ingrid's hand tightened on mine. At last two SS escorted us along the Matthäistrasse. Roehm's house was surrounded too. The SS had set up a machine gun on the roof. Carlo came to meet us in the embassy courtyard:

"They fired," he told me. "On Roehm's house. They arrested everybody in it."

Carlo shrugged.

"Always this politics, they're all in the same party and they treat each other like enemies. Do you understand it, Mr. Naldi?"

It was too long a story, and I only grasped one side of it no doubt, of the hatred between men in power. All of it for each of them. Antonetti was pacing back and forth in his office.

"What you're asking of me is inconceivable, Naldi. Frau Wirth is not Italian, I can give her neither passport nor protection. Is she asking for political asylum? We'd have to refer it to Rome."

Ingrid had sat down, suddenly leaped up:

"I'm not asking for anything. Marco, I'm going."

I ran into the hall after her, grabbed her arm.

"We've got to know first."

We found an empty office. I telephoned Strang, he was always well informed. He confirmed what I already knew, von Baulig abducted by the Gestapo, Maestricht arrested in Bremen as he was about to board a ship for Madeira, the SA chiefs taken too.

"They're beginning the executions, Naldi, don't hang around

in the streets, the SS and gangs of killers have got full powers."

"What about von Wirth?"

"Didn't you know? Shot down at home, somebody rang at the door, he tried to fight they say. Wiped out. Like Schleicher. Two generals, you see they're not just playing around. Schleicher's wife killed too. I don't know anything about your friend, if I hear something . . ."

Ingrid replaced the listening device. She was still perspiring. I took her arms, forced her to sit down. Her eyes were fixed, dilated.

"They've no right," she said. "Hindenburg . . ."

I stroked her cheeks. She had been lucky.

"You wait here," I said.

She shook her head no.

"I want to see Werner."

They had certainly removed the body far from any morgues, autopsies, or inquests. The door was flung open: Ferri, Antonetti behind him, Ferri beside himself.

"Naldi, what are you doing, do you realize?"

Antonetti nodding: "I was compelled to notify His Excellency," he said.

I leaped at him and pushed him out the door.

"Get out of here!"

"Naldi, Naldi," Ferri was saying, "you've lost your senses!" I shut the door and turned the key.

Ingrid sat there, indifferent.

"Naldi, I order you."

Ferri moved toward me, then made as if to open the door. I grabbed his wrist and forced him back toward the desk.

"Ferri, I want, you hear me, I want a passport in the name of Mrs. Naldi and the embassy car with Carlo. Right now."

Ferri looked at me:

"But Naldi, passion . . ."

"A deal, Ferri, just a simple deal."

I was up against him, my fist on his chest.

"A passport and the embassy car or else, listen to me, Ferri, this very evening I leave for Rome and ask to see Ciano and we will talk about Elsa's death. I can say anything, Your Excellency, fairy tale or truth, you know Ciano, he'll listen to me."

Ferri stepped back.

"But what are you imagining, a . . ."

"Fairy tale or truth, I don't even want to know, but I'll tell."

His expression relaxed, he was pale, gnawing at his lips.

"What's your plan?"

"The Danish frontier. We'll get there easily by tomorrow morning."

He began pacing.

"You're compromising me. Antonetti knows."

A few more seconds of silence. Ferri watches me, looks at Ingrid.

"Congratulations, Naldi," he says. "I accept, for a woman's beauty."

He laughs, lights a cigarette.

"Thank you, Your Excellency."

Our eyes meet, he looks away first.

"Let's hurry, since you don't want to waste time."

Antonetti was waiting for us in the hall, with two secretaries. Ferri shouted:

"What's all this body guard, Antonetti, where do you think you are?"

I had taken Ingrid's arm, was almost carrying her. She leaned against me, saying under her breath, "I don't want to, Marco, I don't want to."

Ferri wrote out the passport in a few minutes.

"Destroy it afterward," he said as he handed it to me.

"I stole it from you, Your Excellency, I'm prepared to admit it."

"Don't hang around."

We left almost at once. Berlin was full of patrols. Reichswehr trucks loaded with soldiers were moving slowly down the Wil-

helmstrasse, von Baulig, von Wirth were paying for having believed in Hindenburg's honesty; they had thought power could
be relinquished, they were conquered. Von Baulig dead too,
no doubt. We were stopped several times on the road. By SS,
who permitted this couple of Italian diplomats, in the embassy
car, to leave town. Carlo drove without a word. Twice, in the
suburbs of Lübeck and Kiel, we met military convoys.

"It smells like war," Carlo said. "All these uniforms. But this
one, Mr. Naldi, I'm not fighting. Their turn."

I talked to Ingrid, tried to explain the rivalry between Hitler
and the SA.

"But Werner," she said.

"They were after everyone who got in their way, von Baulig,
von Wirth, or Maestricht, liberals or overactive or overambitious
nazis."

"It's not possible," Ingrid said. "I want to see him."

"You'll come back. First, you've got to get to safety."

The night was short, pale as dusk. Where was safety? At
Magliano, one rainy day in 1917 I had met violence, then it had
spread over all Italy, and I had seen Africa, then Germany, and
Pierre de Beuil and his men were trying to take over Paris. The
war had been the first sign, the center, now all of Europe was
infected because four years of murder hadn't been enough. And
another war could come. I saw it in the helmeted soldiers ex-
amining our passports at the frontier. Their guns gleamed. They
were laughing among themselves as I had laughed with my comrades in Venice. The white and red barrier went up and we drove
onto Danish territory. Still a haven of peace. A few hundred
yards into the forest, when night was turning to day, we
stopped. An inn. Ingrid leaning on me. The smell of trees, cool
breeze, silence. Carlo sat in the grass.

"Sky's white," he said.

Ingrid telephoned Stockholm. Someone would come for her.

"Don't leave your room under any pretext," I said. "They
don't give up."

She nodded. Then threw herself against me, shaking with sobs for the first time. Who, what was she crying for? Berlin, the chalet by the Griebnitzsee, General von Wirth? Me? She was alive and that was the main thing. We walked a little way under the trees, along a dirt road covered with straw. I let her cry. Caressed her blond hair, her cheeks covered with tears. Then took her back to her room.

"Try to get some sleep," I said.

She kept saying it was impossible to part like this, impossible for Werner to be dead, impossible for her not to see him again, not to see me again. What did she know about what was possible?

"Maybe it won't last," I said.

She needed some words of illusion. I finally left her. Carlo was in the back of the car. I wanted to drive. Stay alert. Feel every one of my thoughts, worries, take the measure of this departure, farewell to a body, a face, a voice.

"I think you've done her one hell of a favor," said Carlo.

We drove back toward the frontier. I had given the passport to Carlo and he tore it into tiny pieces and scattered them along the road.

"She did me one too."

At least now I knew I was capable of action.

We drove through a deserted landscape, frozen in white vertical summer light; the air coming into the car was sticky, full of insects. Patches of shadow, a few trees here and there in the distance. Five or six miles outside Berlin I stopped, I needed to walk a little. Carlo came with me, his jacket over his shoulder like the peasants I used to meet in their Sunday best, coming back from the village along the Magliano path. We sat under a tree. Carlo held out a pack of cigarettes.

"We've known each other a long time, Mr. Naldi, you were just a kid, a bit full of yourself."

The years had scarcely touched his face, but they had hollowed Ferri's and deformed Elsa's.

"Neither of us, Mr. Naldi, was made for that, all that, war, people fighting each other, killing."

Then a long pause. The hum of insects in the tufted air.

"You'll drive to Berlin," I said as we got back into the car.

I sat beside him, he took his time, finished his cigarette, started the motor slowly.

"We weren't made for it, Mr. Naldi. And believe me you can't change the way you were made. You can try."

As we neared Berlin the road and countryside became more populous. Carts, cars, groups of cyclists, a Sunday of habits, and along Unter den Linden the terraces of the café Kranzler, colorful, the waiters' white coats going from table to table, people walking under the trees. But two Reichswehr trucks were stopped at the corner of the Wilhelmstrasse and the Dorotheenstrasse. And sitting, motionless, guns between their legs, the black, helmeted SS.

"Things look quiet," Carlo said before going back to the embassy.

Darkness, the cool staircase. I went up slowly. Opened the door. Two of them in black coats, hats over their eyebrows, one seated and the other standing, his right hand in his pocket, two of them in my apartment. One came toward me, shut the door, and searched me rapidly.

"I am Italian, an Italian diplomat," I said, trying to get loose.

The other stood up and went behind me, took hold of my shoulders. I felt a gun barrel in my back. One went through my passport. They pushed my face against the door. One of them telephoned. I listened.

"*Hauptsturmfuehrer* Gildisch. He's here."

A pause. Click of the receiver being replaced. A brutal shove. I see drawers pulled out, my papers spread across the floor. On the stairs, one holds each arm. A car in front of the door. A few seconds to cross the sidewalk, stumble against pedestrians, the startled, frightened eyes of a woman. The car starts. Unter den Linden, the terraces of the café Kranzler, the same white jackets, my death maybe, the deaths of other men, von Baulig, von Wirth, and a quiet town. Empty streets, the Tiergarten, I recognize the Gestapo headquarters, 8 Prinz Albrechtstrasse. Deserted sidewalks, a group of SS outside the entrance, young and smiling, gauntleted. Stairs, corridors, office, Hitler's portrait and a swastika on the wall. The two men stay close beside me. They click their heels, salute Heydrich, who sits behind his desk. I had seen him at embassy receptions, a face all in flat planes, smooth skin, almost invisible lips. He waves the two men away.

"Be seated, Mr. Naldi."

"I . . ."

He stops me with a gesture.

"I know, you are going to invoke diplomatic immunity, you are Italian, a fascist government official."

Folds his hands.

"We know you very well, Mr. Naldi."

His eyes narrow, a wrinkle on either side of the mouth, a smile.

"Von Baulig, Maestricht, von Wirth, odd that you should be so close to those three men."

"Three dead men."

He rises. In uniform, high shining boots. Sticks his hands through his belt.

"Death is catching, Mr. Naldi."

Sound of boots on parquet, Heydrich stops in front of me.

"You crossed the frontier last night."

"I did not leave Berlin."

Suddenly, why, how, my will to get out of this, fast, not to die here on the Prinz Albrechtstrasse, for nothing, after hugging the ground under fire so many times on the Piave.

"Heydrich, you're not forgetting that I am here in Berlin as a representative of Minister Ciano, the Duce's son-in-law, you're not forgetting that, are you?"

The sound of boots. He sits at his desk.

"They would be highly surprised," he said, "to learn . . ."

"What do you know about it?"

He narrows his eyes again, observing me. I see the hesitation again, the uncertainty that is the disease of all men in power. One mistake and they can lose everything.

"I know von Baulig, von Wirth, Maestricht, but I know Minister Goering too. Careful, Heydrich!"

He fingers the pages of a file. A bell. The two men enter, take me away. Heydrich hasn't moved. I am shoved into a little room, one chair, bars on the window and heat like dirty dust sticking to the skin. Time. Ingrid must be on her way to Stockholm. Maybe Ferri denounced me to Heydrich and is waiting too. The two men, their hats over their eyes again, hands in their pockets. Hauptsturmfuehrer Gildisch takes my arm. Corridors, a man whose brown SA shirt is covered with blood, dragged along by men like those flanking me. The street, the sun like a reflection in a mirror. The car again. We go down the Wilhelmstrasse. Outside the chancellery a happy crowd, children carried by their fathers, women waving scarves, and shouts: "Fuehrer, Fuehrer!" Helmeted SS holding back the crowd. We stop outside Goering's residence on the Leipzigerplatz. In the grounds, heavily armed SS, I see men lying on the rooftops in firing position. Inside, officers and from the far end of a gallery Goering's voice screaming, "Shoot him, you're just a pig, a pig, you're going to be shot!" Goering is there, a white shirt hanging out over his military breeches, black boots almost to mid-thigh. Fists on hips; in a corner an SA slumped half on the ground.

"Pig," Goering continues.

All in black, silent, watchful eyes behind gold-rimmed glasses, Himmler, white file cards in his hand. Gildisch has stepped forward. Goering turns to me, a theatrical gesture of sarcastic greeting.

"My dear Mr. Naldi, what a surprise!"

Then the voice rises, shouts:

"What do you think you're doing, trying to interfere with us, you want to end up against a wall? Nothing will stop us, Mr. Naldi, nothing!"

An officer runs up, holds out a message.

"Don't let him get away, you hear, you'll answer for him with your life."

Then Goering sinks into a chair, his voice quiet, suddenly tired.

"Mr. Naldi, really, you are imprudent. You know these gentlemen of the Gestapo would willingly have taught you a lesson?"

He leans both hands on the arms of his chair, painfully hauls himself to his feet again.

"But in memory of Venice, I absolve you."

A laugh, motion of the hand, unctuous as a benediction. I am on my way out. In the gallery, an SA leaning against the wall, hands over his face, shaking with sobs. I cross the courtyard, an SS officer and two sentries bar the way. I try to convince them I have permission to leave. They don't even look at me, black, throat strap taut, empty men. Gildisch comes out. A few words. They step aside. Funereal puppets controlled by an order. I walk along the iron fence of the Goering residence, turn into the Wilhelmstrasse, the crowd outside the chancellery, the cheerful SS and the shouting: "Fuehrer, Fuehrer!"

All night long there was killing, and the executions continued in the courtyard of the Stadelheim prison in Munich and the Lichterfelde military academy, people were shot down in doorways, in the streets of Bavarian towns, and Karl Maestricht, taken in Bremen, was executed at Lichterfelde.

"He died shouting 'Heil Hitler,' the fool!"

Strang was speaking softly, both elbows on the table at the Taverne. Merry Groves was smoking silently, leaning against me, and her familiar hair against my hand, the warmth of her skin under the light cloth, were gradually calming me.

"They never realized what was happening," Strang went on. "Neither Maestricht nor Roehm nor von Baulig. All wiped out, there's no room for opposition. You remember, Merry, that saying by some guy from the West, can't remember who it was: the only good Indian is a dead Indian. Here it's the same thing."

We drank. The doors of the Taverne were open to let in a little fresh air. We heard shouting, chants, cheers.

"They're happy," said Strang. "They think the Fuehrer has been saved from a conspiracy."

Merry turned to me.

"You're not very talkative, Marco."

She stroked my cheek tenderly.

"Ingrid?" she asked.

I nodded yes. It was easier to explain my silence by Ingrid's departure, otherwise I'd have had to talk about the pain in me that came from those shouts of joy in the streets, the crowd gathered outside the chancellor's residence, the children being held above their fathers' heads so they could catch sight of Hitler, the children of sacrifice being held out to the executioner all that night of the long knives. I saw Werner von Wirth again, von Baulig leaning against his bookcase and that man in the Gestapo headquarters with his shirt covered in blood.

"Now," Strang said, "nobody can get them out of power. They'll do whatever they please. War, no doubt. And that's what will destroy them. I hope, Naldi, that Italy will come in on the right side."

He stood, saluting with his hand.

"Come on, Merry, let's leave our fascist to meditate."

She wanted to go. I put my hand on her knee. She looked at Strang:

"I'll stay with Marco," she said.

"Angel of consolation," Strang said.

We walked slowly. I didn't want to go back to the Dorotheenstrasse, to the mess, the broken images of von Baulig and Ingrid. In the streets of Berlin, basking in the milky warm night we wandered, speaking occasionally, my hand on Merry's shoulder. Along the Wilhelmstrasse, Unter den Linden, the Reichswehr trucks were still lurking; the SS had got out and stood talking in groups of two or three; their heads didn't turn but I felt their eyes following us.

"They frighten me," said Merry.

"They die like anyone else."

But they may be harder to kill.

Our footsteps echoed in the empty streets, fatigue was gradually gaining on me. At Merry's I lay down too weak to take off my clothes. She leaned over me, untying my tie, lifting me to help me off with my jacket.

"You're exhausted, Mr. Naldi," she said, maternal and sardonic. "Stay there, don't budge."

The sun woke me at dawn. Merry was sleeping nearby. I closed the shutters and went out, crossing the Tiergarten filled with patrols. The first editions of the papers were announcing the discovery of a plot by the chiefs of the SA, against the Fuehrer. Obergruppenfuehrer Maestricht had been arrested just as he was about to flee abroad; Generals von Wirth and Schleicher, accomplices of the SA, had been shot while vigorously resisting arrest. In a pension at Bad Wiessee, SA generals had been found in bed with young soldiers. Mud, filth: "The abscess has been lanced," Goebbels had said and Hindenburg had sent Hitler a telegram: "You have saved the German people." The tin soldiers were back in place and von Baulig was dead.

At the embassy Antonetti greeted me as usual. Discretion and a short memory were the cardinal virtues of diplomacy. Ferri was waiting for me, friendly.

"Problems?"

"Nothing for you."

"Who's talking about me?"

He came forward, pointing to a chair facing his.

"What have I done to you, Naldi? Elsa?"

He was gnawing at his lips.

"You and I, Marco, have got to forget Elsa Missini. A woman has nothing to give to a man, you know. She used you. She used me, and then an accident. She drank, how many times did she fall down, but I was always there. Carlo will tell you."

He spent a long time talking about Elsa, to convince me. But all that seemed very far away. Elsa: between her and me there had been this night of murder.

"They've asked for you to be sent back to Rome, not right away but as soon as possible. Goering notified me," Ferri went on. "But you've got plenty of time."

He came to the door with me.

"This is not an official move but you know the custom, one is made to understand. They would prefer to know you were somewhere else. Or dead."

"Somewhere else, it'll be."

"Of course, of course. But take care of yourself. They won't hesitate. You saw Maestricht, Roehm."

Was this a warning? A threat? Ferri was smiling. He was no man to hesitate, either. I didn't want to die. There were still too many things I had to understand: myself first, why I had become this personage, ventriloquist, and so many questions about these crowds milling under the balconies. "*Sieg Heil, viva il Duce,*" there was that to understand and this feeling, so strong, that I had hardly begun to live, that there was, held in by hidden dams in the very depths of myself, a heaving flood that would surge up one day and maybe then my two voices would become one, maybe then my thoughts would become acts. I didn't want to die. I had learned to hug the ground on the Piave. I had learned to know killers in the service of power. Those who had stabbed Matteotti and those who had taken me to Gestapo headquarters. I didn't go back to the Dorotheen-strasse. From the embassy I went to the Taverne. That evening, I moved in with Merry Groves.

"You're taking a risk," I told her.

She laughed, gave me a whiskey.

"You know," she said, "I've got a passion for you."

The telephone rang several times. Merry cried, "Say something!" and there was always silence. They were trying to find out. We didn't open the door at night. In the morning I saw a car start up behind me as I was coming out of Merry's: then I decided to sleep in the embassy. I didn't want to die. I asked Rome for a transfer.

"They'll understand," Ferri said. "Of course I support your request."

He had to leave Berlin too. They were promising him London. Talking about Paris for me. On July 13, I received notice of my departure. That evening Merry Groves and I went to lose ourselves in the crowd accumulating outside the Kroll Opera, where the nazi politicians were meeting. In the distance behind the trees the mass of the Reichstag was visible and the projectors playing around the opera house sometimes picked out the girders of its ruined tower. The fire was the first act; the curtain fell with the night of the long knives. Hitler talked, the crowd swelled with shouting: "Shoot, burn live flesh, kill at once," the Fuehrer was saying. I saw von Baulig's face. I took Merry's arm and led her away, it was hard to get through the crowd. I was disturbing their enthusiasm, going against the current. We were finally alone, in a dark alley.

"They're mad," she said.

They were following their master, obeying, howling, marching in rhythm. Would each of them go through what I had, since the days in the streets of Milan when I shouted "A *noï!*"

I stayed with Merry that night, we made love like two old lovers, old friends meeting again with their bodies a little wearier but rediscovering each other with the pleasure of habit. We smoked in bed, lying side by side on our backs.

"You're a funny guy," Merry said.

"And you're a funny girl."

We laughed together.

"I'm leaving tomorrow."

"You know we'll always meet again. In Rome or somewhere else. I'm going to stay in Berlin awhile," she said.

"You've got Strang."

"Strang, sure. But I like you better. You've got a façade, and then something else behind it. I want to find out more. And you change all the time. I always want to know more. I'm never bored with you, Marco, even when you don't talk."

"I'm your background material for a big article. You began it one evening at Elsa Missini's."

"Unpublishable. Too personal."

She took the cigarette out of her mouth and kissed me gently.

"Pity you don't love anybody," she said.

"And you everybody."

We laughed again, Merry hiccoughing, then she stopped, laying her head against me.

"Too bad, I was getting used to you. I'm going to be lonely."

"You've got Strang."

"Yes, I've got Strang."

Two days later I was in Rome, the city staggering in the heat. The ministries were empty. Ciano traveling abroad. The Duce at his Riccione estate. I spent my days in the apartment on the Piazza Barberini, shutters closed, in a dense semidarkness, unable to bring myself to go to Magliano, not knowing where to go. On July 25, fortunately, Rome came back to life. The Nazis had just assassinated Chancellor Dollfuss. An invasion of Austria was feared. The Duce and the fascist press roared their indignation. Ciano hurried home, summoned me to the Palazzo Chighi.

"Naldi, you saw it coming," he said. "The Duce is beside himself. He told me this morning, now listen to this . . ."

Ciano held out his arm, froze, started again:

"This morning the Duce said to me, 'Hitler is a horrible sexual degenerate, a dangerous madman, and the Germans are all apes.' The Duce, you hear, Naldi, will never allow Germany to enter Austria. It would be the end of Italian security. The end."

I had nothing to say, my place was to listen, agree. Manacorda brought in the press review.

"You saw the headline of the *Popolo di Roma*, Your Excellency: 'What Are Nazis? Killers and Homosexuals.'"

"All right, all right," said Ciano.

He was worried. Had they gone too far? Was that what the Duce really wanted? Then he repeated Mussolini's words, gave me a little praise.

"Naldi had already said all that."

I was his man of the moment. I had been played off against Ferri, now I was being played off against Germany. A pawn with no real importance, but for Ciano at that moment I was priceless. Thanks to me he could prove that he had foreseen all. A month earlier, when Hitler landed in Venice, my reports were insignificant. Now, because the Duce had spoken, they became archive documents.

"Tell them in Paris, make them see, all those pen pushers, that we Latins must join forces against these barbarians."

His chest swelled, he folded his arms, raised his chin.

"'They still didn't know how to write when the Latins had Caesar, Vergil, and Augustus,' the Duce said. The patrimony we share, Rome and Paris."

So I left for Paris.

Paris, where I met Maud.

6

The embassy was in a town house on the rue de Varenne, at the end of a long dark passageway opening onto a quiet garden, an inner sea surrounded by ivy-covered walls. It might have been a palazzo in Rome or Venice, and the whole of the Left Bank of the city seemed to me a continuation of my cities, Venice, Rome; I found the same slanting streets hemmed in like canals, narrow gashes joining the river, and a sense of space and openness. Paris, my city from the very first day, a city my memory seemed to recognize, a city I could live in, I knew, as though I had lived in it before.

I moved into an apartment on the rue du Bac; my windows looked out onto a garden, more ivy, the courtyard was paved. I worked out my special route through this district in which the streets weave in and out of one another like the lazy meanderings of a river. I walked, rue d'Assas, then the Luxembourg, like the lagoon after the canals. I had an office in the embassy where I went every day. A Parisian press review to compile, and Lanvoni to meet. I saw him at the end of the day, carried my report into his dimly lighted office. He was sitting in front of the window.

"Ah, Naldi!"

He held out his hand, white and thin like his face, took my report. Waved me into a chair. The footman came forward discreetly, Lanvoni ordered coffee and while waiting leafed through the press cuttings I had assembled. Then we drank in silence.

"The count asked me how you were getting on," he said at last.

He set down his cup, watched me. He was feared in the embassy, he was Ciano's friend, the man responsible for confidential reports, discreet contacts, corruption. He had a special bank

account. I wasn't a career diplomat so they had attached me to
his service.

He rose, hands bracing his back, walked to his desk, slightly
stooped.

"You're getting on beautifully, Naldi. Beautifully, despite a
certain moral reticence, which is all to your credit."

He smiled a moment, then, swiveling in his armchair, took out
his filing cards from the open cabinet behind him. He shook
one of the white cards in his fingertips, it was covered with black
marks, his careful, round writing, one card selected from the
rest, a name, an amount, a fact, the crossroads of a destiny, the
choice of a man.

"That one, I've got him," he said.

Passed me the card. Journalist, elected to parliament, wife,
this fissure in their lives written down here, scarcely a shadow,
but for Lanvoni a lever, a means of widening the fissure, transforming a man or woman into a tool.

"See Bernard tomorrow."

Lanvoni placed a card on his desk, isolated like a target on
the black leather.

"I telephoned him," he went on, "he's expecting you."

He never raised his voice, both white thin hands placed palm
down on either side of the lone card.

"Be tough," he said. "Scare him, make him cough up his information. Otherwise, don't pay. Never forget, Bernard is
a whore, he sells himself."

Lanvoni came with me to the door of his office, arm across
my shoulders.

"I know, Marco, I know, this is not classical diplomacy, but
neither of us is a classical type, and is this a classical age we're
living in?"

I went home. The branches tapped at my windows; I went
through the rooms, in the winter I would light all the shaded
lamps the landlord had placed in every corner, one by one, yellow and pink intersecting cones of light; in the summer I would

let night invade the rooms little by little, sitting alone in the silence with the newspapers in front of me, incapable of reading, carried away by the current of words inside me. I had thought I knew power and the men who fight over it. Elsa, her hungry face stretched toward me: "I want that embassy." Lanvoni was leading me into a new circle of hell called corruption. For him, power meant the disintegration of a will, the conviction that nobody resists gold and men are unstable as quicksand.

"They're all for sale," he would say with a smirk of distaste.

But he smiled, raising his head, his eyes motionless as though lost in a dream.

"Naldi, demolishing a man is a question of money, patience, organization, nobody resists. You simply have to find his soft spot."

He brought his hands together, fingers rounded: I saw the fruit.

"There's always a spot, a stain, all you have to do is see it: there, the apple is beginning to rot, that's the spot that interests me."

I said nothing.

"You still have principles, Marco."

He straightened, stifling a cry, clapping his hands to his back and tightening his jaw, speaking through clenched teeth. He had been wounded on the Piave and still suffered.

"Read."

He held out a letter. I recognized names: Alatri, Calvini.

"Those two innocents have formed an antifascist bloc and we already have two or three informers in it. All it took was a little pressure, not even that, just the jingle of a few coins."

He replaced the letter in his files.

"The little spot, Naldi, with that we can do everything."

Bernard was one of our informers.

"A curious creature," Lanvoni had told me early on. "A man rotten to his very fingertips."

I met him two or three times a month in a bar near the Opéra. I would walk from the rue du Bac, trying to forget what I was going to say and do, whom I was going to meet, trying to erect those watertight partitions that make it possible to live. I was involved in politics, but it might just as easily have been a game of billiards, anything, it didn't matter. I would exchange words with Bernard, leave bank notes on the table, touch his fat, thick hand. A job. Then there would be the street, I would forget, erase everything, including the rue de Varenne and the memory of Bernard. I was just an intermediary between him and Lanvoni. One had to make a living. I had a little more independence than the office clerks and salesmen crossing the avenue de l'Opéra in hordes. I knew some truths they didn't. Bound together, they read *Paris-Soir*, bought the latest edition, "Threat of War Between Italy and Ethiopia Averted?" They looked at the picture of the King of Kings in his black cape. Words had one meaning for them, but I knew they had to be turned inside out in order to be understood. I knew. That was my superiority. Yet I needed to be just a salesman too, an office clerk approaching Bernard and Lanvoni with the same unconcern as one of those anonymous figures who come up to you behind a counter, precise, present, and so remote. To act without being concerned, that had to be my law. Because I knew the dice were loaded. And there was no way out; every man, as Lanvoni said, was marked with a little rust-colored spot which power could enlarge in order to turn him into a pawn, a stool pigeon. And Alatri would fall into the trap.

I pushed open the door. A waltz melody, girls at the bar moving only their eyes, Bernard already there, his alcoholic's face with the softened features, his too-pink lips, the expression of an old woman still trying to be seductive, his fat hands playing in front of me and his high homosexual tenor.

"Dear Mr. Naldi, how can I . . . ?" he began.

"No point in talking, then, we'll find someone else."

I pushed back the chair, raised a hand to call the waiter. Bernard grasped my wrist:

"You're so nervous, you Italians, you're as sensitive as women!"

He laughed.

"I hope I don't offend you, my dear friend?"

If the world had been different, if words made sense, yes. I should have thrown my glass in his face, called on those around to witness his spinelessness, shouted that another time would come. Yes. I had only to look toward the bar, those object-girls, and beyond to the street, to Rome, Berlin, further still to Moscow, any street, any city, everywhere relationships were rotten. Rotten the century, men, power. Everywhere confrontations, treason, the same comedy, Hitler against Roehm, Goering against Maestricht, Ciano against Ferri, Stalin against Trotsky. The scenery changed but they were all in the same play. Von Baulig, von Wirth, Matteotti fell. Mercy on all who take stage dialogue for real words. Alatri perhaps. Nitti. This woman Bernard was telling me about.

"Here," he said, "you want information: that journalist, Maud Kaufman, who's into every story, she's a fanatic, a little Jewess, she plays a close game but mark you, Mr. Naldi, she's a Trotskyist, clandestine of course, underground."

Mercy on Maud Kaufman.

"Only," Bernard went on, "they shoved a guy between her legs who works for Stalin, a tough boy from the Comintern, and the cunt married him. Cornered."

I walked along the avenue de l'Opéra. Please rise up, watertight partitions. Let me forget this damp winter, rotten weather, rotten relationships, Maud Kaufman, ridiculed, duped, a tool to reach Trotsky. She believed in words. Married that Comintern agent. Poor ass, mercy on her. Who to believe in except oneself, who can one listen to except oneself? Superiority and solitude. My two cheerless retreats.

"I don't understand the Trotskyists," Lanvoni was saying, swiveling his chair from side to side. "What are they after?"

He had just filled in a card on Maud Kaufman.

"Real communists like to win. But this other bunch, behind their old prophet, talkers, innocents. Naldi, I believe they want defeat, persecution. They choose to lose. It makes them feel pure. Pure."

He smoked as he scribbled on Maud Kaufman's card.

"Pure; only the elements are pure. Men, you know them like I do . . ."

He stood up.

"Not quite as well, you're younger, Marco. But you've had a lot of experience already."

Every day, one more piece of evidence. Pierre de Beuil: Lanvoni and I saw him, discreetly, in my apartment. Lanvoni hadn't come yet, Pierre de Beuil full of confidence, his walking stick in his hand.

"My dear Naldi, what a pleasure, it's all going to be so easy now, for you at least know me. Your ambassador is ridiculously cautious. You're an artist, Naldi, you know how to choose your settings, this courtyard, these trees, I could believe I was in Rome. . . ."

Playing with his gloves.

"You were there when Elsa . . ."

I served liqueurs.

"A stupid accident," he went on. "But that's all over. What matters is the future and we must . . ."

Lanvoni came in. Now I had only to keep quiet, listen to Pierre de Beuil explain his plans.

"February 6 was just an abortive mob scene, a rehearsal, more or less."

He held out his hand to us.

"An improvisation, in fact, but highly instructive. What we need now is a party on the fascist model, and I am capable; here . . ."

He handed Lanvoni some sheets of paper.

"This is a draft, for the Duce, but the core of it isn't there, we need . . ."

A pause.

". . . Italy's moral support, her example, but also material assistance."

The last words spoken more firmly, like a demand, to hide the embarrassment. Lanvoni glanced at me.

"You want money?" he asked.

Pierre de Beuil leaned back in his chair, spreading his arms.

"Well, yes, yes, material assistance."

"Money," Lanvoni repeated.

"What else should it be," said Pierre de Beuil, "money, of course. Do you think you can make a party out of speeches?"

He stood up, began pacing.

"Mr. Lanvoni, I was in Italy from 1917 to 1926, Naldi can bear me out, and the Duce assuredly remembers my role, the role of France in financing fascism. It was a small movement then."

"That's a long time ago," Lanvoni said.

He laid the papers on a table, took out a pen.

"You understand," he went on, "I can't ask Rome for anything without a specific request on your part, if you would care . . ."

Pushing the papers toward Pierre de Beuil.

". . . to word it in your own terms, of course this is a secret document, that goes without saying."

Pierre de Beuil in the web, the spider edging toward him. He hesitates.

"If you are undecided," Lanvoni begins, "we can arrange another meeting, but you're a soldier, you know how to take risks."

Pierre de Beuil sat down, wrote one sentence, signed.

"Is that sufficient?"

" 'I ask the Duce for both moral and financial support,' " read Lanvoni. "Perfect, nothing ambiguous about that."

Lanvoni folded up the papers, slipped them into his pocket.

"Of course, we'll have to discuss the amount of our contribution, the allocation of funds, not that we wish to dictate to you . . ."

Lanvoni smiled.

". . . but, as you were saying, a matter of experience, we have succeeded."

Pierre de Beuil snapping his gloves on his knee.

"Of course you succeeded, but when we go into action we will wipe them all out and we will go further; believe me, if you give us any real assistance the Front Populaire will not win. And it's in the Duce's interest, Mr. Lanvoni, I hope you are convinced of that."

As soon as he left Lanvoni unfolded the papers, holding them out to me. Pierre de Beuil had signed in a rage, his pen had gouged the paper.

"We'll lead that man around with a ring through his nose."

Every day, one more piece of evidence. In October 1935 the war we had been preparing for the last ten years broke out at last: Italian troops were marching on Addis Ababa. The League of Nations accused us of aggression, there were diplomatic and commercial sanctions against us. We needed the support of French public opinion, for our "civilizing" campaign in the land of the King of Kings. Lanvoni juggled his cards, I saw journalists, politicians; Pierre de Beuil, in the daily paper he had founded with money from our special fund, wrote how we were defending the West out there on the high plateaus. Provi, transferred to Paris, was amazed at my amazement.

"Lanvoni amuses me," he said. "What he's doing is entirely traditional, there's nothing new about it. Classical diplomacy, Marco. You're wrong to be indignant."

On the boulevards, Pierre de Beuil's men chanted slogans in our support: "Abolish the sanctions!" they shouted. "*Vive l'Italie!*" Pierre de Beuil had seen the Duce in Rome. He returned resolute and enthusiastic.

"A few weeks more. You'll be in Addis Ababa before the rainy season."

Our troops advanced. Ciano, Ferri, the Duce, Lanvoni: history made them right. One evening in his office Lanvoni detained me as usual, after looking over the press review. He had opened the windows onto the garden. It was March, still chilly but a clear sky.

"I've got a problem, this girl who keeps annoying us with her denunciations, as though there'd never been a bombardment in a war before."

He took a card.

"In fact, it was you who brought this in, try to find out what can be done, she'll have to keep quiet or busy herself with something else."

He read the card:

"With her husband, for instance. You have complete freedom to act."

He was going to Ethiopia. He had been given permission to take part in the final offensive that would end in the occupation of the capital. He held out the card. Of course, it was Maud Kaufman. Almost every evening I came up against her articles —accurate, incisive. Our gas on the fleeing population, our bombs on the warriors in white shammas I had seen lying on the terraced plateaus. But then Maud Kaufman was not just a name, she was that dark, short-haired woman with the quick movements whom I had seen in an art gallery in Montparnasse, a gallery run by an old friend of my mother's; I sometimes went to see Emilia to talk. Maud, scornful, who had snapped:

"I hate frivolous people, I hate polite gentlemen, diplomats."

At home, I lay on the sofa I had placed opposite the window so I could see nothing but sky and trees, forget the wall, the façade of the building across the courtyard. I was spending more and more time alone. Breaking dates; boredom came more from others than from myself. Sometimes I forced myself to wring an assent from some woman, she would come here, sit in the leather armchair, I'd give her a drink, one had to talk, wrap sentences around her to fill up the time until it would be permissible to undress her. Boredom, and then after a brief joy, the too brief explosion of pleasure, that necessity of going to sleep near her or waking up to see her in the morning. No doubt about it, I was growing old.

"You're an odd person," Bernard told me. "You have no vices, you hardly drink, you don't even seem to see these women here."

He put his arm around the waist of one of them, she leaned over us, her white breasts so close.

"If Charles saw me now," he said.

He pushed her away with a laugh. Charles, his lover, attaché in the private office of the Ministry of the Interior, through whom Bernard had access to the files. And so, we were able to fill in our cards.

It was lying near me, Maud Kaufman's card, propped against the copper ashtray. Maud Kaufman, wife of Jacques Morin, painter, his real name Jacques Paillet, Comintern agent. Maud had hugged Emilia when Emilia had told her Jacques Morin's paintings had been sold. Duped, swindled. Honesty must be her soft spot. I called Emilia. She gave me Maud's telephone number.

"Marco, you're not going to, she's so much in love," said Emilia.

I hung up, let time pass and night come. Now I had grown to like the slow numbness, neither daydream nor sleep, a tranquil somnolence, thoughts, questions becoming muffled. The war would go our way, we would occupy Ethiopia, the League of Nations would revoke the sanctions. The Duce would proclaim the fascist empire. Then what difference would Maud Kaufman's articles make; mercy on her, she thought she was free and was nothing but bait for Trotsky, the old prophet as Lanvoni called him. I was half-asleep, an open book on my chest. The ring of the telephone made me jump. Laborderie. We were meeting regularly: I was "his" fascist, he said, and he "my" anti-fascist journalist.

"See him," Lanvoni had said, "I know he likes money. If he bothers us, you'll jingle your coins."

But he was not one of the most hostile and in the end we did not try to buy him. Laborderie was inviting me to dinner.

"An evening just among friends, my fortieth birthday, ghastly, my dear Naldi, ghastly."

It was to be that weekend.

"Two or three charming young women," Laborderie continued. "Do you know Maud Kaufman?"

"You want me to invite her? She's married, you know, but I'll be glad to, if she's free."

Laborderie talked with his usual nervous speed, I had had only one sentence to say. The wheels turned.

"You do realize," he went on, "that she is distinctly to the left of me."

"I didn't ask you anything."

He laughed:

"Naldi, we've known each other for years now, don't tell me your question was innocent, I read her articles like you do, they're the only ones that bother you, the details she gave about your aviation using gas. . . . You'd like to seduce her but it won't be easy, I'd like to see it. Until Saturday, any time after eight, nine."

Silence. It was not easy for me to realize that words led to acts. I knew my failing, distrusted it and most of the time tried to keep quiet, not to toss out the harpoon of a word for an act to hook onto. I had said Maud Kaufman and it was already Saturday.

I was one of the first to turn up at Laborderie's on the rue d'Ulm, a small, warm, pink apartment, slightly feminine and affected, with Indian objets d'art; Laborderie showed me around.

"Brought back from an assignment in Mexico."

And a sword with a swastika hanging on the wall:

"Berlin, Naldi, before I was thrown out. You remember Venice, Hitler at San Niccolo in that shopkeeper's suit, the night before you got so paralytic drunk."

In the living room, angry voices. I hear:

"I'm telling you Beuil was in on it."

"They're talking about the attempt on Blum," Laborderie said. "I'll leave you with Anne."

He introduced a young woman with blond curly hair.

"One of our fashion editors, she won't accuse you of being a fascist. Anne and politics!"

Bare arms, red lips, a fine-boned face, shyness hidden by a smile.

"I'm just beginning," she says, "I've only been with the paper a few weeks."

With one look I sense her body, the quick sharpness of youth. She seems fragile, available. I offer a cigarette.

"What is this about Blum, this morning," she asks, "I didn't . . ."

Léon Blum's car on the boulevard Saint-Germain, a procession of nationalists following the coffin of Jacques Bainville.

"Blum was recognized."

She listens, her face attentive. The skin of her wrist and arm, I can guess the softness of her breasts. It's been a long time since I've held a woman, suddenly I want this girl next to me.

"You're very tan," I say, "do you ski?"

She laughs, there's already a collusion of voice and body between us.

"You were telling me about Blum, what happened to him?"

I shrug.

"The nationalists gave him a beating. Fortunately, there was a building site there and some workers; they got in the way and protected him. I don't think it's serious. He'll be all right."

A touch on my shoulder. Laborderie is behind me, Maud beside him, and a little behind them, tall, heavy, jet black hair growing low on a lined brow, a man who must be Jacques Morin.

He observes me, then looks away. Maud interrupts Laborderie, who was beginning to make introductions.

"I have already met Mr. Naldi, he's a very witty diplomat. You heard him, he's sorry Blum didn't suffer the same fate as Matteotti. They're more efficient in Rome."

She turns her back. Jacques Morin follows her. Laborderie makes apologetic noises, raises his arms in a show of helplessness.

"She can't bear people to joke about some things," he says, "you were unlucky. We were just coming in, she heard you, the Blum affair is a scandal obviously, fascist methods, forgive me but there is no other word for it."

Laborderie hesitates, takes off his glasses. He's afraid he has said something that will cause a break between us. But I don't want to give words any more than the puny weight they have. They don't reach me. I look at Anne's breasts. Words don't concern me. There is this girl, the arm she's moving, her breasts rising. That's real. To play with my body, that is truth. I want the girl. My only will is for her. A will that involves no one but me, and her if she accepts; the most limited of wills, the simplest, the briefest of acts. But Blum, the men, Pierre de Beuil among them no doubt, the killers shouting against the car windows: "Jew, murderer, to the gallows!" opening the doors, rage in their mouths, "Death, death to the traitor!" They were still shouting when they hit him; what can I do against them? Fighting them means altering the whole order of things, changing history, one gesture, even a simple word and the avalanche is rolling uncontrollably. All I want is one woman's body. Anne, whom my knee is touching and who does not move away.

"They wouldn't stop," Laborderie was going on, "Blum, you've seen him, he can't defend himself, they cut open his temporal vein, a miracle they didn't kill him. Frankly, Naldi, can you, you, approve that?"

"Who says I approve?"

"Well, get out of it then and take a stand."

Laborderie had sat down near Anne, who moved away; he kept taking off his glasses and putting them on again. Maud Kaufman came, put a hand on his shoulder.

"André, you're wasting your time. Mr. Naldi has chosen, detached collaboration. He's an aesthete."

Standing behind her, Jacques Morin. What had he chosen, what was he waiting for, except the right moment to slash another temple, that of the old prophet? What did Maud Kaufman know? She was living in an illusion.

"My dear lady, there are different forms of collaboration," I said. "There is a kind one controls and a kind that transforms you into an unconscious tool. I try not to be a tool."

Passion in her eyes, body, the toss of the head, the black hair she shakes to one side of her forehead. I'd have liked to grab her by the shoulders, shake her, pull her loose, shatter her certainties.

"But you are one, a tool of your government," she replied.

Of course I was. Who wasn't? She. Morin. All of us in the mechanism that carried us all, pushed us into one another, ground us up to the sound of fanfares and turned us into *"Sieg Heils,"* outstretched arms, raised fists.

"What do you think of Jean Gabin in *La Bandera*, have you seen it?" asked Anne.

"And what do you think of General Franco, who massacred the workers in the Asturias in 1934?"

Maud had turned on Anne, speaking in a mocking, little bird voice.

"You don't know," Maud went on. "You don't know that *La Bandera* is a camouflaged defense of Franco? Ah, but you need to know, mademoiselle."

"I'm not very interested in politics," said Anne.

"But politics will be interested in you, believe me. You . . ."

All of a sudden, after my anger, I felt like laughing, with Maud Kaufman, saying she was right. In spite of myself I liked her abrupt way of speaking, her sentences like a slap in the face, her way of openly attacking everyone. She spoke with her body, nervous, her shoulders, her hands moving, and the hair she kept tossing to one side as though to underline a sentence. I watched her, and I wanted to see her again, to listen to her talking again because it made me feel good, made me want to stretch my arms and legs as you do in the sun. I must have smiled without realizing it, she must have felt the attention in my eyes, then she stopped in mid-sentence and I saw her relax, smiling too and we remained like that, facing each other long enough, long enough to know that we were moving toward each other over all the obstacles.

"That being said, I do love the cinema," Maud added, "I can't resist the Marx Brothers."

She related one of their gags in A *Night at the Opera*, laughing with her whole face.

"I love to laugh, that screwball film, it's almost like our lives."

Somehow, that laugh had been just for the two of us. We looked at each other again long enough, long enough for her to turn her head away and go to Jacques Morin, who was waiting for her in the hall. He helped her on with her coat, she held out one arm after the other, confiding. Jacques Morin went out behind her, his heavy figure hiding her.

"She's a strange person," said Anne. "Aggressive. Passionate about things. I don't understand that kind of woman who seems to live like a man."

I was turning back to Anne, her wrist, arms, breasts, curling blond hair, and her yesses and no's and nods. Did I still want her? I tried to imagine how the night would be, a taxi, a bar, some whispered words, her wrist, her arm, two or three dances maybe, another taxi, rue du Bac, the paved courtyard. We were already in the courtyard.

"I don't know," Anne was saying, "why I came with you."

I held her to me, there was a resistance.

"Yes, you do," I said.

I pushed her ahead of me. A slender, quick body, young. Maud's laugh in my memory. I lit only one little lamp.

"It's hot," said Anne.

She looked around, watchful, trying to find me out from my furniture, rugs, papers lying on the chairs and sofa facing the window. I was home, I no longer really wanted her. But since she was there, I went over to her, there was her wrist, her arm, her breasts.

"I don't want to," she said, wriggling away.

Later in the night, afterward, when I knew, I understood her fears, her anguish, those little rushes forward and away. Later, while she was sleeping next to me, I thought of the prostitute at the Aquila Nera who first showed me how, and Ferri who had led me to her. Time. Now I was doing the initiating. Time. My body seemed heavier. The pleasure I had felt when this slender girl lay in my arms, anxious, longing and fugitive. The time since the Aquila Nera, since Ferri. What had I done?

The branches were thrashing against the windows in the wind; lights, the apartments across the courtyard. I never closed the curtains, I liked to see the night. Anne slept at my side, an arm over my chest, her hand around my shoulder.

What had I done? Just moved ahead, grown older, tried to understand, to be what Maud Kaufman had said, a detached collaborator. Nevertheless, a tool. But I had neither tilled the soil nor drained the swamps to make them into fields, as the Naldis had done before me. Nothing. Had let myself go with the current, since it had torn me away from Magliano. Had not met my true woman, my wife. Giulia incomplete, destroyed. The others, confused silhouettes, friendly, hostile, Elsa Missini, Merry, Ingrid von Wirth, and the rest that memory and the night hid or flung toward me. Anne woke up.

"I was very scared," she said, "it's stupid, you understand?"

Mother was the same age as Anne. "If she hadn't married Aldo," Emilia told me, "your mother would have died." Mother, that same searching fright, no doubt, but also her whole life she was committing. Time. The body grows heavier. The ties between people change. Make love like a drink of water. Anne, though, a body which she must, one time or another, offer to somebody. Some chance body she must choose or be chosen by. An act I thought was simple, and even there you get stuck in the mire. An act: an avalanche too, that was burying me.

"Do you want us to meet again?" Anne asked the next morning.

Gray, damp, fog, chill hugging the windows like a coat of varnish. She had made coffee, humming. Before I said anything, she went on.

"I'd like to."

A tie, a body. Words. She watched me as she held out a cup.

"Of course."

We drank, sitting on either side of the table, with the wooden surface between us. I stretched out a hand to her face, touched her cheek and lips. She kissed my fingertips.

"I'd like to," she said again. "I was very lonely, you know, this job, everybody thought I was very free, imagined I had lovers, but now you know the truth. This evening?"

"If you like."

So my life took another turning, there was a voice near me helping me not to hear my own, a body I surrounded with my arms, and thus I knew that reality existed, and she put her arms around me and thus I knew that I existed.

Weeks. After the army entered Addis Ababa, Lanvoni had come back to Paris. On the Piazza Venezia the mob was shouting "Viva l'Impero!" Hands on hips, in a black uniform, the Duce replied, "Our flag flies over the conquered citadel of the King of Kings." History. Rumors from Nuremberg, nazi troops moving up to the Rhine.

"Strasbourg is within cannon range," Lanvoni said, "if the French don't react, it's the end."

They didn't react. "Tout va très bien, Madame la Marquise,"

Anne sang in the morning listening to the radio. Laborderie was optimistic.

"You're going to get married," he concluded. "I can see it. And you'll become French. I can get you naturalized very quickly. Naldi, you must break with fascism, war is coming and believe me, either Italy will be with us or she'll be conquered along with Germany. And Germany will be crushed, as in 1918."

Symbols. Processions rolling past, fists raised: "For bread and freedom!" chanted the women, "Work!" "Make the rich pay!" They marched along the cobblestones of Faubourg Saint-Antoine, voices clashing. "*Vive le front populaire!*" "*Vive la Commune!*" and portraits of Blum and Robespierre sway past. A gap between the groups, I hear the song that rang out in Bologna when the threatening procession was coming toward me crowned with red flags. "*Avanti popolo, bandiera rossa, bandiera rossa.*" Cheers, shouts, beneath an enormous portrait of Matteotti, men and women, and Alatri and Calvini in the front rank.

"Italians," says Anne. "Not your friends."

They move along arm in arm, forming a chain, Alatri leaning toward Calvini, whose red scarf is thrown over his shoulder. I am in the crowd, Anne holding my arm, they don't see me, they move away under the "antifascist bloc" banner. They're singing.

My last songs were in Milan in 1918, shouts of joy and the illusion of brotherhood, we were going to seize the future in both hands and build a new country. They were singing. I knew the strength you can get from the warmth of a comrade marching beside you, those walks over the Venetian beaches during training, when Ferri led us through the dunes at dawn. The trucks we crowded into, lurching over the roads behind the front lines, and we sang. Anne is talking to me. What is one voice? We were walking in the thick of the crowd, toward the Seine.

"Would you come on holiday with me?" Anne was asking. "You promised."

I had chosen a life on holiday, I had done so little since the war, there was that one night when Carlo and I drove to Denmark with Ingrid von Wirth at my side. I was like some force in quarantine. Was it conceit, cowardice draped in good intentions that made me refuse to act, either with those arms trustingly upraised to the Duce, those fists brandished by the processions, or these arms linked together like those of Alatri and Calvini. Or because the time for the real fight had not yet come; or no opportunity; or was it wisdom. Or was it all an illusion, and I an aesthete like Maud Kaufman had said, and was I a gear in the fascist machine, and what did my inner monologue matter anyway?

"What do you see me as?"

Anne seemed surprised.

"You?" she asked.

"Me."

We were sitting facing each other in the rue du Bac. She huddled into my bathrobe, bare-legged, her feet arched inside my slippers.

"You're reliable, you don't say much but you mean what you say. People can count on you."

She got up.

"Inside, you're solid. I see so many journalists, men, around me: nothing, they're nothing."

She sat on the arm of my chair, her legs against mine.

"That's why, the first evening . . ." she added.

Maybe that is how she saw me. She didn't guess at that fissure I seemed to feel, the uncertainty. But she had the new-opened eyes of youth, before you begin to hear another voice quivering inside.

"What about our holiday, Marco?"

We went. Pebbles, white waves against the rocks, the dry clap of the waves and dull suck of the ebb, the steady rhythm. Anne, a scarf on her head, waving at the cyclists we met. One morning the Paris papers' black headlines, "War in Spain" and photos of the first battles. Franco's proclamation, appeals of the Frente Popular.

"I don't understand," said Anne, "they were legally elected."

"You liked *La Bandera*," I said nastily.

I was hearing Maud Kaufman's voice, remembering her laugh when she was telling about the Marx Brothers, and the heavy figure of Jacques Morin.

"Yes, I liked *La Bandera*," Anne said.

Empty. She was empty for me, this girl now become a woman. A body, unseeing eyes. We were staying in a hotel at Le Trayas. The red rocks of the Estérel, the road above the sea striped with white, and heat like a misty reflection on the roadway.

"You're driving too fast," Anne said, "what's the matter with you, it's not this business in Spain?"

War, Spain, it was that, and the discovery that I couldn't tolerate an empty body next to me. I had to have a voice tuned to mine, otherwise it was better to keep to the bodies of chance encounters or the numbness of solitude.

Anne was in the hotel room, I was shutting my suitcase.

"Marco, what did I say, what have I done?"

"Stay, stay here, you've got time. I have to get back. Spain. You'll phone me."

I kissed her vaguely, she came down behind me.

"I could have left with you, here . . ."

"You'll swim. The weather's perfect, look."

The beach, a deep blue sea with green patches, and in the cove the red reflection of the rocks. In the distance, islands.

"You'll be back in Paris soon enough."

I left. A road between drought-yellowed fields. I drove all night long in a sort of fury, angry with myself for having put up with that empty presence for so many months. Nothing but a little pleasure, self-indulgence, male vanity. The prostitute of the Aquila Nera had more self-control than I, when she pushed me out into oblivion the next morning. At dawn, after weaving in and out of the Morvan, I stopped at Saulieu. Café just opening, smell of warm milk and hot bread. A poster on a wall, black letters on a red background announcing Jean Gabin in *La Bandera*. And for coming attractions, the Marx Brothers.

"You look cheerful," the owner said serving me coffee in a bowl. "Though what with these war rumors everywhere . . ."

I was laughing to myself, thinking of Maud Kaufman and the sarcastic tone of her voice talking to Anne at Laborderie's. I was laughing and thinking that it was no time for merriment.

Paris and heat. Big photos in *Paris-Soir*: Bodies lying in the squares in Spain, barracks courtyards, kneeling women praying outside a church in a town taken by Franco's troops and there, on the steps of a convent in Barcelona, standing skeletons, open coffins, and then in *L'Illustration* the streets of Irùn overrun by the nationalists, a woman waving a white shirt and eyes full of fear. The courtyard on the rue du Bac is a well of coolness. I sit at the window with the branches nearby, I read, the peace is breaking up everywhere and the earth is already gorged with blood. Lanvoni has come back too, from Rome, where he was spending his vacation. We meet every day.

"Now the big fight is starting," he says, "soon the masks will drop off, make way for His Majesty the cannon, as the Duce says."

More white cards in his fingers.

"We'll have to bring our little world back to heel," he says. I meet Bernard. He sighs, makes apologies, begs.

"Since the '*front popu*' Charles is out of the ministry, it's so much more difficult, you understand, explain to Mr. Lanvoni."

I get up, months have passed and we still have to act the same comedy.

"Please, don't be impatient, I have other informers, nobody is incorruptible but these people are more expensive."

He mops his brow, a pink handkerchief, too strongly perfumed.

"Blum is going to help the Republicans, there is a telegram from Madrid and Blum has committed himself, he has the entire Jewish community behind him. Have you read Henri Béraud's article, remarkable."

He shakes out his handkerchief in front of me, declaiming: " 'The seed of Abraham and Jew's pitch . . .' "

He repeats the words, seems to listen to them again for his own pleasure:

"Great classical prose, a lash on the back of the Levantine scum," he added, laughing.

War, blood, rising hatred. I recognize the sour reek of 1922, 1933, hear the SAs shouting outside the Reichstag, Goering bawling in his residence on the Leipzigerplatz, "Shoot, shoot the pig!"; the two men in gabardine waiting for me at home, on the Dorotheenstrasse. And the gangs of 1922, the peasant woman with her skirt tied, Nitti's marbled face, Nitti not speaking. Von Baulig leaning against his bookcase like a target. And the body of Elsa de Beuil on the tile floor, she too a victim of power, dead by chance or because Ferri, one morning . . .

"You know your friend Ferri has just been appointed to London," Pierre de Beuil tells me. "He has remarried, a Cantoni, chemical products, a fortune."

Beuil's first words, before he even sits down.

Lanvoni had asked me to arrange another meeting in my apartment. Pierre de Beuil was talking more loudly, his features expansive, confidence in his gestures and voice. He stands, sits, leans against the window.

"Have you seen who they dared to appoint minister of the interior? That Salengro, a deserter, he escaped the firing squad but we'll get him, believe me Naldi, I'm looking after it myself."

Articles in *Gringoire* every day, against Roger Salengro, accusing him of having fled the French front lines in 1915, of treason. And despite the socialist minister's retorts, the mud kept flying.

"Twelve bullets for him."

Beuil snapped his gloves like a riding crop.

"Now it's a race between them and us. You won in '22, Hitler in '33. Franco now. We won't lose."

Lanvoni comes in, Beuil hardly pauses, begins again, indignant, red-faced.

"But we must have the means to carry out our policy. It's in the interest of fascism."

Lanvoni smokes calmly, legs crossed, one hand on his knee. I know that expression of contempt, almost imperceptible, a sort of attentive half-smile.

"The time of legality is over," Beuil goes on. "I am a reader of Malaparte, yes indeed, I have reflected on the *Technique of the coup d'État*, and if we want to win we must take action."

Lanvoni spreads his hands, rises, closes the window.

"It's your decision," he says, "you alone can judge, but as it happens you lost the election and the new government is now established for several years."

Beuil shrugs.

"You're a fascist, Lanvoni, a soldier, you talk to me about elections, what counts is the preparations to take over the government, and that costs a lot of money."

He stands again.

"I am not begging, make that clear to Ciano and the Duce, I am proposing a political alliance. We have the men."

He explains, infiltration of the army and police. Political assassinations being planned.

"With sufficient resources, trust me, I'll wipe out the communists, socialists, and put our Revolutionary Action Committee in power. We'll make a Latin alliance, Paris, Rome, Madrid, and let Hitler take the eastern countries. What do you think of it? But the means, the means . . ."

Pierre de Beuil sits, drinks the glass I hold out to him.

"Such heat!"

Then his passion seizes him again:

"So, you send planes and troops to Franco, that's essential."

While he talks I watch Lanvoni, who stubs out his cigarette, stretches, leaves Beuil to orate; now he'll spread his net.

"Tell me, my friend, speaking of infiltration networks, Spain, and your needs, the extent of which I appreciate and we can meet them in part, but as you yourself said, this is an alliance."

"An alliance, of course," repeats Beuil.

"Exactly; you know an Italian antifascist brigade is being formed in Paris and preparing to go to Spain to fight Franco's troops, and ours. Here, Naldi, would you read that, please."

Lanvoni holds out an Italian paper, *Giustizia e Libertà.* The entire front page is in big print, an appeal by Alatri and Calvini in the name of the antifascist bloc. I translate slowly:

"'Spain today, tomorrow Italy! We have reached the moment when the two struggling worlds, the free world and the world of dictatorships, are about to confront each other in armed combat.'"

"The usual style," says Pierre de Beuil.

"Of course," Lanvoni begins; "that is not what concerns us. But a movement begins, you know as well as I do, and then who knows how far it can go?"

Lanvoni lights another cigarette, leans forward.

"In the beginning a movement, a party, is just a few men, a few leaders, Alatri, Calvini, imagine . . ."

A long inhalation.

". . . imagine that the Duce, Hitler, yourself had been disposed of, what would fascism and national socialism have become, what would become of your Revolutionary Action Committee?"

Beuil glances toward me. He rises, Lanvoni has sunk deeper into his chair.

"You want us to remove your two jokers? Is that it?"

"My dear Beuil, I don't want anything, but you're talking to me about an alliance, that's all."

I can't move, can't look up, there they are in front of me,

their bodies riddled with knife wounds, the mutilated bodies of Alatri and Calvini.

"All right," says Beuil. "This is simply a technical problem. I need some information. You fought in the war like me, my dear Lanvoni, Naldi too, and you know what an operation is, it has to be planned."

Lanvoni gets up too.

"The main thing is that we agree on the principle, isn't it?" he says. "For the time being, there's no hurry. Naldi will be in touch with you."

I go to the door with Lanvoni, he gives me a wink.

"He'll get nothing for nothing," he says under his breath.

Alatri, Calvini: the price of a few weapons, some money. And me in the gears, like one of those dogs they use to flush game in the hedges at Magliano, and then come the shots and then the knives sink in.

"You're implacable, you people," says Beuil, "you're the heirs of the Renaissance, conspirators, Machiavelli. You just went straight ahead with Matteotti, and now these two, really . . ."

He was in the door.

"It's war, isn't it, Naldi? Them or us. Well, I'll be waiting."

He shakes my hand.

"I'll be waiting," he repeats.

I, too, was beginning to wait, at the end of that summer when war was creeping into the newspapers and the streets. Ruins of the Alcazar of Toledo, abandoned child, bleeding, in a street where General Franco's *Tercios* were marching, and the first refugees, old women in scarves crossing the frontier and arriving as though they had been walking toward me ever since the day in October 1917 when I left Magliano in the rain and Ferri drove along the columns of intermingled women and soldiers. I was waiting for the moment when Lanvoni would ask me to notify Beuil and his Revolutionary Action Committee would have to act.

Early in the morning I went down to buy the first editions of the papers. Alatri and Calvini were intensifying their activities in the left-wing press. Alatri among the delegates from Republican Spain, raising his fist in front of the statue on the place de la République, Calvini speaking beside André Malraux at a meeting for the defense of Madrid. "*No pasaran,*" Calvini repeated. But General Varela and the Moroccan *Regulares* had entered the ruins of Toledo, the circle was closing in around Madrid. Alatri christened the Garibaldi Battalion of the International Brigade, which was beginning to leave for Spain. They were asking for death and I was waiting. Maud Kaufman was sending articles from Madrid. Accurate as in the days of the Ethiopian war, passion in the form of sobriety. Floor by floor, there was the fight in the university campus and the *dynamitero* rising and hurling his charge, heroism, trenches dug in the street. But in the next column was news of the execution of Zinoviev and Kamenev in Moscow. "It's Trotsky they're after," they wrote, and I saw Maud again, holding out her arms to Jacques Morin in the hall at Laborderie's. The flood of war and violence was rising, the perimeter shrinking. I wait.

Ferri came through Paris on his way back to London. He had asked to see me. We walked along the paths in the grounds on the rue de Varenne.

"You know I've married again?"

He took my arm familiarly.

"Marco, do you want me to look for someone for you in Francesca's circle, some money, someone cultivated."

He laughed.

"No career without a wife, Marco."

Then he began to speak softly, leaning forward, hands behind his back.

"They've sent me to London because they're afraid of me in Rome, I've got an alternative policy and people behind me. Through Francesca, you know the Cantonis, the chemical industry."

A glance at me.

"Tell him if you want to, tell your protector, the great Minister Ciano."

I denied with a shake of my head.

"I'm only joking. But the thing is, *he* has become senile."

He was the Duce.

"The victory in Ethiopia has gone to his head. And . . ."

Ferri led me to the end of the garden, far from the embassy windows.

"There's Petacci, that bitch is wearing him out, and sharks all around her, a whole clan. He's lost his sense of reality. An old man with a slut under his skin."

I could tell Ferri's mood from his fuming voice. For weeks he had been looking for someone to confide in, to tell his hatred to. But he was surrounded by enemies, ambitions. He had to keep wearing his contented courtier's mask. At heart he must know I wasn't a stool pigeon, so he was talking to me.

"Do you know what he said to me when he saw me yesterday, to me, his ambassador to London? Listen."

He stopped to face me and took hold of my shoulder.

"He said to me, 'Ferri, the English have no importance any more. The country's lost. A country with eleven million people over the age of fifty doesn't exist, and besides, they bury dogs and drink tea!' And all that in perfect seriousness, you understand Naldi. And we have to obey, put up with it!"

The Duce still being acclaimed by the crowd, an ever larger crowd, better organized, one hundred thousand in the Roman Forum with arms outstretched for the anniversary of the March on Rome. And the German delegation like a black brick at the foot of the platform.

Ferri went to London. I was waiting. Lanvoni didn't seem in any hurry. Every evening he added a detail to his cards in his office, commented on some article.

"You haven't been able to do anything about Maud Kaufman? Of course. She's stubborn, but I hope Stalin means to take care of her soon."

In Moscow the purge was continuing. By the thousands. Millions, Provi said. We often walked home together down the rue de Varenne, I went with him as far as the Champ de Mars.

"Power has its own logic, Marco. Hitler, Stalin, two opposites who will copulate. Believe me, Mussolini is the lesser evil."

Nevertheless, he was worried. Ciano had just met Hitler at Berchtesgaden. Mussolini was proclaiming the Rome-Berlin Axis.

"If we hitch ourselves to the German tank, it's war. And soon."

Sometimes I was tempted to tell him about Alatri, Calvini, then decided not to. That was my business, to deal with myself. One day early in November, Emilia rang. She was surprised, never saw me any more. That evening she was opening an exhibition of Jacques Morin's work, a private showing, a few friends.

"You know Maud and Jacques," said Emilia. "Maud spoke to me about you yesterday. I was complaining that you had vanished, she told me you must be in Spain, on the wrong side, of course."

Emilia laughed and so did I. It had been a long time. That evening in the gallery I saw Jacques Morin first, sitting with his elbows on a table signing lithographs, drawing. Jet black hair over a broad skull and the hands of a worker, flat fingers. An impression of strength. He raised his head. His eyes were lively, gestures rapid, face heavy, and that look. A confession, for me, who knew about his other identity. He went back to his signing but I felt his eyes on me and caught him watching as I moved forward among the groups. I saw Maud's back, a black pullover and pleated skirt, I saw her hand and heard the voice.

"Madrid won't capitulate," she said. "I promise you."

Suddenly she turned around. Surprise. An ironic smile. She raised her glass.

"I thought you were in Spain," she said. "With your legionnaires."

"I thought you were there too."

"I was. But your friends couldn't manage to kill me, as you see."

"So much the better."

"You're not logical, Mr. Naldi."

For a moment we were left alone face to face.

"Are you going back?"

"My paper finds my stories a little too partisan."

She still had that same gesture of tossing her hair to one side of her forehead.

"I'm not objective enough," she went on. "Objectivity means never talking about the causes of events, you have to stick to the surface."

I saw Laborderie coming over, wave of his hand. I saw Jacques Morin watching us as he talked to Emilia.

"I may need to meet you, in a hurry. Just you."

She began to laugh.

"A political matter," I added.

There was no ambiguity in my expression.

"Just me," she said soberly.

"Yes."

"I'm always at the paper around eleven, before the editorial conference. Ask for me, say it's from Emilia if you like, that will be less obvious."

Laborderie was in front of us, holding out a glass.

"You're not drinking, Naldi, take this. You're going to need it. I know Casanova was an Italian but really you might take a little better care of your conquests. Maud, you remember that young woman at my place, Anne Villemur, she was with Naldi."

That was true, I had forgotten Anne. She had rung up once or twice since her return and I had brushed her off with a few words.

"Naldi takes her on a holiday, walks out on her, and the idiot tries to commit suicide, she imagined she was pregnant, fortunately a guy from the paper noticed her absence and they brought her around. You were lucky, Naldi. Don't sweat like that, it's over now, she's all right, I meant to let you know before but I was too busy. So much happening, I had to go to Spain."

I was sweating. There were big drops on my forehead. The simplest act of all, it involves only my body and that of one woman, and this havoc too, this avalanche, Anne, whom I had treated like an object without even meaning to, led her to my bed, taken her, accepted her, rejected her.

"A poor news item," said Laborderie, suddenly embarrassed. "Perhaps I shouldn't have," he went on.

"I'm an oyster," Maud said.

She was looking at me, a smile.

"You were behaving like a good fascist, virile and uninvolved," said Maud.

"Words, words."

Laborderie was talking nervously, watching me, sure he had said too much:

"Maud, don't go mixing everything up, she's a little goose, she's had her little drama."

"How is she?"

"Fine, Naldi, honestly, it happened more than three months ago. A girl trying to get some attention. She's as pretty as ever and don't try her again, I think she has somebody now."

"Here," said Maud, "drink to her health."

She took a glass from a waiter's tray and held it out to me. I went home along the boulevard Montparnasse, a damp breeze, showers. Life like a billiard game, one ball hits another and who can follow the path of that one, which will strike a third; ricochets, taps. One act, any act; one word, any word; my will, however narrow, and the whole world moves. I thought I had shrunk into nothing, disappeared, ceased to weigh, and here is Anne, an empty form for me, screaming she exists too, I can't reduce her to nothing, go away, leave a void, my imprint, a pain driving her toward death. I smoked all night long in the dark. Thought of commitments. Choose an open action, find some other Africa, remote and lost, or bury myself in the Foreign Legion, become an anonymous mechanism carrying out other people's orders with no knowledge and no motive. A mercenary, regaining innocence through obedience. Going to the farthest extreme of what I already was. Images the night wove together, but in the morning, habit and the newspapers, Lanvoni telephoning.

"Naldi, would you see what Beuil's organization amounts to? They're demonstrating on the Champs Elysées."

They're not ready yet: Pierre de Beuil is alone in front of his flag bearers, his decorations on his black coat, armband, bareheaded. The men march in step in front of him, all wearing the same beret, not fascist militia yet or SAs but already the same men, the same love of parades, the same heavy tread. In a nearby street Marcel Bucard's Frankists in brown uniforms. All they needed was to take over the power, and the crowds would gather in the stadiums, the projectors' beams probe the sky. And they were nibbling away at the power, placing their accomplices, making room for the fear that will hand the mob over to them. Some explosions, the first efforts of the Revolutionary Action Committee.

"Well," Lanvoni asks, "do they exist?"

"Veterans, some attempt at organization, units, and Beuil watching them like a general reviewing his army."

"Too much posing," Lanvoni says, "not enough action. You'll have to see him before the end of the week. Quietly."

He takes an envelope out of his cabinet. Large, blue, sealed.

"Give him this. He must destroy the paper in your presence. It doesn't matter about the photos. Nothing compromising anyway, but it's safer."

The footman came in with two coffees. We sat down face to face.

"Apart from that, my good Naldi, what else is new?"

"That" was Alatri's and Calvini's death. I go home, the

envelope in my pocket. Like Maud Kaufman's card months before. In between, two times, two voices: one of them arranges
meetings with Beuil in the quiet bar where I meet Bernard, the
whores' bar, and the other talks about the deaths of Matteotti
and von Baulig, Nitti's face and Alatri's on the station platform in Bologna. And Anne too. And Salengro, who committed
suicide this morning in Lille, couldn't take any more of those
words they were shoving down his throat. And more processions
assembled, silent, their breaths forming a kind of mist above
their heads in the cold.

I sat down at my table and removed the wax seal. Two sheets.
On one a few words: "A. and C. will go to Marseille on December 20. Black Ford." License number, address at Aubagne, name
of the antifascist they will stay with, time of the meeting. An
efficient informer, that one. On the other sheet, glued side by
side, two photos, Alatri and Calvini. And underneath, two typewritten words, "Operation Alliance."

I telephoned Maud at her paper, saying it was Emilia calling,
on the morning of the day I was to see Beuil.

"Today," I said, "it's urgent."

"Really?" said Maud.

I interrupted:

"I swear it. Today, as soon as possible."

We met in a restaurant on the boulevard Beaumarchais near
the Bastille. I chose a table in the second room, I had been
there a long time when she came, waved, disappeared, finally
sat down, out of breath.

"I telephoned, had to cancel engagements, the editorial conference went on forever, I'm terribly late but you didn't give me
much notice."

She didn't look at me, seemed to be reading the menu, talking fast, finally she looked up a moment, to toss her hair to one
side.

"Why don't we order," she said, "then we'll be left in peace,
for you must have very important things to say to me."

Could I say that I wanted to tell her my whole life, to understand it by telling it. That I trusted her, I felt so close to her, she too, in a different way but unconsciously, was cornered, trapped. Maybe that's why I was there. Or else simply because the two or three times I had been near her I had relaxed, and because I liked that face, too long, too dark, her way of smiling, from the eyes all the way to her mouth, her face breaking into a thousand wrinkles, and then that way she had of barging ahead unprotected, colliding with other people, with me, Anne.

"Was your family German?"

She leaned her head on her fists, elbows on the table.

"My father's German, a German Jew, my mother is Turkish, my first husband American, the second French, a painter, I am French by marriage and stateless by vocation."

She leaned back, a peal of laughter, leaned against the empty chair next to her, her arms very brown, muscular, short, her breasts outlined under her pullover as it stretched. I knew I liked her. Not just her voice and her laugh, but her body too. She saw my look. Her expression became severe.

"You know I haven't much time," she said.

I wasn't there to tell her how one day in October 1917 I had been dumped out on a road that had led here; how, in order to try to understand that road I had had to shed ambition and the comforts of power, and Ferri, that officer I had seen with his cape slung over his shoulder outside the farm at Magliano, who took me to his dead friend, my father. I wasn't there to tell her why I agreed to go on being this fascist government employee who was sitting opposite her. Not there to look at her like a woman whose hand one wants to hold, whose skin one wants to touch because it's calling. I pushed away the dishes. Took out the blue envelope Lanvoni had given me.

"Do you know the men of the Italian antifascist bloc? Alatri and Calvini? I thought you could warn them. Here."

I held out the two sheets. She read, looked, read again, looking up at me now and then.

"Beuil's men are instructed to kill them during this trip to Marseille. They should be warned. But . . ."

She had taken a cigarette, was holding out the pack to me, light, slender fingers, quick, nervous gestures.

". . . they mustn't know the source of this information. And there mustn't be any noise about the matter. I think I can trust you."

We smoked in silence, forgetting the meal, ordering coffees.

"That's why I was so anxious to see you today. I needed an intermediary and I thought of you. Will you remember?"

I took back the papers and put them in a new envelope.

"I'm seeing Beuil this evening. He's going to set it up."

"You're financing him, aren't you?"

"Could you doubt it?"

She smiled.

"Confirmations are always useful."

She ordered another coffee, drank it slowly, looking at me over the rim of the cup:

"Why are you doing this?"

"You remember one evening at Laborderie's, you accused me of being a detached collaborator, a tool."

"I remember very well. You were with that young woman."

"I talked about controlled collaboration, and this business now is one of my limits. I don't collaborate here."

She leaned her face on her fists again, and looked me straight in the eyes. Maybe I had chosen her in order to convince her, too.

"You could go further," she began.

Her face didn't move, caught between her fists; only her dark lips.

"Join those men, Alatri and Calvini or some others, a different camp."

"Why?"

Suddenly she became heated:

"Why? Why, because you have to be against fascism, it's a

political necessity, historic, moral, I don't know. You want to be lumped together with Beuil and his killers?"

"You want me to lump you together with the people who are purging in Moscow?"

"That's not the problem. Besides, I'm not on the side of the judges, I'm only on the side of socialism. For me Stalin's just a red Bonaparte."

"Then, Maud, what side are you on? Socialism is only a word."

I was waiting to play my card, I realized I had also wanted to see her for that. I hadn't thought about it, but now, facing her, I couldn't keep silent. Oh, of course, I wanted her to know, and I also, no doubt, unconsciously wanted to drive her away from that tall, heavy figure of Jacques Morin, who must enfold her every night in his thick worker's hands. I let her talk. We went out, taking the boulevard Henri IV toward the Seine. She was rather stocky, she raised her head to me, using her hands when she talked, her heels striking the ground.

"There is another reason why I wanted to see you."

I had interrupted her.

"Also important. It concerns you."

She stopped.

"Me?"

"You must listen until I finish without interrupting. You can talk afterward."

I began, we were walking slowly along the boulevard, then we crossed the pont Sully and turned into the Île Saint-Louis; another river, a grayer sky, with these damp gusts, and yet this island, these arms of water, Rome, Venice, steps in my memory. Maud was walking beside me, I felt her looking at me but didn't turn my head, I looked at the water, the dirty white façades, entrances and carved wooden doors, I said Bernard, the information he had given me about her, how I knew she belonged to a secret Trotskyist organization and this was proof that I wasn't joking or making it up, and then in the archives of the ministry of the interior there was a file on Jacques Paillet, a Comintern agent, a "tough guy" as Bernard said. His mission was to get inside the Trotskyist organization by any means. I didn't turn my head, I looked at the water and talked, we went deeper into the streets of the Île Saint-Louis. Any means. He had become Jacques Morin, married her, there might be a chance to reach Trotsky through her, of course she was free not to believe me but was anything impossible in this age of Beuil, Hitler, and the Moscow trials?

"You've got a name, Jacques Paillet, up to you to check on it, Maud. I've been carrying that around for months. Long before I ever met you. Then I did meet you. You know there are limits to my collaboration."

We walked, turned, we were back on the pont Sully again.

"I'm going to take a taxi," she said.

I looked at her but she turned her eyes away. She lowered her head.

"I won't forget, for Alatri and Calvini. I've got a very good memory. Count on me. They'll be warned this evening. And don't worry. I'm an oyster. Good-bye, Marco."

Her gloved hand in mine, my first name. She hailed a taxi, saying:

"It will be done."

I went home along the quays. Had I talked about Jacques Morin, had I told her? I began to wonder, I had to recall the sentences I had spoken, the streets on the Île Saint Louis. Had she heard me? Had she believed me? That evening I met Pierre de Beuil in the bar.

"Queer notions you've got, these whores, you'll compromise me, my dear Naldi."

I took out the envelope.

He opened it, I took back the envelope and tore it up while he was looking at the sheets.

"To destroy once you've read it."

"Naturally; I keep the photos."

He folded them and put them in his notebook.

"It doesn't look very difficult. If we aren't capable of that. I bet the idiots aren't even armed. Besides . . ."

He began to laugh.

". . . they're aliens, they're not allowed to be."

He ordered a bottle of champagne.

"To our alliance," he said.

I let him go, sitting on in the semidarkness of the bar with the bits of paper in front of me between the champagne glasses. The lives of Alatri and Calvini. A girl came and I went out with her. Then other evenings, other girls. I found my way back to the prostitutes, because I had to wait and there was no sign from Maud. Because I was seeing Bernard and having to face Lanvoni every evening. At last, December 20 came. The papers announced no grisly discoveries, no disappearances. Early in January, at the window of his office, Lanvoni held out a photo. It showed Calvini at the front line in Madrid handing a flag to the Italians of the International Brigade, red scarf over his shoulder.

"That stupid fool Beuil," said Lanvoni. "Play-acting and an appetite, and our informer unmasked. These French need a lesson. Fortunately, they're getting ready for it back there."

"Back there" on the other side of the Rhine, behind the Alps. Goering was in Rome. "The common front between our two countries," the Duce was saying, "has already been made concrete in the common military front in Spain." What could I do but lurch from body to body, girl to girl, or sleep. But there was the radio, the papers to be read, Bernard, Beuil to be seen, the undermining progressed day by day as I watched. The security police fired on the crowd, place Clichy. Bernard smiled.

"I don't know the details, but you should ask your friend Pierre de Beuil, he will certainly know why they opened fire so quickly. The head of Blum's personal staff was wounded. You know, dear Mr. Naldi, I don't believe in chance very much, in stray bullets. Neither do you, I daresay."

Shooting in Paris, explosions, caches of arms found in the sewers and, in Moscow, men accusing each other, disappearing. Then Guernica. The city in flames and a dog howling its lungs out by a cadaver in the middle of a street.

My life, too, like a ruined city crumbling under the days. My body filled with stifled shouts, I wanted to talk, more than wanted, I needed to, there were rumblings that couldn't force their way out and grew louder in the silence. Probably I had held myself down too long and one night I dreamed I was peeling off my skin layer by layer until I was raw at last, my body bleeding and free. Delivered. At peace. A nightmare of cries, pains, leaving me exhausted and sweating. I tried to talk with my body alone, but nights with whores gave me nothing but brief fatigue and an ever greater need for friendship.

"You're not well," Provi said. "You've got on your sulky face, your chin's sticking out. You're not well, Marco."

He gave me a friendly thump.

"Come with me."

Rue de Varenne, the sun running straight down the street, the Champ de Mars, trees at last and the sky opening up, a marvelous perspective. Provi was talking.

"I don't understand you, Marco."

I didn't understand myself, still wavering between extremes and certain that it was futile and illusory to choose at all. I was a spectator in the game that was already tearing the world apart, wearing the costume of one of the sides, yes, but so minimally involved, trying not to add my weight. And yet, and yet, I had to tie down my hands to keep them from rising, I had to gag my mouth to keep from shouting; why did they need to strike, to shout? One day, it was because of Goering's squadrons who left alive in all of Guernica only one dog howling its lungs out; another day, because of the prosecutor in Moscow who pointed his finger at Karel Radek and demanded death for the traitors with a shrill executioner's voice. And behind Radek, Trotsky. I fumed against conquerors and conquered, masters and slaves. The Duce crying in the downpour in Berlin, "To-morrow all Europe will be fascist" and the million Germans who listened in spite of the rain. My loneliness. No camp to choose, only unclean ones, ambiguities, and yet my hands and voice, and their revulsion against inactivity and silence.

"I don't understand you, Marco," Provi was saying, "at our level one can do so little. And besides . . ."

We slowed down crossing the Champ de Mars, Provi took my arm.

"Besides, who really decides or chooses? Hitler, the Duce? More than we do, of course, but behind them there is such a tangle of forces. Herr Krupp, maybe? Not even. History escapes men's grasp, the machine was set in motion thousands of years ago, it's speeding up and you and I are in it with the rest. You should get married, Marco, make your little island, give yourself some weight. Take root."

Provi made a gesture signifying the futility of all things.

"Afterward, afterward, you know, everything becomes rela-tive, you have built your historic universe around yourself, you've got your own history, Mr. and Mrs. Naldi and their chil-dren, everything else moves at another speed and then physi-cally, too, it's important, stability."

I dined with them often. Provi, Mrs. Provi, and their son Pietro, an Italian servant who waited at table, smiling, some-times Mrs. Provi's sister Angela who was there for the taking—in church, of course. And I fled. Another contradiction. I pre-ferred my solitude, my bad dreams and my nights with the whores.

But in that case one was alone when one opened the tele-gram the embassy runner brought late one morning. I had read the papers, written my report. Windows open, the voice of the concierge in the courtyard talking to her cats. Gentle hours, a languid September, the refrain of a hit song somebody kept playing over and over again on the phonograph, "*C'est un mau-vais garçon,/Qui a des façons,/Pas très catholiques . . .*" and

I was humming too, a peaceful, routine morning, sheltered, a simple report, Hitler's sentence greeting Mussolini was in every newspaper: "Here is one of those unique men whom history does not make, they themselves make history" and the bell ringing: Provi on the phone. He was sending me the runner with a telegram from Magliano. I opened it, solitary, the name of Nitti after two words: "Mother deceased." Nothing.

Train, conversations, laughter. And a numbness I was burrowing into. A refusal to think, a meal in the dining car, I ordered extra dishes, I remember that desire to eat, eat more, move my muscles, numb myself, stuff myself with food, eat in order to keep the words down and keep down the tears that were climbing up my throat. Venice. The road, the sun multiplied in the canals and reflected back and forth by marble, gold, stained glass, a sun ricocheting on the lagoon, ponds, rice fields.

"The coffin had to be closed," the doctor told me. "With this heat, you understand."

In the bedroom the smell, density of wood and memories, corridors of the hospital in Venice. The same desire to vomit. Hands I shake, words I repeat, words held out to me. Fortunately, all there is is this smooth wood marked with a shiny copper plate. Mother disappeared, changed into wood, and the crumbling black earth of Magliano on top of the wood.

"What are you going to do with the land, Marco?"

My uncle, not seen for years. Came back from the cemetery with me, talking nonstop while I looked at his profile. "My brother looks so much like me," mother used to say, "that when we were children people took us for twins." Childhood in a wooden box and earth on top of childhood.

"Sell, Marco, the Nittis are too old, the new farmer's no good, I kept telling your mother, but you know her, she's stubborn."

He was still talking in the present tense, life prolonged the length of a verb.

"She wanted to be a Naldi and the Naldis are the land. You know her, stubborn . . ."

I didn't know anything about her. Since Emilia had been talking to me, maybe I could half-imagine the young woman she had been, hanging on my father's arm and I would pull at her hand, "Leave him, come with me." I tried to pull her away, my father laughed, then she took her hand away and I was alone, far away from them but they were watching me, alone and I started to run and her cries after me, "Marco, Marco!" never stopped me, I kept running and often I fell down, scraping my knees, and lay there with my face on the ground howling, at last, at last she picked me up with her hands and in spite of my father's voice, so high and far away, saying, "Let him cry, he's exaggerating," she would hold me to her and rock me and smooth my hair and wipe my mouth and eyes with her big embroidered handkerchiefs and the sweet scent of her perfume got mixed up with the salty taste of tears. I didn't know anything about her, I had bent her to all my whims, never giving her the right to exist, she was my mother so I made her my slave, dispossessed her of her life to reduce her to mine. And then left her. The order of things. A toy you use and throw away. I had been her life. And had claimed the right, by not staying at Magliano, to refuse her her life. Now I saw her again, an object, wood, earth. And because I had grown older, no doubt, and because Emilia had talked to me I knew she had been more than two arms reaching out for me, an existence reduced to the state of my servant, had been a whole labyrinth of passions, regrets, doubts. A woman.

"You've got to sell," my uncle was repeating, "you'll give a little something to the Nittis and they'll be pleased, anyway it's your right, fortunately the time of leagues and unions is over otherwise you'd have had a hard time with that Nitti but he's calmed down now."

He began to laugh.

"Some pressure was put on him," he added.

A woman. All I could do now was imagine her, I had missed the opportunity of knowing her. I had let her life go as you let water sink into the sand; I had preferred to stay in Venice with Elsa, to go to Cairo or Bombay, or to Le Trayas with Anne; I had been running away from her since the autumn of 1917 when her pain told me she loved somebody else besides me, my father. Unbearable pain. I ran away from her to punish her for that confession she couldn't hide; I hadn't watched her gestures or her eyes, hadn't tried to give her life back to her by letting her talk about herself; I wanted her reduced to that comfortable presence, so full for me, so partial for her: my mother. Now, now, I was left with objects, the house, a desert around me, childhood well and truly dead, father, Giulia, mother.

"I'll think about it, don't worry," I told him.

"You know I'm a buyer and you could always come back, of course I'd leave you the house, I had already suggested it to your mother."

He lit his pipe. How did he manage to take death so easily. Maybe he too was a mirage, the rituals of life, his pipe, buying land. I went to his car with him then came back, lingering by the poplars, outside the shed. I knocked at the Nittis' door. Mrs. Nitti opened, in black as always. Seeing me, she burst into tears. It had been so long that I had lost all recollection of it, it seemed to me that hadn't happened since the days when I used to fall down and scrape my knees, father shouting my name; and I cried too, holding Mrs. Nitti, so small, against me. I touched the wool of her shawl, her shoulders, and was tempted to give way forever to that hurt, return to the age of tears, childhood. The sound of a chair. Nitti getting up, touching his hat. I moved away from his wife.

"Nothing will change," I said. "I'm keeping Magliano. Naturally, you'll stay. I'm the only one now. If anything happens to me you'll still stay. I'll arrange it."

I don't know what Mrs. Nitti murmured. She crossed herself. Nitti didn't budge, his hands crossed in front of him, his face in the shadows of the low-ceilinged room.

"I think this land is yours too," I went on, "you worked it.
I didn't."

I went out, annoyed with myself for those last words, too
simple and pretentious. I sat down at our long black wood
table in the big room in the silent house, the sun tracing bright
bars through the shutters, marking the walls. How long did I
stay there? Long enough to walk beside mother through the
alleyways of Venice, long enough to feel her hand on my forehead when I had a fever and she came to sit near me, any
time I opened my eyes she was already there: "What do you
want?" I wanted her, her, alone and completely, and when I
asked for a toy, a glass of water, when I demanded things it
was still her and only her I wanted. Sitting at that table, long
enough for the bright bars on the walls to fade and night to
come.

There was a knock, the door opened. Nitti stood in the doorway.

"Shouldn't stay alone," he said. "Come have a bowl of soup
in the house."

He didn't wait for me to answer, went out leaving the door
open.

I spent a few days at Magliano to deal with the business of
the inheritance, arranging an annuity for the Nittis if I died.
I had dinner with them in the evenings, in the room where I
used to play with Giulia. Not many words, every one led to
too many traps, released too many memories. Mrs. Nitti served.

"Eat, Mr. Marco, eat," she said.

That was her joy, her mission, preparing and giving food. First
she filled my plate, then Nitti's. She ate standing up, her plate
in her hand.

"Sit down, Mrs. Nitti."

She smiled, shook her head. Nitti said sharply, "Sit down."

She still refused and he shrugged, not speaking throughout
the meal. The last evening, as I was leaving, he said:

"Tomorrow morning I'll take you over the fields if you like."

We left very early. There was no fog, but a cold north wind. Nitti walked ahead, pointing out the new canals with his spade handle, the ponds he had begun draining with Matteroni, the other farmer. We climbed up a fill planted with poplars, the border of our property. The sun was rising, sliding along the gray wind-wrinkled water. Nitti stopped, leaning on his spade. He shaved only once or twice a week and his beard was already long, stiff gray and white hairs in his dull-hued skin.

"You're in politics, Mr. Marco, you think they'll have this war?"

I didn't answer, a shrug of uncertainty.

"You want me to tell you?"

He pointed a finger at me.

"They'll have it because they can't do anything else. You heard him talking about eight million bayonets, and the other one in Berlin saying cannons are better than butter."

I had been with him for days and he had never spoken, suddenly he was talking, open and heedless, aggressive and exact, as though it were a speech he'd been reciting to himself for a long time and was finally making aloud.

"They'll have it, Mr. Marco, but I was wrong once, in '18, I thought that was it but this time if they have the war it's the end, fascism, nazism, we'll wipe them out, you'll see, they'll pay, Mr. Marco, and the revolution, this time, believe me, you've seen in Spain, what the antifascists gave Mussolini's legionnaires, in the ass, at Guadalajara, in the ass, Mr. Marco."

His eyes dropped suddenly and looked straight into mine. He wiped his mouth with the back of his hand.

"Okay. There's the fields, Mr. Marco. I'm going to work."

He smiled.

"Don't get much chance to talk around here. But that doesn't stop it going on inside. One day it'll come out."

He saluted me, two fingers in front of his hat.

The next day I was back in Paris, another world, of Lanvoni,

Beuil, Bernard. Another camp. During my absence Provi had written the press review for me. I questioned him:

"Nothing important."

He leafed through the reports.

"Oh yes, one news item, here."

Underlining the words, he repeated:

"A news item."

I took the report he held out to me and read. Calvini had been found murdered in his car at the side of a road near Caen. Doors open, blood, body half-stuffed into a ditch hidden by a hedge. Twenty knife wounds in his chest. A red scarf caught on the hedge, a girl passing by surprised to see an abandoned car, a red scarf, pushes aside the hedge and finds the body. Lanvoni had succeeded. With or without Beuil's men. I felt like vomiting again. Another part of me that had grown familiar, Calvini calling off the marchers at Bologna, Calvini alongside Matteotti, Calvini next to Alatri, Calvini, whom I had tried to protect.

I closed the file. Went out. Street, city, mother's death and Calvini's, the dead of the last bastion of the Asturias, those prisoners the Frankists hauled into a plowed field, you saw them walking forward in white shirts between men carrying rifles. Those dead were filling the world, and the street and the city were indifferent. I telephoned Emilia. Had she seen Maud Kaufman? No, it was odd, she hadn't seen her for months but something was wrong, Jacques Morin hadn't come to collect his paintings. Their phone didn't answer.

"And," Emilia said, "Maud has left her paper, they don't know anything about her, they told me she might have gone to Spain. She's crazy."

I wanted to talk to Maud, she seemed to have believed me. If Emilia ran into her, would she ask her to ring me, it was urgent. Emilia laughed.

"I saw, I felt there could be something between you two, you're like your mother, one look and you're on fire, be careful

Marco, Maud is not easy to get along with, I'm very fond of her but I think she's mad."

Days. Paris burying Calvini. Thousands and thousands, men and women, black crepe on their lapels, the tread, pressure of bodies, slow progress between the gray façades of the boulevard Voltaire. I joined the crowd.

Pushed by it, imprisoned by its silence, I went toward Calvini's face, an immense gray photograph held by men under the platform. Then, suddenly, a song like an oath of vengeance, fierce and determined. I managed to work my way out of the procession, suddenly uneasy. No uniforms, though, none of those distorted faces on the Piazza Venezia or the Wilhelmplatz but that song, that sudden surge through the crowd, fists rising like proof that it, too, could break loose in the blindness of certainties.

Laborderie telephoned, beside himself:

"Naldi, this crime is signed, you can't subscribe to it. Do something. It's a question of self-respect."

"In Berlin, you remember, you suggested that I meet Alatri."

Laborderie stopped me, I could imagine his gesticulating hands.

"Arrange something at your place, all three of us," I said.

"Bravo, Naldi, bravo."

Wait. How far could Laborderie be trusted? A chatterbox, a journalist who loved gold, Lanvoni said. But since Maud wasn't there I had to use him. Wait. Then his ring, the pink apartment on the rue d'Ulm.

"I've had difficulties," Laborderie was saying. "Alatri's a communist, you know. He never acts without consulting his comrades. If he has accepted that means they agree. And it's very important. Highly significant."

Laborderie was talking softly, unable to stay seated for ten seconds. Giving me drinks, smoking, then stubbing out his cigarette almost as soon as he'd lit it. Alatri came with a stranger, a young man with a massive face and cropped bushy hair. They stand in the entrance. Laborderie comes over to me.

"The party insists that Mr. Gasparini be here. You must know," he whispers, "they all check each other."

What do I care. Alatri and Gasparini sit facing me. Alatri looks at me, always the same ironic, mildly scornful smile.

"So," he said, "the coincidences of history."

He lights a cigarette.

"You have proposals to make?"

Laborderie leaves the three of us alone.

"Proposals?"

I was hoping for an open conversation. Innocence. What does the past signify—Venice, the Piave—in the days of long knives?

"I'm only a walk-on, you said it yourself, and I speak only in my own name. I have nothing specific to say."

Gasparini crosses his legs. He has placed a little notebook on his knee and is taking notes. Suddenly I feel empty, futile. What is one voice? What importance have my moral dilemmas, interrogations, hesitations, half-treasons? The army has the floor now, Gasparini and Alatri are soldiers, like Lanvoni.

"I thought you'd moved toward us," Alatri says. "Events might have opened your eyes. Matteotti, Ethiopia, Spain, Calvini. The bigger and bigger role being played by the nazis. You've been in Germany?"

I nodded. Have I moved toward them? Am I ready to change camps? Maybe I'm just a deserter. They're waiting, I have to say something.

"There's one point, the Calvini affair. I know a few details. And you're threatened."

I mention Beuil, his organization. Alatri interrupts me.

"We know all that, Naldi. And also that they already tried something on Calvini and me, we were supposed to go to Marseille but we have our informers."

I say nothing. Why tell them I am their informer? Alatri watches me, pleased with himself, that attitude of the serene

older brother he had already adopted in the barracks the day
Ferri took me to Bologna. Old irritations rise up, I think of
Maud, too, and Jacques Morin.

"But go on," says Alatri.

I shake my head.

"That's all, you know as much as I do."

"What you say is not totally useless. The party will take it
into account. Besides, we can talk to fascist officials like you,
who are well-meaning, who have made a mistake but are ap-
palled by the policy they are being forced to carry out."

He talks a long time. Gasparini nods agreement. I don't listen.

"You can easily return to Italy, can't you?" Alatri asks, ending his monologue. "If the party trusts you, we'll give you letters.
But later, much later. We've already had some unfortunate experiences."

He laughs.

"We've learned to be careful."

"No. Not letters."

I get up. Between us this evening, nothing is happening.
Words thrown at me. Empty words, even if they're telling truth.
I look at Alatri, that self-satisfaction, that smile, I think of
Lanvoni. Different policies, contrary. But the men resemble
each other.

"Think it over," says Alatri. "Think it over. We won't always be underground, outlaws."

"I only wanted to do you a favor. Warn you. You."

Alatri gets up too.

"I don't exist without the party. Get rid of your individualist
ideas, try to understand the age we're living in."

"Of course, you approve of the Moscow executions, the persecution?"

Alatri laughs as I've never heard him laugh before.

"Naldi, really, you are inimitable. You are going to give me
a lesson in justice and human rights, you, me?"

He comes closer, looks at me over the tops of his glasses, stern.

"You know the setup in fascist prisons? Those of the government you work for?"

"That doesn't change anything."

"The Moscow trials are our business. There are always traitors. And sometimes justice goes by the board. You worry about Rome."

"Words. I might as well be listening to a speech on fascist law."

Alatri takes another step forward. Gasparini holds him back.

"What do you want?" Alatri says. "To argue? About the meaning of history, the guilt of Zinoviev and Radek, Trotsky's role in the Russian Revolution? Honestly, do you think this is the moment?"

"For me it is."

"But you isn't much. What do you represent? Yourself. It is the masses who count. And you're so far away from them. You hesitate, as always. You haven't made much progress. You like your shell. Your little individual emotions."

He opens the living-room door.

"Try to remain a walk-on."

Walk-on? How is it possible not to be? How can you have the nerve to drag other people with you in the faked game of history? Walk-on! The word was no insult to me. It wasn't my cowardice, it was my dignity. My refusal to be shouting with the killers one day, whether they wear black or red. You shout "A noï!" in a happy crowd, you march with a comrade at your side, you feel the warmth of an arm linked in yours, you sing your lungs out, it's Milan one foggy day in November 1918, I'm going through the streets and then the curtain rises on violence, courts of justice, prosecutors, assassins. From then on I refused the gangrene of collective certainties. I wanted to act in accordance with my little individual emotions, when history turned into a name, a flesh-and-blood being—Ingrid von Wirth, whom I was driving to Denmark, von Baulig, whom I was trying to convince, Alatri or Calvini, whom I was trying to warn. Maud, whom I did warn. I distrusted ideas when I couldn't see their faces. I had gone toward Alatri in memory of the prisoner I had seen on the station platform in Bologna, Alatri of my memory. Maybe I was driven by a hidden hope that I would be convinced and carried along, that I'd forget Jacques Morin and my doubts, my day-by-day choices. That the adolescence of fire and fury would return. But Alatri as he was now, divested of his remorse, a voice too dry, an untroubled self-assurance, a condescending scorn, a blindness. His choice of executioners, as though one lot were fairer than the other. And that wasn't the main thing. Maybe you did have to choose to kill because it was a killing age; but his joy in his choice, his tranquillity: that was what kept me from joining him.

Both of us had changed since Venice and the Piave. I had abandoned my convictions, the simple ideas the Naldis had bequeathed to me along with the land; torn off Ferri's hero's mask to discover power as a maze of sordid ambitions and rivalries, or a conjunction of hate-filled and often criminal associations. Him, Alatri whom I had dragged through the Piave mud when he was wounded, what had he become? Repeating other people's words, those of his party, words fashioned in Moscow by men who were just as tainted by power; was that enough to fill his heart and mind? Being a flawless voice, a weapon, a certainty; did that give him the right to lead others? Still a gulf between us. Different from the old one but just as deep. Being a walk-on was indeed my choice, my unglamorous solution, the only possible one for me.

I was still meeting Pierre de Beuil, Lanvoni, Bernard, learning that the peace was still disintegrating and new tin soldiers being set up behind this stage setting, the next act was already beginning.

"You noticed Laval's silence," Bernard was telling me. "Don't be deceived by that. They say he's pushing Pétain. You understand the maneuver, Pétain will be the Hindenburg of the French Republic, simple, isn't it?"

As in 1922, as in 1933. I listened, passed on to Lanvoni.

"First rate, Naldi. The spot is spreading. The fruit is rotting," Lanvoni said.

He was drinking his coffee delicately, looking up at me smiling, playing the part of someone about to win.

"When the moment comes, we'll hand them the bill."

He identified himself with power, fascism, history. He took his roots from them, like Alatri or Pierre de Beuil. I was interested in Maud, Morin, myself.

"You remember Maud Kaufman," Bernard was saying. "She's disappeared. Jacques Morin's been found out. Cut his ties with the Comintern. And the other fool has gone off to get herself shot in Spain."

"Dead?"

"I don't know. But it's inconvenient to be a Trotskyist out there."

He laughed, aiming his folded fingers at me.

"If the Frankists don't get you, the moschettieri will. Little cunt. As if getting screwed weren't enough for her!"

Be quiet. Think of Maud, her short arms, the toss of her head to move her hair to one side. Maud, there history was flesh and blood. I telephoned Emilia, who still hadn't seen her.

"She's mad," she kept saying, "I'm sure she's in Spain. This war is driving you all out of your minds!"

Maud: one of the shapes I saw being dragged out of the ruins of Barcelona one evening when I had gone into a cinema to get away from my obsessive thoughts. But the present leaped out of the newsreels, sirens, screaming, buildings collapsing in a cloud of dust, the streetcars in Barcelona derailed and overturned and the bodies being dug out of the rubble. I went out, the film had hardly frosted over those images, I walked, crossed all Paris, nocturnal Paris, futile and hustling, went from street to street, sometimes from body to body, the geography of my weariness and loneliness.

One evening in May, in a cinema over on the boulevards I

recognized the self-satisfied strut of Ciano, the Duce was welcoming Hitler to Rome and on the Piazza Venezia fascist militia paraded in goose-step, a grotesque posture copied after Nuremberg. Somebody sitting near me shouted, "Carnival!" A happy, hardly aggressive voice, a scatter of applause, laughter, and different images already, a fashion show, white cars, a woman in a bathing suit and approving whistles from the house. I didn't wait for the feature. Went back out onto the boulevards, late afternoon, horns, women alone, blue filtered light, that mild, light peace, in suspension. Walked to the rue du Bac. Too many truths to shout. One day the carnival in Rome and Berlin would come dancing here: Beuil, Bernard, Laval, Pétain were getting the production ready. Then their laughter would freeze on their faces, but who listens to Cassandra?

Rue du Bac. Home. Too early, cats in the courtyard lying in the last rectangle of sunlight. I was like one of those stormy days on the plains near Magliano when you wait for the sky to burst at last. Sometimes, as this evening, I even wanted the war to start. Because then everything might be simpler for all of us. I telephoned Provi, hoping for an invitation to dinner. The Provis were out. The servant said, "I'll tell Monsieur you rang as soon as he comes in."

An illusion of peace at the Provis'. A semblance of order and security. And why not marry Angela? Forget questions. Go to sleep. Cigarette after cigarette; leafing through books. The phone. Provi. Let it ring or answer? A gesture. The receiver in my hand.

From the far end of that tunnel of months, the depths of that Spain where she died in my thoughts a hundred times, and was buried, all the way to the interrupted sentence on the pont Sully. It was Maud, ringing from a café.

"You're never at home."

She had tried to reach me several times, in the evenings, and it had to be this chance, those newsreel pictures, that brought our voices together at the end. She wouldn't keep me long, she said.

"I don't have a phone yet, you know, I've moved, changed my life a little."

She laughed.

"A little bit because of you, you remember, some valuable information, very accurate, I wanted to thank you."

She mustn't stop talking, I mustn't lose her again, it seemed as though all the words I had accumulated, everything I had wanted to say to Alatri, to Nitti, to Provi, to the friends I didn't have and couldn't have, I might be able to say to her. Maybe because she was one of those Lanvoni called the conquered, those who choose to lose, because she was a long way from power, from the reigning powers, red or black, and then she had been betrayed. I needed her. I was becoming increasingly certain of it with every vibration of her voice.

"I must let you go," she began.

She must not let me go because she was alive and she was talking. I insisted, she kept piling up dodges that weren't really refusals. At last, her address, rue du Cherche-Midi. I laughed, the street so close to me, such an odd name.

She laughed too. "I'll leave you now."

She mustn't leave me. I began holding open the sentences she was trying to close, pushing out another idea, another word. Finally she gave in. A few hours to wait, I was in the street. We were going to have dinner together. Chance giving me one tiny chink in the wall. At the end of a narrow green path, four floors to climb, steep and gloomy. No name on the door, a hesitation, the door opens. Maud, bare arms, tanned, small.

"I heard you coming up and I didn't know with that courtyard if you'd find the way."

She ran her hand through her hair.

"A mess here . . . you wanted to come."

Clothes on a chair, suitcases, and the sky like a blue panel behind the glass bay. A balcony, a studio that reminded me . . .

"I lived on the Dorotheenstrasse across from the Tiergarten, a studio like this, belonged to a Jewish sculptor, Meyerson, gone to London."

She picks up clothes, disappears in the narrow inner staircase, talks to me from the loggia.

"You were right about Jacques," she said, "but you know he wasn't very dangerous, in fact I think he'd been caught in his own trap, he loved me, I loved him too, that was that. Excuse me a minute."

A creak, she was opening a cupboard.

"That's all," she resumes. "Jacques is a romantic. We turned the page, he disappeared, gave up politics."

She was coming back down, a new dress, blue, moving easily: "We're both starting over, each on his own. But thanks."

"And Spain?"

She sat down across from me, elbows on her knees, face in her fists.

"Spain's lost, the revolution's lost. They're all ganging up together to strangle us. I was fired at in Barcelona, I'm a Trotskyist, I've got the plague, more dangerous than a Frankist. But they'll fight to the end. And the real war will start. Everything points that way, doesn't it?"

Maud got up, set down a glass near me. What was she saying? She was talking about Austria, Hitler wanted to annex it, the Sudetans threatened, Trotsky hunted, Stalin slowing down the revolution. Then the persecutions. Her father hadn't been able to leave Germany. What was she saying? What you read in the papers, what I was thinking, but she gave life to the words so often pronounced, worn out, and I liked to see her, to follow the movement of her lips.

"It's gone completely dark," she said all of a sudden, interrupting herself and getting up. "I'll put on a light."

She passed near me as I was getting up too and because we needed each other, us, our hands, bodies, voices, we found ourselves next to each other, her hair against my mouth, her head on my chest. The sweetness. To talk, my mouth against her breasts, and her skin. The sweetness of her voice, peaceful when she talked a long time later when the night was there for good and I was lying next to her on the unmade bed.

"A funny story," she was saying.

Voice slow. She was smoking, a red dot above her face.

"Don't you think?"

Too many words in me, bumping into each other, my life like a flood forcing its way out, I had to tell. But I liked her voice, soothing, telling me too, and in a Berlin in revolt I followed a little girl running after her father among the sailors and soldiers who believed in the revolution.

"I was ten," she was saying, "it was in '18 or '20, in the winter, I thought the sailors were giants."

She talked and we let the night glide past, sometimes interrupting it because our bodies were talking another language that slowly stopped our voices. The day woke us. Me first. I didn't know this peace, the pleasure of having shared, shared, a new word, my body, my life, and having received, to share, Maud's body and life.

"A funny story," she said, stretching beside me.

She was watching me, one elbow on the bed.

"I wonder if it really will be a funny story."

She didn't give me time to answer, she was already leaping out of bed, naked and happy.

"What do you have in the morning? Coffee, tea?"

Maud was calling from the kitchen below. I went on lying there. From the loggia all I could see was sky, caught between a roof and the ceiling, I felt at home like at Magliano with that night already behind me, profound as a continuous past. I went down naked, with a new body it seemed natural not to hide.

And we hid nothing. For the first time I was confessing my interrogations, doubts, monologue, my history to a woman. She talked about herself. We poured our memories together. And for a few weeks we forgot the present. Paris was in the sovereign soft light of May. We went away two or three days every week, along straight roads tunneling into forests. I had notified Provi, who replaced me at work. Maud had managed to get a free-lance job at her paper, so it was possible for her to leave Paris.

Early in the morning we would come out of a village inn, walk in the woods, Maud swiftly ahead of me, and I liked to follow her, to imagine the movement of her nervous legs under her skirt. What she liked was a panorama, a boulder or hummock from which you could see the forest like a woolly dark sea, and what she wanted was the wind in her face.

"Space," she said, "I need space. Paris stifles me. Space, wind, that is freedom."

She inhaled loudly, laughing.

"Breathe, breathe," she told me.

She moved over closer.

"I'm not making any demands on you yet, but don't think I've forgotten what you are, you're nothing but a fascist."

She put her arms around my waist and squeezed until it hurt.

"Is it worse than a Moscow spy? Explain to me, Marco, why do I, who am so definite and uncompromising, why do I attach myself to twisted creatures like you and Jacques? Why?"

We went back to Paris at the beginning of the week. I left Maud at rue du Cherche-Midi and returned to my courtyard, cats, and concierge, who held out an armful of papers.

"Things are bad, you know, they're mobilizing."

Big black letters, the shadow of war on the front page. Hitler threatening to invade the Sudetens. France calling up the reserves. The telephone rang. Maud.

"Have you seen? It's war."

I reassured her. War of course, someday, but I didn't want to admit it, I would have had to choose.

"What are you going to do?" asked Maud. "You can't stay with them."

"Have to wait."

She hung up. Another war was beginning, between us. She wanted me to change camp, give up the embassy.

"We'll go to Norway or Mexico, we'll join the Old Man," she said.

Why should I choose Trotsky's camp? Because it was the loser?

"Maud, there aren't any camps, there's you and me, let's leave France if you want, but for Switzerland, to forget."

"Deserter!"

She became angry, insulted me, pushed me out of bed.

"That's what fascism does to a man, a broken reed, go to Spain, join the brigade, there!"

"To be a fool? Again?"

She lay back down beside me, cuddled against me, then I could talk to her about the peace that might last after all.

"We've got to wait, Maud."

Wait. I had been waiting for years. Now I knew those years hadn't been completely in vain. I knew it existed, that foreign body that soothes you, that other person who listens to you and who hears you, that woman who is not just a shape, a friend, a meeting in bed, but who seems to have come out of your childhood, a playmate, your adolescence, long ignored and suddenly discovered and you meet again. In Maud I found Giulia again. Different; but when I was telling Maud about the shed, the smell of apples, Giulia's wet hair, I seemed to be reminding her of things she knew too. Maud the witness of my life. With her I had closed the circle, understood that feeling that had driven mother to my father: "Your mother would have died," Emilia said to me once, "if she hadn't married your father." With Maud I had discovered my own time, my own country, with her I set foot on a peaceful island where days would flow past and when she said, that autumn of 1938 when we came back from Venice where we had spent a happy week talking and making love, when she said:

"And what if we had a son, Marco, to say we'll go on living, you know, to show we have faith?"

I knew I could accept it. But my reason kept inventing obstacles and I said nothing. Then Maud went on:

"A son, Phillip, Phillip Naldi, why not, can you imagine, Marco, what madness, you and me, a fascist and a Trotskyist!"

It was our soap-box opera, our farce, we played with it, laughed at it, and yet when the word took form, "A son,

Marco," where did my shiver come from, my anguish and joy?
A son. The word filled my chest, made me want to laugh. I did.
And yet I kept saying:

"We have to wait, Maud, wait."

Good sense, reason, Provi's advice. Fear and refusal, impos-
sibility of conceiving the future. War, what was it? Yet I had
seen the Reichstag burn, heard Beuil calling for the purifying
violence, to purge Paris and France.

"My dear Naldi, Jewish blood must flow. They are the killers
of God, France must be purged, there are no other words."

Italian bombardiers were flattening Barcelona, the wall of fire
was moving across Europe. Hitler was in Prague, then Madrid
fell. Maud held out the papers:

"Read, read it aloud if you dare."

I read. On the Piazza Venezia the black bawling parade,
swords of the militia raised to heaven, Mussolini welcoming the
legionnaires on their return from Spain. The Duce showing an
atlas to the crowd: "This atlas has been open for three years to
the page of Spain," he shouted. "Now that is enough. But I
already know I must open it at another page." "Duce, Duce,
Duce," chanted the militia, waving posters on which you could
read "Nizza, la Savoia, la Tunisia," and the word that was my
sickness, "*Guerra!*" Maud was angry again:

"Well, say something, what do you have to say about it, you
read their speeches and believe in peace, you dare?"

I wanted to believe in peace, believe it was possible not to
lose Maud, not to enter the savage time when men grappled
and killed one another. I tried to take her in my arms. I said:

"Maud, you know . . ."

Then she insulted me, called me spy, fascist, murderers' accomplice, bastard. It was still spring. A year already since I had
found her. I looked at Paris, rue du Cherche-Midi, white and
respectable, Paris I could glimpse beyond a wall. I wanted
Maud and me to be, both of us, just two of those passersby,
seemingly without a past, their lives set in their habits, who
walked across streets and times and wars. But one day Maud

had learned, when, maybe in Berlin in the twenties, because of Karl Kaufman, the father who was lost in nazi Germany, Maud had learned to look beyond a street, a district, beyond her own life. And I knew she was right when suddenly, breaking, she sobbed into my arms.

"They don't see anything, they don't understand anything. And you don't understand anything either, Marco."

I did understand, I did know. But I kept trying not to reach conclusions, to stretch out the time that was left to us. To live to the end that vague compromise in which I had been wading for years. And then I imagined there was still a chance, in spite of everything, war might not come in spite of the Duce and his shouting, Italy might stay out of it.

"I'm confident," said Laborderie. "Hitler is isolated. He won't fight for Danzig. Prague of course, but Warsaw is like striking Paris, Moscow, London and Rome too. No, I'm confident, the Duce is a bastard but he's a shrewd politician, he began in the Socialist party, didn't he?"

Laborderie. I wanted to believe him. Paris was so calm. But Maud was growing nervous, irritable. She insisted that I choose and not wait any longer.

"I need to know," she said.

She was losing weight, tense, a line across her forehead, at peace only when making love, as though oblivion filled her then. I asked her.

"Why, there's no hurry. I swear that when I have to, I'll . . ."

"Decide now."

It is not easy to cut a life in two. To know one is going to cross a frontier that can't be crossed; before, after. I had Magliano, Venice, my memories fastened to a row of poplars and a shed back there. The land my mother lay in. My land, my country, my family. Words I didn't say aloud but they were turning into a single face, mother's, or sometimes father's, or Giulia's. And I couldn't make up my mind never to see Magliano again, or that I had to become something different. As I had done so often, I was waiting for other people to decide for me, waiting for war to force me to choose. But other people was Maud, impatient, exigent, absolute. I can see her, that April evening. Ciano had flown over Tirana. The king of Albania, betrayed, had fled to the mountains with his young wife. I knew from Lanvoni that Ciano, entertaining a few close friends, had stated, laughing, "King Zog will give in. I am counting heavily on the impending birth of his child. Zog loves his wife. . . . Frankly, I can't imagine Geraldine, nine months pregnant, running through the mountains in the middle of a battle." But Zog and his wife were clambering up the steep paths as the fascist troops disembarked.

"Have you chosen?"

Paris was peaceful. She had given me her hand a moment, then tossing her hair to one side of her forehead she asked me to call a taxi. The line between her eyes was deep. She was staring at me, her lips tight together, her mind made up, and to me she looked like a sulking child who refuses to cry. Only this time, she didn't let herself go against me as she had done so often at her apartment or mine. She closed the taxi door. And then without raising her voice, as I was leaning over the open window:

"Marco, it's finished."

She was pregnant, she was leaving me. She kept the son, the word that frightened me and gave me joy. With one sentence she left me completely alone. I was without her and there was my monotonous solitary voice again talking endlessly inside me. Paris overnight was sinister, a stream of closed doors, dead valleys, mute faces. A night, a day. Hardly time to look for her. To make sure, because Emilia and Laborderie talked to me about her, that Maud had existed anywhere except in my memory. Had been real. And then I was deported, an inspector came with me as far as Modane, I was crossing the frontier, looking at Manacorda again, the fascist militia, Venice and the gondolier who was staring into the muddy greenish water in the Grand Canal and saying:

"The tide, dirty sea, sand everywhere this year, it's rising."

7

Magliano, the poplars and the shed, Maud lost who had never come here, but I was seeing her at every step. I had told her everything in my life and together, rue du Cherche-Midi, on those long Sundays we spent lying motionless on her bed in the loggia, we had taken inventory of all my memories. With her I had walked down the streets of the Berlin of her memory, then Boston, where she had lived for a few years. Now she was with me, part of these blurred images of mother and Giulia. I avoided Nitti, locked myself into my wanderings, past, dream, future. Mrs. Nitti made dinner for me and served it to me in the big room on the black table. She didn't say much because with one look, as soon as I arrived, she saw that I had come to sit in a corner, my head between my arms, and sick animals are best left alone. She just shook her head, wiped a tear with the back of her hand because for her, since 1917, since Giulia, every day was a wound. Sometimes at the end of a meal, before she left, I would take her by the shoulder and pat her on the back.

"Don't worry, Mrs. Nitti, don't worry."

It was myself I was trying to comfort. I went out, walked, sat with my back against the shed. The sun had warmed the stones and above the trees I followed the cottony stream of white spring clouds. I went out heading nowhere yet every day I ended up on the path to the cemetery, the grille, the gravel walk straight in front of me and way at the end, almost up against the gray wall, the little squat house, the tomb of the Naldis and in front of it two slabs, one already worn and the other insolently shiny, new, father and mother side by side. I went back, through the village, asking the postman. I had sent telegrams to Maud, Laborderie, Emilia. Only Emilia had answered. She had gone to the rue du Cherche-Midi. Maud had moved out one morning in two or three hours and then vanished. No address. Not a word. Then I wandered from one memory to another, from a trace to a sign, from the poplar-edged road to the shed and since Maud was nothing but a name now, a series of waves inside me, of despairs that never dared to become sobs breaking on a shore, I mixed her up with my other memories. She came into the shed with me in the days when I loved Giulia, I ran along the buildings with her and across the courtyard, I imagined her sitting at the table. And sometimes, not knowing any more where was the beginning and the center of my pain, I imagined she was that, too.

I didn't read the papers, I had gone to earth and was rotting. In the evening I put a book in front of me and tried to escape through some other thought but all it took was one word, one emotion to bring me back like a boomerang crashing into my own despair. Yet I knew I would have to tear loose from the self-indulgent gray spiral I was wrapping around myself. Or else dig in for good. Deliberately. Two or three nights I walked the countryside with the temptation to silence the questioning voice, with one squeeze of a finger and one shot to join the tomb of the Naldis at the end of the straight gravel walk. Two or three nights of adding up balance sheets of misfortunes, circumscribing doubts and frustrations, measuring, mostly, the depth of the pain, mother, Giulia, father, and maybe Maud as well, all dead for me, life escaping, the arms you hold out too late to people who have turned cold as stones. Was that my only real question, my one authentic wound, death staring back at that adolescent in the hospital in Venice, father's cheeks covered with fuzz that looked like mold. But I had seen that soldier's head opened like a fruit by a shell in the trench, more than once I had held death in both hands, but that wasn't enough to make me admit it. It was an obscure, denied, evident presence. End oneself to get away from it. Get away from the faked game, life, history. Two or three nights I hesitated. It seemed to me that I owed nothing any more. I could flee without leaving a mess. Mother dead too. Maud lost. The son she didn't think me worthy of. So why not? Put an end to the weariness and doubts. Before the war that was coming, that I wasn't responsible for but it would involve me. Why not? One man less, me. Who had no importance for anyone but me now. A death limited to myself, the image of my own life.

Two or three nights I hesitated. The last one I took father's gun out with me. Not sure. I was coming to the end of the interrogation. A very clear, almost a white night. I crossed the courtyard. Matteroni's dog didn't like me and barked furiously. I began walking toward the shed, the poplars. Footsteps behind, catching up with me, Nitti. His hand toward his hat in a gesture of greeting, then he walked beside me, stooped, hands in the pockets of his corduroy trousers, his shoes scraping the dry earth. We walked on, side by side, toward the end of our fields, there where he had started talking about the war from the top of the fill. I stopped, not sure what to do. He rolled a cigarette, held it out to me, rolled another for himself. I knew his big copper lighter, the tall flame.

"Better for you to go away," he said. "Magliano, right now . . ."

Shook his head.

"No good to you."

I was leaning against a tree, Nitti in front of me in the middle of the path, smoking slowly in the glow of the night.

"If I was your age, with your education and if I was where you are, you think I'd let them do whatever they please? And then . . ."

He turned up his jacket collar:

"To be able to understand, to see, where you are you must know lots of things, even if you don't do anything, one day you can tell it. Don't you feel the damp? We'll catch our death out here, and it would be stupid to die like that for nothing."

We went slowly back. Nitti stopped in front of the shed.

"You remember in '17? I threatened you but I knew you wouldn't turn me in. Men are like trees, they grow straight or crooked. You grew straight."

Now we were in the middle of the courtyard.

"And you should have grown crooked, look around, where you are, people like you. And to think for once there was a straight one."

He laughed. When had he laughed before?

"Don't you feel the damp? We'll go to bed."

Hit my shoulder.

"Come on, we'll go to bed," he said again.

Early the next morning I left for Rome. I didn't see Nitti again, at dawn he was out in the fields.

There was the big apartment on the Piazza Barberini, the soft Roman colors and that first evening I stayed leaning on the balcony for long hours, watching the colors fade and angles and roofs, calm, knowing I could go on living with the memory of Maud as I had consented to go on living with those of father, Giulia, mother. I watched the sky darken, zone after zone like a tide rising imperceptibly, creeping farther up the sand every time, the night coming, the first calm night I was to spend since my return to Italy. At Magliano I had gone through another barrage, behind were all the others I had passed, accepted, milestones in a life, often a death was their sign, father, mother, Giulia, but also a body yielding, the whore at the Aquila Nera, Elsa my first woman long beside me, Anne too, then Maud, the revelation of our bodies, the joyful need she had for me and I for her, love then, passion then, the worn-out words new for me thanks to Maud. Then another barrage at Magliano and life that a single shot can exhaust, one gesture, a river draining into a chasm. I'd got through that, a gaping crack, thanks to a few words of Nitti, to chance, to my own impetus. And there I was on the balcony, the night gradually covering Rome, there, older and more hollow, with a feeling of settling inside me but also an obstinate decision to live that would push me to the natural end of the game.

A calm night then walking, the following days, along the Forum, on the Via dell'Impero that had been opened up and led to the ochre Forum wall, between cypress and marble. I was waiting for an interview with Ciano, who wanted to see me. Listening to the rumors exchanged in low voices in the cafés on the Via Veneto; Ciano had turned anti-German, he was afraid of the war in which the nazis might easily involve us.

"We're not ready," said Manacorda, following his chief. "The military people are all bluff, tragic bluff, Naldi, the Duce is being misled. In Albania the count saw how disorganized our troops were."

True, I felt a quiver of independence in Rome, an intuition that the alliance with Berlin would lead to disaster. But it was only a soft whisper of words. Goering had been welcomed in triumph, had just left Rome. Ribbentrop had been received by Ciano in Milan. The count, Manacorda, like me, we bent our heads accepting, each carrying his excuses around inside, his reasons, his personal diplomacy. We were all obedient Machiavellis. I felt I wasn't going to be able to do it much longer, was going to have to end the compromise. Choose a straighter way, more bitter one. I'd understood that too, those nights at Magliano.

It was Manacorda who ushered me into the count's office in the Palazzo Chighi. He introduced me, holding my arm, protective and friendly.

"Your Excellency, here is our deportee, Marco Naldi."

Ciano had put on weight, his expression was sullen and a little weary, the shadow of a smile, his eyes veiled.

"Naldi, it's been years . . ."

He waved me to a chair.

"Berlin, Paris: you're the eternal outcast, they're always throwing you out."

He got up from his desk and came to sit across from me. His

face looked bloated, like a spoiled child granted his every whim and caprice.

"Which way's the wind blowing in Paris, what are people saying, ready to fight?"

Paris pacifist, Paris apathetic. If the Germans want Hitler let them have him and leave us alone. If the Germans demand Danzig, after all it's a German city, give it to them and leave us alone. That's Paris, Paris consumed by gangrene, the Paris of Bernard, Beuil, Laval, and Pétain.

I talked, thinking about Maud, Laborderie, the thousands of men who had followed the coffins of Salengro and Calvini in silence. But why recall those faces, their breath like mist over their heads, the raised fists and the huge portrait of Calvini carried by the men. They were those thousands, the losers: Paris, the official and anonymous Paris, the Paris that accepted, the Paris of common sense and the easy way—that Paris wanted peace.

Ciano listened, rose, shrugged.

"That may be, but what they're going to get is war."

A few steps.

"They want to win the lottery without buying a ticket. That's the French for you. And François-Poncet says it himself. Did you know him in Berlin?"

I had often seen him at embassy receptions, elegant, chatting with Ferri. Ciano seemed to be thinking.

"Naldi, your trouble in Berlin," he started, "that affair."

"Ingrid von Wirth, Your Excellency, could I let a woman be murdered?"

Now he was speaking to Manacorda.

"Then add Naldi to the list of our delegation to Berlin. And refuse to take him off it, even if they insist. We're not their valets."

He turned back to me.

"They think we're polishing their boots, well, no; you'll look after the press."

That was Ciano's defiance. But when, walking alongside Hitler in the whirlpool of uniforms, the reflections of the chandeliers on the marble of the new halls, huge, austere, chilly, of the Reich Chancellery, Ciano moved forward between two rows of helmeted SS, the sullenness had faded from his face. I was far behind, at the rear of the procession beside Antonetti, but I could see the back of Ciano's head, sometimes his profile, he was as I had seen him in the newsreel that evening already so long ago when Maud had telephoned me for the first time. He sat down, the film projectors dazzled me, he signed the Pact of Steel, our chain, a chain around Europe, me, Maud, Nitti, millions. Then we met him back at the embassy, loquacious, pleased with himself, speechifying.

"This is the first time," he was saying, "I've seen that woman Ingrid von Lappers, twenty years old, regular features, splendid body, the Fuehrer can't take his eyes off her. They are seeing each other privately. Absolutely beautiful, just a girl, you can tell, but a woman's body already. All the better, the Fuehrer is becoming humanized, coming down from the mountaintops."

Then there was the Ribbentrop-Goering incident. Ciano laughed:

"Naldi, you who know Goering so well; there were tears in his eyes when he saw Ribbentrop with the collar of the *Annonciade*. Von Mackensen had to listen to a whole scene afterward, Goering stamping his feet, 'I was the one who deserved that decoration.' . . ."

The laughter tore my throat but I pretended to be gay too. But Goering, but Ribbentrop, but these men, who had taken to themselves the powers of gods, one day, whatever the cost, they would have to kneel down and bow their heads, they who shouted, "Shoot the pig, shoot him."

I had one more evening to spend in Berlin, went back to my old haunts, the Tiergarten, Dorotheenstrasse. The studio looked lived-in, brilliantly lit; above, von Baulig's apartment closed, a black bar across the façade. Merry Groves had asked me to dinner, Strang dropped in. He was sick of Berlin, the noise of boots, concentration camps, Jews still trying to escape; sometimes one managed to get inside the embassy but he had to go back out again and usually was seen no more. Suddenly I had a hope, believed in chance.

"Karl Kaufman, an architect, socialist, do you . . . ?"

Strang searched his memory, said he'd have to see in the embassy, but offhand he didn't recall. I asked him to look, write me in Rome. Without reason, because I didn't know where Maud was. But it was one more tie I could hold out to her, to her past life that had become mine. Then Strang left and Merry and I stayed behind, deep in armchairs on either side of the cone of light from a lamp.

"So; your life?" Merry asked me.

She hadn't changed much. She was the kind of woman you told yourself wasn't young any more but you found her child-like. The smile, maybe, the very short hair. Merry looked a little like Maud, an unfinished Maud without the energy, the personality, the color.

"My life? Yours first," I said.

We laughed. And began drinking lukewarm whiskey.

"I wear glasses now when I type, apart from that, nothing. . . ."

She took a long drink, her eyes seeming to disappear in the glass.

"Strang? A friend?"

"A faithful friend. A good comrade," she said without looking at me.

I saw the void inside her deepening, I knew the feeling of being unable to catch hold of life as it goes by, it's slipping past, you know it, you see it, and there's this glass window, transparent though, but you keep hitting against it and your hands stay open, flat against the cold glass. On the other side is the other person, the others, inaccessible.

"And you?" she asked.

She was trying to smile.

"You're more self-assured," she went on, "calmer. A woman? Am I wrong?"

I would have liked to say, my wife, to tell her, explain to Merry that even now, when she was gone, Maud had left me more than a name and the stir it always caused inside, she had left me different, I knew someone else existed who hadn't given birth to you but was still flesh of your flesh. Another to share with. That discovery stayed inside me. Helped me to understand Merry, too, even Nitti. But how was I going to say all that to Merry?

"Yes and no. I lost her," I said.

Merry gave me another drink.

"Marco, I think we're loners. You're luckier than I am but you're still there alone, like me. Who was it?"

Merry had crossed her path in '38 in Barcelona when she had had to leave Berlin for a few days for a story. They stayed in the same hotel.

"The only one, everybody stayed there, you used candles during the alerts."

She knew Maud wrote for *Le Populaire*.

"Not pretty, Barcelona," said Merry. "It almost made me homesick for Berlin. Maud came in one evening, I remember, she'd been fired at from a car outside the hotel. Communists, Trotskyists, anarchists, they're all at each other's throats. Not nice."

Lift up the flag, underneath a pus-filled wound. But if that's the law. Of history. Like death is the law of life.

"Aren't you trying to find her?"

I explained Maud's decision, my deportation, the silence.

"You didn't dare choose, she chose for you. You cared more about the past than about the future and now you've got nothing."

I let her go on hurting me. Her bitter revenge. But because she was trying to hit, her aim was good. I hadn't dared, tangled

up in my cautions, cowardices, my idea of Magliano; I had
traded Maud for some images, a precarious security I didn't even
want. But having lost her, I had learned. The lesson cost me a
lot. A hole in my life I'd nearly fallen into.

"I know," I said, "I know, Merry. Only, I'm not going to
be wrong any more, I'm becoming tougher with myself."

She began to laugh, hiccoughing a little because she had had
a lot to drink over the hours.

"Marco Naldi the intransigent, you can guess what that
means, it means risking your life. Your life, Marco."

She put down her glass and came over to me, not too steady,
her finger pointing, touching my chest.

"Your life, Marco, your life."

She slid her fingers inside my shirt. I took her on my knees,
I felt old, sympathetic, and detached. I held her and rocked her
like a baby.

"By-by, Merry, by-by."

She let herself go, laughing, putting her whole hand on my
skin.

"Marco, why?"

She stopped laughing and repeated:

"Marco, why?"

Why was there only the connivance of habit between us,
friendly and superficial, why the sense of failure Merry carried
inside her when, after a few drinks in the middle of the night,
came the time for nondeforming mirrors and confessions, why
could I do nothing, why did our bodies, though, skin against
skin, go to each other and why did we let them go, without
illusion and almost without pleasure?

We parted in the vague dawn, Merry holding out her cheek
to kiss:

"Bye, Marco, if war comes you'll see me in Rome again."

She hugged me:

"They scare me here," she went on, "neutral or not, with
them the laws of war . . ."

I went back to the embassy, the delegation, the official carriages on the train, listening to Ciano and Manacorda. We got to Rome. Crowd on the platform, officers' commands, dignitaries, Ciano pirouetting about to offer his face, salute, hand. A localized belch, satisfied and loud, some decorated passions; but a few hundred yards from the station the calm, peaceful city. At home, a letter from Emilia. Maud had come by, heavier, Emilia said so I would understand. Emilia told her about my deportation, my telephone calls the last day. Maud was not really listening. "She was play-acting," Emilia wrote, "you know how proud she is." But all I saw in the letter were the last lines: "Maud has decided to go to the United States. She didn't leave any messages for you. She's as mad as ever."

Frontiers and the coming war: as if those obstacles weren't enough. Now there was distance, too, losing her for good because I knew nothing about the country she said she was going to. I couldn't even imagine her there. Then began a dreary time in a mute, indifferent Rome. Sometimes I rang Merry. I couldn't stand not to talk any more. Sometimes I drank, methodically, to reach the peak where there is nothing in front of you except night like a moving ocean. Sometimes I spent hours at one of the terraces on the Via Veneto. I would hang on to a face, a woman, Manacorda too. Through him I could glimpse Ciano whose reflection he was, could measure the anxiety of the minister and his jackals. Their triviality, hesitations between servility and realism. Manacorda waved his hand when he saw me:

"Ciao, Naldi."

Sat at my table, leaned toward me.

"Extraordinary," he began.

Mussolini had just seen the new ambassador from England. A dignified, pink and blond gentleman.

"The Duce was so violent," Manacorda went on.

Rubbed his hands. I could imagine the stupefied Briton trying to recover his breath all along the long walk I too had taken across the Sala del Mappamondo in the Palazzo Venezia, my heels echoing on the marble. The Duce hadn't even looked up, hadn't answered the ambassador. And Manacorda was laughing.

"Percy-Lorraine," he was saying, "he was red, apoplectic, twitching with a nervous tic. He looked like a man who had been slapped in the face, he was talking to himself. Slapped."

Their victories. Trivial. Listening to them, following events, persuading myself that war really was the disease of these bespangled men, they needed it, and that individual murders were no longer enough for them, I decided Maud was right to get out of Europe. Let her go away, she and the son I would not see, far away from our madness. Then I began to worry again: had she really left Europe, or was that just a story, to put me off the trail? For I couldn't imagine her giving up, letting people fight on alone here, running away from the rising tide of war that was submerging Ciano and Manacorda. They were struggling now, caught in their own trap.

"It's not possible, Naldi, Hitler can't want to go to war over Danzig, too many risks," Manacorda argued. "He's bluffing, I'm certain of it."

Nevertheless, their faces were contorted with fear. If war really came it wasn't going to be another of those games you could play without risk, where you could pick up your chips and walk out, so they were trembling for themselves, for the power they held and were going to have to put out on the table, win or lose. In mid-August, Ciano decided to meet the Germans in Salzburg. He wanted to read his own future in the eyes of Ribbentrop and the Fuehrer. I went with them. Behind the windows of Fuschl Castle I saw Ribbentrop, impassive, walking with Ciano.

"Implacable players," Manacorda said.

In the evening we met in the bathroom of Ciano's room at the Oesterreichischer Hof in Salzburg. We turned on the faucets of the bathtub so the Gestapo couldn't pick up our conversation. Ciano, panting slightly, mopped his brow: heat, fear, a sudden awareness of his responsibilities, also the discovery that he was powerless.

"I said to Ribbentrop," Ciano began, "'What do you want, what does the Fuehrer want, Danzig or the Corridor?' And Ribbentrop, in his calm voice, 'More than that,' he said, 'dear Ciano, more than that, we want war.'"

Ciano drank, exploded:

"No matter what they're given," he went on, "they'll attack anyway, they're possessed by a demon of destruction."

Salzburg was wreathed in humidity, it seeped through the hotel, stuck to your skin. I went out and walked along the river where there was a cooler breeze coming down from the Alps. Cars were parked near the Oesterreichischer Hof; even in that heat the men standing by them, leaning on the cars, wore their long leather Gestapo coats. They were protecting us. Like they protected me in Berlin. One of them walked behind me, openly. Maud: let her lose herself, forget me, flee this Europe and these men. How could I find out where she was, make her understand? If I could be sure she'd gone to the United States. The questions came back when Ciano talked, during official banquets, in the great hall of Fuschl Castle hung with gloomy tapestries, halberds, and old swords. Helmeted SS motionless between suits of armor. Only the clink of forks and glasses and Ribbentrop's voice suddenly.

"Dear Ciano, I'll make a bet with you, clear, precise, fair."

Silence. Ciano's eyes questioning.

"Here it is," Ribbentrop went on; "if the English and French intervene in our war with Poland you win a collection of antique weapons, if not you give me an Italian painting."

Ribbentrop leaned back against the high wooden chair:

"I'll let you choose the period, dear Ciano."

Von Mackenson, the German ambassador to Rome, shook his head.

"I'm afraid . . ." Ciano began.

"No, no, don't be a pessimist, my dear, you'll get your weapons."

"Antique?" Ciano asked sourly.

Ribbentrop laughed.

"You Latins are never serious."

Then Ciano saw the Fuehrer at Berchtesgaden, the maps of Poland already spread on the table facing the mountains. The Fuehrer, pointing out the axis of his future offensives with a ruler, hardly listening to Ciano's questions. Bormann and Ribbentrop flanking their master.

"He's irresponsible," Ciano said that evening.

The count was sitting on the edge of the bathtub, depressed and humiliated. Manacorda, his back to the wall, was watching him in terror. I was in the doorway. Water was running in the bathtub. These are the men who decide the fate of nations.

"He called me a Latin, him too," Ciano went on. "Well, in that case I can't understand why he, the Fuehrer, has this pressing need for wood from the Polish forests. Do you hear?"

He got up.

"They've misled us, they've lied. But our hands are not tied. We must remain neutral."

Too late. The vise was tightening. The sky above Rome was red. At Magliano when Mrs. Nitti saw those splotches of blood dyeing the clouds in the hot plains twilight, she used to shake her head and cross herself. A red sunset presaged violence, disaster, hurricane. In Rome the sunset was red. I learned that Ribbentrop was flying to Moscow, Stalin and Hitler were shaking hands over Poland. If Maud had not left Europe she would be cornered, enemy of both, defeated before the war ever started. It was then that she wrote to me. She had gotten my address from Emilia and the letter was posted from Paris. Maud had thought it over, was wondering whether she had been right to leave me like that, with so few words. She had let time pass, to make sure. Now she was sure, she and I were not meant to be together permanently. It had been better to end it then. She wanted to write me this to terminate our "funny story" without ambiguity. Not a word about the United States, not a word about the child, not a word about what she intended to do. Just one last blow to finish me off.

I walked to the Palazzo Chighi, the newspapermen were shouting about the signature of the German-Soviet pact. Farcehistory, tragedy-history, putrescence-history. Maud, Alatri, Jacques Morin too, who had given his self, his face, to a faith that was now cynically shedding its veils. What had become of those thousands I had seen parading with upraised fists, what had become of Alatri, Gasparini? How did they explain this? And Maud wasn't leaving, Maud was caught, staying inside the mousetrap, in the morass.

I walked under the arcades of the Piazza Colonna and talked out loud to myself. In front of a newsstand two or three militia were bullying someone who had bought the *Osservatore Romano*, the organ of the Vatican that was being accused of something or other, pacifism or liberalism. I grabbed the sleeve of one of those men and shook it violently, shouting, "Haven't you had enough yet, haven't you had enough?"

People around moved away in astonishment. I was wearing decorations, intervening, I must be powerful. The militia moved off. I went on toward the Palazzo Chighi. Intransigence, the end of juggling with words; I was completing a period of my life, I would still see the journalists, but only for a few minutes more.

I was jumping into the mousetrap too. The time was coming when we would have to pay with our bodies. Get ready to be kicked. Give them your skin. Back in October 1917 I had known that moment of acting without thinking, had gone to the war like a kid running to meet his father, hanging on his neck asking to be picked up. Today, the same moment, again. Because I had shaped and transmitted too many words and, lined up one after the other, they made a long chain, now mine to wear.

In the evening there was a security blackout. Merry had just come from Berlin.

"It's due any time now," she said. "I didn't want to be caught there."

We leaned over the balcony on the Piazza Barberini. Above the rooftops a red sky striped with purple, the evening still clear but the Roman twilight was slowly strangling it after the flare of the day, like inevitable death.

"If war comes, I'm asking to be sent to the front."

Merry turns around.

"Are you serious?"

Silence.

"Are you doing that for Maud Kaufman?"

The question annoys me, I go back inside the apartment. Merry doesn't move. I'd like to tell her, but how clear is it to me? I begin. She soon cuts in.

"You're mixing everything up together, politics and passion. You're not a fascist any more. You're hurt because you were abandoned, you the father, the Latin, so now you're going to have your little tantrum. You're an eternal adolescent, Marco, if you were grown up you'd find a safe corner somewhere and wait until it's over."

"No, Merry."

Finding a safe corner means death and rot. That's what I am learning, it's taken me long enough.

She comes over, caresses my face and hair.

"I'm always moved by you," she says, "the older I get the more moved I am. So you're going to fight for the fascists, for the nazis, in their army? Great solution."

"Merry, just be like anybody, you understand, in the ranks with anybody."

"You're not just anybody, you can't help it."

I must be, though, if the time to die was coming, the time for smashed faces. I could have told Merry that, about the great slaughter, the trenches, all those who hadn't decided anything that other time, all the Carlos of the war, whose lives were rubbed out by a bullet and a thud. What right had I to protect my life, my skin, in the name of what pride? One dead man is worth as much as another. A universe disintegrating, with one blow things that hung together scatter, run apart, fall, die too. At Magliano, in mother's room, each thing in its place, a ball of black wool and red needles on the arm of a chair, lace doilies, a photograph in a gilded wood frame. She and father holding hands among the pigeons on the Piazza San Marco. She in a big hat with a rose on it, he with a walking stick. Nothing left, scattered stones, a world decomposed. And war going to trace its path among men, overturned, sliced, wiped out. All those worlds that each of them loved, the ties, the universes destroyed. I had nothing left, I who had marched in the wake of the conquerors, I was reduced to myself. I couldn't stay out when others, when Maud . . .

"You're a fool, Marco, a fool," Merry said.

The streetlights were turned on again in the Piazza Barberini, the geometry of the streets came back, dotted with winking lights, Italy was neutral. But war was driving into Poland, horsemen charging behind their lances and the horses' chests torn apart against the steel of Panzers. Warsaw fell. Ciano came back to Berlin, some people were already talking of a compromise peace.

"Hitler is either a visionary madman or a genius," said Ciano, hypnotized like a hunted animal.

I went on with my duties, the months passed, I waited, certain the war disease would infect the government. Merry believed in the neutrality, she was dreaming.

"After all," she said, "I adore Italy, why don't we get married, Marco? You don't mind me, at least I answer back."

I laughed. I was fond of Merry. She was already part of my past. I made promises, convinced they were pointless because war would come. We arrived together at the Villa Cantoni, where Ferri had moved after his recall from London. He was building up a following, criticizing the government, the Duce. He drew me aside, we walked along the patio colonnade. He was bald, heavy, wearing an English suit. Sweating. Time had murdered the young captain I had seen motionless in the rain at Magliano.

"Marco, one has to have the courage to face reality. Even Ciano has seen it. The one person responsible, the obstacle, is the Duce."

He lowered his voice.

"He's surrounded by a bunch of prostitutes and pimps, and syphilis, Marco, that's the key, syphilis."

Ferri was smoking a cigar, speaking English to Merry Groves. But the blond soldiers of the Wehrmacht, helmets dangling from their belts, were laughing now in the ripe wheat of the Beauce; and France, like the rotten fruit of Lanvoni's imagination, was letting itself be squashed.

In the first week of June the Duce called a meeting of the ministry staff in the Sala del Mappamondo.

"It's been decided," Manacorda murmured to me.

We crowded together, the Duce in uniform paced back and forth in front of us.

"Gentlemen," he began, "the battle is coming, His Majesty the cannon is about to speak again."

He turned his bulging eyes on us.

"From now on you are working for me."

Our group splits up and the Duce moves about among us. He takes Ferri's arm, I overhear a few words.

"The people only know how to follow, Ferri, they have to be directed, kept in uniform from morning till night, they need the stick, stick, stick."

Ferri smiling. Ferri silent. The Duce speaking loudly so we would all hear:

"The people are like a prostitute, she loves the strongest man."

We were going into the war, but France had already been cut

in half. Lanvoni came in from Paris, triumphant. Provi is pre-occupied. He stops by to see me often on his way back from the Palazzo Chighi. We drink with Merry.

"It will be a long war," he says. "The English will never give in. And then . . ."

He turns to Merry.

". . . there are the Americans, they'll come in."

Merry has begun to cry, quietly, no fuss, with dignity.

"You know Marco has applied for active duty," she says.

Provi looks at me, questioning. I nod, go out on the balcony. The June days are endless, they stretch out over Rome cloudless, the still light, twilight no more than a blue veil. Provi has come out to me.

"The dice are loaded, Marco, you know that; our military preparations are nonexistent, the men they sent to the Alps would have been massacred, luckily the French were already beaten. It will be worse than on the Piave in '17. You know that?"

I say yes.

"That's the thing. Because I do know."

"You're unforgivable, pull out of it, Marco, quickly."

"It's all done," I said, "I'm waiting."

Ciano and Manacorda had received my official application. But the war moved away again, French delegates came to Rome for the armistice. I went from the Villa Incisa to the Palazzo Chighi, where I talked to the journalists. Villa Incisa: in the distance, the ruins of the Empire, cypresses, and Noël, the French ambassador who goes past pale, playing nervously with his gloves, General Huntzinger behind him, clenched jaw, haughty, peaked cap in hand. They were signing the protocol of agreement. Days passed. Suddenly Rome burning under a white sky, like a reflection in a metal plate. July, the beginning of August 1940. Maybe I had missed my chance to break away. Maybe the war would be soaked up by passing time like a puddle of water by sand. Merry was hopeful, laughing again. We went to Ostia and lay on the beach.

"You're too old," she said, "forty, Marco, that's old for a soldier."

I renewed my application. Manacorda was annoyed.

"Out of the question, Naldi, out of the question just now. Lanvoni is going back to Paris and the count was thinking of . . ."

The rest of the sentence got lost. A chance to find Maud again, maybe, a hand held out, a reprieve.

"You can be useful there," Manacorda was saying.

I didn't say anything to Merry until I was sure, until the morning in mid-August when Ciano saw me in his dark office, shutters closed. The count was wearing an air force uniform, Lanvoni came in soon afterward, congratulating Ciano on his military exploits over Calvi, Bastia, Nice.

"A few bombing missions," said Ciano, "routine."

He was delighted. He opened a file.

"There are new men in Paris, and you know them, try to get in touch again."

I didn't have the courage to mention my application for active duty. The new men were Pierre de Beuil, Bernard, others I had met in Laval's circle at the time of the Ethiopian war. They held Paris, were already on the throne in this gorgeous August that glared down the empty avenues where the fanfares of the Wehrmacht resounded. I moved back into the rue du Bac. The cats were still in the courtyard, looking for shade now, hugging the walls or crouching under the tree. The very first day I went to the rue du Cherche-Midi, without illusions. But I did have illusions, they grew with every step in the street, on the steep staircase. Door closed. No name. I rang, knocked. It was ridiculous, but I had to go all the way and if I could have, I'd have kicked in the door to make sure Maud wasn't there spying on me, teasing or asleep. I had to go back down; the concierge was under the entrance, as on that morning in April 1939, the last day.

"I know you, remember you very well," she said.

She was leaning against her door.

"You coming back now?"

Wiping her hands on her dirty apron.

"Miss Kaufman?" I asked.

"The trouble I've had over that one . . ."

She moved as if to go back indoors.

"You ought to know because you're not French either, it's easy to tell, you know."

"If you don't want to say anything . . ."

My tone was threatening. I would have shaken her until she talked.

"Me, what difference does it make to me, that's a fine way to talk. First the French police came, several times, about a year ago that was, just after war was declared, only she was already gone, then a fortnight ago the others came, those men, the others, the Germans. You ought to know."

She shrugged.

"I'm not paid to know where tenants go when they move out."

Rue du Cherche-Midi, the passersby who walk across it and the era, the war. Soldiers trying to find their way from a subway map, rue de Rennes; the newspaper stand at the corner of the rue Notre Dame des Champs, the vendor's hat down over his ears, dead cigarette at the corner of his mouth. The same papers posted. I lose my way among these signs, this present that is only the end of my past. In *Le Matin*, at the bottom of the front page, an article: Trotsky supposedly assassinated in Mexico, with a mountaineer's pickax. My past breaking like that smashed head and here is the present spurting out. Maud hunted. They killed the one she used to call the Old Man, to whom she was supposed to lead Jacques Morin, who had agreed to be an assassin.

The present, Emilia embraces me, holds my hands.

"If you knew," she says weeping, "if you only knew . . ."

She has lost weight, her hair has gone white.

"They arrested me in August, the French, weeks in a camp, Italy was still neutral; afterward, they released me."

I let Emilia talk, but she interrupts herself.

"Have you come about Maud? She was supposed to go to the United States and then, mad as ever, she came here one day, I was just back from the camp . . ."

Emilia stops.

"She was pregnant, heavy, but it suited her, she looked younger, her face all filled out, an apple. I forget what she wanted, to find safe places for later, later, when the Germans would be here. I couldn't tell her anything. In her condition, mad, mad."

I walked through the streets, looked into the women's faces, Maud maybe, since chance had brought me this far, why not. I talked out loud, I resented her stubbornness, why wasn't she just a mother, curled around her son to be born, why wasn't she a woman hemmed in by the four corners of her own heart, I insulted her, idiot, madwoman, ass, trying to sacrifice herself, and her head would burst open too with a blow of a pickax or a bullet. The same day I went to the rue d'Ulm, to Laborderie. Door closed also. Another concierge, who took me into her room.

"Are you one of his friends? The Germans have already been several times. He must have known. He hasn't come back."

She talked softly, her eyes on the door. I leave a tip, which she tries to refuse.

"Just think; Mr. Laborderie," she keeps saying.

More soldiers around the Pantheon, standing in the middle of the square in the sun that is flowing down the rue Soufflot. The people walk furtively, keeping close to the buildings. A sudden anguish comes with the dusk and I try to drive it out by walking fast, crossing the Luxembourg, but it has me by the shoulders and won't let go. Maud, Laborderie, it's as though I'm feeling my way along like a blind man and my hand touches nothing but empty air. Return to Paris: not a reprieve, but final proof that Maud is lost. If I could I would leave tonight, put on a uniform, march in a row, anonymous, like just anybody. But I've got to see Bernard, Pierre de Beuil, try to renew connections.

"We must," Lanvoni was saying, "place our men. Not go against the Germans, but not drop out either. For the present, allies."

He was negotiating with the occupying authorities; I met Beuil at the office of a new paper, *La Volonté française*, which he was running.

"My dear Naldi, here you are at last."

He gets up, offers me a drink.

"We're rebuilding, believe me, the people who drove you out in such a disgraceful manner will pay for it. We're going to clean up Paris first, then France."

He was listening to his own voice. He didn't hear a word I said. He was talking about the New Europe.

"The Fuehrer has seen the importance of France very clearly. We must not disappoint him. And our good Ferri, I'm told he's turned antifascist since his stay in London?"

Pierre de Beuil laughed.

"I am informed. My own little police. And you, Naldi, what are your plans?"

The telephone rang, secretaries came in. Power for Beuil, at last. He came to the door with me.

"Come this evening, I'm counting on you, my home, a reception, just our people. You'll get back in touch with Paris."

My job. My last promises. Lanvoni and I went to Pierre de Beuil's home on the avenue Montaigne. Good-humored groups, Luftwaffe officers with pretty women, others pausing in front of eighteenth-century paintings, Bernard coming over.

"Naldi, Naldi, what a surprise, I didn't know you were back
in Paris."

We were no longer important. The masters, the providers of
money, were the occupiers. Lanvoni tried to approach Pierre
de Beuil, talk to him, but he was interested only in the officers
of the Wehrmacht, a glass of champagne in his hand.

"You remember," I began to Bernard.

I couldn't help it, if there was any chance, why not take it.

"Years ago you told me about a journalist, Maud Kaufman,
it's not really important but if you could . . ."

Bernard wrinkled up his eyes. I was exposing myself.

"She interests you? That little Jew, oh yes, the girl a Comintern
man had married, by the way you saw they got Trotsky, clever
and tenacious people, those OGPU killers. Do you want me to
find out? Maud Kaufman, I'll try, unless these gentlemen . . ."

With a smile he waved at the German officers.

". . . have already taken care of her, with a name like that
she's more for them than for you."

A weapon. To feel its weight in your hands, know one squeeze
is all it takes. That evening there was violence in my fingers. I
turned my back on Bernard. A woman smiled at me, blond, and
walked over.

"Don't you recognize me?"

"Anne, of course."

Of course. A few years to fill out her body, give her this ease,
this swaying walk.

"What are you doing here?"

The narrow world we move in, bumping into one another,
the privileged, the sheltered. I can't talk to her any more. Time,
a break, oblivion. She is someone else.

"And you?"

She laughs, mocking.

"I'm still in the fashion business," she goes on. "In Paris ele-
gance never loses its powers."

Anne talks, talks, the new paper, she has complete charge of the fashion pages, complete, she repeats. She was sitting next to me at Laborderie's that evening when Maud. And our interrupted holiday when war broke out in Spain.

"You haven't changed much," she says. "I was very much in love with you."

Laughs again.

"I was a silly girl discovering Paris. Ring me sometime."

Her hand lingers on my arm a moment. We lived together for weeks, then, Laborderie said, she tried to kill herself. Now we moved past each other scarcely remembering. I sat in a corner of the room. I could see Beuil surrounded by German officers, Lanvoni listening to Bernard, Anne Villemur followed by a young man who was too short for her and had to look up when he talked to her. Our futile gesticulations. One of the first things Maud had ever said, "I hate frivolous people." I hated them too that evening. Because of her, or of my amputated youth, dragged into the war. For years, though, I had tried to go with the current without paying much attention. To live on the surface. But what remained? Not even the image of one face. Anne hardly recognized, a mild embarrassment stifled by indifference. Nothing, in other words. As though the weeks, the pleasure we had truly experienced, had left nothing. A memory that matched the futility of our relationship. What you win, in life, depends on what you bet.

"You're very pensive, my friend."

Bernard was sitting beside me.

"I've been looking for you," he went on. "You spoke about that Maud Kaufman. I asked that fellow over there, *Sonderfuehrer* Maier."

He pointed to an officer with a turned-up mustache and heavy tortoise-shell glasses.

"He is in charge of the *Propaganda Staffel* and he knows his people, because he was a journalist in Paris before."

Bernard laughed.

"They are remarkable, they had everything planned. But your

Kaufman, vanished, my dear, and I am led to believe they looked for her very carefully, they wanted her badly."

A chance for Maud, to escape. Maybe she had gone to Jacques Morin's house in the unoccupied zone, at Arles.

"If you have any information for them, they're interested."

There was nothing more for me to do in Paris, but I hung on nearly two months. The city was quiet, cyclists pedaled by, one heard sounds of voices and footsteps, sometimes of fife and drums. The red emblem with the black insignia floated above the buildings. I met Beuil, Bernard, others. I saw the first rally of the Volontaires Français. Beuil shouting into a microphone, facing an audience of uniforms: "We shall remake France, we shall build Europe, a purified Europe, cleansed of the Jewish gangrene." The carnival of Rome and Berlin had reached Paris. From Rome, Merry wrote that she was trying to get permission to come to Paris. I didn't discourage her, but for me the reprieve was ending. War over London, war in Egypt. The dead. I couldn't juggle words any more, chat in drawing rooms while other men were dying in the sand. I renewed my application to Lanvoni, who thought it was a matter of patriotism.

"Naldi, I understand you, a soldier's place is at the front. I wanted to take part in the Ethiopian war, but this is a front here, too."

Merry came for forty-eight hours. We went through Paris in the autumn. The horse races had started again at Auteuil. Elegant ladies and officers in the russet light of the weighing-in post.

"I can't imagine war," Merry said as she left for Rome again.

A few days later the Duce ordered an attack on Greece. And the first defeat. I decided to go back to Italy. I went over my old tracks once more, rue du Cherche-Midi, rue du Bac. A farewell with no regrets, Paris was a desert for me. Emilia kissed me.

"Don't get yourself killed," she said.

"I'm too old now to die in a war."

"If Maud . . ."

"Tell her we'll meet afterward. And that she's mad. And also that I've decided to hate frivolous people."

Emilia didn't understand. Besides, I didn't think she would be seeing Maud again. Lanvoni gave me permission to go. Rome again. On a siding at the entrance to the station stood a train, white, blood-red crosses painted on the sides. I saw the wounded inside.

I had to choose, anything. Or else agree to be the same as Ferri, Beuil, Bernard, all of them. Ciano or Manacorda, Ribbentrop or the Duce.

"You're crazy," Merry Groves said. "You could wait quietly here, what's one soldier more or less."

We were finishing the last bottle of whiskey. In a life there have to be stages, moments definite as cliffs. Before, after. That's what makes a life. Merry came over to me. She was going back to the United States.

"You'll come back, you'll marry Strang, journalist-and-diplomat. A vast experience of Europe."

She didn't feel like laughing. I clinked my glass against hers.

"Merry, it's always the others who die. Why should I worry?"

PART THREE

E·L·I·S·A·B·E·T·H

8

Since leaving Modena the train had been going through villages with gilded church spires and tall forests rising out of white sand. Sometimes it slowed to cross a wooden bridge guarded by unconcerned sentries, then rolled on under the impassive summer skies until suddenly, with a shrill squeaking as of human cries, it stopped on the edge of the plains, the moving yellow open sea that joined the sky at the horizon. Ruined hangars, rails disappearing into fields of sunflowers and rye, and silence after days and days of rhythmic lurching, silence, a refrain, a tune on a harmonica, a few voices singing of mountains, love, and the soldier's melancholy wait. An officer came running past, interrupting the song:

"Unload, unload," he cried.

The men leaped down among the sunflowers, topping the tall stems, fragile and sun-dried. I gave orders. Pralognan, a fair-haired young lieutenant, thin, whom I looked at as in a mirror, kept saying:

"What's happening, Captain, you think . . ."

"We'll see, Pralo."

He went off, and with Luigi, the sergeant, gave orders to unload the mules, the artillery carriages. Pralognan, like me in another war on the Piave, so close, within memory's reach, needed a few words of reassurance, the ones Ferri spoke the first time we crawled out past the barbed wire. One after the other the carriages were emptied. We sat among the crates, bags, weapons, staring at the steppe, the rye and sunflowers, following the train that was beginning to back away, throwing up jets of steam and leaving an empty horizon before us, that wide empty space in which a man could get lost. Not a village, not a tree, but a wind laden with heavy sweet smells, skimming the ground, an inexhaustible wave from the east, bearing a black dust that hid the sun. I went from group to group looking for Marghella. I had found him at Modena on the platform, unchanged since Addis Ababa, commanding a battalion, amazed and overjoyed to see me.

"You, Naldi, you're coming with us, you . . ."

He grabbed my shoulders, shaking me affectionately.

"I'd have sworn you'd hide yourself behind some desk in Rome or were in some embassy in Switzerland or Sweden!"

He took my presence for heroism but it was only submission to the laws one makes for oneself, decisions one takes oneself. Pride, too. A refusal of those private capitulations between self and self which I couldn't put up with any more. Merry had understood when she left Rome shortly before the declaration of war on the United States. She was going to Spain.

"It's the nearest place," she said. "Don't get yourself killed. You're too old."

I had drifted from barracks to barracks a few months longer; met Ferri in Rome, he was acting as commander in chief and His Majesty's aide-de-camp for the duration. He had inspected our unit, taking me aside:

"Do you want to join His Majesty's staff? That's where everything will be decided. It's time to mop up the place, finish off this whorehouse."

We were in the middle of the courtyard, the soldiers standing at attention in the sun, and Ferri was pulling me aside.

"You saw the whore's sister's marriage?"

The whore: the Duce's mistress. Ferri was furious.

"A crime, an act of provocation," he said. "Everything is rotten. The Duce's nothing but an old syphilitic. We've got to get rid of him, Marco, everything's going to hell."

Defeats. Addis Ababa already in the hands of the English. The dead.

"Well?" said Ferri.

Pralognan, one step ahead of the men, at attention, Pralognan like me in the other war. I said no.

Now I was looking for Marghella at the edge of this Russian steppe, among the soldiers lying in the sunflowers under the black-veiled sky. I saw him leaning against the wall of one of the hangars, smoking casually, hardly looking at Colonel Berenini, who was waving his arms and shouting:

"Might as well have dumped us in the submarines!"

Marghella came over.

"Here we go, Naldi, Berenini's in a rage."

At Modena a few days before our departure, Colonel Berenini had called the regiment together. A fine speech, heroism and patriotism. We were going to the Caucasus, we the mountain troops, the Alpine soldiers with our mules, light artillery, hobnailed boots, pickaxes and ropes, we were going to storm the glaciers of Elbruz. And here we were in the plains, sunflowers and rye and the sickening smell of crushed stalks.

"We're going to march on the Don," Marghella told me. "Higher orders! Bah, fight there or somewhere else, why not the Don?"

Far away, beyond the Ukraine, which we had to cross, a river with gray banks, and on the other bank, beyond the sparkling water, the Russians. We set out, plunging into the open space. March one hour, ten-minute pause, march one hour, ten-minute pause, night after night, dust over us like a scorching fog, drying out throats, cracking lips, gradually covering us over, faces turning into grimacing masks. Sometimes a village, a few carbonized isbas, carcass of a tank already rusted, helmets half-buried in the ground, debris of weapons and the trail among the sunflowers, the column of which I couldn't see either beginning or end. I marched, Pralognan near me, marched, my step in an anonymous footprint, I was anybody, every tread of the heel on this sandy ground where your feet slipped was destroying the Marco Naldi who was a juggler of words and wearer of masks, the Naldi of Rome and Berlin, and the Naldi of Paris.

What was left were Magliano, Maud, the poplars and the shed, the Piave, as though I had marched out of one war into the next. In the evenings I walked away from the camp, sat down at the side of one of those narrow depressions, shallow dents that waved across the plains. Pralognan was smoking nearby, waiting for my questions.

"Well, Pralo?"

Often, one last gust, a whirl of wind that enveloped us in dust, and raindrops heavy as ripe fruit came smashing down on the black earth. I listened to Pralognan's report. A voice from the past, my voice, certainties from the past, illusions still imprisoning him. Would he need twenty years, too, to learn how to make his way, even as clumsily as I, among the stage settings and the masks? Pralognan my double, my mirror, wandering as I had wandered, blind as I had been. And maybe he'd die before he ever learned that words were hollow. Listening to him drove me to despair. I thought of Maud, of the child she had carried, to whom I could never explain anything, my voice closing in upon itself, useless. An unbearable thought. I tried to talk to Pralognan, to tell him about Salzburg, Ribbentrop, and Ciano. But he didn't understand, all he knew was you had to fight, and I was locked inside the trap I had built for myself.

"But why are you here, then?" he asked. "You were in the reserves, nothing was forcing you."

Then I had only one piece of advice to give him:

"Try not to get yourself killed, Pralo."

We marched on. The trail. Dust. Sunflowers. Shifting backs ahead of me. Sometimes German tanks overtook us, dirt hit our faces and crept inside our closed eyes. March. As though the track across the Ukraine had no end, an escalator tread in a slot-machine landscape. March, away from yourself, step after step on this hot earth that burned leather, through the dull, dry days, heart and fatigue beating together in your throat in step with the march, seeing more clearly a shy, impulsive boy who began to run away one day in the autumn of 1917. Run away from the hospital ward in Venice, the gray sack, the shortest, bloodstained. To run away, confused, torn, inconsistent. I felt sorry for you, I sympathized with you, Marco Naldi. You had put on a man's uniform, learned in one day that it is possible to die and necessary to kill and you laid down your life for the war to take, if that was the price of loyalty. Then afterward, you had to live. With this cumbersome existence, desires, ways among which one has to choose.

Where was loyalty, where was sacrifice?

Step after step in the black Ukraine darkened by storms or reflecting in a thousand leaning suns the high fixed sun, I was discovering in the center of my life those two questions, my two wounds, seeing as never before that far-off and familiar face, my own, and I had time, the endless time of the march in which to question that look, my look that Maud used to say wouldn't hold still anywhere, it was veiled and anxious.

Step after step, my life.

We marched, silent, harassed, three hundred miles through the extreme mid-continental summer. Pralognan wasn't talking. I tried to slide myself inside him. To understand. But he sent me back to myself, to the choice I had made once again, to be here in the war trap, with no alternatives but fighting or death. Who knows, maybe that was my last running-away, the last offering of my youth to father's body. Another solitary, private sacrifice dressed up as a virtue. Adolescent, Naldi? Still. Still ruled by pride and imposture. A prosecuting attorney seeking the guilty party in himself and sentencing him to risk his life. Again, as before. Marching here, like just anybody. Pralognan, Luigi: mountaineers from the Piedmont equipped for rock climbing and being forced to march across a powdery steppe, sent out with their light arms, pickaxes and ropes, to tackle the screeching steel of tanks. Step after step in the plains, like just anybody. In vain was my private road, in vain my silent cry, in vain my conscience, in vain my revolt. I was marching in the flock of victims. And if the war cut me down I'd be just a baffled body, like father's, like Pralognan's. As though I had never lived or understood.

We were crossing the Ukraine, the fields of rye and sunflowers, traveling toward the Don. I was traveling away from myself. Forty. The time it takes to see yourself, identify, follow the trace of the years, the furrow that an accident can rub out, what you are. That march across the plains, time given to retrace my own route by going backward. The end of my adolescence, a change of skin, the beginning for me, maybe, of a time with no prosecuting attorneys and no guilty parties.

If life were left to me.

One evening brought the end of the sea, the other side of the steppe, another blood-red twilight and a row of hills like a beach, trees we were marching under, soft moss and the cool moisture of the night. Marghella had left the ranks and was watching us pass, calling out the officers.

"The Don," he said. "The Russians are on the other side."

Marghella pointed to the far side of the wood, a ridge beyond which began silence, the river and dying. A German officer came up. Thin, his skin taut and yellow, feverish eyes. A weary smile.

"Welcome, gentlemen," he said. "It's quiet. Sometimes they set off mortar fire, then there are their night patrols, they want prisoners. For information. Routine."

He leaned against a tree, folding his arms, not looking at us.

"The worst," he added, "is winter. One night, farther north, we had seven thousand men frozen to death. In a single night. They were like wood. In their tents. That was the first winter. We didn't know."

He struck the tree trunk with his fist.

"Like wood."

If life were left to me.

War. The chill of fear, the chill of the weather. We dug ourselves in, a complete network of galleries three yards underground. Luigi, Pralognan, the men, we all dug, shoved down tree trunks, built stoves out of the brown clay of the riverbank. With only our eyes topping the ridge, the sparkling water below the slope of the banks and beyond, gray earth, a line above which other eyes watched. Some machine-gun fire. Some wounded. At night the barbed wire we had set up suddenly vibrated unleashing a jingle of bells, the flames from our machine guns, sometimes a quickly stifled cry, flares, the water glimmering for a few minutes, shapes like big twisted branches being ripped to pieces by bullets. Night. Then rain. As at Magliano and in Venetia before, mud in front of the shelters, life like a circle, the Piave, the Don, from one river to the other. Pralognan was sleeping nearby. I listened to his regular breathing, beating the time, the years since 1917. Pralognan my double. I so close to him, as though I hadn't been able to shake off the Venetian mud, falling back into my own tracks, my rut, starting the same experience over again.

But only if life were left to me.

I lit my lamp, a flash, time to relieve a sentry—Pralognan was sleeping. I could see his face half-hidden under the collar of his coat, the blond beard didn't age him, fists together under his cheeks, for he lay on his right side with his knees bent, like I did. But I could never manage to go to sleep just like that, like a curtain falling. There were all those years to live through again, Ferri, Elsa, and Maud. She had judged quickly, without hesitating she had left me standing on the sidewalk. One April day. How could I have taken the responsibility for a son when I was getting ready to be born myself, to break through the envelope of pride and timidity, my cast-off adolescent clothes. A son. You've got to be able to. And Maud knew, Maud who had come too late for Marco Naldi of the rue du Bac, too soon for this one now. Too soon, too late, question of luck.

If life were left to me.

The rain, icy. Men running head down along the communication trenches. Marghella called me to his command post in the woods below the ridge.

"Things are bad," he said. "The Americans have disembarked in Africa. Those jerks in Rome, your friends, Naldi, they don't know anything about war."

We had gone out under the trees. The first snow was lying on the ground, it was already hard, crackling underfoot. In the morning Pralognan showed me his mess tin full of ice.

"Blessed be Africa," Marghella went on, "you remember?"

A silence, to recall the embassy garden in Addis Ababa, our rambles on the trails across the high plateaus.

"The Don's going to freeze, then they'll attack, with tanks. They'll cross on the ice, and we've got nothing."

Nothing. Fear contracted my muscles. Cold. Silence. Flights of wild geese overhead, white triangles in the gray sky. We gathered around our clay stoves; huddling together in the same shelter, Luigi, Pralognan, Giuliano, our chaplain. Shoulder to shoulder, we waited. When we had to go out, our breath froze. On Pralognan's beard it turned into white lumps like big teeth. The wine froze. The body froze and the blood beneath the skin was ice-colored. Wounds: the flesh pulled tight, white like cracked plates; skin stuck to steel leaving fingers and hands peeled, raw, skin like a glove pulled off. Legs turned to stones, toes breaking into pieces, left inside shoes like clods of earth. Silence. We went outside a few minutes. Time for a round of sentry duty. Long as a death agony. Ice on the Don reflecting the low sky.

"The tanks can cross now," Luigi said. "Can't they, Captain?"

Don't answer. A word shows fear, emptiness.

"What do we stop them with?" Luigi went on.

"Be quiet."

Don't say. Pralognan was watching us. Luigi and I were older. Luigi from Turin, had fought in Ethiopia.

"Not enlisted," he added. "Sent there, Captain. You know?"

Giuliano kept his gloved hands on the copper cross hanging from his neck. Luigi questioned him, without looking at him, in a serious voice.

"You think war can be blessed, Father?"

Then a glance at me. Complicity can be no more than that, a glance.

"You have no faith, do you?" asked Giuliano.

Luigi didn't answer.

"And you, Captain," the chaplain went on, "what do you think?"

That voice, when mother made me kneel in the church at Magliano, the priest touching my cheek and mother leaning over me reciting prayers that I said after her, and just a murmur, "Our Father who art in heaven."

"You have faith, haven't you?" he asked again.

All my life I'd made gestures with the others but so many gestures imitated, yes, no, two little decisive words that meant nothing. And these bodies turned to mud, the cheeks turned to stone, mother reduced to nothing, living in my memory alone, and Giulia. The lives of others, dead or far away, mother, Maud, did they exist only in the heads of the living?

"Life is sacred, that's all I know. Only we're here to kill or die. Comic, really."

"Comic?"

Luigi looked at me.

"Weird sense of humor you've got, Captain."

"You want us to start crying?"

"Might be better, Captain."

Pralognan was silent. Suddenly he stood up.

"I'll take the duty," he said. "If the Russians come, then, yes, we can cry."

"After all, it's their home here," muttered Luigi.

But Pralognan was gone.

More days. Were they days? Little more than a slit of light in a long night, two or three gray hours soon invaded by darkness, torn by the wind that chiseled flesh and silence. Waiting. The other bank like a darker band of the night. And around mid-December, Marghella came into our shelter. All I could see were his eyes, the lower part of his face protected by an ice-frosted scarf.

"Naldi, departure in two hours, regroup in the woods, the Russians have attacked farther north, we're in danger of being cut off here."

Then we abandoned our shelters, their precarious warmth,

and marched as though we were naked in a crevasse of ice, ice bristling with lances we tore ourselves on and the wind flung a hail of needles against us. Night or day? Who knows? The column, a tottering black streak, a mule falling exhausted, men running at it, tearing at the raw meat, biting. That was days later, after we had finished our rations, gone through villages, heard the cries of the wounded heaped inside a burning isba, seen the crazy eyes of a soldier naked to the waist who was singing at the roadside, bayonet in hand, threatening anyone who came near him. That was days later, after we had met the tanks with the red star that flattened the men on the ice, leaving them like black prints in the ground, after we had seen trucks loaded with German soldiers go by, shooting at any of us who tried to climb on. Up there, farther north on the Volga, the pincers were squeezing Stalingrad and here on the Don one of the jaws was grinding us up. At the entrance to a village we threw ourselves into the snow and our stomachs became stone, men tried to storm their way through, sometimes the Russians fell back, sometimes they came after us and we poured back down into the crevasse that was cluttered with dead and wounded, weapons already half-covered in snow. Sometimes two or three isbas, the men piling into them to get out of the wind and others coming up with bayonets, sticking them into a body to take its place, and others crazy from cold and rage throwing grenades and going wild with the cries and fire. Eat, breathe, live, march. Days, days.

Maybe it was in the village of Slavianska, almost intact, isbas standing close together and when we opened the doors the wounded and dead, another column had gone through before us. We shoved them aside to lie down with them and then, how much later, night, day, it was all gray, everything dark, shots, the squeak of tank treads. Pralognan in front of me, we go out. Russians in white snowsuits. We have to run, a tank farther on blowing up the isbas, knocking them over with one push, they open, screams, then the gray and white mass flattens wood, snow, and cries, pivots on planks and bodies, I push Pralognan to make him run faster but he stays there standing straight, I grab his shoulders, he shakes his head. Two Russians in front of us. I jumped into a ditch, I left Pralognan. Pralo my double. His arms were hanging, still shaking his head, he bent over, hands on his stomach, falling on his knees. A few seconds, the whoosh of the wind, bullets. The men beyond the village, the march. Luigi next to me.

"The lieutenant?"

My double whose breathing marked the time of my memories, my years, and who was sleeping inside me on his right side with his knees bent, fists under his cheek. Pralognan, one of those black milestones we left behind us, soon changed into little white hillocks like pimples on the earth. He wouldn't turn back to retrace his tracks. They stopped in the village of Slavianska, cut off, and he knelt down with his hands over his stomach and his eyes dazzled by the lie of history. Blind forever. Victim forever. Assassinated like Matteotti and Calvini.

"You all right, Captain?"

Luigi had caught my arm, holding me up. I wrenched away.

"You were talking to yourself and then you fell down."

I was dazzled too.

More days. A clear road and then the noise of tanks and chatter of machine guns. We had to storm through and we left more Pralognans in the snow. It must have been twelve days we marched westward. Then a road, a few signposts, an armored car sitting there; around a fire, Marghella and Colonel Berenini. They came toward us shouting:

"You got out, it's over, it's over!"

Marghella walked beside me for a minute, handing me a fistful of sugar lumps.

"You're here, Naldi," he kept saying. "It's over."

I let him hug me. I was somewhere else, with Pralognan in the snow. With the wounded whose cries were stifled by steel treads, with those black and red spots imprinted in the ice, men laminated under forty tons. Over? Two syllables. My memory would be over only with my life.

In a dirty isba Luigi sat down next to me near the stove. Other men were leaning against the wooden walls, sleeping. Slowly we stripped off our solidified clothes, impregnated with snow, blood, fear, dirt. The colonel came in. He was touring the isbas.

"You're going back to Italy," he said. "In a few days, as soon as there's a convoy."

He nibbled at his mustache.

"Italy can be proud of you."

Luigi went on taking off his clothes, slowly, head down.

"There'll have to be a report, won't there, Captain?"

"Of course, a report."

Words, to tell about Pralognan and the soldier singing bare-chested in the snow. Words to tell death, our death. And what if, while death were queen, the time of words should come to an end, and acts begin to govern? Death against death.

"I've put you all in for decorations," Berenini went on. "Italy must know what her soldiers have done."

Luigi looked up.

"And what's been done to them, Colonel," he said, "does she have to know that too?"

Berenini took a step forward, clenched his fists.

"You're still a soldier, don't forget it, and insubordination in a soldier is never excusable."

Luigi had gone back to cutting up his socks with a wooden-handled knife and at the ankle the skin came off, sticking to the wool, the bone laid open.

"Get out of here, get out!"

I had shouted; Berenini drew back, red-faced, hesitant, finally going, leaving only the sound of snoring soldiers.

"Which decoration will you choose, Captain?" Luigi asked me.

We looked at each other. In front of me was a heavy Russian revolver Pralognan had given me. I oiled it, slowly wrapping it in a cloth, and put it in my bag with a handful of cartridges. It mustn't always be the same ones who die.

9

Again the tall forests rising in white sand, again the villages with gilded spires, but we were going westward in half-empty carriages, lying on straw, and it was days before we began singing in a chorus, to the tune of some old mountain song, a few words, a soft lament like a lullaby, that one of us made up:

> *Farewell the steppe, farewell soldier,*
> *Farewell my comrade.*
> *Here's the wooden bridge again*
> *You crossed in June so glad.*

Never had I felt so close to other people, to these men with the hollow cheeks, to Pralognan my lost double, to Luigi lying next to me.

"What are you going to do?"

Both his feet were bandaged, one ear gnawed away by frost, his skin stretched taut over his skull.

"Me, Captain? Like before, if they let me out. Work; I'll make guns so other guys can go get killed."

Luigi was massaging his knees and calves slowly, with the precise gestures of a worker or peasant.

"That's all the factory does any more," he went on, "make guns, machine guns, ever since 1934, around the clock, it'll have to go on, no reason why it should stop since we're all mules. Worse. Don't even know how to kick any more."

The train was crawling through valleys still smothered by snow, it was the end of February 1943, but the air was already mild and we left the doors open to see the peaceful slopes, the calm villages, children sometimes, women.

"And you, Captain?"

All I had was memories, an empty steppe in front of me, a

trail to make that shouldn't be a continuation of the years before. The snow had covered Pralognan. It had covered Marco Naldi too, the one who thought for so long that it was possible to stay outside, almost uncompromised. I was tired and decided. No more talking: doing. The Ferris, Valsecchinis, Marco Naldis, Mussolinis and Cianos and fascism were born out of one war. Let this one bury them.

"What about you, Captain?" Luigi repeated.

"Kick."

I held out my pack of cigarettes and we smoked together, backs against the carriage sides, watching the trees go past, joining in with the others in the refrain of that lament:

> *Farewell the steppe, farewell soldier,*
> *Farewell my comrade . . .*

Each man was murmuring it for himself, shoulder to shoulder, swaying to the rhythm of the song and the monotonous regular lurching of the train. Towns, Kielce, Vienna, Salzburg, Rossenheim, Innsbruck. At last, after a narrow valley, the open expanse beaten by the wind, a white mast, a flag, carabinieri. I helped Luigi down onto the soil of our country. The Brenner. All the men had jumped off the train, some were embracing. Our country. The carabinieri came up.

"Inside, inside," they were shouting. "Close the doors. Forbidden to open them."

They pushed us. I stepped forward.

"I am an officer," I said.

The carabinieri saluted.

"Orders, Captain, and they apply to officers too. The people must not see you in that condition."

We were the real face of the war.

"Morale, you understand."

Some soldiers were protesting but the carabinieri were forcing them slowly back toward the train. I saw Marghella, who was watching the scene with his arms folded, I went over to him.

"You hear that, you see that?"

"Morale," he said, "after they've been repainted they can be shown."

He smiled.

"If you want what we did back there not to be wasted, the country has to hold together, so might as well hide our mugs. You understand."

He took my shoulder.

"Come with us, Naldi, we've got a good carriage, cognac and cigars. We'll celebrate our return home."

I twisted away.

"Great day, it really is, some homecoming. Your health."

I jumped into Luigi's carriage and we stayed side by side as far as Udina. Trucks were waiting there, in the middle of the night, a deserted station. We were the untouchables. A few days in a barracks to count us and try to indoctrinate us. Marghella called me into his office, friendly and sympathetic.

"Of course, of course, sometimes they go too far," he said.

He sat on the corner of his desk.

"I was there too, with you, you know that Naldi, good, well, I think the command is right, after all."

He held out a circular addressed to the officers. They were to advise the men not to talk while on furlough; and a reminder that we had to fight until the final victory. I put the paper down on the desk.

"What I have to do, Marghella, from now on, nobody but me is going to decide. I've learned that. Earned the right."

I went out without waiting for his answer.

Luigi was discharged. I went to the station with him. He was leaning on me, thin in his new uniform that was too big for him.

"You know, Captain . . ."

We were outside his carriage.

"I think we think the same way. And I like that. It was easier for me, I've always thought that way, my father already, but you, an officer. That's good, it makes me feel good."

We embraced. I was taking the train to Venice. A long furlough. At first, the city rediscovered, hesitating between the tenacious winter, still foggy, and then spring, sudden gusts of wind lacerating the sky into long streaks, leaving a sparkling blue above the canals, and the sun brilliant on the pink and white marble. I stayed nearly a week in Venice. Walked the narrow streets, found peace again, time incrusted in the stone, history effaced. I had myself taken to the Dogana di Mare, the Punta della Salute. Watched the motor launches moving up and down the San Marco Canal. Went back slowly, from bridge to bridge, up to the Ponte di Rialto and then down the Grand Canal on the other bank; I needed these façades, these canals, fossils deposited by history, needed the presence of people, their city noble as a challenge. Venice the antidote, after the empty steppe, the bare yellow sea we had crossed marching east and then the long crevasse of ice we tore ourselves to shreds in, fleeing west. I went into the Palazzo Dandolo, empty, idle waiters, an aged dozing doorman I chatted with.

"Ah, the war, sir . . ."

Beginning his litany, his lament. His son gone to fight in Russia.

"You must tell me, sir."

A pimple on the earth, a wrinkle in the snow like Pralognan's body. Maybe one of those soldiers I'd seen flinging themselves on some bottles of cognac unearthed in an isba, who ran off drunk, weaving into the night before they toppled over with their arms flung out and a smile on their lips, the snow covering them so quickly.

"There have been so many prisoners, you musn't worry about it, he'll come back, believe me."

Lie: I was trapped again. But how could I confess to those lives the steppe would never give back? So I listened to the doorman telling about his son, the future buried in the snow.

"You understand," he said, leaning over next to me and facing the Grand Canal, "after the war everything will be motorized, gondolas, everything. So that's why I wanted him to be a mechanic, not like me, I don't know how to do anything, he can take a Fiat motor apart with his eyes closed, so when he comes back . . ."

I leaned a hand on his shoulder. Lying with the pressure of a hand, too. At last, I went to Magliano. To get away from the doorman as much as to see the dark room again and the paved courtyard and the paths behind the poplars and the shed. I got there around noon, the Nittis' door was open, Mrs. Nitti at her stove. I saw her shrunken body swathed in black cloth, the gray chignon, the odor of fried oil. She turned, put her hand to her mouth, beginning to cry and throwing herself on me.

"Mr. Marco!"

The voice of my childhood, still so amazingly present, rubbing out the years, Russia, bringing back the dream of a return to that time before death, that frozen time where father and mother stood eternal, pink and white marble statues:

"You must have suffered," Mrs. Nitti was saying. "You're so thin, you're so thin."

She wiped her tears.

"You've got to eat, Mr. Marco, you must, I'll kill a hen, some broth for you, that's what you need."

Nitti came in later. He was having lunch in the field, I didn't want to go out to meet him. I stayed by the stove listening to the flat voice of Mrs. Nitti that interrupted itself now and then to shed a few tears. What it told was trivial life, the past she lulled me with, a slow warm murmur sweet as milk. Nitti shook my arm, wiped his nose with the back of his hand, winked at me.

"You've come back alive, that's what counts. Old Mustache gave them a beating, Moscow, Stalingrad. You didn't deserve to stay out there, to pay for them."

He was rubbing his hands.

"Some wine."

Mrs. Nitti brought a bottle of *lambrusco*, that wine with the pink froth father used to let me taste. Nitti poured, the foam overflowed and spread across the wooden table.

"My eyes aren't so good any more," he said.

But he seemed happy, younger, more talkative than I'd known him before.

"It won't last much longer, you know, Mr. Naldi, this time won't be like after the first war, the other one."

Mrs. Nitti was shaking her head.

"What was it like out there, bad?"

"Bad," I said, "bad."

He filled my glass several more times. Time became muddy, like a swamp, facts, names, places were superimposed on top of one another, Maud was here close to me in my childhood and Ferri sitting in grandfather's place in our dark room, leaning against the high back of the chair, I was running along the path toward Maud and she was handing me Pralognan to hold, who resembled her like a son. When I opened my eyes, the first thing I saw was Mrs. Nitti crossing herself.

"You frightened us," she said.

Nitti was leaning against the wall with his hat shoved back on his head.

"It was my fault, the wine, you're still weak."

I straightened up. Once again Magliano was no good for me. My mud, my footprints. I took the cloth-wrapped package out of my bag, the Russian revolver Pralognan had given me. A handful of cartridges. Both in the middle of the table. I pushed them over to Nitti.

"Maybe that could be useful here. I'll get another one."

I went out before he undid the wrapping and the next morning I left for Rome. The train was jammed. Soldiers, women. A Black Shirt was trying to force his way along the corridor. The soldiers refused to see him, didn't budge, prevented him from moving. He was young, his cap down to his eyes. Finally he began to shout:

"I'll kill you," he bawled, "I'll kill you!"

A murmur, women's voices protesting:

"Let him go to the front if he wants to fight, there's room there in Russia, in Africa."

He backed away and disappeared into another carriage. A woman stood up screaming, a peasant woman dressed in black.

"You heard him, the butcher, the son of a murderer!"

Other women tried to quiet her.

"What do I care, the murderers, they killed mine."

Then she started sobbing. In Rome, the atmosphere was the same. Lines in front of the shops in the Trastevere. I walked, learning the city again, the colors of the Via Giulia in the spring. The streets often empty, silent. Sometimes an alert, waves of bombers you heard first and then saw, silver sparks in the blue and white sky. The city was afraid, drawn into itself, waiting for some event that would release it, fill its lungs after the long years of silence. In the Piazza Barberini apartment I was met by dust, the smell of my past, I opened the shutters onto the roofs, domes, and the hills in the distance, sharp lines against the pale horizon. The second evening, the concierge came up. The same old woman, shrunken now, holding her chest, leaning on the railing.

"Mr. Naldi, I didn't know you'd come back, a lady came by, there's a . . ."

Maud. Hope, joy for an instant, as though to show how much of my life was amputated, empty, inert since I had lost her.

"Who? Did she . . . ?"

"Who, who? How should I know. She left you a letter."

I went down behind her, I would have carried her, knocked her over, but she was clutching the rail, step by step, fumbling in a pile of letters in a drawer, couldn't find it. At last, an envelope. Not Maud's writing. I went slowly back up. There was plenty of time. Why open it? I lingered on the balcony, incurious, a sense of revulsion. Work to do, the work of living, trying as well as I could, who knows why, to have done with the people who forced Pralognan to kneel in the snow with his hands over his torn stomach. Pralognan and I and Maud and so many others, all those lives diverted, truncated, separated.

Night fell in an instant, without dusk. A decapitated spring day. Cold wind over the dark city, the sky pitted by the beams of antiaircraft searchlights. I went in, drawing the curtains, not putting on any lights for a long time. But I'd have to make up my mind. Tore open the envelope. Several pages. A signature, Emilia, and on the first page the name leaping out at me, Maud. Emilia had come back to Italy. People were starving in Paris, she'd have an easier time in the country with her sister, above Florence. She had seen Maud once, by chance, on the boulevard Montparnesse outside the station. Maud had lost weight, bleached her hair, she was blond, wore glasses. Emilia wouldn't have known her but Maud had taken her arm and they had walked down the rue de Rennes to Saint-Germain. Maud was traveling a great deal. Emilia had underlined that. She couldn't stay in one place. Emilia underlined that too. Another time, a month later, Maud had come to the gallery. She had slept there. "She never mentioned you," Emilia wrote. In her opinion, the child must have died. Maud never said a word about it. "I'd like to see you," Emilia added, "I'll explain."

I took another train. Just getting to Florence was an adventure in itself. Viaducts were blown up, military convoys had priority. The trains stopped, the passengers walked over bridges, waited for other trains. Sitting by the tracks we talked together, about the army that was retreating in Tunisia, the strikes that had paralyzed Turin and Milan. In low voices, a few words to sound out the other person, then if you felt you could trust him you added, "It can't go on." Too late for Maud, no doubt. Emilia's letter had revived my despair because for a few seconds I had believed it possible that Maud herself had come here for me, alive. But there are no miracles. I knew it when I saw Emilia, I knew by the way she took my hand so we could walk under the cypresses, a long drive that led from the house away to the horizon.

"I am glad to see you," she was saying.

Clinging to me.

"You're alive, your mother would be so happy."

I didn't ask questions, let her approach her revelations in her own way, with detours and pauses.

"You got my letter, yes? Of course, how stupid of me, since you're here, I'm an old woman, you know Marco, I'm losing my memory."

Trying to laugh.

"Did you read, about Maud?"

"Yes, so here I am."

"Yes; well, I saw her again, two or three times. She left packages. She warned me."

Tracts, papers, the resistance.

"I hid them behind paintings, and Maud told me, 'I won't talk, don't worry.' I trusted her. For a month I didn't see her. One day . . ."

She came in, said, "I'm going to introduce someone to you in case anything happens to me, you understand?" Another month.

"I didn't know what to do with those packages that nobody ever came to collect," Emilia went on, "and then the young man she had brought with her came."

He had sat down, smoked. Emilia asked him.

"They got her," he had said. But she hadn't talked. "You have nothing to fear. We've waited as long as was necessary."

Emilia squeezed my arm.

"It was better for me to tell you, wasn't it? After that I left, mostly because of that, I was afraid and then Maud's memory, I was fond of her, a little mad but warm-hearted."

We went along under the cypresses, toward a promontory overlooking the hills. It was still cold, because of the wind that was turning the sky a deeper blue. Emilia blew her nose, biting her lips. We didn't talk. In the distance, on a red-earth hillside, a village with the smoke streaming horizontally, running in the wind.

"Mad; she should have hidden, she a Jew, throwing herself into all that, insanity. It was a thousand times more dangerous for her. Marco, Marco, this war, the horror, when will it end?"

I went back the same evening. Needed to be alone. Go over the story for myself, imagine, see Maud again, understand the passion that had separated her from me, from her child, hurled her into this war where she fought with her bare hands, a Trotskyist Jew in occupied France, minority among minorities, earmarked for every executioner and yet refusing to be a victim, sure to win one day, she or those with her.

I felt so poor, alone, empty-handed, without that wealth of a shared passion. I had husbanded my life like a Magliano land-owner, trying to increase my capital, get the wheat in before it rained, selfish and careful. Only two or three little attempts to reach out, thanks to Maud; when I chose in spite of everything this war among other men, Pralognan, Luigi. A clumsy commitment, crablike, still blind. But at least I had shed skins. I had found the fraternal voices, the soldiers in the train going to Udina, Luigi beside me and both of us singing:

Farewell the steppe, farewell soldier,
Farewell my comrade . . .

I shut myself into the Piazza Barberini apartment for several days, writing to Maud, to myself: for the first time I brought words out of me and gave them the weight and reality of written sentences. Why at that moment this violent outpouring of my life, to whom, for whom? To me, for me, the need to put the past in order, the past that stopped on the steppe back there, on the banks of the Don; to draw Maud's face with words, to tell her, to tell myself how much I had loved her; the words came up and back and back, made new in the process of being written down, and others came with them because they were all chained together in long phrases that began at Magliano one day in October 1917 when Ferri, his cape thrown over his shoulder, stood waiting for me motionless in the rain. Page after page, a furious burst that shattered the hours and finally flowed into the spring of 1943 and Rome, where I was.

Then I rubbed my eyes. The ashtrays were full, the light was on, daylight filtered through the closed shutters in broken white stripes. Pages in front of me. A wall as high as all those words, closing off my past. I opened the shutters. Sun. Brilliance on the domes. Outside me the city, other people, a present to make.

I ran a hand over my cheek; growth of beard like after a high fever. I took a long time to shave, wash. When we reached the first organized camps after the retreat we were deloused and then stood in scalding showers, trying to let life return. After these days of darkness in Rome I had the same feeling, water running over me, into me. I went back to my desk, collected the ashtrays, cleaned off the table, and then I picked up the pages, the words, and tore them up without regret. Maud was dead, who could read? Me? I knew it all. The wall was inside me now. That evening I phoned Provi.

In his home facing the Pincio there was the same tranquil atmosphere as in Paris before the war. A different servant. And Angela was married. After dinner we sat alone in the drawing room, the Pincio like a darker pool shaken by the wind, the trees etched in black for a moment by the brutal beams of a searchlight.

"They've set up antiaircraft guns in the gardens," Provi said, "but they won't be needed, it's the end now."

He was smoking a cigar, his eyes half-shut, watching the smoke, telling me about the Duce's isolation.

"You know he fired Ciano? Sent for him at the beginning of February and simply said, 'What would you like to do now?'"

I said nothing.

"Obviously, the morality of all that . . . but when the ship is sinking you know what the rats do. And they're right."

Around the Duce there remained only a little knot of the faithful, who either didn't realize or were too heavily compromised or who had chosen the German camp: Valsecchini, who used to be head fascist in Venice, had become secretary general of the party; and Lanvoni.

"Now he's Himmler's man here," Provi was saying. "He hopes Ferri and Ciano will try something against the Duce, the Germans will intervene, occupy the country, drive out the king, and it will be Lanvoni's moment of glory."

Provi got up, poured clear liqueurs into ballooning glasses like the one Maud had drunk from that last day in April, in Paris.

"The Germans are the Duce's only chance," he went on.

The government was cracking up again, like dried plaster, flaking and crumbling, strikes in Turin, Milan, in the munitions works. Luigi. The Duce, Provi was telling, had called a meeting of the executive of the Fascist party.

"They were all there, Ferri, Ciano, Valsecchini, the faithful and the dissident."

Manacorda had heard it from Ciano. The Duce was furious. He cursed the police because they hadn't ordered the armored cars to open fire on the strikers.

"Ferri and Ciano applauded with the rest but the moment they got out of the palazzo they started plotting again; as for the Duce, he's sick, completely in a dream world."

Provi drank slowly. Those bodies like scarcely visible hummocks so swiftly covered, back there on the steppe, by the snow.

"What about you?"

Provi widened his eyes, smiling.

"Me? You know my attitude. My dear Marco, I have obtained a long leave of absence, an unexpected illness, strategic if you like, and although I wouldn't presume to advise you, if you would like to be infected I know an excellent doctor."

Maud. Pralognan. The drunken soldiers falling with their arms spread-eagled. And so many others since 1917. Matteotti, von Baulig, Calvini, Maud. No more hesitations, only one question I asked myself: which was the best weapon, the most effective place? To fight death with death, it was the law of the age.

"You, Marco, what have you decided?"

"I'm still a soldier, not discharged yet."

Provi shrugged, I only had to ask, he said, a mere formality. I got up. Soldier, maybe that was a weapon. I like steel better than intrigue.

"As you please, Marco."

Provi took me to the door, kept me a moment.

"You were lucky in Russia, Marco, don't try for the jackpot. It'll all be over soon. Try to be there at the end, that's the main thing."

I knew that speech, it belonged to my past. But I had built a wall, changed skins, forgotten the words of moderation and caution. Empty.

I spent April in Rome, looking for some means of action. Ferri asked me to the Villa Cantoni, paternal and pleased, it appeared, to know I was alive; fulminating against the Duce.

"That massacre you saw, Marco, that's him," he shouted, "he alone wanted it because the old tart was hoping to seduce Hitler, you saw the results."

Ferri had shed years, rubbing his hands nervously, smoothing his sparse hair, opening his jacket:

"Look . . ."

He showed me a pistol in his belt, rubbed his hands again:

"You never know, they won't stop at anything. Valsecchini is a killer. We have to rid Italy of these people, then at last we'll establish a new order like the one we used to dream of, my policy is all prepared . . ."

He paced back and forth in the drawing room that was sheathed in white marble halfway to the ceiling.

"With the king's support," he went on.

"What can I do?"

He came nearer, I knew his half-closed eyes, knew every one of his ambitions and cowardices but if I didn't want to act alone I had to turn to him. Afterward, if the opportunity arose, Ferri would have to go too.

"Bravo, Marco, bravo. Sit down, tell me, where are you now?"

"Officer, on furlough until the end of April."

In Ferri's plans the army was to play a decisive part. Most of the generals were loyal to the king, and our defeats had won over the fence-sitters. The Duce, infected with every vice, responsible for every decision, had become the sole scapegoat. The accomplices were all turning out to be innocent. Like Ciano, like Ferri, like Manacorda or Antonetti.

"Come back again, I'll think of something."

Someone was running after me in the grounds of the villa, calling:

"Mr. Naldi, Mr. Naldi . . ."

Carlo, his chauffeur's cap in hand, breathless:

"I was parking the car, I thought I recognized you."

"Always me, and always you."

He laughed, turning his cap between his fingers and saying, "I'm glad to see you, glad to see you, I knew you had gone out there."

"People come back."

What had we to say? So many times before Carlo had been close to me, our lives intersecting, friendship growing out of a few words half-spanning the gap between our worlds.

"Lousy war," said Carlo.

Long ago on the road to Magliano he had cursed the war. He came to the gate with me.

"But it's back again, your war, you swear at it but here it is."

"I don't know, I don't understand what's the matter with them all, the ones who give the orders, I mean, they ought to know."

Lives crawling between walls, blind, like so much of mine. All of Carlo's. Pralognan. All those lives groping their way, moving ahead because they happened to be standing on the slope somebody else wanted. A crime. Tear the walls down, let lives be clear and everyone decide for himself, know where he's going, why he has to go there. Then would remain only the other crime, the incurable wound of the dead. Pralognan. Maud, mother and the gray sacks in the dirty light of the hospital in Venice in 1917. I went back through the Pincio, along drives shaded by parasol pines. To live and grow old means leaving a dead forest behind you, trees blackened as by fire, denser and denser, closer and closer I could feel it around me.

April days. I slept, walked, revived, in the Roman spring. A kind of peace. In spite of the news and the war closing in on Italy and the alerts often punctuated by antiaircraft fire, futile white sprinklings in the sky. I saw Manacorda, Antonetti, Provi, a few women. Marghella too, now a colonel, called me to headquarters. Decorations on his uniform, like so many certainties displayed.

"You know I put you in for the gold medal? Yes, Berenini was against it, seems you insulted him or threatened him."

A wave of the hand:

"But Berenini doesn't count any more, he's out of it. You'll get your medal."

I watched him. What did he want?

"Naldi, I don't get it, I wanted you assigned here with me but there's this order that's just come from the supreme command, transferring you to the Fourth Army in Nice, do you want to become an occupier?"

I hesitated.

"You can turn it down," Marghella said, "I'll support you. The order is signed by the general in chief. But I have influence."

He winked, held out cigarettes.

I remembered Ferri.

"Discipline," I said.

"All right, all right."

He stood up, suddenly severe.

"Naldi, don't let yourself get mixed up in those little plots, in the end we're the ones who'll win. Don't forget Germany."

That same evening Ferri told me he needed a contact in the Fourth Army, in France.

"You'll be at staff headquarters," he said, "you'll act as a liaison with me, I have to have somebody I can trust there. I have confidence in you."

For the time being my goal was the same as his, our paths were parallel. My mission order came in the second week of May; a few days before I left, Mussolini had spoken to an enormous crowd from the balcony of the Palazzo Venezia, they were waving posters and shouting "*Vinceremo.*" The Duce's voice was strained: "We shall return to Africa, fellow fascists, we shall conquer." This imposture in which my life had been bogged down too long had to stop. That mouth had to be gagged, the militia had to be dispersed, their arms taken away.

Imposture. Everywhere. A sickness that infected us all, I recognized it in the gestures of the carabinieri in the train taking me to Nice, the words of the staff officers of the Fourth Army.

"Ah, you've come from Russia, dreadful, isn't it, dreadful."

A sentence, hardly touching their lips. Imposture. And Pralognan my double, my comrade, dead for that sentence, that farce. For these elegant, vain, futile officers, whom I caught combing their hair and whistling as they emerged from their offices.

"You'll see, Naldi, in a few days you'll be a happy man, the women of Nice hold no grudges."

Imposture. A few whores, a few girls without enough to eat. Sham passions. A sham army, corrupt, basking in the sun; a sham occupation, too many ties between town and soldiers. Sometimes I missed our trenches on the Don, our nights shoulder to shoulder, equality in suffering and in fear, oblivion all around us bringing us closer together. No: nonsense, those regrets; madness. This town was better any day, this quiet, useless army waiting for the end, deaf and blind, disorganized.

I moved into the fourth floor of a requisitioned hotel on the promenade des Anglais. Awoke at dawn, facing the sea. I loved the slowly expanding horizon, the bay, the sour smell of the soft-oily sea. And fishermen going into the water with their trousers rolled up, heaving boats up on shore in front of the hotel, a soldier running to help, starting a conversation. At army headquarters I drew up lists of units. Waited. Like the town and the army. Then Elisabeth walked into my office. A mannish look about her, hair pulled back, broad shoulders, how old could she be, young, never mind the rest. My orderly grinning idiotically as he introduced her.

"A young woman, Captain, she wants to see you, Miss Elisabeth Loubet, should I . . ."

She came in.

"You're Captain Marco Naldi, is that right? I was told you were here. I'll sit down, rode my bike from Vence, it's a long way and it's hot."

She was mopping her brow.

"Can you come outside, we need to talk, only in that uniform, what about civilian clothes?"

Elisabeth talked fast, left me no time to answer. Rocked back on her chair to see if the door was completely closed.

"Ambassador Ferri," she said, "there; we should talk."

I met her later on a terrace near the place Masséna, then we walked under the plane trees, she hardly looked at me.

"I was told you were to be the liaison with Rome. I've got news for Ferri, urgent."

Then began a time of action for me, travels. I went to Rome. Came back. Colonel Valeri imperturbably signed mission orders. He got me a car. I chugged up to Vence, stopped in front of our barracks outside the town, old buildings surrounded by figs and olive trees. Got out, lost my way in the narrow streets, taking care not to be followed; and came to Elisabeth's villa. She lived

alone, she worked in her garden; sometimes I came upon her
spade in hand under the noonday sun in that dry, clean July,
made austere by the heat: a bra, long khaki shorts, tanned skin.

"You're very English," I said one day, laughing.

"But I am English, my mother was."

We had time that day. The liaison agent, whom I didn't know,
was late. We talked in the garden.

"Give me some tea, then."

Since I had come back from Russia this was the first woman
I had felt like talking to, for more than a few minutes and without any specific purpose.

"I could sleep here," I said, joking, as I was getting ready to
leave.

"Why not?"

She didn't look away, and said again, "Why not?"

We sat down under the trees, shoulder to shoulder, a violent
twilight slowly overpowering the hills, blurring the sea, creating
silence.

"You're not afraid?" I asked.

"Of you?"

"Of the police, the OVRA, or the Gestapo."

Shrug.

"I'm careful, and then why live if you don't take chances?"

Put my hand on the back of her head.

"You're so young."

I was feeling old, tired, worn out sometimes. All those years,
voices, von Baulig, Maud, Alatri, those dead, the snow and
now the waiting for the collapse, the end of the war.

"Me?"

She patted my knee.

"Don't you worry, Marco, I promise you I feel old enough
inside and just as crazy as you are."

Her body was friendly, giving, soft; a soothing, peaceful
love, slow-moving, her arms around my neck like a soft, warm
piece of material. Sleeping beside her, being inside her, like an

ultimate expression of friendship. When I awoke she was already
up, I heard the crunch of the spade in the dry earth. I walked
out into the white, burning sun. She hardly looked up, called
out that breakfast was ready in the kitchen.

"Hurry up, the guy's here."

Later, she sat down on the bed, perspiring, holding out an
envelope.

"For Ferri, you've got to leave, I think."

She lay down, sweat glistening on her brown stomach, heaved
a sigh of weariness, I kissed her, she stayed there with her arms
flung out, drowsy, abandoned, and vigorous.

Then the road again. Rome, Ferri. The Villa Cantoni deserted, paintings, museum pieces, bric-a-brac vanished, Ferri's
drawing room appearing immense, the shutters half-closed. He
caught my look.

"I've put a few things in a safe place, one never knows."

Tore open the envelope, called his secretary, rubbed his
hands.

"Only a matter of days now," he said. "The Americans agree."

I listened, silent, the heat, the trip over roads cluttered with
military convoys traveling south, toward Sicily where the Allies
had just landed. Soldiers were surrendering on the island by
tens of thousands, towns and fortresses capitulating.

"Everything depends on the Germans," Ferri was saying.
"We've got to watch out for them."

His wife had already left for Spain. He was hoping to take
over, with the support of the king, after the Other had been
disposed of. The Other: the Duce we now knew was trapped
in his Palazzo Venezia, a dark mass in the brutal July light.

I cross the empty piazza, go up the Via del Corso, a few
pedestrians, militia in the shade under the arcade of the Piazza
Colonna, suddenly an eruption of noise, a clamor, low-flying
planes, the wail of sirens. I run home. From the balcony I see
the city, a glitter within a gray haze, still the sirens, the sputter
of antiaircraft guns, shatter of glass, walls and balcony shudder-

ing, dull explosions, close my eyes: the Piave, the Don, our trenches, but it's only Rome being bombed for the first time, the haze thickens over the city, sirens, silence, and just above the rooftops, rending the sky, planes. Instinctively I throw myself down on the floor. Silence, sirens, cries in the street.

Before leaving that evening I saw Ferri again.

"I hope they've understood," he was saying.

Among the rubble, under stone and plaster, caught between steel girders, beneath torn, jagged metal, in the steam of gutted boilers spurting out in a scalding hiss: fifteen hundred dead and six thousand wounded. The smell of blood mingling with the heavy dust stagnating above the ruins of San Lorenzo, Tiburtino, Appio Latino, demolished districts through which walked the pope, the king, and the haggard crowd. Fifteen hundred dead and six thousand wounded so that the fascist leaders, the hesitant, cautious jackals, would understand that they had to make up their minds. Fifteen hundred dead and six thousand wounded, the trump-card Ferri was being offered by the American air force. But other people paid for it.

Back in Nice two days later, Elisabeth, Colonel Valeri.

"Soon, now, won't it be?"

He was waiting, like the town, like the Fourth Army. He saw me in his office, gave me a drink, leaning out the window.

"What a country," he said, "a stage setting. I'll come back here when the war's over. The air is as pure as in Naples and it's cooler."

Who knows? Maybe when the thaw came some peasants had found Pralognan's body between the floorboards of the isbas and hidden it under the earth before the next snow. Who knows?

"I've always thought the Duce was mad but I'm an officer like you, Naldi, we obey."

We had raised our arms, shouted, accepted, served, and there had to be these dead in Rome, Greece, Russia, Pralognan, Maud before we could see the madness in the fixed, staring eyes of the Duce.

"Nothing to do now but wait, is there?"

I walked around in civilian clothes, wandered through the streets of the old town, the markets, between the lines outside almost empty shop windows, went back to Vence. Elisabeth and I sat under the lime trees in front of the entrance to her house.

"Tell me," she said, "explain to me, how could you become a fascist?"

The abyss of age. When she was born I had already known the Piave, was hanging about the streets of Bologna meeting processions of workers, learning the body of Elsa Missini. I talked to her, to myself, we stayed up at night until the cool came, frogs croaking in the pond, the countryside asleep, our bodies finding and calming each other. In the morning I went back to Nice, the office. On July 26 all the doors stood open, men and officers running. Valeri grabbed my arm:

"Where have you been, I've been looking for you all night."

He shouted:

"It's done, Naldi, it's done, they've arrested him."

Insane days began then, the men shouting and throwing their caps in the air: "*Finita la guerra, a casa!*" and Field Marshal Badoglio, the new head of the government, repeated, "The war goes on." Insanity. The Germans were entering Italy. Insanity. The army was firing on civilians in Rome, Turin, Naples. Ferri had fled to Spain. Ciano put himself under the Germans' protection. The Duce was under surveillance. The town was still waiting. Groups gathered around the soldiers. "What are you doing here, go home now!" The first convoys began repatriating men and equipment.

One morning on my way to the office, a stranger stopped me. Fifty years old, the look of a manual worker, strong arms, tobacco-stained teeth.

"Are you Marco Naldi? Can I speak to you?"

I was in civilian clothes, hesitated. He smiled:

"I come from Ferri, you see, I know who you are."

I followed him along a little street near the place Masséna. An apartment on the fifth floor, bay windows overlooking the whole town, the red-tile roofs, white terraces. I had asked no questions.

"Can you wait?"

I sat down. An easel, canvases. An hour, looking at the sky and roofs.

"So, Naldi, is this a surprise?"

Alatri in front of me. A mustache, tortoise-shell glasses. He sat, held out a cigarette. The past. So many encounters like this one had dampened my capacity for surprise.

"We meet again," he said.

He wasn't the man to bring up old memories, he hadn't sought me out in order to see my face again. These weren't days for friendship.

"What do you want?"

"We haven't often been in agreement but, you see, events have pushed us onto the same side. I know what you've been doing with Ferri, against the other one. Will you help us?"

There were several communists trying to get back into Italy, needing papers, contacts.

"It's not over yet," Alatri was saying, "the Germans are coming in; so there'll have to be a fight. We want to be in on it."

I stood up. Years ago, before Russia, I'd have tried to talk, to get through to Alatri again, but I had grown too old, knew him better, or else had lost any hope of going beyond simple acts.

"Tomorrow, tomorrow morning you'll have a series of mission orders. I think you'll have to cross the frontier pretty quickly."

I felt the mousetrap ready to spring. A few days later, outside the staff headquarters, I saw the men in gray gabardine I had first seen in Berlin. The Gestapo here already, worming their way into our occupation zone. Colonel Valeri was growing nervous.

"I'm going home," he said, "I don't want to be caught, the Germans will have no pity on us, we're traitors in their eyes."

It was crumbling daily. On September 8 the armistice was announced; then I watched an army in panic, soldiers requisitioning cars, guns in hand, military stores plundered by civilians, Valeri running down the corridors.

"Burn your papers," he was shouting.

I watched terrified officers made ugly by fear, decimated, livid, all masks off. I was in no hurry. I was in civilian dress, watching the columns of soldiers who had been marching since Toulon, the mules hauling, the officers crowded into cars, the faces of a country too long fed on lies, the end of one imposture. I wasn't going back with them. Later, maybe.

I took one of the last bicycles at headquarters and set out for Vence. I pedaled slowly, meeting overloaded army trucks, disarmed soldiers groggy with fatigue on their way to be taken by the Germans no doubt, sooner or later, in some railway station or at the top of a mountain pass. Alatri and his men had got through in time. Clever. Far-seeing. Determined. They'd survive. Or die with their certainties. But the rest, these peasants and workers disguised as soldiers, blind, would fall in their ignorance. Like Pralognan.

And then, I didn't like to run away, to be part of this disorder reeking of fear and panic. I'd go back later. Or stay and fight here. Or else, though I wouldn't admit it to myself, I didn't have the courage to be alone again, to abandon another woman. Her body and her voice. Her gentleness.

At Vence peasants were transporting bags of flour, cheese forms, piles of blankets on carts; helmets were rolling in the streets; our barracks, when I went past, were swarming like a corpse in an anthill. I crossed Vence. Elisabeth's house stood by itself at the end of a dirt road, slanting cypresses seeming to point to it. The wooden gate, lime trees, house empty. Elisabeth wasn't there.

I lay down. What bound me to her? My loneliness? The need

for a woman's body, her friendliness; or her youth, the surprise still in her eyes, the feeling so strong when I looked at her, that she hadn't unfolded yet, discovered herself, my desire to watch her grow up and out? Or was it simply the pleasure in an active body, a smooth stomach with the moisture of perspiration on it? Or my fear of myself, my past, and the need to deny those years that weighed so heavily, Elsa, Maud, Calvini, so many more, all my wanderings, my failures, my need to be reborn since I had built that wall between myself and the other past. Elisabeth, a different world, a different age, one more pillar holding up the dam between me and me. She knew nothing of Magliano, Maud, Merry, Berlin. Nothing. She was new in the world. New in me. For her, the Piave didn't exist. I clung to Elisabeth so that she would protect me from myself. Help me to get away from the dense, close, black forest of my dead years.

"Hello, Marco."

She jingled her bike bell. I watched her coming, swerving along the gravel path, waving, smiling under a big straw hat. And in those days of defeat when men were being herded like cattle on the roads and handed over to German guards who were waiting for them with machine guns in their fists, I recognized that gush swelling in my body, rising in my throat, a feeling of choking, living at last, again, breathing with the heart: the pleasure of watching Elisabeth ride toward me.

"Hello, Marco," she says again.

Drops her bike. I get up. Maybe life was that, first of all, always, a woman. The rest just emptiness, noise, death, wars.

I moved into the house. An interlude of happy days. I dug in the garden and watered the flowers. We went nowhere. In the evening the English radio, fighting between Italian and German troops. Then Mussolini's escape, the German broadcasts repeating, "Mussolini has resumed leadership of fascist Italy." And the Duce's voice like a scratched record: "The state to be built will be yours. The traitors will be sentenced. Ciano,

Ferri, they will all pay for the damage they have done to the country." End of interlude.

Elisabeth worked for the resistance, in liaison with the English and Americans. I got a set of false papers in the name of Julien Delvert, asked to join a French maquis unit. Weeks went by. Suddenly it was cold, fiercely, clear, freezing the trees; now and then a German convoy, two or three trucks and some motorcycles came along the road to Nice, we could see it winding along the hills below the house. The Germans had occupied the region, were tracking down Jews who had hidden there under the Italian occupation. Two or three times we took in families who exhaled fear, then disappeared into the mountains. I thought of Maud. One woman, dark like her, older, who never stopped trembling.

"They kill us," she murmured, "I know it, they kill us. For them we're nothing, not even insects."

She looked at me:

"But what have we done, tell me, what have we done?"

To become a victim and die, it is not necessary to be guilty. A peasant came to guide her. She was wary, questioned me.

"You think I can trust him?"

I looked at the man, the closed face, a gray beard. He looked like Nitti. I reassured her, they left. Later I learned that he had robbed her and left her alone on a mountain path above Castellane. The gendarmes had found her and taken her to Nice. And she had disappeared, swept away, lost in one of the German convoys.

I couldn't stay any longer at Elisabeth's, waiting.

One evening we lit our last fire, two big crossed logs, twigs snapping. There was a group of partisans near Moustier-Sainte-Marie. Elisabeth had finally got the information, I was going to join them the next day. We sat on either side of the fireplace, silent. Only the sound of the bark crackling in the heat.

"After the war why not go on, get married," I said.

"That's a long time from now."

She crouched down, blowing on the twigs.

"But what if it was tomorrow, Elisabeth?"

"Why not?"

We came together, I put my arms around her neck, my hands on her stomach. Maud. The son I had missed. Maud I had lost. Try with Elisabeth. I had let myself drift for too long, with Elsa, with Ingrid, with Merry. With Maud. You had to want, decide, choose. Accept, also.

I left in the night, on foot at first, until I came to an old mill. There a peasant took me, in a van, along little back roads. Then on foot again across dry, red plowed fields where the lavender was beginning to sprout. At last, on a plateau framed by bare mountains, a big farm, two men coming toward me with hunting rifles over their shoulders.

"I'm Julien," I called out.

10

One morning before the darkness began to loosen its hold, they surrounded Elisabeth's house. One word in a file, one word was enough for me to imagine the men in gray gabardine, in leather coats, I had met in Berlin. One more word in a file I was going through, later, in a Gestapo office in the Hôtel Atlantic we had just occupied, one more word showed Elisabeth running through the garden, trying to climb over the stone wall, but on the other side the low car was there, and suddenly the headlights went on, I could hear the men shouting while she raced across the terraced fields, leaping from plank to plank until they fired in the first dawn light, and she had fallen among the bare vines. Winter, the brittle earth, smooth trees. Their voices above her multiplying the pain, the car, the cellars of that Hôtel Atlantic in Nice, her delirium and pain and their questions like more wounds. The words I was reading in the file: "Elisabeth Loubet, transferred to Paris."

"You see," Leblanc was saying, "there's still a chance."

Between the two of us there were unfinished confessions made in barns, and the cold and fear, and the Gelas glacier we crossed to avoid being encircled, and those shelters buried in snow where we uneasily slept. Then the descent into the valley, Nice like a bouquet of joy, the final skirmishes, Vence, Elisabeth's home a shambles and some peasants coming up to me.

"They arrested her, sir, in January, one morning, we couldn't do anything, it was, you know who I mean."

The file in the Hôtel Atlantic. I left Leblanc.

"Don't do anything stupid," he said.

I had long since passed that barrier, nothing would stop me now until I came to the end of my course, alone if need be. I went out of the hotel. In the streets were armed groups, young men wearing armbands with the French colors firing into shop fronts, a woman, elbow raised to protect her face, being man-handled, other women around her spitting words of filth and hatred, slut, whore, whore, and another one they dragged to a halt sometimes so that she would have to take the words, the blows, the spitting, and one youth saying,

"We're going to shave her head, we're going to shave her head."

He pulled her hair to make her raise her head. I walked to-ward the sea.

In front of the barbed wire closing off the gardens a little crowd of gesticulating men, one woman hiding her eyes and crying. I came closer. Under the orange trees, a hundred yards away in the garden, a man lying down, moving his arms.

"A mine, he's blown up, a mine, the bastards stuck them everywhere. Can't just let him die."

Voices shouting "Can't let him," "Do something." I went over the barbed wire. The grass where the man had walked was still flattened. I went straight toward him, walking in his foot-steps. Maud. Pralognan. Elisabeth. Why not me? Just keep to your course, not cautious, not careful or careless either. He was on his back, broken branches around him, his legs as though mashed, mixed up with the cloth that had turned red. I pulled him, slowly, to the barbed wire. An ambulance came. They took him away. People around me, voices, voices, words like chains.

"All you had to do was follow his footsteps," I said.

"All the same, all the same . . ."

"If we got hold of those bastards we'd make them take those mines out with their teeth."

I wasn't in a mood for talking. They let me go and I walked on toward the sea, past the concrete walls closing off the streets, finally reached the deserted beach, the shining expanse nobody dared set foot on yet. Lay down in the sun. The feeling that the war didn't need my death. If I had escaped in the Ukraine, got through the cold, not gone down on my knees in the snow, I wouldn't die here. The war had chosen to kill me second by second, to begin over again every second, father, Giulia, Maud, Elisabeth. I had war in my heart but I was still alive.

I stayed at Vence a few days. Summer. I learned things about Elisabeth, there were her cupboards the Gestapo had ransacked. I closed the doors, hung up dresses, picked up books and arranged them above the fireplace. A period of silence, like others I had known before in my life, after Maud left, after mother died. My voice for me alone, as when I came back from Russia, in Rome when I put my life in order again.

I watered the garden, lay in the sun, light and heat making the days all uniform, time like a burning block into which I dug; but that cold and snow, Russia, the Gelas glacier, my memories like the wind beating across the steppe: the heat did not thaw them. They stayed inside me, solid masses, jagged, and I had only to move one word, one idea or image, to catch myself on them and be hurt. Only one thing helped: to sleep in the sun. But Leblanc telephoned.

"A guy wants to see you, American, do I send him out?"

It was Strang in uniform, tossing his cap on the table under the lime trees, giving me a thump on the back.

"Naldi, I've been looking for you for months. What heat!"

Cicadas, like the rustling, irritating presence of the heat. He unknotted his tie.

"I only found you thanks to Ferri; Ferri, Elisabeth Loubet, anyway here I am. You know she was working for us?"

Ferri was living in Lisbon.

"He's preparing his plans for after the war. Who doesn't have plans? He's been lucky and he's got a good nose. Did you see about Ciano?"

One day at the end of January, when I had stayed late outside the shelter, Leblanc had called me in. I heard only the end of the story that was coming over the English broadcast, Ciano tied to a chair with other fascist officials accused of high treason, de Bono, whom I'd seen in the days of the Matteotti murder;

chairs side by side on the firing range of the fortress of San
Procolo near Verona. And the squad missed, Ciano was only
wounded and it took several shots to finish him off, Ciano whose
ambition had killed him, who delighted in flying over Tirana
and bombing Calvi and machine-gunning Ethiopian warriors.
Ciano crossing his arms and raising his chin like the Duce.

"Shakespearean," Strang was saying, "a family drama, the
Duce sacrificing his son-in-law and in Verona, too, what a set-
ting. A certain grandeur about it. You're not saying much,
Naldi."

Snow, Pralognan on his knees.

"Getting to the top by climbing up on other people's dead
bodies, Strang, that's always their way. I call it cowardice."

"You know," he began; "what is there to govern with except
other people, they're the pawns, you push them out and
swoosh!"

Strang made a move as if to sweep the table. Among the isbas
the tanks were grinding up floorboards and wounded together.

"The law of society, my dear Naldi, the rule of power, either
that or you dream; but sometimes I wonder if you aren't a
dreamer first, Naldi."

Dreaming of the end of the actors, impostors, the stage sets
are falling down, the puppets are dying. Here are men without
masks, without uniforms. A dream?

"Come on, Strang, was it only friendship that brought you
out here?"

He laughed, wiped his forehead, lit a cigarette.

"You're as frank as ever, Naldi, the first time I ever saw you,
in Rome, you attacked right away. You know Merry's in Paris?
If I tell her you're here, you can expect a visit."

Some of us, Merry, myself, Laborderie, who, Strang told me,
was a member of the provisional government, Alatri editing
Unità in Rome, some of us, me first of all, walked across time
and met again as if there had been no Maud or Pralognan. Hard

life—implacable. You have to see and play blind to keep living.

"Well," Strang said, "I can't hide anything from you."

The war, he was saying, would end, six months sooner or six months later, that was the business of the military men, but after that? He got up, back in his role, his certainties.

"You understand, Naldi, you're a man with experience, you can become indispensable in Rome, politically you already are. You haven't been tainted by fascism, you've been in the war and the resistance and you aren't a communist, understand me, Naldi, I've got nothing against them."

He held out a cigarette.

"You and I lived through the last after-the-war, remember? And what are we going to do in this one? What will it be? Red instead of black or brown, like Rome or Berlin in '22, '33? That's no better, you've been to Russia, you know the communists as well as I do. Think about it, Naldi. We can help you. It's our policy and in your own interest."

Reknotting his tie, fanning himself with his cap.

"Elisabeth Loubet, you cared for her, I believe, we'll look for her. Call me in Paris."

He had left his jeep at the end of the path under the cypress. The driver, a Negro, was leaning against a tree with his legs spread apart, the sun cutting his body in half.

"Kiss Merry for me, Strang, but tell her not to come."

A few days more alone under the vertical sun. From Rome, Provi contacted me. He was reorganizing the ministry, asked me to take Paris as acting ambassador. Manacorda was going to London, Antonetti was posted to Moscow. Provi himself was in charge of the secretariat at Palazzo Chighi. Loaded dice, he used to say. He had won. Survived. They were all finding their way back to the path of honors. A few crazy fools still holding out: Lanvoni, minister of the Fascist Republic—a state surviving on the shore of Lake Como in fog and anguish; Marghella, who had become general of the fascist national guard and was hunting down partisans; Valsecchini still secretary of the party. They had been wrong. Bad cards. Provi sent me a telegram. He wanted an immediate reply. Loaded dice. Playing with them, I knew, you could save your skin but it would be empty. Two words for Provi, "Refuse. Naldi."

A few days more, then I went down to Nice on Elisabeth's bicycle. "Hello, Marco," she had said and put down her bike on the gravel path. I was free and alive on that road where the breeze carried the sweet smell of figs. She, who knows?

Leblanc at the Hôtel Atlantic, listening to me. There were groups of partisans fighting in the Italian Alps behind the Germans. Sometimes, to get out of a pocket, they would fall back into France before returning to the mountains.

"Okay," said Leblanc, "if you want to."

Dirt paths, shelters, the fog coming in with the silence, fires we lit in the hollow of a rock. Then snow. I found the war again, the quiet men, attack and retreat. Found death again, bodies in a farm burned by the SS, and this peasant talking to me:

"You're a veteran of Russia, I knew another one, Luigi his name was, got himself killed, a grenade, just like that."

Here or on the Don.

> Farewell the steppe, farewell soldier,
> Farewell my comrade . . .

Maybe a different Luigi, but once we were dead we all looked alike. Weeks. Winter. Valleys choking in fog. Weeks. Unexpected SS counter attacks, burning two or three villages then disappearing. Weeks. March, fight, eat, sleep. I commanded half a score of men. Their lives in charge. Them between me and me. In the spring we began working our way down the valleys. The Allies were attacking in the Apennines. Back in Berlin, the death agony.

We went into the villages and little gray Piedmontese towns, women threw their arms around us. Joy. The fatigue that drowned me at night. The next morning another village, another town. Then the open roads. Speeches on a square surrounded by an arcade. The end. Everybody embraced.

"What are you going to do now, Naldi?"

Our last evening in a carabinieri barracks. A colonel in the regular army:

"You're a diplomat, I believe?"

We were taking possession of our old uniforms, personalities. I wanted to see Magliano again, and Nitti, the poplars, the shed. My memories. The colonel got me a car, a mission order, and I left without sleeping, in the rain, overtaking troop convoys; then sun, the paving stones of the suburbs of Milan, barrages of partisans:

"You can't go any farther," they shouted.

I asked why not.

"See for yourself, see for yourself," they answered, laughing.

I parked. Streets, groups running, men shouting, children. At the end a square and a mob swarming around a scaffolding of iron girders. Black, like the Piazza Venezia when the Duce made his speeches. From the girders, bodies hanging. Sometimes a burst of machine-gun fire to keep the crowd away. Men spitting from a distance. I recognized a face. The groups in the street were calling to one another, "Mussolini over there, hung up with his whore," and making obscene gestures. I had seen Lanvoni too. Hanging by his feet, the face already marbled.

I drove on. Crossed Reggio Emilia. There, how long ago was it? Yesterday, I had met Elsa, the black-shirted militia laughing near her and the peasant they had gorged with castor oil, where was she? The road. Stopped in Bologna. The town was filled with American army jeeps, soldiers singing in the streets, but they were disturbing my memories, only yesterday and now them, their shouts, their arrogance of youth.

The road. To get back to the silence more quickly, my voice, Magliano, the trees and Nitti, one place preserved, perhaps, at the end of this war, to make the connection. Recompose, organize, aim my life. Here in this courtyard I was entering,

where I used to play with Giulia, to reassemble all I had lost.
Maud and Giulia.

The Nittis' door was shut. I looked in through the window. A
step behind me. Matteroni, the other farmer, cap in hand, short
pipe in the corner of his mouth.

"Mr. Naldi, aren't you? I'm glad to see you. I'll open up for
you."

He left me alone in the courtyard with a growing certainty
that the war had come here, too. I sat down in the big room
with my elbows on our long table. Matteroni stayed on his feet
despite my urging.

"You knew Nitti better than I did," he was saying, "he had
his ideas, after '43 when they arrested Mussolini, well, he
wanted to fight. At his age. Only, they got him."

The Germans. The fascist militia, the hunted partisans.
Months before this spring of 1945.

"They got him, I don't know just where, he was armed, they
killed him outright."

Mrs. Nitti had died a little while later.

"We didn't know what to do," Matteroni was saying, "where
you were, we didn't know."

The war struck in ricochets, that pistol I had given Nitti,
Pralognan had pried it out of the clenched fingers of the body
of a Russian officer back on the banks of the Don. Matteroni
was talking, plans, the state of the crops, men to be hired, I was
back with Nitti in the shed when he was waving his gleaming
bayonet at me, or later on the path above the embankment
when he was hoping that after this war things would be different. But war had caught up with him.

"What are we going to do, Mr. Naldi, are you staying here?"
I stood up. Here? Nothing. A pit. Later, maybe.

"Keep on, do the best you can. Keep the house up. I'll write
you."

I left again. Venice, what for? Another swamp. I drove hour
after hour, accumulating my fatigue like an antidote against the

poison of time. I went through the Apennines in a driving rain, interrupted by cave-ins, shelled homes, and I had to get off the highway, take dirt roads, get over to the coast, go back up the valleys and through ruined villages and others the war had ignored. History like a sieve. Some die, some live on. War like the essence of chance. I stopped to sleep in the car while the rain was beating. Then on. Don't think, get away from Magliano and this country, begin again somewhere else.

Rome at last. Soldiers had taken over the squares, as in Bologna, followed by ragged urchins and painted women. My apartment on the Piazza Barberini. A neighbor who tipped his hat to me. Like before. And Provi, who welcomed me in the Palazzo Chighi, in the office where Ferri used to reign. Provi, friendly.

"You've got a tough hide," he said coming toward me. "Naldi, our hero. Here."

He held out a typewritten sheet. My name, for a series of decorations.

"Don't say anything, they've already been awarded."

He interrupted himself to sign some documents a footman brought in.

"We've got to put everything in order," he said without raising his head.

Then he took me outside into the grounds, holding my arm; we walked slowly under the trees, the air so light.

"You were wrong," Provi was saying. "You should have accepted Paris. Anyone could have fought in your place in the mountains. And now you'd be in Paris not just provisionally but established in the post."

A bench under an orange tree with shiny leaves, fruit still green, the bitter taste of a leaf I bit into.

"What is your aim, Marco? You know what they're saying?"

He lit a cigarette.

"Don't be surprised."

I shrugged.

"That you might run for election as a representative for Venetia, you're the perfect man for the communists, a patriot, in the resistance, you don't frighten anyone, you're not in the party, so? It's a career and you're holding good cards, the wind's shifted to the left."

I listened. My life they were taking over again, dispossessing me of it, to play out among themselves, in their game that was starting all over again.

"If you get an opening," Provi was saying, "don't hesitate. Now's the time. Once you're elected you can always slide, a little to the right, a little to the left, all you need is a nose."

He laughed.

"Just come and ask me."

We walked among more paths, Provi talking; he understood, of course the war had left its mark on me, Maud, Russia, but after all.

"You're only forty-four, Marco, you've got a career ahead of you, your life is still to come."

War in the heart. Since the autumn of 1917. I had paid. Leave me alone. A career? So many events since that autumn, so many faces seen, bodies abandoned. Let me continue my descent, far from the noise. I had done my share. Alatri was insisting too. I agreed to see him at party headquarters near the Piazza Venezia, Via delle Botteghe Oscure.

"I wanted to thank you," he was saying. "We got through. Just in time. You took risks. We aren't forgetting. Believe me."

Portraits on the wall, Togliatti, Stalin, Gramsci. Alatri's smile broader, relaxed.

"In the end, Naldi, we were right."

He was leaning on the desk, holding out a book.

"Here, read this, I think you've got some questions, maybe in there."

A history of the Italian Communist party, pages, words.

"Answers," Alatri was saying. "We've known each other for years, Naldi, I've never told you because . . ."

A vague gesture.

"But I've always respected you, you were looking for the right way, but alone; and you were wrong, one can't do anything alone, or not much. Think about our proposal."

Young men in the corridors, brochures piled against the walls. Alatri coming down the steps with me and outside, as far as the Piazza Venezia.

"You're certain to be elected. We'll support you."

I let them talk, Provi, Alatri, others. Merry came to Rome for a few days, I was very happy to see her, she made me laugh again, and in the evening we sat on the terraces of the cafés on the Via Veneto to talk about the past, tell stories.

"You're not made for politics, Marco," she was saying. "You know that."

We were old friends. We kissed each other on the cheek. Then Strang telephoned: Elisabeth was being brought to Paris.

"You'll get married," Merry said. "You're ripe for marriage. A quiet life."

She was helping me pack.

"I've always missed my chance with you, I'm never there at the right moment."

I telephoned Provi. I had to have something in France, anything. Embassy footman. Rang Alatri too. I was just about to leave, the door rang, there he was, grave.

"I really don't understand you," he said. "You have political responsibilities, whether you like it or not. People are counting on you. And you back out. Bring her with you, live in Rome with her. Who's stopping you?"

I wanted to break off. Get out of the game for good. Had paid my debts. The Piave had flowed into the Don. I wanted to live in exile, in exile from myself. It was my right. Alatri stopped answering, suddenly.

"All right, you've chosen, you'll stay alone. No historic con-

science, no ambition, why should you fight when your little
private ethics aren't stimulated? Give me a drink."

We sat down, Merry, Alatri, and I, on the balcony. So many
times, this fragmented sun reflected in the cupolas.

"Does anybody change," Alatri murmured. "You remember,
Ferri, Venice, you're the same, I'm the same. So short, a life."

He leaned on the balcony, turning his back to the street, the
city.

"Time; I wonder if we've understood how much time it takes
to change a man. It'll be long. Longer than that."

That was the first time I ever heard him ask himself a question in my presence. He emptied his glass with one swallow.

"All right," he said, "that's the way it is, and not otherwise.
Addio, Naldi."

11

My course. Years in Paris, how many? Over a quarter of a century. Is it possible? Erosion, day by day, ever since that morning at the end of May when Elisabeth held out her hand above her stretcher, with a smile in her eyes. Her arm, her fingers were trembling, with effort or emotion. She had come from Sweden, evacuated from Ravensbrück by the International Red Cross in mid-April. Months before she would be able to walk again, leaning on my shoulder. Then we went to her house at Vence and gradually her strength came back, but as though measured, worn, shrunken. Sometimes she sat near me with her eyes open; what was she looking for beyond the walls, trees, horizon?

The war; she too had it in her heart.

Between us, without ever speaking about it, a convention of silence grew up. It was as though there was nothing before we met on the platform at the gare du Nord, when she had held out her hand. Nothing for her or for me. We were trying for oblivion, deliberately. We got married. "You won't have any children, Marco," she had said. So be it. I'd end with myself. Then Paris. Day by day, erosion. An apartment on the boulevard Raspail, which I left in the morning for the Italian press agency I ran, thanks to Provi. News on the teletype, the chattering world in front of my eyes. In the evenings, Elisabeth. Maybe we should have confronted our pasts, mixed them together as Maud and I had done, our memories. But it was too late. Between us already, at the end of those months, silence like a wall. Merry came to see me at the agency.

"You don't look very happy," she said.

My course. Made of refusals. No more evasion. Live to see, to understand. I read. Wrote a few articles. Friends came, Strang,

Provi. Laborderie, who now was nothing more than an ex-minister I met one day for lunch at his place.

"Listen, have a look around will you, I'd like to know, about Maud Kaufman. Whether she had a son."

I gave dates, the name of Jacques Morin, Arles too. He phoned me a few days later. Maud shot at Mont Valérien, no trace of a son or of Jacques Morin. Maybe he'd left the country. The information was reliable, Laborderie said, one of his friends in the ministry of the interior had done the research himself.

So. Read, understand. All I have left of this quarter of a century is a few books, a few events. Bernard's execution. The trial of Pierre de Beuil. A big show. I ran into Anne Villemur, who was there as a witness for the defense. My past like the surf, in waves. Arguments. Alatri staying in Paris and I gave a dinner for him with Laborderie. Alatri remote, mute, Laborderie shouting.

"But you can't deny the existence of the Soviet camps, we have dozens of eyewitness accounts, it's plain as day, admit it for God's sake, the U.S.S.R. has corrupted the very idea of socialism."

New waves. And the wall between Elisabeth and me. Why? Sometimes, at Vence, we would recover our old vitality, of the days when we first knew each other. Then I would feel the solid, compact zone grow between us again, like water hardening, words weren't getting through any more. Maybe to do with bodies, with fear, maybe if we had agreed to talk we could have opened, cut it out like an infected wound. Elisabeth tensed when I came near her, I could feel her shoulders tightening, her fists closing, could hear her breathing grow hoarse. Why? What hell inside her since the war?

Then the erosion of days. Paris, Vence. In the garden under the lime trees, when I saw her slowly loosening up in the sun, I tried to find out, but she tensed up again at once.

"I warned you," she said.

I didn't push her. Not wanting to arouse, to hear confessions, laments. My cowardice, maybe. Then our final break when she suggested that we adopt a child. My anger, refusal. The memory of Maud, a child of my own. Pride, unfair pride. Years later, because time passed, I tried to suggest it myself once at Vence, it was too late. Elisabeth said so, with a tired smile:

"Now, Marco, really it doesn't interest me any more."

We were two companions, each day a little more isolated from the others. Our habits. Our jobs. Elisabeth translated novels for an English publisher. I read dispatches, compiled, wrote sometimes. Between us and the world, words, phrases, the means we had chosen to protect ourselves, to muffle the noise of time. Elisabeth and I were survivors, our lives, for both of us, seemed an imposture. A theft. I had gradually learned to follow her eyes beyond the lime trees, to sense what she saw, the heaped-up bodies, mutilated women, the truck that parked in front of the barracks every morning at Ravensbrück and left again for the gas chamber. As for me, ever since the hospital in Venice, the shortest sack, bloodstained, since the soldier with the face sliced in half, since Maud and Pralognan, since those black milestones, the bodies of comrades we had left in the snow that covered them so quickly, what was I except someone death had overlooked, and maybe that was why Elisabeth and I were living in the margins of time like casualties, convalescents. The words we manipulated, surrounded ourselves with, books, dispatches, life seen in reflections. I refused a post in New York, another in Rome. I wanted to stay in Paris, it was Maud's city. I refused to be associated with all those contradictory campaigns: for peace, Alatri wrote me; against barbarism disguised as socialism, Laborderie explained. I lived a quarter of a century from the outside. Once or twice a week I saw Merry, alone, for the pleasure of hearing her talk about me, for her smile that reminded me of another planet, Elsa, Berlin, Maud.

"I knew you as a man of action," she said. "Alas, you've turned into a French intellectual, ghastly. You're getting worse in your old age, Marco. I'm going back to America."

We were drinking in her little apartment on the avenue Mozart. She was scraping by, a few columns for West Coast papers, an inheritance being nibbled away. Then I went home.

"Hello, Marco."

It was almost the same voice. Elisabeth putting her glasses up on her forehead, stretching, yawning. I kissed her.

"Have you been drinking? With Merry. What on earth do you two find to say to each other?"

We talked about a novel she was translating; we went out to dinner. A film. A play. Culture. Merry was right, I was becoming an intellectual.

In the spring we went to Vence. I read, Elisabeth went on working. She always got up very early. Hoeing, cutting, watering. I listened. Sometimes when she was alone with the earth in front of her, in the morning, she would sing. A low, determined voice. Why did she stop when I opened the shutters? I was breaking into her song. Then I stayed inside the closed, cool house until Elisabeth started the car, to go to the beach.

"I'm ready," she called.

May. The roads still empty, water cold, blue steel. Elisabeth swimming out to sea alone. We had lunch at Antibes. One year, in May, it was the coming to power of de Gaulle. Another year, in May, the students revolting in the streets. Each time leaving Elisabeth, I returned to Paris at once, to watch the news day by day. A spectator of the battles of a country that was not mine, in an age in which I was a leftover.

Then that stopped too, came days without a ripple. Farewell ceremony at the agency. Retirement gift from the journalists. A speech. Telegram from Provi.

"What are you going to do with yourself?" said Merry. "Write, since you've become an intellectual. That's all you need: your memoirs to fill in the time when you retire."

We spent longer periods at Vence. Elisabeth was translating faster and faster. A fury for work, for silence and written words. She sat in the sun in a big straw hat, open books in front of her, bare arms, the blue number 35000 indelible on her skin. Like memories. I walked among the olive trees, toward the horizon that gradually disintegrated between the concrete cubes that were rising side by side. The town nibbling, proliferating. I kept telling myself that one day before I died I would have to find out what they had done with Magliano, the poplars, the paths. But I kept putting off the trip for another season.

One day in May I went into the museum in Antibes. I was alone. Elisabeth at Vence. The museum empty. Suddenly a painting I seemed to recognize, life like a flood pouring through me, a painting I had seen at Emilia's, years, centuries before. Two initials: J.M. I asked the curator; he explained his policies, finally came to the painting:

"An interesting painter, practically unknown," he said. "I discovered him in Arles, his house is a sort of municipal museum, part of it, there are people living in the other half. He bequeathed the whole thing, paintings, building, I'd call him an austere realist. You'll be hearing about him, you'll see."

"Dead?"

"Not long ago, a year or two, a singular person, mysterious, he came back after the war, from America I think, Morin, is that his real name? He called himself Rougerie, Paillet, I don't know what all. But incontestably a painter. He'll endure, he only needs some critic, or better a dealer, to discover him, if ever you go through Arles, a handsome house, splendid line of plane trees, it's worth a trip if you like painting."

Enthusiasm. In itself, a project. I had a project. Went back to Vence, driving fast, jamming on the brakes on the gravel of our drive. Elisabeth coming toward me, her glasses up on her forehead, hat in hand.

"What's the matter?"

"I'm taking you back to Paris, I have to go to Arles, an extraordinary painter I want to see."

"A painter?"

"Morin."

We went to Paris. I was silent, she asked questions:

"But Marco, explain."

I knew her, she didn't like me to escape from her eyes, her

silence. But it was too late to tell her, for her to understand. I went to Arles two days later, after yelling at Laborderie over the phone, demanding information. I went to see him in the office of the paper he edited, he held out a card, data on Jacques Morin:

"Here, the fellow came back only ten years ago; before he was in the States."

I read. Words underlined. A son. Phillip Morin, journalist, French correspondent for an American television network.

"So, you've got what you want?"

Enthusiasm and the fear of arriving too late, there was the deadline that was coming closer, my death; rebellion, thinking of all those years that had slipped away for nothing, a quarter of a century.

Then the plane tree drive, shaded, the house, the cypresses, the well and I leaned on it. The caretaker taking off his beret, putting it on again, slowly rolling a cigarette.

"At our age, everything makes you tired," he said.

You lived here, Phillip, then Jacques Morin managed to get to the States in 1942 and you stayed behind with his parents. A few months later you joined him. Because he was the man for missions, straight lines that bend only when they break. And he had promised Maud. So, he saved you. Bit by bit, I put it together during the months that followed my visit to Arles. While Elisabeth prowled around me anxious, interrogating, realizing that I was escaping her, where, why. I tried to reassure her. But did she still exist? My eyes were full of those paintings, those wide bars of color, sharp, stony, Jacques had painted and they were the background to your life. I was with you, with Maud. I followed your trace, reeling in your past, not trying to see you, trying only to understand who you were, the son of Maud and me, who had escaped from us but was alive. I used Merry and Strang, I learned how you managed to get Daria out of the U.S.S.R. in 1966 in order to marry her. And at the agency I found an item I had missed before, a little scandal, a bundle of dispatches telling about your mix-up with the police, the

ministries, on account of this Russian Jewess you were in love
with. I had loved Maud Kaufman, but I hadn't known how to
cut, choose.

For weeks I hunted you, reconstructing the visible elements
of your life. But I didn't dare try to meet you. I had thought
you were dead. I had killed you inside me, buried you under
the debris of the days that were my life for the past quarter
of a century. Then you were there. Knowing nothing about
me.

"You're so nervous," Elisabeth said. "Have you seen a doctor? You're smoking too much."

I spent whole evenings without moving in the corner of our
living room, the warmth of a cigarette on my lips, endlessly, the
bitterness in my throat.

"At your age it's not wise."

She watched me. What could I say to her? That I needed
to talk to you, to find myself again by talking to you, that she
hadn't been part of that past, maybe because I was somebody
else since 1938 when Maud had left me and taken you with her.
Since then a wandering, an averted death. And Elisabeth, an
illusion mutilated by the war. I needed to talk to you, Phillip, to
go back to Magliano, to my house, where you were without
ever having been there.

Elisabeth tried to prevent me from going. An intuition that
I was rejecting her. Unfair to her. Then she suddenly quit
trying.

"After all," she said, "do as you please, you're insured, I
suppose."

After so many years I saw Venice again, Magliano. A little
girl, Carla, jumped on her bicycle and I saw her riding off
down the dusty road.

Two months I've been here writing to you, Phillip, my son,
on this black table, finishing these pages, my life, you'll do what
you like with it. Tomorrow I'll mail the package and go back to
Paris. Without anguish. My life in order. Now it is perfectly
clear. Because I've written it, for you, thanks to you.

GLOSSARY

Terms or names that are followed by an asterisk (*) denote that the character, place or event is imaginary. However, in creating them the author has made use not only of his imagination, but also of many real-life models from which he has borrowed certain characteristics or details.

The glossary is divided into four sections:
  I. Characters (in alphabetical order)
 II. Places (in alphabetical order)
III. Events (in chronological order)
IV. Other terms (in alphabetical order)

I. CHARACTERS

ABRUZZES, Duke of the: Reigning member of the Italian royal family. Goes to Ethiopia in 1928 to convince the Emperor that Italy is *not* preparing military action against Ethiopia.

ALATRI*: Son of a general noted for being tough, Alatri is a communist. Naldi first meets him in the Arditi. Alatri becomes a journalist on the *Unità* (the communist newspaper), is arrested by the fascists and escapes. Naldi saves his life. Adversaries at first, Alatri and Naldi are on friendly terms after World War II, but in 1945 Naldi refuses Alatri's proposal to go into politics. (Alatri is then editor of the *Unità*.)

ALATRI, General*: Father of Marco Naldi's companion in the Arditi. Famous for his attack-whatever-the-circumstances policy, and for his toughness and lack of concern for the fate of his men.

ANTONETTI, Count*: Italian diplomat posted in Berlin when Ferri (the ambassador) and Marco Naldi (Ciano's representative) were also there. He is "in" with Berlin's high society of aristocrats and is flirting with nazism. After the fall of the fascists, appointed Italian ambassador to Moscow.

AUWI, Prince August Wilhelm, called "Auwi": A son of the Kaiser who sides with Hitler; one of the group of German aristocrats who choose to join the nazi movement.

BADOGLIO, Field Marshal: Italian; loyal to his king, he serves fascism, which gains him the rank of Field Marshal for commanding the forces in Ethiopia. Deserts the fascist cause in 1943 and becomes head of the Italian government under the king's authority.

BAINVILLE, Jacques: (1879–1936) French historian, ultraconservative, and monarchist. His funeral procession meets the car of the socialist leader Léon Blum, who is on his way home, and the procession degenerates into an assault upon Blum, who is badly beaten up and seriously injured.

von BAULIG*: German diplomat in the Ministry of Foreign Affairs in Berlin. Marco Naldi rents an artist's studio from him, located near the Tiergarten, the famous park in Berlin.

    Brave, liberal, and an enemy of the nazis, von Baulig is one of the first to learn of the existence of the concentration camps, and tells Marco Naldi and André Laborderie about them. He relies upon the Reichswehr and Hindenburg to drive the nazis out of power, but is assassinated by them on June 30, 1934.

BÉRAUD, Henri: Extreme right-wing French political writer, who violently attacks the Front Populaire in the weekly *Gringoire*. Antisemite and antirepublican.

BERENINI, Colonel*: Italian officer in the Italian expeditionary force in Russia in 1942.

BERNARD*: Informer working for Lanvoni, who has a hold on him. Alcoholic and homosexual, Bernard is a petty right-wing politician who serves Italian fascism and works for the Germans during the occupation. Shot after the Liberation.

de BEUIL, Major Pierre*: French officer, brother of Elsa de Beuil (wife of Prince Missini), French military attaché at the French embassy in Rome. Has strong sympathies with fascism. After being made a colonel and allowed to retire by the government, which fears his action, he founds a fascist-oriented political movement, composed chiefly of veterans, in Paris in the 1930s. His movement is partly financed by fascist Italy, and in exchange some of his men assassinate the exiled Italian socialist representative Calvini. Collaborates with the Germans and is sentenced after the Liberation.

BLOMBERG, General: A German officer who chooses to support the nazi cause; Hitler's Minister of War.

BLUM, Léon: (1872–1950) Leader of the French Socialist party and head of the Front Populaire government of 1936–1937.

His beliefs and Jewish origins make him one of the French politicians most virulently attacked by right-wing parties.

BUCARD, Marcel: French politician, founder of the fascist movement known as *francisme*; receives funds from Italy and Germany. Executed after the French Liberation.

CALVINI*: Italian socialist representative. Marco Naldi encounters him several times. In the 1924 Parliament, he is one of Mussolini's chief adversaries. In exile in Paris, he leads an antifascist group, fights in Spain in the International Brigades, and is assassinated in France by French fascists acting on orders from Rome. Calvini's fate makes a deep impression on Marco Naldi.

CANTONI*: Prominent Italian family that controls the chemical industry. Francesca, one of the Cantoni daughters, marries Ferri, who thereby becomes connected with the economic rulers and subsequently reflects their views.

CARLO*: Captain Ferri's orderly, who follows him throughout his career, in Rome, Berlin, and London.
   A man of the people, uprooted by the war—his wife abandons him —he submits to his fate.

CAVOUR: (1810–1861) Italian statesman, the most skillful and energetic architect of Italian unity under the Piedmontese kings.

CIANO, Count Galeazzo: (1903–1944) Son of one of the first fascists, he marries Mussolini's daughter Edda. Minister of Foreign Affairs at thirty-four. He is fascinated by the Duce and imitates him; ambitious, superficial, power- and pleasure-loving, after 1938 he becomes aware of the peril into which nazism is leading Italy and tries to restrain Mussolini. Votes against Mussolini in 1943 and is thus one of those responsible for his downfall. Hated by many leading fascists, accused of treason, and shot in Verona in January 1944—by the fascists, but on the orders of the Germans.

CIANO, Edda: Mussolini's eldest daughter. On April 25, 1930, marries Galeazzo Ciano, son of Admiral Costanzo Ciano; his promising career ends tragically in January 1944 with his execution, carried out with Mussolini's blessing.

CITTADINI: Italian general, head of the military establishment of the King of Italy at the time of the March on Rome.

DARIA*: Wife of Phillip Morin (Marco Naldi's son). Russian and Jewish; Phillip Morin, correspondent for an American television network, succeeds in getting her out of the U.S.S.R. in 1966.

de BONO, General: Officer of the Italian army who joins the fascists and organizes the March on Rome in 1922. Chief of Police in Rome at the time of the Matteotti assassination.

Executed on Mussolini's order in 1944, for having voted against him in July 1943.

DUMINI: One of the *squadristi* (members of the *squadre*) who abduct and then assassinate the Italian socialist representative Matteotti in June 1924.

EMILIA*: A friend of Marco Naldi's mother, runs an art gallery in Montparnasse (Paris). Marco Naldi first meets Maud Kaufman there; Maud's husband Jacques Morin is a painter.

FERRI*: Bologna lawyer. Ambitious, brave, and violent as well as intelligent. A friend of Marco Naldi's father, he is a captain in the Arditi. One of the first fascists. Works closely with Mussolini, is appointed Secretary of State for Foreign Affairs. Marries Princess Elsa Missini. Rival of Count Ciano, the Duce's son-in-law; later ambassador to Berlin, then to London. His second wife is Francesca Cantoni, daughter of the Italian chemical industry magnate. Instrumental in the fall of Mussolini in 1943. At his embassy in London, establishes relations with British and American circles.

Plays a decisive role in the life of Marco Naldi.

FRANÇOIS-PONCET, André: French diplomat, ambassador to Berlin during the nazi regime. Brilliant and elegant; Marco Naldi meets him at a reception at the Italian embassy in Berlin.

GABIN, Jean: Famous French film actor.

GASPARINI*: Member of the Italian Communist party who accompanies Alatri to his meeting with Marco Naldi.

GILDISCH, Hauptsturmfuehrer: SS killer; during the "Night of the Long Knives" he arrests and executes several SA leaders. It is he who arrests Marco Naldi.

GIULIA*: Daughter of the Magliano farmer, Nitti; Marco Naldi's childhood love. He leaves her to enlist after his father's death. She dies in the influenza epidemic which rages across Europe after 1918.

GOEBBELS: (1897–1945) Originally a journalist and German intellectual, one of the first to join the nazi camp. A gifted, intuitive man, he sets the stage for nazism, with processions, etc. and creates a highly efficient ministry of propaganda. Commits suicide in April 1945 in Berlin, with the Fuehrer.

GOERING, Hermann: (1893–1946) When Marco Naldi first meets the man who later becomes Field Marshal of the Reich and chief of the Luftwaffe, he is still only a captain with a price on his head. Seriously injured in the abortive nazi coup of 1923, Goering takes refuge in Venice where Naldi makes contact with him on behalf of the Italian government. To allay the pain caused by his injury, he begins to take drugs. During the "Night of the Long Knives" (June 1934), Naldi meets Goering again, in Berlin.

GRAMSCI, Antonio: A founder of the Italian Communist party. A brilliant thinker, imprisoned by Mussolini; nevertheless, he succeeds in producing an important body of writing which is only just beginning to be known today.

GROVES, Merry*: American writer for the New York *Times*, then the Chicago *Tribune*, and later for West Coast newspapers. Meets Marco Naldi in Rome in 1923, becomes his friend, and encounters him in various places, including Berlin and, after the second world war, Paris.

HANFSTAENGL, Putzi: Descendant of a Munich family who becomes one of Hitler's closest associates.

It is the Hanfstaengl family that introduces Hitler into the world of riches and high society during the dark, prepower years.

PHILLIP of HESSE, Prince: A German aristocrat related to one of the reigning families; he is a companion of the nazis, and of Goering in particular. On very good terms with the Italian royal family, especially with Mafalda, daughter of Victor Emmanuel III. Hitler uses him on several occasions to announce decisions implicating his Italian ally, but which Hitler has taken without consulting him.

HEYDRICH, Reinhardt: Himmler's second-in-command and one of the founders of the Gestapo; a former naval officer, highly ambitious and a brutal fanatic. Shot down by Czech resistance agents in 1942, in Prague. He interrogates Marco Naldi during the "Night of the Long Knives."

HIMMLER: Chief of the Gestapo, founder of the SS and Reich Minister of the Interior, he symbolizes all the cruelty of nazism. Master of the concentration camps, the empire of the SS. It is he who initiates the "final solution" of the Jewish problem. Commits suicide in 1945.

HINDENBURG, Field Marshal: (1847–1934) A German World War I hero; becomes President of the Republic in 1925. A nationalist, he allows himself to be persuaded to appoint the man he calls the

"Bohemian Corporal Hitler" as Chancellor. Dies in 1934, whereupon Hitler takes over full powers.

HITLER, Adolf: (1889–1945) Marco Naldi sees Hitler on several occasions while posted in Berlin; in particular, he watches the enormous parade celebrating Hitler's arrival in power on January 31, 1933, and is present at Hitler's speech after the burning of the Reichstag in February of that year.

HUNTZINGER: A French general who takes part in armistice talks with the Italians at the end of June 1940.

von KAHR: Minister in the Bavarian government at the time of Hitler's attempt to seize power in November 1923; he defeats that attempt, and is assassinated by the nazis in June 1934 during the "Night of the Long Knives."

KAMENEV: A Russian revolutionary accused of treason by Stalin and sentenced during the Moscow trials held to destroy the Bolshevik old guard, beginning in 1937; executed.

KAUFMAN, Maud*: Jewish, German-born; a journalist based in Paris. Her father is a German revolutionary. First married to an American, then to Jacques Morin. Trotskyist, passionate, she leaves Morin after being told by Marco Naldi that her husband, acting for Stalin, is trying to use her as a means of getting to Trotsky. She loves Marco. Pregnant by him, she leaves him because he can't take action.

She joins the French resistance movement and is shot by the Germans at Mont Valérien, near Paris.

She is Marco's one great love, but he is not able to keep her and suffers remorse on that account for the rest of his life.

KAUFMAN, Karl*: Maud Kaufman's father, who takes part in the attempted revolutions of 1919–1920 in Berlin and elsewhere in Germany. Architect and socialist.

KRUPP: Prominent family of German industrialists from the Ruhr; they support Hitler.

LABORDERIE, André: French journalist. Special correspondent for the *Epoque* in Germany, with antinazi views. Deported after Hitler's final victory. Naldi first meets him in Berlin, then again in Paris, and becomes acquainted with Maud Kaufman through him. During the war, he joins the resistance. Minister in Fourth Republic governments, then newspaper editor.

LANVONI*: In the Italian embassy in Paris, so much a fascist that he is not quite a diplomat. In charge of information and allocation of secret funds to French fascists. Organizes destruction of antifascists such as the former representative Calvini. A cynic; Marco Naldi's direct boss.

Remains loyal to Mussolini to the end; the Germans' man—and especially Himmler's—in Italy.

Arrested by partisans, executed, and hanged by the feet alongside the Duce in a square in Milan, in April 1945.

LAVAL, Pierre: French politician, favors an entente with fascist Italy and nazi Germany. Collaborates with occupying forces during the war, shot after the Liberation.

LEBLANC*: Leader of the French resistance unit in the south of France which Marco Naldi joins to fight the Germans.

LOUBET, Elisabeth*: Part-English, she works for the Anglo-American information services in liaison with Ferri. Meets Naldi and becomes his mistress.

Arrested by the Gestapo and deported to Ravensbrück; marries Naldi upon her return. But, having been traumatized by her experiences in the concentration camp, she cannot have children. Becomes a translator and lives buried in herself, more beside Naldi than with him.

LUDENDORFF: (1865–1937) German general, World War I hero. On November 8, 1923, leads the nazi forces in their attempt to seize power in Munich. His presence does not stop the Reichswehr from opening fire and scattering the troops.

LUIGI*: Factory worker from Turin. Soldier in the Italian army in Russia, where he meets Marco Naldi. Possibly killed fighting the Germans in a partisan unit in the Alps, after his return from Russia.

von MACKENSEN: German ambassador to Rome.

MAESTRICHT, Karl: One of the founders of the Nazi party. Meets Marco Naldi in Geneva in 1923 and obtains financial assistance for his party from the fascist government. After Hitler's failure in Munich in 1923, flees to Venice with Goering. When the nazis come to power in 1933, becomes Obergruppenfuehrer of the SA (the Sturmabteilungen, or Stormtroopers). But, with Roehm, he wants a "second revolution" (the first being the seizure of power) and is liquidated during the "Night of the Long Knives" (June 30, 1934) together with other SA leaders, on Hitler's orders as carried out by Himmler's SS.

de MAISTRE, Joseph: (1753–1821) French political author, theoretician of authoritarianism. Condemns the French Revolution and becomes a source of inspiration to partisans of strong government such as Charles Maurras or Pierre de Beuil.

MALAPARTE, Curzio: Italian author, originally a fascist, involved in the March on Rome. Wrote *"Technique of the coup d'état,"* an analysis of conditions for seizing power in the twentieth century; also *Kaputt,* a firsthand account of war in Russia.

MALRAUX, André: French writer, later minister of General de Gaulle. Organized combat aviation for Spanish Republican government; his novel *Man's Hope* is based on his experiences in the Spanish civil war.

MANACORDA*: Official in the Italian Ministry of Foreign Affairs, under both Ferri and Ciano. As Director General in the same ministry, he continues his career after the fall of fascism, having successfully maneuvered to ensure his future, and under the new regime is appointed ambassador to London.

MARGHELLA*: Italian officer whom Marco Naldi meets in Somalia, where he is military attaché in Addis Ababa. They meet again in Russia in 1942. After the armistice in 1943, Marghella chooses to go on fighting for the German cause, remaining with Mussolini in the Fascist Republic of Salo. At that point he is general in the fascist national guard, fighting against the partisans and thus against Naldi.

MARIA, Signora*: Owner-hostess of the "Aquila Nera" brothel in Bologna.

MATTEOTTI: Italian socialist representative. With Calvini, speaks out in Parliament against the first Mussolini government in 1922. In 1924, by denouncing the fascists' illegal and violent election tactics, he incurs Mussolini's wrath, and is assassinated in June 1924. The ensuing inquiry soon reveals that Mussolini's government is responsible, and for some weeks public opinion deserts fascism; but the cunning of men like Ferri, and the support of the king and Mussolini's own shrewdness enable them to regain control of opinion and of the country. The Matteotti affair, in which Marco Naldi is indirectly involved, is one of the last expressions of antifascist feeling.

MATTERONI*: A tenant farmer—Nitti's successor—on the Naldis' land at Magliano.

MAURRAS, Charles: (1868–1952) French writer and editor of the newspaper *Action Française*. A monarchist, he plays an important role between the wars as critic of the republican system, and he sympathizes with the fascist cause.

MEYERSON, Karl*: German Jewish sculptor who has opted for exile in England; Marco Naldi rents his apartment in Berlin.

MISSINI, Princess Elsa*: Née Elsa de Beuil. French. She marries the aging Prince Missini, who has an estate near Parma. Ambitious and passionate, she sees herself playing an important political role. While mistress of Marco Naldi, she gives brilliant receptions at her palazzo on the Via Giulia in Rome. She then becomes Ferri's mistress, marries him after her husband's death, follows him to Berlin, and dies in Venice in June 1934, under somewhat mysterious circumstances.

MORIN, Jacques*: Second husband of Maud Kaufman. A painter and Komintern agent. His real name is Jacques Paillet; his mission is to infiltrate Trotskyist groups in order to approach Trotsky and thus arrange his assassination.

MORIN, Phillip*: Son of Marco Naldi and Maud Kaufman, who bears the name of Jacques Morin in whose care Maud leaves him after separating from Naldi. Brought up in the United States, he works as French correspondent for an American television network.

MUSSOLINI, Benito: (1883–1945) The Duce of fascism. The founder of fascism (March 23, 1919) was originally a socialist. Ambitious, with a predilection for violence, he strongly favors Italian entry into the war in 1914, quarrels with the socialists on this point, and joins the nationalists. After entering the government in 1922, he slowly gains complete control of power. Popular until 1936, when his alliance with Germany, followed by his entry into the war in 1940, turns the public against him. Overthrown by his own fascist executive in July 1943 (this is the work of Ferri and Ciano), arrested by the carabinieri at the king's order, then freed by the Germans and placed at the head of a nonexistent state (the Republic of Salo), he is finally executed by partisans in April 1945. Marco Naldi sees his body hanging upside-down in a square in Milan.

MUSTACHE, Old: Nitti's nickname (and that of Italian antifascists) for Stalin.

NALDI, Aldo*: Marco Naldi's father. A landowner, and an energetic man, fond of hunting and swimming. In 1917, a major in the army, he is wounded in the Austrian offensive and dies in hospital in Venice, where his son goes to see his body.

His death is the decisive factor in Marco's life.

NALDI, Marco*: Born 1900. Tall, slender, sensitive, and dreamy-eyed; his father's death in 1917 drives him to enlist in the army. He is influenced by Captain Ferri and becomes his secretary after the fascists come to power, but tries to avoid compromise. Sent to posts in Somalia, Berlin, and Paris, he fights in the army in Russia in 1942. Joins the resistance after 1943; later becomes director of the Italian press agency in Paris. Marries Elisabeth Loubet in 1945. In 1970, learns that he has a son by the journalist Maud Kaufman, whom he had loved in 1938; he tries to locate the young man, Phillip Morin.

NITTI*: The Naldis' tenant-farmer at Magliano. A "Red," proud, with socialist ideas. He deserts after the defeat at Caporetto. Later, after amnesty is proclaimed, he returns to his old job at Magliano. Persecuted by the fascists, he is protected by Marco Naldi; but he is killed by fascists in 1943 after Mussolini's fall.

NITTI, Maddelena*: Giulia's mother and wife of Nitti; loves Marco Naldi like a son.

von PAPEN: Chancellor of the Reich in 1932, this former German officer and intimate of Hindenburg imagines that he can keep Hitler in check. He is Vice-Chancellor of the first Hitler government in January 1933 and actually encourages Hindenburg to appoint Hitler as Chancellor. Quickly loses power and is threatened during the "Night of the Long Knives." Drops all pretense of opposition and becomes the nazis' ambassador to Vienna, where he prepares the Anschluss for Hitler.

PERCY-LORRAINE: United Kingdom ambassador to Rome.

PETACCI, Claretta: Mussolini's young mistress, beginning in 1933. Executed with him in 1945. The fascists accuse her of exhausting the Duce and having a very bad influence upon him.

PÉTAIN, Philippe: Maréchal de France. World War I hero whose love of power drives him into politics. Men like Laval use him to disguise their policies and mislead the public, who trust the old officer.
    Beginning in 1940, he heads the Vichy government and sets up the French State, thus becoming the enemy of General de Gaulle. Sentenced to life imprisonment after the Liberation.

PRALOGNAN*: Italian lieutenant serving with Naldi in the expeditionary force in Russia in 1942.
    Killed during the retreat.

PROVI*: Italian diplomat. Marco and he become firm friends at Addis Ababa, where both are employed in the embassy. They meet again in the Italian embassy in Paris. A career diplomat, cautious and clear-sighted, Provi avoids all open commitment. Diplomatically ill at the "showdown," he has plans for the postwar period. Convinced that the dice are always loaded, he is a skeptic. In 1945, becomes Secretary General of the Italian Ministry of Foreign Affairs.

RADEK, Karel: Bolshevik revolutionary, executed after being charged with treason during the Moscow trials held by Stalin from 1937 on.

RAS TAFARI, King of Kings, Emperor Haile Selassie, Negus: Titles of Haile Selassie, the ruler of Ethiopia. In 1935, he personifies his country's resistance in the war with Italy. Manages to escape from Addis Ababa in 1936 and is restored to power by the English in 1941.

REICHENAU, General: German officer of the younger generation who see nazism as a way of revitalizing the Reich, the young, and the army.

RIBBENTROP: Nazi Minister of Foreign Affairs, who favors the war. Naldi meets him in 1939.

ROBESPIERRE: (1758–1794) French revolutionary honored by left-wing parties in France.

At the time of the Front Populaire (1936), his image, like all things related to the French Revolution, is much in vogue.

ROEHM, Captain: German officer, a founder of the Nazi party—he recruits Hitler. Creator of the SA or "Brown Shirts," his political plans and ambitions are a source of concern to Hitler and other top nazis (Goering, Himmler), as well as to the army. The "Night of the Long Knives" marks the destruction of the SA by the SS and the army. Roehm and the entire SA staff are executed. Karl Maestricht perishes with him.

SALENGRO, Roger: Minister in the 1936 Front Populaire government of France. Accused by the ultraright-wing press (*Gringoire* in particular) of having deserted the front during the first world war. The smear campaign ends in his suicide.

SCHACHT: Brilliant German financier who, in conjunction with German economic and banking circles, enables the nazi regime to establish a solid currency. Supports Hitler.

von SCHLEICHER: German general, Chancellor in 1933; he tries to govern by splitting the Nazi party into rival factions. Von Papen opposes him for reasons of personal ambition. Schleicher is the main victim when Hitler is brought into power by the von Papen-Hindenburg duo.

The nazis remember his opposition to Hitler, and he and his wife

are both killed during the "Night of the Long Knives." The Reichswehr, to which he belongs, does not protest.

von SCHROEDER: Big German banker from Cologne; supports Hitler.

SHIRER, William: American journalist and correspondent in Berlin,
where Marco Naldi meets him together with Merry Groves and Norman Strang; has since written a monumental history of the Third
Reich.

STRANG, Norman*: American diplomat, first seen in the United States
embassy in Rome. Friend of Merry Groves, through whom he comes
to know Marco Naldi.

    Subsequently posted to Berlin at the same time as Naldi. Contacts
him in 1944 in an attempt to convince him to go into postwar
Italian politics.

STREICHER: One of the first nazis, a fanatic antisemite.

THYSSEN: German industrial magnate who supports Hitler.

TOGLIATTI, Palmiro: A founder of the Italian Communist party; after
World War II, favors independence from Moscow.

TROTSKY: (1879–1940) The one his followers call the Old Man; lives
in exile between the wars, driven out of Russia by Stalin and hunted
down by the dictator's agents, who are determined to kill the revolutionary; with Lenin, he is a founder of the U.S.S.R.

    Lives in France, Norway, and lastly Mexico, where he continues
to denounce Stalin's policies. Assassinated in 1940 by a Soviet agent
who infiltrates his circle.

VALERI*: Italian colonel, Naldi's commanding officer at the Fourth
Army headquarters in Nice.

VALSECCHINI*: Representative of the Venice *fascio*; later, secretary
of the Venetia fascist federation and general in the fascist militia.
Remains loyal to Mussolini, becoming secretary of the party at the
time of the Republic of Salo.

    Marco Naldi intimidates him into leaving his farmer Nitti, per-
sistently persecuted by local fascists, in peace.

VARELA: A Spanish general, one of Franco's collaborators during the
civil war.

VICTOR EMMANUEL III, King of Italy: (1900–1946) Anxious to
maintain his prerogatives, fearing for his throne, he supports Mussolini's action in 1922 although he dreads fascism as well. Supports
the regime so long as it is successful, abandons it in 1943 and has
Mussolini arrested in July of that year; abdicates in 1946.

VILLEMUR, Anne*: Young Parisian fashion-writer, who has a superficial affair with Marco Naldi.

VOEGLER: German industrial magnate who supports Hitler.

VOLPI: One of the squadristi who abduct and kill the Italian socialist representative Matteotti in June 1924.

von WIRTH*: A German general, subordinate of General Schleicher; opposed to the nazis, relies on the Reichswehr to drive them out of power. Married to a Swedish woman, Ingrid, whom he meets while military attaché in Stockholm. She becomes Marco Naldi's mistress, and Naldi saves her from the nazi killers who shoot the general on June 30, 1934, during the "Night of the Long Knives."

ZINOVIEV: Russian revolutionary, member of the Bolshevik party. Tried and sentenced by Stalin during the Moscow trials designed to eliminate the "Bolshevik old guard." Accused of treason and executed.

ZOG: King of Albania in 1939 at the time of the Italian attack.

II. PLACES

ADDIS ABABA: Capital of the kingdom of Ethiopia. Marco Naldi is posted to the Italian embassy there.

AQUILA NERA: ("Black Eagle") Brothel in Bologna run by Signora Maria and frequented by Captain Ferri; Marco Naldi's first sexual experience takes place there.

ARLES: Town in the south of France; Jacques Morin owns a large home there, where he hides for many years. It contains most of his paintings and he bequeaths it to the town.

ASSAB: Capital of Eritrea, Italian colony on the Red Sea coast. Marco Naldi spends some time there.

BAB EL MANDEB, Straits of: Separate the Red Sea from the Gulf of Aden.

BOLOGNA: One of the handsomest cities of northern Italy, capital of the province of Emilia—one of the richest in Italy. A city where passions run high: in the early part of the century conflict between fascists and socialists is intense. Bologna gives birth to the first fascists (Ferri is a Bolognese lawyer); and just after leaving the army, Marco Naldi first encounters socialist violence there.

CASTELLANE: Village in the south of France.

CONSULTA: Seat of the Italian Ministry of Foreign Affairs, later transferred to the Palazzo Chighi.

DANZIG: Free city, inhabited by Germans and separated from Germany by a corridor belonging to Poland.

  In September 1939 German claims to Danzig and the corridor initiate the second world war.

DJIBOUTI: Capital on the coast of French Somalia on the Gulf of Aden. Commands the Straits of Bab el Mandeb.

ERITREA: Italian colony on the Red Sea, in the north of Ethiopia. A base for action against Ethiopia in 1935. Marco Naldi spends two years there.

FAUBOURG ST. ANTOINE: Famous main road in northeast Paris, leading to the place de la Bastille. A district of small shops and tradespeople, the faubourg St. Antoine is a revolutionary center during the French Revolution (1789–1794) and the Paris Commune (1871). Marco Naldi watches parades of working-class people on the faubourg in 1936 and 1937.

GALLERIES, VITTORIO-EMMANUELLE: Famous glass-roofed arcades in Milan, full of shops, opening onto the piazza du Duomo.

  Political demonstrations are held there. During the armistice celebrations in 1918, Marco Naldi first sees Mussolini addressing the crowd, many of whom are Arditi, in the Galleries.

GELAS GLACIER: Spur of the Alps in southern France.

IRÚN: Spanish town in the Basque region near the French frontier. In 1936 France witnesses the conflict there between Basques and Franco's Moorish troops.

KAISERHOF, Hotel: in Berlin; Hitler stays there before coming to power, and his followers parade outside it.

LANDSBERG, Fortress of: After the unsuccessful 1923 Munich *putsch*, Hitler is incarcerated here, and writes *Mein Kampf*.

LIPARI Islands: Italian islands near Sicily, to which Mussolini deports dissidents.

  Alatri is sent there but manages to escape and rejoin the exiled antifascists in Paris.

MAGHERA: Mainland district outside Venice.

MAGLIANO*: The Naldis' large holding in Venetia. Farmed by tenants—first Nitti, then Matteroni—it is to the Naldis a symbol of themselves. Marco Naldi's grandfather often vaunts to his grandson the qualities needed to build up a large agricultural holding such as Magliano.

MASSAWA: Town in Italian Eritrea, a port on an island in the Red Sea; Marco Naldi spends time there.

MOGADISHU: (Mogadiscio) Town in Italian Somalia where Marco Naldi stays.

MONTECITORIO: Seat of the Italian Parliament in Rome.

MONT-VALERIEN: A hill outside Paris where the Germans shoot members of the resistance after torturing them. Maud Kaufman is executed there. Today a monument has been put up in memory of the martyrs of the resistance and deportation.

MORVAN: A region of France, north of Burgundy, on the road from the Mediterranean to Paris.

MOUSTIERS STE.-MARIE: Small town of Provence in the south of France.

NICE: Town on the south coast of France claimed as Italian by the fascists (it has been French since 1860), and occupied by the Italians until September 1943.

Marco Naldi is based there at the Fourth Army headquarters.

NUREMBERG: Nazi party congresses are held there, against a background of music, lighting effects, and Wagnerian and medieval-inspired festivities.

OBBIA: Town in Italian Somalia where Marco Naldi stays.

PALAZZO FARNESE: Home of the French embassy in Rome.

PALAZZO VENEZIA: Under the fascists, this palace becomes the symbol of Mussolini's power. The Duce gives audiences in the Sala del Mappamondo there.

The fascist Supreme Council also sits in this Renaissance palace. The Duce makes his speeches from the balcony to the crowd assembled in the square below by his propaganda services.

Marco Naldi's audiences with the Duce take place in the Sala del Mappamondo.

PIAZZA VENEZIA: Square in Rome where fascists and Romans gather to hear the Duce speaking from the balcony of the Palazzo Venezia.

POTSDAM: Residential suburb of Berlin. The von Wirths live in Potsdam, and Marco Naldi goes there often to meet Ingrid von Wirth while the general is in Japan; the nazis are careful to remove him from Germany after coming into power.

QUIRINALE: The royal palace in Rome.

RAVENSBRÜCK: German concentration camp for women; Elisabeth Loubet is deported there.

REGGIO EMILIA: Italian town in the Emilia region, where Marco Naldi first meets Prince and Princess Missini.

SOMALIA: An Italian colony in East Africa, south of Ethiopia on the Gulf of Aden. Marco Naldi spends several years there making preparations for the Italian offensive against Ethiopia which takes place in 1935.

TIERGARTEN: Large park in Berlin.

TIRANA: Capital of Albania. Ciano flies over it during the Italian offensive in the spring of 1939.

LE TRAYAS: Beach resort on the French Riviera, where Marco Naldi takes Anne Villemur in July 1936.

TRIPOLITANIA: Today part of Libya. Conquered by the Italians in 1911 after a fierce struggle; the nationalists are very excited by this colonial scheme. While out walking with his grandson, Marco Naldi's grandfather praises the aggressive and nationalistic virtues of Italy in the Tripolitanian war.

VENCE: Little town in the south of France; Elisabeth Loubet lives there.

VIA VENETO: The most elegant street in Rome, lined with sidewalk cafés; one can see all the fashionable people of Rome there.

WILHELMSTRASSE: Street in Berlin on which the Ministry of Foreign Affairs is located.

III. EVENTS

THE MARNE: A battle takes place in September 1914 along this river to the northeast of Paris. The French troops manage to halt the German offensive there, and counterattack. At the time of the Battle of the Marne, Italy is not yet in the war and does not enter until May 1915.

THE PIAVE: A river northeast of Venice. During the Austrian offensive of October 1917 and after the disaster and rout at Caporetto, the Italians manage to establish a line of defenses at the river, thus stopping the Austrian advance, which would otherwise reach Venice.

The Piave has become a symbol of Italian resistance, of military heroism. Marco Naldi and the Arditi are at the Piave front.

AUTUMN 1917: The crucial moment of the war for Italy. The Austrians are attacking around Caporetto, the Italian front is giving way. This is the setting for Hemingway's novel A *Farewell to Arms*. Marco Naldi's father is killed at the time of the defeat.

CAPORETTO: Site of an Italian defeat in October 1917. See Hemingway.

THE ARMISTICE: Following an Italian offensive, the armistice is proclaimed on the Italian front on November 4, 1918, one week earlier than on the French front.

Fascists and nationalists make great use of this week's discrepancy in singing the praises of Italy and her armies.

NAPLES CONGRESS: The last congress of the Fascist party—October 24, 1922—is held in Naples; there Mussolini announces the decision to make the March on Rome.

MARCH ON ROME: At the end of October 1922, the fascist squadre begin a march on Rome intended to force the king to put Mussolini in power.

Fascist mythology notwithstanding, it is not the March on Rome that makes possible Mussolini's nomination as President of the Council (October 28, 1922), but the negotiations conducted behind the scenes by his subordinates.

NOVEMBER 8, 1923: The Munich *putsch*, when Hitler and the first nazis (Goering, Karl Maestricht, General Ludendorff) try to seize power by imitating the March on Rome. Hitler is arrested and sentenced to five years' imprisonment (during which he writes *Mein Kampf*). Goering, injured, flees to Italy where Marco Naldi meets him, with Maestricht, in Venice.

THE MATTEOTTI AFFAIR: The abduction, followed by the discovery of the corpse of the Italian socialist representative, releases a wave of antifascist feeling in Italy in the summer of 1924. The discomfiture of Mussolini and the fascists, compromised in the assassination, lasts several weeks. But liberal opposition—as expressed in papers such as *La Stampa* and the *Corriere della Sera*—looks to the king, who, having called Mussolini to power, cannot reverse his decision two years later. Thereafter all opposition is handcuffed, and the fascist backlash becomes intensified beginning in the autumn of 1924.

JANUARY 3, 1925: In a violent speech, Mussolini assumes full responsibility for the Matteotti affair in front of Parliament, and announces that all opposition will be eliminated; this, occurring two years and three months after the fascists first come to power, represents their total and definitive conquest of the country. Marco Naldi, a witness in the Matteotti affair, now chooses to leave an Italy henceforth bound and gagged.

DECENNALE: In 1932, ten years after their arrival on the scene, the fascists organize a great demonstration to celebrate their first decade in power. Political prisoners are granted amnesty. The regime is genuinely popular and accepted. At this point, after spending several years in Africa (Somalia, Eritrea, Ethiopia), Marco Naldi returns to Italy.

JANUARY 30, 1933: Field Marshal Hindenburg names Hitler as Chancellor of the Reich. Marco Naldi, then posted to Berlin, watches the torchlight procession, massive and rapturous, celebrating this event.

BURNING OF THE REICHSTAG: February 27, 1933. An event almost certainly staged by Goering. The Parliament House—the Reichstag—burns during the night of February 27. Left-wing opposition (communists and socialists) is immediately blamed for the crime. An arsonist—van der Lubbe—is arrested and confesses. Opposition members are hunted down and their parties outlawed. But as von Baulig informs Marco Naldi, there is an underground passage connecting the residence of Goering—then President of the Parliament—and the Reichstag, and it is through this that the arsonists gain access to the building.

FEBRUARY 6, 1934: Riot in Paris. Ultraright-wing movements, fascist groups, and the generally discontented try to storm the Chambre des Députés (Parliament) and precipitate a crisis for the republican regime. They fail, and left-wing reaction follows, culminating in the victory of the Front Populaire.

MEETING OF HITLER and MUSSOLINI, June 14, 1934: The first meeting of the two dictators, in Venice, is not a success. Hitler is fascinated by Mussolini, Mussolini is disappointed by Hitler. The two countries are rivals for influence over Austria.

It is on this occasion that Elsa Ferri is found dead in a hotel bathroom by Marco Naldi.

NIGHT OF THE LONG KNIVES, June 30, 1934: In power since January 30, 1933, Hitler decides to destroy all opposition within his own party. The SA are the victims of this purge, carried out by the SS. At the same time, liberal or military enemies are also done away with. Naldi thus witnesses the disappearance of von Baulig, von Wirth, Maestricht.

ASSASSINATION OF DOLLFUSS: Austrian Chancellor, murdered by the nazis on July 25, 1934. This is the nazis' attempt, one month after the "Night of the Long Knives," to take over Austria. But the assassination of Dollfuss arouses international protest and the wrath of Mussolini, who denounces nazism as a barbarian movement and shifts his position closer to France and Great Britain. Hitler backs down and postpones his annexation of Austria until a later date.

ASTURIAS MOVEMENT: October 1934. The workers' uprising in the Asturias (Spain) is ruthlessly repressed by the troops of General Franco, who is then no more than an officer loyal to the central authorities of the Spanish Republic.

ITALO-ETHIOPIAN WAR: October 1935–May 1936. Italian troops attack the kingdom of Haile Selassie and quickly conquer it; the offensive is carefully prepared for many years, from Eritrea and Somalia. It avenges an Italian defeat in 1896; but it also precipitates a serious international crisis. France and England denounce the war, Italy moves back toward Hitler, and the Italo-Ethiopian conflict heralds the approach of world war.

REMILITARIZATION OF THE RHINELAND: March 1936. In defiance of the Treaty of Versailles, Hitler decides to reinstall troops on the east bank of the Rhine.

The French, although directly threatened, prefer not to intervene; this is Hitler's first spectacular success.

FRENTE POPULAR: Spanish left-wing coalition. Its success in the February 1936 elections precipitates a revolutionary upsurge throughout the country and incites military circles to the coup d'état which is consummated, on July 17, 1936, by the civil war.

FRONT POPULAIRE: Movement arising in France in 1934; the elections in June 1936 end in victory for the left-wing parties descended from this movement.

The ensuing government, led by Léon Blum, is short-lived (1936–1937). The front populaire leaves the country profoundly shaken, torn by fierce rivalry between right and left.

Men like Pierre de Beuil prefer occupation by Hitler to government by the front populaire.

SPANISH CIVIL WAR: Devastates Spain from July 1935 to March

1939. General Franco's troops from Spanish Morocco, supported by Italian fascists and nazis, set out to achieve the methodical reconquest of the country in defiance of the legally elected republican government. They meet with fierce resistance for three years. The Spanish war splits public opinion all over the world.

Calvini, Alatri, Maud Kaufman are all active in Spain, on the republican side, during the war.

ROME-BERLIN AXIS: A policy of alliance between fascist Italy and nazi Germany. The word is first pronounced by Mussolini in November 1936, when the war in Spain is already in progress.

ALCAZAR OF TOLEDO: A famous episode in the Spanish civil war, when troops garrisoned there, having sided with Franco, are besieged by the republicans and hold out until Franco's own troops manage to recapture Toledo and free them. This Frankist exploit has been celebrated by all Franco's followers.

GUADALAJARA: Battle in the Spanish civil war, in 1937.

Mussolini's fascist troops, coming to the aid of Franco, are defeated by the International Brigades, and by the Italian antifascist battalion in particular.

CLICHY: District in Paris where, in 1937, left-wing demonstrators clash violently with the Gardes Mobiles—a contradictory situation, since the *front populaire* government—i.e. a left-wing government—is then in power.

Pierre de Beuil's men may be behind the incident.

GUERNICA: Town-symbol of the Basque country. Ferdinand and Isabel of Castille took an oath there to respect the freedom of the Basques. In 1937 the German air force under Franco's orders destroys the town; international feeling runs high. Picasso paints his famous mural.

ANSCHLUSS: Reunification of Austria and Germany, achieved by Hitler in March 1938.

ITALIAN AGGRESSION AGAINST ALBANIA: April 1939 (Good Friday); proof that fascist Italy has no more respect for international rules of play than nazi Germany.

STEEL PACT: May 1939. A treaty between Berlin and Rome, allying Italy and Germany.

Naldi is present for the signing of the treaty in Berlin.

CIANO-RIBBENTROP MEETING: Salzburg, August 11, 1939. At this meeting Ciano, accompanied by Marco Naldi, realizes that Ribbentrop is not seeking fresh advantages for the nazi Reich (e.g. Danzig), but is bent upon war with Poland, convinced that England will not intervene. Ciano, alarmed, then tries to keep Italy out of the war.

RETREAT OF THE ITALIAN EXPEDITIONARY FORCE IN RUSSIA: Mussolini convinces the German high command that Italy must take part in the war against the U.S.S.R. The troops he sends out are ill-equipped, and when the Russians launch their late-winter offensive (1942) to disengage Stalingrad, Italian resistance on the Don is annihilated. A murderous retreat then begins, in which virtually the entire Italian army in Russia is lost.

MAY 10, 1940: Full-scale German offensive to the West; France is quickly defeated.

JUNE 10, 1940: Italy declares war on France.

JUNE 14, 1940: The Germans enter Paris.

JUNE 22, 1940: Franco-German armistice.

JUNE 23, 1940: Franco-Italian armistice.

JULY 10, 1943: English and Americans land in Sicily.

JULY 25, 1943: Mussolini arrested on the orders of the king of Italy.

SEPTEMBER 8, 1943: Italy signs armistice with the Allies.

VERONA TRIAL, January 1944: Fascist extremists, now regrouped in the Republic of Salo, try and sentence fascist dignitaries accused of treason.

Among those tried is Count Ciano, the Duce's son-in-law, who is executed on January 11, 1944.

FASCIST REPUBLIC OF SALO: January 1944–April 1945. After his release by the Germans from the prisons of the king of Italy (July 1943), Mussolini founds a mock Republic at Salo on the shore of the Lago di Garda, which survives on words and German assistance.

It also fights Italian partisans hostile to Germany.

Lanvoni, Valsecchini, and Marghella are members of it.

MAY: May 1968 in France. Period of student unrest and industrial strikes, more widespread than any recorded in French history. One of the most important events in postwar France, leading to the fall of de Gaulle in 1969.

IV. OTHER TERMS
(Groups, parties, newspapers, etc.)

A NOI: Rallying cry of the Arditi (it means "To us!"), which becomes a fascist slogan.

ANTIFASCIST BLOC*: A unit in Paris, set up by Calvini and Alatri, in which Mussolini's enemies regroup. Lanvoni places informers within the unit.

ARDITI: ("the bold") Special Italian troops—something on the order of commandos—employed in the most dangerous missions on the Piave front in 1917; they crossed the river, attacking the enemy rearguard. They are given special treatment. Fascism finds many followers among their ranks. Men and officers in the regular army dislike them, regarding them as mercenaries and pirates, which in many cases they are.

ASCARIS: Italian colonial troops made up of natives recruited in Eritrea or Somalia. They fight the troops of Emperor Haile Selassie in the war against Ethiopia in 1935 and 1936.

AUSTRIANS: Until 1866, they dominate the whole of northern Italy, and in the eyes of Italians from Venetia they symbolize the loathed foreign invader, whose return the defeat at Caporetto in October 1917 seems to presage.

L'AVANTI: Italian socialist newspaper whose offices are raided and destroyed by fascists in 1922; later, the newspaper is banned.

"AVANTI POPOLO, BANDIERA ROSSA": ("Forward, masses, with the red banner") A famous Italian revolutionary song, the anthem of the Italian socialists. Marco Naldi hears it for the first time in Bologna in 1919, when he encounters a procession of socialist demonstrators.

BLACK SHIRTS: Name given to the Italian fascists who, in 1919, adopt a black uniform taken over in part from that of the Arditi. Hitler's "Brown Shirts" are a German adaptation of the Italian original.

BROWN SHIRTS: Members of the Storm Troopers (*Sturmabteilungen*) in Germany.

CARABINIERI: Italian regular army troops whose loyalty to the king is unshakable. They play the part of a military police force.

CLUB OF LORDS: (Herrenclub) In Germany, the closed circle of aristocrats—the "junkers," or Prussian noblemen—largely big landowners, nationalists, and army officers.

COMINTERN: See Komintern.

THE EUROPE OF VERSAILLES: The treaty of Versailles—which the United States does not ratify—draws up a map of Europe, and defeated Germany has to accept this "decree"; but, like Italy and like Russia, Germany wants the treaty "revised," and Hitler and Mussolini are prepared to use force to that end.

FASCIO: Local branch of the Fascist party in Italy or abroad; in most large cities, including New York, there is a "fascio."

FASCISM: Movement founded in Milan by Mussolini, on March 23, 1919.

FRENTE POPULAR, FRONT POPULAIRE: See listing under "Events."

GARDES MOBILES: French domestic police units.

GESTAPO (*Geheime Staatspolizei*): German secret police whose headquarters are at 8, Prinz Albrechtstrasse in Berlin.

Led by Heydrich and Himmler, it gradually comes to control the entire Reich, engages in a war with Roehm and the Storm Troopers and obliterates them during the "Night of the Long Knives."

GIUSTIZIA E LIBERTA: Italian antifascist movement. Calvini belongs to it; its leaders, the Rosselli brothers, are assassinated in France by French agents in the pay of Mussolini.

INTERNATIONAL BRIGADE: In the Spanish Civil War, volunteers from several countries form units to fight on the republican side. Among them is one Italian antifascist unit, the Garibaldi battalion.

Cf. Hemingway, *For Whom the Bell Tolls*.

ISBA: Russian country cottage built of logs.

KOMINTERN: Communist international organization set up by national parties to coordinate activities.

It sends agents throughout the world—such as Jacques Morin—and after 1930 ceases to be a revolutionary instrument, becoming instead a tool of Stalin.

LEAGUE OF NATIONS: Set up immediately after World War I with headquarters in Geneva, the League of Nations is intended to arbitrate disputes between states.

When Italy attacks Ethiopia in 1935, the League denounces Rome and issues diplomatic and economic sanctions against Italy, but is unable to enforce them effectively.

MEMORIAL OF SAINT HELENA: Las Cases, Napoleon's companion in exile on St. Helena, assembles the former emperor's statements in this "memorial." Naldi's grandfather, like many other Italians who believe that Napoleon, coming from Corsica, was really an Italian, is fond of reading the work and admires the Emperor of the French.

MOORISH: To carry out his reconquest of republican Spain, General Franco uses units from Spanish colonial armies made up of Moorish soldiers renowned for their savagery.

MOSCHETTIERE: The Duce's musketeers. This elite body of men—in black uniforms, armed with daggers—is Mussolini's private guard. Always on duty in the Palazzo Venezia.

"NO PASSARAN": ("They shall not pass") Slogan of Spanish republicans during Franco's siege of Madrid in 1937.

OBERGRUPPENFUEHRER: Rank in the SA or SS corresponding to that of general. Maestricht is promoted to this rank and put in charge of maintaining order in Berlin.

OGPU: Soviet secret police, now called KGB.

L'OSSERVATORE ROMANO: Vatican newspaper read by Italians because it provides better news coverage than the fascist papers.

OVRA: Italian political police; the Italian equivalent of the Gestapo.

PANZERS: German armored units owing their effectiveness to the fact that their tanks move as collective units, rather than providing isolated support for infantry.

THE PARTY: The term used by politically aware people in Western Europe (France, Italy) to designate the Communist party.

POPOLO D'ITALIA: Mussolini's newspaper. He founds it in 1914 after leaving the Socialist party, when he wants to campaign for Italian entry into the war.

It remains the organ of the Fascist party until Mussolini's death.

LA POPULAIRE: French socialist newspaper for which Maud Kaufman writes.

REGULARES: The troops in General Franco's army, chiefly Moroccan.

REICHSWEHR: The German army, before taking the name of Wehrmacht in 1938. The Reichswehr plays a decisive role in Germany between the two wars; after preventing a left-wing revolution, it allows nazism to be established in 1933 in the hope of strengthening its own position with a view to a war of revenge.

SCHUPOS: Berlin ordinary police.

SERIAL NUMBER: Elisabeth Loubet, like everyone else deported by the nazis, has a number tatooed on her arm.

SQUADRE: (squadrons) Small fascist units organized on military lines, which scour the Italian countryside and assault antifascists. Their members, the squadristi, are often ex-Arditi troops. They wear black uniforms and purge their enemies with castor oil.

SQUADRISTI: Members of the *squadre.*

SS: (Schutzstaffel) Select paramilitary organization headed by Goering and Himmler, emerges triumphant in the conflict between nazi factions which ends in the "Night of the Long Knives."

STORM TROOPERS: The SA of "Brown Shirts." Created by Roehm to keep order during nazi meetings, these small units grow into an army of several hundred thousand men recruited from the working classes—the unemployed, former communists. The Reichswehr and nazi leaders view this army with mistrust; it is taken in hand by Hitler after the "Night of the Long Knives," when Himmler's SS move into first place above it, and relegate the SA to a subsidiary role.

SUDETENS: A German minority within the Czechoslovakian state. Hitler announces his intention to annex it in 1938, and it is granted to him by the Munich conference in September 1938. This marks a new phase in the capitulation of the democracies, and another success for Hitler.

TERCIOS: Units in General Franco's Spanish army which are partially composed of Moorish.

"TOUT VA TRÈS BIEN, MADAME LA MARQUISE": Famous French comic song which says that everything is just fine, when in fact everything is in chaos.

TROTSKYISTS: The followers of Trotsky. Although few in number, they are extremely active in France and Spain between the two world wars. Persecuted simultaneously by governments, who regard them as revolutionaries, and by nazis and fascists whose enemies they are, they are also hated by the communists.

They maintain their revolutionary faith despite everything; such a person is Maud Kaufman, who belongs to a Trotskyist organization.

L'UNITÀ: Italian communist newspaper for which Alatri writes.

WEHRMACHT: The German army, previously known as the Reichswehr, was renamed in 1938.